T0354883

GENESIS

THE UNITED STATES
FIGHTS TO SURVIVE
AS EUROPE GOES MAD
WITH WARS AND REVOLUTIONS

A CARROLL FAMILY SAGA

ROYSTON MOORE

Order this book online at www.trafford.com
or email orders@trafford.com

Most Trafford titles are also available at major online book retailers.

Note for Librarians: A cataloguing record for this book is available from Library
and Archives Canada at www.collectionscanada.ca/amicus/index-e.html

Printed in Victoria, BC, Canada.

ISBN: 978-1-4251-8564-0 (soft)
ISBN: 978-1-4251-8565-7 (ebook)

*Our mission is to efficiently provide the world's finest, most comprehensive
book publishing service, enabling every author to experience success.
To find out how to publish your book, your way, and have it available
worldwide, visit us online at www.trafford.com*

Trafford rev. 9/21/2009

 www.trafford.com

North America & international
toll-free: 1 888 232 4444 (USA & Canada)
phone: 250 383 6864 ♦ fax: 812 355 4082

READ OTHER BOOKS BY ROYSTON MOORE

FIVE BOOKS IN THE CARROLL FAMILY SAGA

FICTIONAL LOVE STORIES IN AMERICA FROM 1690 TO 1850

MARYLAND – a Rags to Riches love story around 1690 – Amelia Eliot and David Carroll begin the Carroll Family Saga

OHIO – The love stories of five couples during the "Seven Year War" – really British and French enemies who became friends

LIBERTY – Carroll descendents and other immigrants still survive and discover love during the American Revolution from Britain

GENESIS – The new United States struggles whilst chaos reigns in Europe. New immigrants helped by Carroll's to discover love.

LEBENSTRAUM –"*Living-Dreams*" - Later Carroll descendents also with others continue the expansion west looking for Living Space – Their part in River, Sea and now Railway transport for growing industry

LOVE 3000 YEARS AGO IN ANCIENT EGYPT

MAKERE – THE FEMALE PHAROAH – QUEEN OF SHEBA

Though written as fiction – It describes the actual life of MAKERE HATSHEPSUT –the only Female Pharaoh of Egypt – yet proves she was, also the mysterious Queen of Sheba – Her actual love for lowly web-priest, Senmut and Solomon, King of All Israel. – Her tempestuous life – so similar to British Tudor Queen Elizabeth.

PURCHASE ALL AT ANY BOOKSELLER OR ON LINE AT AMAZON.COM OR DIRECT AT TRAFFORD PUBLISHING

FOREWORD

A romantic story of love triumphing during the Genesis of the birth of a new United States, whilst it fights to survive, as Europe goes mad with wars and revolutions. This the fourth book in the five book saga continuing the lives of the two Carroll families descendents of protestant David Carroll and Roman Catholic Edgar Carroll. Following the previous three books, 'Maryland', 'Ohio', and 'Liberty'.

The first country with a democratically elected President, instead of a King. Having won its independence, trying to survive and prosper, attempting neutrality as the world lapses into chaos.

The saviour for many men and women escaping from war torn Europe to settle and expand this new country. Including the aristocratic Hapsburg Prince and Princesses whose scandal threatens them with death, to those exiles escaping death by the guillotine in France, and the many settlers beset and in danger from indian attacks.

Yet it is essentially a story of romantic love and lovers, of new emigrants and those resident here for many years. How, in their own way they endeavoured to establish this new country, providing a refuge for many new families coming from England, Ireland, France and Austria, forgetting their previous nationalities and becoming Americans.

All events are all historically correctly described, including the despicable treatment of many women. How the descendents of Edgar Carroll helped establish the industrial revolution and steam river boats, whilst Daniel Carroll continues to help the Irish descendents of his grandmother.

Then on a single day in October 1803 the United States doubled its size by the 'Louisiana Purchase'.

Enjoy this story of love of many men and women in America at the end of the 18th. Century.

ROYSTON MOORE

THE CARROL FAMILIES SAGAS IN AMERICA

MARYLAND – *Is the first of Five books set in America from colonial days in 1688 to 1694, and to the United States in 1850.*
This book introduces readers first, to the Protestant Carroll family going to America from Somerset to join the Roman Catholic Carroll family living there since they emigrated from Yorkshire.
It is a Rags to Riches story of love in the late 17th. Century

OHIO – *This second book covers the period from 1748 to 1763. the time of the Seven Years War between Britain and France – the first global war. It covers the life of five sets of partners, both British and French who, though should have been enemies, but due to their presence in this new land of Ohio, are drawn together and become friends. Continuing the Carroll Sagas, now with Daniel Carroll, grandson of Amelia and David Carroll.*

LIBERTY – *The period of 1770 to 1789 – The events leading to and the actual War of American Independence from Britain. Many characters from the previous books and the valuable assistance Daniel Carroll and his wife Michelle gave to George Washington during the bleak times of the war. Continuing the sagas of both branches of the Carroll families but introducing many new persons.*

GENESIS – *The New Country. The period from 1793 to 1803 when in a single day the size of the United States doubled with President Jefferson's 'Louisiana Purchase' from Spain. The problems besetting the United States - a country ruled by an elected President and not a king, attempting neutrality, whilst Europe descended into chaos with the French Revolution and the many European wars. Now we meet the numerous off springs of two Carroll families, and their love* affairs, again concerning the life of Daniel Carroll, his wife Michelle and their children, and many new emigrants from Europe.

LEBENSTRAUM– Covering the period from 1826 to 1850. The expansion Westwards – Texas and Mexico and events in California. The development of an industrial America and the vital part played by both Carroll families in both river and rail transport. Again dealing not only with their love affaires, but those of the many new emigrants coming the America and settling in love there.

THE CARROLL FAMILIES & RELATIONSHIPS TO 1803

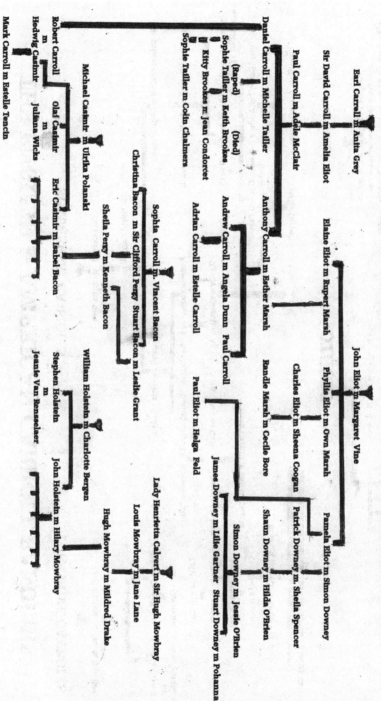

Earl Carroll m Anita Grey

Sir David Carroll m Amelia Eliot

Paul Carroll m Adèle McClair

Daniel Carroll m Michelle Tailler

(Raped)   (Died)

Sophie Tailler m Keith Brookes

Kitty Brookes m Jean Condorcet

Sophie Tailler m Colin Chalmers

Robert Carroll
m
Hedwig Casimir
m
Mark Carroll m Estelle Tench

Michael Casimir m Ulrika Polanski

Olaf Casimir
m
Juliana Wicks

Eric Casimir m Isabel Bacon

Anthony Carroll m Esther Marsh

Andrew Carroll m Angela Dunn   Paul Carroll

Adrian Carroll m Estelle Carroll

Sophia Carroll m Vincent Bacon

Christina Bacon m Sir Clifford Perey   Stuart Bacon m Leslie Grant

Sheila Perey m Kenneth Bacon

Elaine Eliot m Rupert Marsh

John Eliot m Margaret Vine

Phyllis Eliot m Owen Marsh

Charles Eliot m Sheena Coogan

Pamela Eliot m Simon Downey

Randle Marsh m Cecile Bore

Patrick Downey m. Sheila Spencer

Shaun Downey m Hilda O'Brien

James Downey m Lilie Gartner   Stuart Downey m Pohanna

Simon Downey m Jessie O'Brien

Paul Eliot m Helga Feld

William Holstein m Charlotte Bergen

Stephen Holstein
m
Jeannie Van Rensselaer

John Holstein m Hillary Mowbray

Lady Henrietta Calvert m Sir Hugh Mowbray

Louis Mowbray m Jane Lane

Hugh Mowbray m Mildred Drake

THE ENGLISH & AMERICAN CARROLL FAMILIES

SOMMERSET CARROLLS

YORKSHIRE CARROLLS

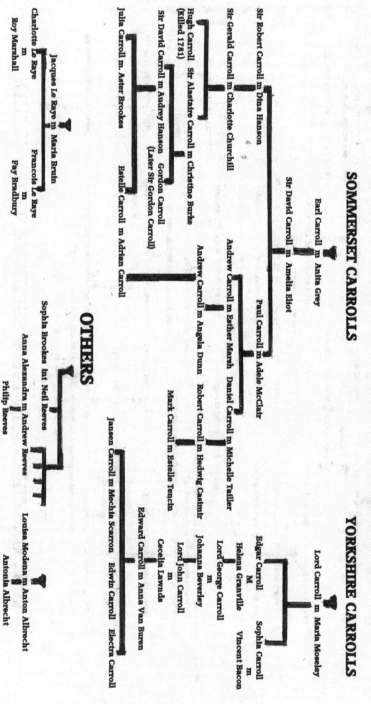

Sir Robert Carroll m Dina Hanson

Sir Gerald Carroll m Charlotte Churchill

Hugh Carroll   Sir Alastaire Carroll m Christine Burke
(Killed 1781)

Sir David Carroll m Audrey Hanson   Gordon Carroll
(later Sir Gordon Carroll)

Julia Carroll m. Aster Brookes

Estelle Carroll m Adrian Carroll

Earl Carroll m Anita Grey

Sir David Carroll m Amelia Eliot

Paul Carroll m Adele McClair

Andrew Carroll m Esther Marsh   Daniel Carroll m Michelle Trellier

Andrew Carroll m Angela Dunn   Robert Carroll m Hedwig Casimir

Mark Carroll m Estelle Tencin

Jansen Carroll m Mechta Scearron   Edwin Carroll   Electra Carroll

Edward Carroll m Anna Van Buren

Lord Carroll m Maria Moseley

Edgar Carroll   Sophia Carroll
M   m
Helena Granville   Vincent Bacon

Lord George Carroll
m
Johanna Beverley

Lord John Carroll
m
Cecelia Lawnds

OTHERS

Sophia Brookes int Neil Reeves

Anna Alexandra m Andrew Reeves   Louisa Modena m Anton Albrecht

Phillip Reeves   Antonia Albrecht

Jacques Le Raye m Maria Bruin

Charlotte Le Raye   Francois Le Raye
m   m
Roy Marshall   Fay Bradbury

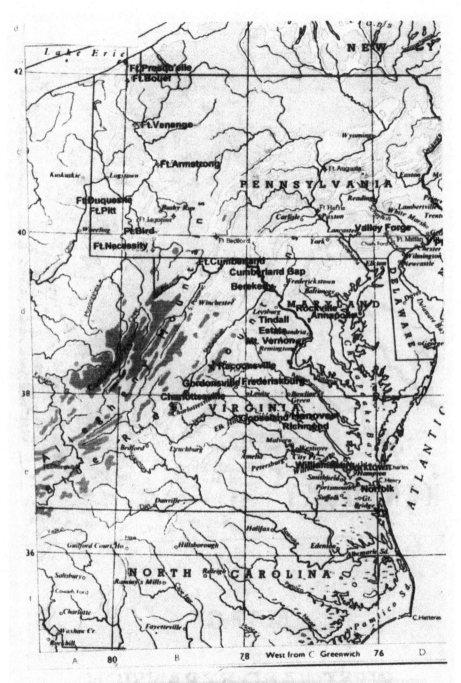

NORTH AMERICA
AREA OF CONFLICT 1700-1800
SOUTH

MAP OF

WESTWARD EXPANSION

Contents

Contents

PART 1

ESCAPE

ESCAPE

Louis Scarron took his wife, Julie, into his arms, trying to comfort her. "Please don't cry. I understand how you feel. We must try to help." They had just learned of the terrible Terror which had been unleashed onto a chaotic France in 1793. Julie refused to be consoled, "But they are murdering our relatives – our friends. It's not just happening in Paris but throughout the country. What can we do. The mob are not just killing aristocrats, they killing priests, and anyone who has any form of wealth. France has gone mad. Tell me how can we help. Neither the Dumas nor the Colbert's have any means of communicating with them. So how could we find them?"

Louis pulled Julie to him and kissed her. "We must go to Daniel. He has friends in England and Ireland who may help. After all, he has the important branch of his family living near Wookey, in Somerset. They are nearer to France. He might even get Lord Baltimore, in Ireland to help. Baltimore owes a lot to Daniel and the Carroll family. I'm certain they will try. Please, Julie, let us go to Racoonsville. I know he will try to help us. If, together, we can find them we must pay to bring them here to live with us. We can give them a new life here."

The United States of America was a very new country, a very different country from most. It had not been recognised by other countries until very recently. It had a government and like Britain it had an elected type of 'parliament', a Congress consisting like Britain of two Houses, a Senate and a House of Representatives. However, unlike nearly every country in Europe, it had no Monarch, no King. Instead it had a President and the first was, George Washington, the man who, as Commander-in-Chief, had led the country to victory against Britain. He had only been elected three years before. So the country was very different from all others in Europe.

However it seemed to America that the world was going mad. There was utter chaos in Europe. Perhaps it was their own revolution which had been

3

the catalyst for what was now developing elsewhere. Perhaps it had planted the seeds, for what was now happening in France. France which had given them so much help and without this, all knew they could never have been victorious, but now was being torn apart in Bloody Revolution. What had been, at first an attempt to curb the absolute power of the king. Then to try to develop a constitutional monarchy, a democratic country with everyone of substance being able to be elected, to help govern the country. But now this had been torn aside.

The first attempt, the National Assembly had been disbanded. The moderate Girondins had been overwhelmed by the militant Jacobins and now terror had been unleashed throughout the entire country, though the center of agitation and murder had been in the capital, Paris. It was here that the guillotine had been set up by which so many people, men and women, aristocrats, but many more ordinary people, lawyers, priests and political rivals, where executed by the severing of their heads. The year 1792 saw the death of many thousands of people. There was no real law only the law of the jungle and ruling by fear. In France there was anarchy such as no European country had ever seen before.

The Sans Culottes marched the streets taking anyone who might seem to oppose the revolution, and giving them mandatory execution. Although the National Convention had replaced the National Assembly it stood for little and Maximilien Robespierre had triumphed over most of his rivals, many of whom had been executed, and now he was the true ruler of France. King Louis XVI and his wife, Queen Marie Antoinette, after their abortive attempt to flee to the boarder and their capture, were now prisoners of the revolution. They no longer ruled France, which had now declared itself a Republic.

Leopold II, King of Austria and Emperor of the Holy Roman Empire, was extremely concerned about his sister, Marie Antoinette, and had demanded France must free her and her husband, and send them to Austria for safety. He did not want war but was threatening it. It seemed it might be avoided. However news had just arrived in America that the France National Convention, believing the down trodden people of the world would now revolt, if assisted, and remove all autocratic monarchs, had decided to act. They thought Austria should be the first to become free and so on April 20th. 1792 France had declared war on Austria and launched an offensive on the Austria Netherlands, which today is the country of Belgium.

The United States, which in the beginning had mainly supported Frances's attempt to free itself from Mediaeval constraints and introduce a system of democracy, now feared France was going mad and tearing itself apart, dissolving into anarchy. They also feared what damage this could do to the rest of Europe. At least they learned the French offensive was not going well. Perhaps its enemies might triumph and bring back sanity to that nation.

The United States found itself in a peculiar position. It owed so much to France for its help in freeing it from the British. Lafayette, who was a hero of America, having helped them so much to obtain their own freedom, had been one of the main supporters of trying to establish a constitutional monarchy and received great support from many Americans, including Thomas Jefferson of Congress. But many ordinary Americans had, also, been his supporter. Now matters had changed. Efforts had been made, unsuccessfully, to free Lafayette, and save him, but now his whereabouts were unknown. It was rumored he was a prisoner in a Prussian jail.

However because of the chaos now ruling France and the murder of so many people, without any kind of justice, the United States wanted to distance themselves from any decisions made there. It was essential, now that war had occurred between Austria and France. There was even more concern, for it seemed that France may soon be at war with Britain. This would place America in a dilemma. Britain, to many, was still the country which had opposed, so long, their own independence, Support should normally be given to France. But this was no longer the France which had been their loyal supporter.

How could they support a country in which a revolution had turned into a massacre of its own people. To most in the Government, especially the President, George Washington, the most sensible course was to adopted a position of neutrality. Yet their were some very important men, who still hated Britain so much, they might force the country to side with France. The United States was a new country. There had never been one like it before. All its actions were without precedent. They had no data to fall back on. Further more, though Washington's position was secure, there were many who now were trying to exert and better their own positions. Very ambitious men, with widely different views.

Two such opponents were Alexandra Hamilton and Thomas Jefferson. Both with very different views on where the country should move in the future. Hamilton was a Federalist and Jefferson considered democracy was more important than a well disciplined society. They were always at loggerheads in Congress providing Washington with difficulties in trying to reconcile their different views.

Washington had always abhorred the party system of British Government, which he believed had lead to America going to war with Britain, which he had done so much to avoid. He wanted to avoid such a system in America, but it seemed that with these two, were at loggerheads. It was likely that sooner than later, a two party system would emerge here. Yet he knew he required the different strengths of each men to help him govern successfully.

This was why he tolerated them and gave them important positions in his cabinet.

Hamilton was a brilliant financier and had successfully dealt with the large war debts, leading to the establishment of Bank of the United States in 1791, so necessary, but opposed as a threat to democracy and solitary power, by Jefferson. However it successfully overcame the problem of the old colonial, and now state debts.. Jefferson again opposed Hamilton's high tariffs and federal aid for public works. The real reason for their differences was their family background, and Jefferson, born as a Virginian, and his respect for freedom, though ironically he believed, firmly, in black slavery.

All this provided Washington with enough worries. Hamilton's Whiskey Tax in 1791, though sensible, had resulted in the Whisky Rebellion. The poor President had enough problems at home for this new embryonic country, untried and without the help of previous practices to guide it. It was a proof of the resilience and brilliance of Washington, that the country had made such progress, in such a short number of years.

But now the United States were beset by problems not of their own violation. With Europe in chaos and engaged in futile war, it now had to contend with new problems which might devastate it, through no fault of its own. However there were more personal problems besetting men like Washington and his friends in Virginia and Maryland, - where he would rather be, - than running this new country. With the war and even before it, Washington felt a responsibility to the many French men and women living in America, coming here since the start of the previous Seven Years war with France.

The Tencin's, Scarron's and many others who he knew must be in desperate fear for their relations living in War torn, revolutionary France. Though he must keep his country free from entanglements in Europe, he still wanted to help his friends of so many years, in trying to save their relatives – at least those who still remained alive. He would use all his possible power to bring as many as possible to America, and knew the Virginian and Maryland friends of his youth would help him.

However the news just received, of the war between France and Austria would make this even more difficult. His duty as the head of his country must take precedent over, even his friendship with the French exiles of the past. This then was the position when America had to prepare itself for a further influx of emigrants from all the countries in Europe suffering from a world gone mad.

2

Austria was at war with France but the war was going well and the Emperor, Leopold II, had no doubt but that his imperial forces would easily defeat the ill disciplined French army, a peasant army led and controlled by men of an inferior class, who had murdered, and displaced the nobles, born to rule such people. Then he would march into France, free his sister, Queen Marie Antoinette and place her husband, Louis back on his throne. Countries could only survive, if governed by Kings or Emperors. Others were intended to obey. The United States of America would never survive controlled by a president and men elected by the people. It was only a matter of time. It had been a bad example which had resulted in the trouble in France.

But Emperor Leopold and his entire court were much more concerned and shocked by the double scandal which had hit the royal court. Leopold was Emperor of the Holy Roman Empire, not just Austria, which had lasted almost a thousand years, and ruled by one family the Habsburgs. However before Emperor, Charles VI died, after his only son had died, he had declared that the female issue should succeed him. So his daughter, Maria Theresa became Empress, but since the constitution demanded a male as ruler, she married Francis Stephen of Lorraine, who became Emperor. From that date the country was ruled by the Court of Habsburg-Lorraine.

That was nearly fifty years ago. Her son, Joseph II, had followed Maria Theresa's long reign but, also, had died and his younger brother, Leopold had taken his place. This, in itself had created a problem, for Leopold was then Grand Duke of Tuscany. Tuscany had always claimed a measure of independence, hence the title of Grand Duke. Now it seemed that it was to be directly ruled by the Emperor. To avoid this Leopold separated the Duchy from his inheritance and made his second son Ferdinand, and his successors, to its lands and title. This now resulted in an enormous proliferation of prince and princesses of the court, related to other direct descendents of the old court, before Charles VI, as well as the many children of Maria Theresa and her descendents, and now the Duchy of Tuscany.

Inevitably this led to serious infighting, each family attempting to achieve a higher status, yet all were expected to perform with decorum within the imperial court. It was almost unforgivable if a daughter of one branch of the family were to attempt to marry a son of another family who was in disfavour with the first family. It could well lead to a duel of honour to decide the issue. Yet now it seemed two such princesses had dared to disobey the unwritten law, one engaging in an affair with a son of a family, which was virtually an enemy of the girl's family.

This was serious enough but almost at the same time another more serious affair had occurred when another princess rebelled and worse, entered into an affair with a commoner, an English tutor. Very quickly the two scandals became known to everyone at, or connected with court. Of course, because it seemed that these two princesses had probably conceived by their lovers, they must be separated and the princesses sent to a convert and forced to take up Holy Orders to help save their souls, for neither were married. – The only difficulty was in spite of the efforts of the entire court, and not just the two princess's family, it seemed neither the princesses, nor their lovers could be found. They appeared to have vanished into thin air.

⁓

Louisa Modena looked sadly at Anton. "You know it will make no difference. They'll never let us marry." Poor Louisa was referring to the fact that she knew she had conceived and was now carrying his child. This was the first couple whose scandal shocked the court.

"I know dearest," Anton Albrecht replied. "Once they know, they will put you in a convent for life. They will send you away and have our baby adopted after you bear it. Your mother and father hate all Albrecht's and every persons who come from Savoy, as I do. - Darling we must get away – we must leave Tuscany, immediately, before it's discovered." Louisa Modena was just twenty and Anton was three years older. Then he added, "I warned you we should not let this happen."

Louisa merely smiled and said, "Dearest you had no choice. I seduced you. I fooled you, deliberately. – You see I want your child – many of them. Why won't they let me have a life of my own with you. – But you are right. We must go -----"

Now Louisa sighed, " I know – I know - but I hate to leave Tuscany but where can we go and not be discovered and brought back here. – It's you I'm afraid for. If I stay and they send me away, they may relent and accept a large payment from your family to prevent them killing you. But if we flee and are captured and returned – my family will have no option. They will have to kill you for bringing disgrace to the House of Tuscany."

Anton took her in his arms and hugged her close to him, smothering her lips in his kisses and then stroking her long hair, as it fell behind her back, attempting to console her, "Louisa I have an idea, but it will mean we must go far away, perhaps never to return here. We are both rich. I know my family will not stop my allowance, but if not I have a considerable fortune in trust in a bank in Venice. We could transfer this anywhere to another bank in the civilised world. – Your personal horde of jewels are worth a fortune. If we were to use these, with my own fortune we could buy land – an estate anywhere."

Louisa broke loose from his embrace. "But Anton if this were anywhere in Europe – however far – they would discover it. The Habsburgs have sufficient power to make that country return us to them."

Now Anton smiled, "But that will take some time – weeks, months – even a year. This will give us the time to plan. I have some cousins in Spain close to Cartegena. They are wealthy and important and more, we could rely on them to kept our secret. Of course if we stayed there we would eventually be discovered. However they also have plantations in Spanish Florida in America. We could buy an estate there and then after a short time travel there to spend the rest of our lives in peace. My cousins would never betray us. However it means you leaving all you love here and travelling thousands of miles across the Atlantic to a new and developing country. – Could you make this sacrifice?"

Now it was Louisa's turn and lovingly embrace Anton. She took one of his hands and pressed it to her breast – breasts she knew he loved to fondle and which gave her such delight. "Dear, Dear Anton if I must leave home, I'm willing to go anywhere, just so long as you are there, with me. – In any case – I want your baby – I shall lose it – and you - if I stay here. You know where I store my jewels – make the arrangements. I will travel with you as soon as you can arrange it."

Now she took him by the hand and led him through the door into the bedroom. Anton did not need an invitation. She said, "But even those arrangements can wait. I'm already pregnant – The damage is done – Give me the pleasure I know you can give me – My body is yours – as it always will be."

3

Tears were running down the face of nineteen year old Anna Alexandra. They were tears of desperation. "Oh! I'm now certain it has happened, Andrew. What shall I do? When the discover my condition they will make me take Holy Orders and banish me to a convent, for the rest of my life. – Worse I shall never know our baby. It will be adopted and sent away. I might as well be dead."

Anna was pleading with Andrew Reeves, her English Tutor, who had been employed by her family to improve her education. Anna was the daughter of Maximillian Franz of Lorraine and his wife Karolina. Franz was the son of Charles Alexandra of Lorraine and his own wife called Anna, the very reason for her being given this name. Whilst Charles' Anna, was one of the younger daughters of Empress Maria Theresa and Franz Stephen I. So Anna Alexandra had the blood of both the Hapsburg's and Lorraine in her veins.

Andrew Reeves was an English man of twenty one, who had been brought from Somerset, in England to tutor Anna, as he was very proficient in both the French and Italian languages, as well as having a good knowledge of Spanish, having acquired these talents in a school in Bristol. He had been teaching Anna, now for some fifteen months, and was very handsome. There was no doubt but that Anna had been attracted to him from the moment he arrived at their ancestral castle in Lorraine.

However the invasion of the Austrian Netherlands and then the war with France, had caused her family to leave their homeland, as it was now unsafe and come to Austria for protection. Her mother and father had gone to live at court in Vienna. However Anna and Andrew had, quickly, been sent to one of the Hapsburg's great mansions in Granz. It was this separation which had led to Anna's present predicament and downfall.

Left, virtually, without chaperones, very soon Anna became very attached to Andrew. With no one to check her, she had happily flirted with this very handsome man, her friend, now, for so long. Inevitably it had gone further and their flirtation had become intimate. Eventually, Anna's desire for him had become so great, and not having any men of her own prestige at Granz, she had succumbed, with the inevitable results. It had only happened once, but now poor Anna had found she was, almost certainly, carrying Andrew's child. This was her desperate situation as she confessed her condition to her lover.

Between her sobbing she added, "Andrew, I have no future – neither have you. They will execute you for what you have done, as soon as they discover it. – Andrew, I know it is impossible, but I do love you, sincerely. – That is why I let you lie with me. It was heavenly. – However, even if this had not happened, you know they would never have considered letting us marry. – Now we shall be parted forever. You will be dead and I may just as well have died."

Andrew, already, had his arm around her trying to comfort her. Now he pulled he to him and hugged her sobbing body to him. Then gently and quietly he spoke to her. "Anna, how really strong is your love for me. I've told you repeatedly I love you, perhaps, even more, than you may love me. – Would it be possible for you to make an even greater, sacrifice. We could run away. Go to England. Once there we could marry. But it would not be the life of comfort you have enjoyed, ever since you were born. – But I would stand by you, and never fail you, and we would be together for ever afterwards."

Now Anna was startled, "What do you mean run away?- How? – You have little money. How could we live without such means. How could we escape from here, let alone find a way to go so far as England. – In any case, even if we arrived there, they would find us, and force the British to return both of us for punishment."

Now he kissed the side of her face. "I doubt if they would ever find us, but it would mean that you would have to forget and annunciate your grand name. Become, simply, Mrs Andrew Reeves. I warn you it would be a very hard life, one, I fear, you would not want to endure. But we would both be alive and, more important, together, both helping each other to earn a living."

Poor Anna sighed, un-believingly. "How could we. – Dearest, if you still want me, I believe I could accept any future other than the one at present decreed for me. Becoming a Nun would be a living death for me. Only my faith would prevent me killing myself and sending my soul to hell. – We could never marry – I am a Catholic and you are a Protestant. In England, I would have to renounce my faith. – Dearest, I could not do this, even to be with you."

Now he kissed her again. "I would never want you to do that. Neither would I become a Catholic. That would only be the case if we stayed in England. – No if we went to America, we could each worship as we pleased.

Maryland, especially and West Virginia allow complete religious freedom. You could remain a Catholic and I, a Protestant. Though you might have to, first, marry me in a protestant church in England.. I swear I would marry you again in a Roman Catholic church in America, though, meantime we could live together as husband and wife. – so our child, when born, would be legitimate."

Anna turned and now kissed the side of his face. "Oh! Please! Tell me how. How can we get to England and then to America. To me it seems it is impossible."

He just smiled, "I've been thinking of this since you first feared you might be pregnant. You have some jewels and I have just been paid. Together we have enough to pay for a passage on a ship leaving Trieste. You know my Italian is very good. We could sail to Bristol and I could take you to my family in Somerset. It is there that we could marry. Only after this would be sail further to Maryland and settle there. We should still have sufficient left to pay for a passage and I know my family would help. – But it would mean leaving this life behind – forever. You must realize it will be a very hard life. One, perhaps, you cannot contemplate."

Again Anna sighed, "But we would be together. Even now, I believe that would be better – no extremely desirable – than my fate if I stay here. Also, it would mean you could live. I would not be responsible for your death. Dearest, you will have to help me – I've had no training for such a life. But I will try. In any case I can keep our child, which will be torn away, if I stay in Austria."

This settled, it was, now, time to be practicable. Together they assessed their asserts. Andrew had enough money to hire a coach to take them to Trieste. There, they could sell some of her jewels, only a few, to prevent suspicion – but enough to pay for a passage to Bristol in England, as they knew many ships sailed there each week. Once in Britain they could sell more and so, especially, if his family would help, they would have sufficient to pay for a passage to America. Even then they thought they might still have enough to purchase some land in America. But it would have to be in the wilderness – the Ohio country. However, Andrew told her he knew there were, now, many people leaving England and settling there. They would not be alone.

Again. It was necessary to explain fully to Anna what sacrifices she must make if she came with him, though he told her he loved her deeply, and wanted her as his wife, and promised her he would never discard or hurt her. She had simply smiled and added. "Andrew I want to live – and live with you, for the rest of my life. I will prove to you I can do this. I will make you happy – yes, even proud of me."

So very carefully they planned their escape. It had been usual for them to go into the countryside most days. No one would be suspicious, until they discovered she had not slept in her bed. In any case, she spread the rumour that she must soon visit her mother in Vienna and would be away several days. It was carefully orchestrated and Andrew went into town and purchased a carriage.

Very cleverly Andrew had the carriage driven to the castle and with some ceremony she boarded it telling everyone she was going to her mother. He joined it a little distance along the road. Once in town, Andrew took the place of the coachman and they set out along their long and difficult journey over the Alps, but it was summertime.

They had arrived at Trieste before anyone at Granz was suspicious of Anna's departure. In fact, very long afterwards they discovered their flight had not been discovered until they were both on a ship sailing to Bristol. They had sold part of her jewels and boarded a ship leaving two days later. So their tracks were already very old, when at last the Austrian court heard of her departure, making it extremely difficult to ascertain where she had gone.

They were not to know it but exactly a week before they left Trieste, Louisa Medina and Anton Albrecht had made their own escape, but their ship had been bound for Spain and later to Spanish Florida. So the scandal at the court became known but they found it difficult to ascertain their destinations. It would be many months before the court even discovered they had both left on ships from Trieste, and they did not even know the names of the ships on which they had sailed.

4

Roy Marshall had entered the mill with the mob who had then set fire to it, but Roy was more practical than the others. Though like them he was thirsting for revenge, he wanted to be more practical and gain something from the man he considered had led to the deaths of both his parents, due to starvation, which, also, had nearly killed him. He wanted Robert Grimshaw to pay heavily. He had found his large safe and used his heavy crowbar to break it open. As expected, Roy found it full of gold coins. He now held in his hands a bag into which he had poured these. He knew, though not a fortune, it was sufficient to keep him alive for very many months, perhaps years.

As the flames were now licking the outside of the office, he made a hastily escape, still carrying the heavy load in the bag, desperately trying to remember the way he had came as the smoke was dense. Roy did not consider he was stealing, only exacting a justified revenge for what that man had done to his family. It was, justifiable, retribution for his wrongs.

For many years his family had earned a reasonable living as hand-loom workers in their house near Gorton, in Manchester. Of recent years they had taken their woven cloth to Robert Grimshaw's nearby house to sell their products. It had been very profitable, so much so that his parents could pay a local teacher to instruct Roy how to read an write, unusual for persons of their trade. Then in 1790 it had stopped.

Robert Grimshaw in league with Thomas Arkwright had set up a cotton mill at Knott Mill, Manchester, mechanizing the industry, using Arkwright's steam engine for power. This resulted in them being unable to sell their own handmade products forcing them into to poverty and then starvation, causing his parents to die. His mother had only born one child, namely himself, being unable to conceive after his birth, so he had been left alone. However his family were only one of very many families who had suffered this way, and as other handloom workers in other parts of Lancashire, were suffering from men like Robert Grimshaw.

Rather than die, as his parents had died, they had come to gather as a mob and today had stormed into the mill setting it on fire and destroying the cause of their suffering. Roy had joined them and had wanted revenge, which he now considered he had enacted. The others had only been concerned with destroying the thirty power looms which were the cause of their problem. Perhaps his little education had taught him to plan and devise a further revenge. Hence his attack on Grimshaw's safe and the valuable acquisition he now held in his hands.

He could hear the sound of rifle shots, even above the roar of the fire, so there must be many who were now suffering. He struggled to find a way of escape, as everyone else appeared to have left. At last he found the door, almost choking with the smoke, he staggered outside into the fresh air. The mob had gone, disbursed by the continued volleys from the soldiers who had hurried to quell the riot. But not all had fled. There were many bodies lying strewn across the courtyard, with others bending over their dead compatriots. Many were women who had come with their men, forming part of the mob.

Roy could see the soldiers now trying to take those they had captured, away to be taken to the local prison,. Fortunately the smoke from the burning building was obscuring many from their view. He knew the way outside from the back, as he had visited Grimshaw many times in the mill during the last three years, trying to get employment, without success. This was his means of escape, for if not he would not only lose his new wealth, but possibly his life or transportation to this new land in Australia.

In the smoke he nearly fell over a young girl bending over a dead man. Yet he could still see she was attractive, possibly in her late teens. She did not seem to notice him and was weeping violently saying, "Oh! Trevor! Don't leave me. I need you. I do not want to live without you. You mean everything to me." So this man, only slightly older than her, was not her father, but possibly a brother, a husband or a lover, and meant very much to her. Whether it was pity or, more possibly because she was attractive, he stopped in his flight and bent down, almost forcing her, against her will, to stand.

He spoke sharply to her, "He is dead. There is nothing you can do. If you stay with him, the soldiers will find you. Then you will land in jail, and may be executed or transported abroad, at the next assizes. Come with me. I know a way out. It's your only chance." She still did not move and tried to bend down again to the man. He was not sure why he reacted. Was it that he pitied her, or did he not want the soldiers to win the day. He had never hit a woman before, but his fist shot into her chin and she collapsed unconscious in his arms as he caught her. Slinging her light weight over his shoulders, still holding the bag of coins in his other hand, he then staggered through the smoke, the way he knew and away from that cursed mill. The cause of all the mayhem.

Taking the back dark passage, he put as much distance from the mill and those soldiers, as was possible, coming at last to the green clearing, almost a mile from the fire which was still raging. He then laid her down and tried to revive her. Slowly, she became conscious. Immediately fear came into her eyes. She knew she had been abducted. Now she feared, what did this man intend to do to her, for she knew she was in his power.

She almost screamed out her fear, "Oh! – Please! – Please do not hurt me." He just smiled and replied, "I've no intention of hurting you." A little relieved she asked, "But why did you take me from Trevor. He is all I've got. His parents and mine are dead. Now I'm alone in this world. It would have been better if you had left me there."

Now he sat down bedside her and, though she shivered in fear, gently put his arm around her, trying to comfort her. "You are not alone – I am here. Please let me talk to you. Please don't be afraid. – I don't know why – but I do want to help you. But first we get away from here. Soon those soldiers will be searching for all of us. We must leave Manchester. I think out best plan would be to travel to Liverpool – now – today. You say you have no one. Can you trust me. – will you come with me. I promise I will not try to rape or hurt you."

Her reply surprised him. She said, "Even if you did those terrible things – it would not matter. I'm already a fallen woman. I'm carrying Trevor's baby. We were to marry next week, so he could take care of me. – If you want me I will come with you, if you want me, you can use me. I've nothing, now, to live for – but how could we travel to Liverpool. It will cost money?"

Again he smiled at her and then very gently kissed the side of her face, so as not to frighten her. Then he held up the heavy bag. "I have the money, enough to hire a carriage. If you will come with me, I will take you with me, for neither of us dare stay here any longer. They will search every house. We dare not return to our homes or they will find us. It was a riot and they will want to punish all of us, to prevent it happening again. – However if you come with me, you must be willing to do all I say. – I promise I won't misuse you. – There is nothing for you, if you stay here. We might even find work in Liverpool – though I doubt it. We may have to go far away. If so would you come with me. I swear I will not attack you – and I do feel sorry for you. – Frankly – I do not know why."

Perhaps it was his last remark which gave her the courage to accept his offer. He was right. She knew no one. He was her only hope. In her condition, she had to trust him. She knew her only alternative was to inhabit a brothel – become a prostitute. Even if he forced her to live with him as his wife – it would be better than that, so she said "Yes! If that's what you want."

To her delight he smiled kindly at her, then said, "In that case, I think I should know your name. I'm called Roy Marshall – but please call me – Roy." She gave a little frighten laugh. "I'm called Fay Bradbury – but you can call me – Fay." Then she started weeping again, "The man I loved and intended to marry was Trevor Reynolds. Our families have known each other for years. We were both hand-loom workers until the Grimshaw's set up that mill. They really caused both our parents deaths. That is why we came here today."

Again Roy smiled, "It was just the same for my parents. I knew Robert Grimshaw well, but he did not help us. Anyway this money in my bag belonged to him. But it does no longer belong to him now. That is my revenge. – Come. Let's go to the stables and hire a carriage. The sooner we can get away from here and get to Liverpool, away from this town – the better. – We can talk on the journey. It will take a least a day. – Perhaps we shall know each other better when we arrive there."

Now more composed, Fay stood up with him and then grasped his offered hand and went to the stables to hire their transportation.

5

R oy Marshall knew where to go. He knew a carriage man, who in their past more affluent life, it had been used by his father, when he needed to travel distances selling their products. The man would "sell" a carriage and horses to them. However when they got to Liverpool, a colleague of his would buy them back from him, with a little deduction for their use. Ray went with Fay and obtained their transport and set out for Liverpool. When darkness came they slept in their carriage next to each other but Roy made no unwanted approaches to her body.

They arrived in Liverpool the next afternoon and Roy bought accommodation for both of them in a good quality inn, knowing the authorities, even if they tried, would hardly look there. Fay had told him to purchase one room and register her as his wife, though she added, "I'm afraid I will not do my duties to you that way." Roy just smiled, "I would not expect you to do so, but it will save money."

That night they had the first opportunity to tell each other of their past lives and how Fay had fallen completely in love with her childhood friend Trevor Reynolds. How it became intimate and when she discovered she had conceived his child, Trevor insisted they should marry. Now it was too late. She sighed, "Now what is to become of me,. I shall be an unmarried mother, with a child?"

So as not to frighten her, Roy took her hands and kissed them. "I will not make any demands on you, but I was brought up to respect women – especially those in need. If you stay with me I will see to and ensure you have the funds to see to your child. That bag of coins is sufficient to keep both of us for much longer than a year. By then I shall have found other ways of adding to it."

Fay was surprised, no, astonished, "You would do this and not expect me to reward you, as a wife should do? Am I not, then, very attractive to you?" He smiled, "No! My dear girl, it is not that. I admit, I would very much like to get to know you better. I am a man, and you are a very lovely girl. I have the same faults as any man – but I would never take a woman by force – nor use my position to demand more. It would only happen, if you wanted it, and you would have to convince me that it was your wish and not for any repayment."

Up to now Fay had not really considered her position. She had accepted coming with him, as she knew the alternative would be much worse, even if he used her. After all she was, already, pregnant, hc could not hurt her that way. Now she regarded Roy in a different way. He must have some affection for her, just to adopt her and help her. She still did not have any strong feelings for him. She had just lost the man she had loved for many years. At that moment she decided she would stay with him and see how things might develop. At least, it seemed he had no real girl friend of his own. Not one with whom he would have wanted to spend his life with.

They went out and toured the town. The papers told all about the riots in Manchester, and other happenings the previous day, in Rochdale. It seemed that the hand-loomers, were not going to accept these new ways of weaving, without protests, but only Grimshaw's mill had been burnt. However they also learned that work was just as hard to obtain, here, as it was in Manchester. So, somewhat desponded, they returned to their inn.

They arrived as a young man and a young woman were registering., booking two rooms, so it seemed they were not married. They had both purchased some clothes whilst they were near the shops, so they opened their wears and dressed, appropriately for dinner. Then went downstairs. The room was busy and they found they must share a table with others. By chance they found the other two at a table were the ones they had seen registering. Roy saw the young women's eyes were red from crying, so she must be unhappy, or unwell.

He felt he must inquire, asking her if this was so. It was the man who replied. "No my sister is not unwell, but thank you for your consideration. No, I'm afraid, it is just that we are so very unhappy. You must have read of the riots in Lancashire. The mob in Rochdale, murdered our father and mother, yesterday, and we were both fortunate to escape ourselves."

Roy curiosity knew no bounds. "Were you then the owners of one of these new cotton mills. Like the one in Manchester, we see they burned Grimshaw's mill, that same day." The man gave a sad smile. "No! But it was my father who made it possible. The owner employed him, at a good salary, to leave our very prosperous handloom industry and work for him. You see my father invented the flying shuttle, which enable the machinery to make the weave. In fact we have become quite rich, in the last three years, but unfortunately many other handloom workers have been cast into poverty."

He continued, "There had been several attacks on the families who worked at the new mill. Then they discovered what father had done. So they attacked my mother and father in the street and beat both of them to death. We knew then they would come and find us and do the same to us. That was two days go. We dare not stay. We knew that father had received communication from a man in Philadelphia, in America, begging him to come there had wanted to use his inventions to start a mill there. Even offering him a partnership. I know my father intended to accept."

Now he sighed, "We had a large share of money stored away, ready, for us to emigrate. I told my sister, we must leave Rochdale, leave the man to whom she had become engaged, and travel to Liverpool, to board a ship to go to America. It was our only chance. I, almost, had to use force to bring her here. – Well that is our story. Tomorrow we will try to find a boat. I shall write to this man, telling him we are coming, and I have my father's invention to trade with him. Now neither of us wish to stay in Liverpool."

Roy looked at Fay, "Would you be willing to come with me to America? I'm certain we could find employment and live a good life there." Though Fay was a little confused at his sudden wish to leave England. She did not want to stay here without him. So she replied, "Roy, if it is your wish, then I will gladly come with you."

As they had all about finished their, meals Roy, suggested they should arise and go to the smoke room to talk. The other two, glad to have company, agreed, and followed him there. Now at last Roy introduced himself as Roy Marshall and Fay as his girlfriend. The man introduced themselves as Huge Foyle and his sister, as Linda Foyle. It was then that Roy could tell them, but not a true story of his recent life. Explaining that his family, like the others had been very prosperous handloomer's. However the coming of Grimshaw's mill had severely limited their wealth. As both there parents had recently died, they had sometime previously intended to come to Liverpool, were there was no mill, and carrying on working there. Saying it was a co-incidence that they must have left Manchester, on -the very day the mob had destroyed the mill, but they would have come here in any case.

Roy concluded his fictitious tale, by telling them they had a reasonable amount of money from their past prosperity, and was why they had come to Liverpool to try their luck there, rather than an impossible life in Manchester. Just a few moments ago they had learned of the other two's idea of going abroad. He then asked them, if they were to come with them, would Hugh, with his contacts there, try to help him to find employment in Philadelphia. He told them he had sufficient money for the passage and for many months in future. If not they would come anyway, as it seemed that prospects there were better than in England.

It seemed Hugh warmthed to the idea and spoke to Linda, who seemed to like the idea, so Hugh agreed and felt sure he could help Roy to find suitable work when they arrived. Before they retired that evening, it was agreed that the next day they would go out together, and try to discover a ship sailing to America, and not too distant from Philadelphia. They sat drinking together for sometime, talking of their past. Roy noticed that Linda's spirit seemed to have improved, talking to a new, and handsome man. Her reaction seemed to please her brother, for up to now, he knew that, without her fiancée, she felt her world had been torn apart. Even her desire to live. Losing him, as well as the parents she had adored, and who had given her such a very happy life, all within the last two days.

As they retired to bed, Linda felt a pang on jealousy, when she saw both Roy and Fay entered the same bedroom. She assumed, though not married, their affair had progressed sufficiently, for it to become more intimate, than just a casual one. Still, she thought, 'On the ship, it would be a long journey, possibly weeks, I might be able to come to know this man more fully." She, determined, then, she would try

6

The Congress of the United States had constantly opposed the imposition of a Regular Army, believing such a force could provide the situation whereby someone might wish to take dictatorial control of the country. Only the rebellions in Massachusetts, then in 1787, Daniel Shay's rebellion and attack on the Springfield arsenal provided Washington and his Secretary of State for War, General Knox with ammunition to demand a Standing Military force. A ludicrously small unit of some 800 men were accepted.

One small but important concession was agreed, assigning all executive power to the President, so General Knox was responsible to Washington and not to Congress. This meant that the President became the Commander-in-chief of the army and navy. Gradually over the years the size of the Regular Army was increased to about 1,300 men. However with the enormous influx of new emigrants into the North West Territories squatting on lands which Congress had granted the indians by treaty, had produced a very difficult situation. The indians had retaliated killing whole families. In 1790 over 1,500 settlers had died in Kentucky and now Miami Indians to the north in Ohio and on new adjacent areas, which was being referred to as the Indiana territory, were attacking southwards from Lake Erie, assisted by the forts still, wrongly, in British control on the lake. Something had to be done.

The Regular force was too small and General Knox obtained Congress support for demanding from each state, a militia of soldiers belonging to the state, and trained by them but giving Congress the right to call on 'every able white citizen between 18 and 45' to form part of that militia. However their time of service was limited, ridiculously, to three months every year.

To deal with the indian situation in the north Secretary Knox ordered Arthur St. Clair, Governor of the North West Territory to appoint General Harmar, who had distinguished himself during the War for Independence, to assemble at Fort Washington, now the locality of the City of Cincinnati, his regular force of some 1,300 trained men, and demanded from the local states including West Virginia, a militia force of at least 1,500 recruits, some of them as mounted soldiers. Where possible the Militia should consist of volunteers. Pennsylvania and Kentucky, near the center of the disturbance would provide the large numbers, but West Virginia and even northern Virginia would contribute a few.

Notices were circulated from all the West Virginian Forts, of Pitt, Necessity, and Fort Cumberland calling for volunteers. It was in this way that twenty four year old, James Downey and twenty year old, Paul Eliot learned of this request. Both lived with the adjacent families a few miles to the south west of Fort Cumberland. Families who had become quite rich breeding and raising horses for sale, which were in great demand as the new west expanded. In fact it had been in the recent War for Independence that Simon and Jessie Downey had come from poverty in Ireland, with their two babies, James and Helen, their passage paid by Daniel Carroll, who wished to extend his grandfather's desire to bring to America any of his wonderful grandmother, Amelia's family, in difficulties in Europe.

However at the same time another descendent of Amelia's, Peter and Elsie Eliot, also with two children, Patricia and Paul, though living in Maryland, were in some difficulties because both their families, were large and the land they worked could not support all of them. Again Daniel had suggested they combine their family with the Downey's. As Simon had been trained in breeding horses in Ireland, Daniel purchases this large stretch of land in what was then called the Wilderness. Land unsuitable for agriculture but excellent for raising horses.

Daniel and his wife Michelle had helped to establish both families on the small estate, even building a homestead with adjacent rooms to house them and helping until they had trained Peter and Elsie, how to rise horses together. Later as the number in their family had increased they had built a similar home nearby. Yet they had always behaved as one large family. Though there had never been any sexual relations between the two families, neither had they ever tried to avoid each other' s view of the naked bodies. In fact it was almost one large family.

Over the years they had persuaded other families, emigrants from Europe, to come and work for them. Establishing homesteads for them but still acting as employees, but also very much their friends. However in spite of these additions, the numbers living in the area were quite small. Even their mothers and fathers realized there were few opportunities for their children to meet and possibly marry a partner.

It was true that both Helen Downey and Patricia Eliot and formed an association with two sons of the families who had come to help them, but neither James nor Paul had found any of the younger females, persons who they might later consider as wives. In fact they had needed to make many visits to Fort Cumberland where there were very well run brothels, to assuage their manly desires.

It is true they had made contact with a number of girls within the rich and aristocratic families in the Potomac valley, but they both knew they were merely the playthings of these rich girls, who would never consider them as suitable long time partners, for they realized their own social standing, nor their wealth, would lead to a permanent relationship. So they enjoyed their sexual relationships with them, but knew it would be short lived.

Now however they had just returned from Fort Cumberland with the request of men like them to join the militia being assembled for service in the North West Territories. Each had completed their annual training and James would probably be offered an officer ship in this force. Both had been trained in horsemanship and would form part of the Cavalry contingent. More important each could look forward to a life, far more adventurous than the one they lived at present, even if a little dangerous.

Of course they still had to persuade both their families to let them go and enlist. It was true that their work would be missed but by now they, as part of the family, which owned the business, they were mainly required to do administrated tasks. In fact it was these tasks they found boring.

They had one persuasive point in their favour. If they joined, not only the two horses they would ride themselves but also they would be allowed to bring for sale six more horses, but only if they had joined the militia. This would in effect add greatly to that months sale of horse, and at a good price. Finally their term of service would be only three moths from the time they arrived at Fort Washington.

Both their families could see it was the desire for adventure and the possibility of meeting more interesting feminine company than was available to them at the homestead. In fact they felt proud of them, though their sisters were loath to see them go, fearing for their lives. They promised their fathers that when their term of service was over they would return home, even if they had meet some feminine company. So at last both sons obtained approval for them joining the militia.

Choosing two excellent mounts for themselves, they drove the six other horses to Fort Cumberland, signed papers as volunteers for three months service. Received letters of credit for the sale of all eight horses which they deposited in the bank in the fort until they returned . Then with a few others who had assembled there, set off on the three hundred mile journey via Fairmount and Parkersburg. Then following the great Ohio River all the way to Fort Washington, arriving at the end of May.

7

Louis and Julie Scarron had gone to Racoonsville to meet Daniel Carroll and his French wife, Michelle, hoping he could help their friends in France, now in danger of their lives. They felt sure that Daniel or his nephew, now the Master of Rockville, the estate which his grandfather, Sir David Carroll, had been given when he first landed in America, would help.

They were surprised, and relieved to find Daniel had, already, set in progress a means by which they could help them. In this he had been assisted, greatly, by the President, George Washington, who was a friend of all of them and who, too, was desperate to help many Frenchmen, who had helped during the American Revolution against Britain. Daniel had told them that he was certain that his nephew, Andrew Carroll, would willingly help financially, if required. Rockville was both the richest and largest estates in Maryland. It was the base from which the present protestant Carroll families in America had originated. However Andrew hated publicity so Daniel preferred not to trouble him.

Cecilius Calvert had been Governor of Maryland, like his predecessors, at the time of the American Revolution. Because of his family in Ireland, his sympathies had been with Britain, and had affiliated with them when they landed at Annapolis. However he had been a lifelong friend of both of them, as he had been of Daniel's uncle, Sir Robert Carroll, and together had tried to avoid insurgency and ensure peace in Maryland, for long after the war in New England had begun. He loved America as much as Ireland, but wanted America to remain British.

So, though branded as a loyalist, when the United States won, George had enabled him to retain his lands in Maryland, after paying reparations for aiding the British, and had promised him that he, or his relatives, would be welcome to come and stay on his land, after he returned to Ireland. As his father had recently died, Cecilius had become Lord Baltimore. He had one son, Frederick Calvert, who had married Lady Diana Egerton, daughter of the Duke of Bridgewater, who had died not long after their wedding. This had devastated him. He never married again, though he did have a few affairs with other women, leading to the birth of an illegitimate son, Henry Harford. Only recently Frederick had died of a broken heart.

Frederick's sister, Caroline had married and had a son Robert Eden, now twenty two years of age, who had come to Maryland with another relative, Horatio Sharpe, to live for a time on the Calvert estate in Maryland. So it had been easy for both Daniel and George Washington, to obtain the assistance of them to use their influence in Ireland to try to give secure to French émigrés fleeing to Britain, and even becoming involved in helping some to escape from France. Lord Baltimore had been pleased to help his friends in America, by allocating large sums of money for this purpose, and fortunately Daniel Carroll knew three young men who lived on his estate, who thirsted for adventure, and good employment, all whom could speak French, and willing to risk their lives by going to France at Baltimore's expense, each offering if they could help.

This was due to a remarkable relationship covering over a century between the Carroll family in America and the Irish family in Ireland. These three men were the descendents of Margaret and Amelia Eliot, again an intriguing and complicated story, concerning, Amelia Eliot, a convicted felon, to serve as an indentured servant in Maryland, and bear four children, out of wedlock, in quick succession. Amelia was Daniel Carroll's grandmother, who discovered love and eventually married Daniel's grandfather, David Carroll, himself an émigré from his, illustrious family, at Wookey, in Somerset, meeting Amelia, and saving her life, on their journey from Bristol to Annapolis.

David Carroll, risking the wrath of his family, had married Amelia, then became, for a time Governor of Maryland, even defying King William III, before becoming a Knight of the Bath and making this peasant girl, Lady Amelia. Then bringing her mother Margaret and several of her families to come a live in Maryland, to work land owned by him. Only two of her family, her brother Sidney, married to Mary and Pamela Eliot married to Simon Downey, had preferred to stay in Ireland, being more prosperous.

Sir David, then Sir Robert Carroll, and now Daniel Carroll, for many years had carried on communication with both Sidney and Pamela's descendants. Of course the growing size of both families had meant financial difficulties as the years passed and now Daniel knew of three young men aged between twenty four and twenty, the fifth generation of both Sidney and Pamela, whose prospect in Ireland, though not poor, were somewhat of a liability to their families, and yearned for a chance to prove themselves, and at the same time obtain good financial success.

Daniel had, through Robert Eden, written to Cecilius Calvert, giving him their names, explaining that he had discovered their desire to go to

France to try to rescue some from the terror. The reason these three could understand French was due the influence of Daniel's wife, Michelle, who during the long absences of her husband during the last war, had passed the time by writing many letters, in French, being of French birth, to all three of them, in Ireland with translations in English and sending money for them to obtain a teacher to enable them to speak the language. It seemed that this pastime would now provide dividends.

Meantime, at George Washington's behest, he had been using his influence and money to discover the whereabouts and the present condition of several Frenchmen of good birth. Two in particular were, Victor, Comte de Lameth and his brother, Charles Francois Lameth, both of whom had helped Washington greatly, during the war against Britain. Washington wished to spare their lives, if they had not yet been executed.

It seemed that Daniel had anticipated Louis and Julie's coming, although he knew of Louis' mother's death in 1783, he knew of his relatives, his two step-sisters Marie, married to Henri Colbert and Catherine, now married to Jacques Lespinasse. He also knew of their earlier difficult life at the Court of Versailles, where, for financial reasons and titles, like his mother they had to make themselves available to rich courtiers for amorous liaisons. Often leading to pregnancy.

Neither Marie nor Catherine were his father's child. At court all noble women in the time of both King Louis XIV and Louis XV, had to be willing to join the king's bed for his pleasure, often with the expected result. Both kings were notorious for the number of illegitimate children they had sired. For their services these poor women received very generous gifts and often titles as a reward for their infidelities. Though not with the king, both Marie and Catherine had needed to sacrifice their bodies to other noblemen to enable them to live financially, with their husband having to accept their lapses.

Both Marie and Catherine had to yield themselves to Comte Guillaume de Lamoignon Malesherbes. Marie, though then married to Henri Colbert, had born him a daughter, Louise and a son Guillaume. Catherine, though then unmarried and young, had born him a son, Antoine. This was before they came to America before the war, to escape from the necessity of further unwanted pregnancies. In spite of this neither Marie, Catherine, not Henri had felt any animosity to the Comte, and, though not necessary, the Comte had sent many letters of credit to pay for his children's upbringing.

The Comte had held many very important positions under King Louis, only resigning from politics after his reform program, along with his friend, Turgot, and had then refused to become further involved. They knew, after thirteen years in retirement, he had felt obliged to act as defender of King Louis XVI, at his trial in 1792. They knew he had been arrested soon afterwards, but did not know his fate. For these reasons Daniel, had already, added his name and those of his family to the list given to Cecilius Calvert.

One other name given by Daniel was Madame de Lamballe, a longtime friend of Louis Scarron's mother. Her life was probably more in danger than anyone as everyone knew she had been Marie Antoinette's special friend for many years. With the king and queen executed they all feared for Madame de Lamballe's life.

So it seemed to both Louis and Julie that Daniel had, already, set in motion a plan to try to first discover their whereabouts, and the then try to extricate all of them from death by guillotine. Robert Eden had told Daniel, that Cecilius had spent large sums of money, merely, to discover where they might be. Now he told them he had sent for the three men, whose names Daniel had given him to provide them with the means, and transport to France to see if they could save any of them.

They were given additional instructions to add to this list anyone associated with the names already given to them, even any servants who might, also, be in danger because of their service to their masters. It seemed, now, that any one connected with nobility in any, were considered as loyalists and might receive the same punishment for their crime. Robert Eden was able to report that the three men had, already, left for France. So Louis, Julie and Daniel would have to wait to see if they had achieved any success.

8

David Downey was twenty four years of age and the fifth descendent of Pamela (Eliot) and Simon Downy. Jack Eliot was twenty three and Stuart Brady was just twenty, both fifth descendents of Sydney and Mary Eliot. Pamela Eliot and Sidney were the elder sister and brother of Lady Amelia Carroll, David Carroll's grandmother. These three men had been sponsored for several years by both Daniel and his wife Michelle, as Daniel was frequently in correspondence with all the remaining relatives of his grandmother, who he idolized, though she died before he was born. He had wished to continue the help to these families which his grandfather Sir David, and then his uncle Sir Robert Carroll, had done.

However all three men knew they owed even more to Daniel's wife, Michelle, herself a Frenchwoman, who during her husband's absence during the American war with Britain, had entertained herself by writing to each of them in French, giving them an English translation. Then sending money to give them a reasonable education and, more importantly, to learn to speak French, as well as a native Frenchmen. Her kind interest in them had intrigued them, and engendered a desire to go to America, if only to meet this wonderful woman. Now there was a chance their wish might become possible.

Their liege Lord Baltimore, Cecilius Calvert, happy to help both George Washington and Daniel Carroll, for the kind consideration in letting him retain his lands in Maryland, which should have been forfeited to the United States, for his help to the British during the war. Two men he both admired and who had been for long his friends. Acting on the requests from them to try to give succor to the families of both George and Daniel, whose lives were now in danger due to the terror in chaotic France.

He had set aside the profits from his Maryland estates for this purpose. employing men to try to ascertain their whereabouts. Now, again, acting on Daniel's request he had called these three men to see him and was offering them a substantial sum of money, if they could use their talents to rescue any of these families, and help them to escape to Britain. As President, George Washington had promised them maximum help from the American Ambassador to France, James Monroe and Robert Livingston. However Cecilius had warned them of the great danger to their lives, and that if caught the Embassy would be unable to help them.

However the Embassy would be able to give them the most recent information about the current state of any part of France. Also the most likely route they should take in their escape, besides giving them the addresses of 'safe houses' to which they should take these families they might discover. The three men knew the dangers but were both young and adventurous. Furthermore they knew, if successful, they would acquire sufficient wealth, not only to travel to America and meet this mysterious Michelle Carroll, but sufficient, also, to set up homes there. They had no qualms in accepting the lordships offer.

They were given large sums of French and English money to use to bribe persons to help them in their quest and pay for the passages of these families to Britain. Also they knew they could obtain more, if necessary, from the American Embassy, so financially, they would have sufficient resources for their task. So they quickly made the journey from Dublin to France going first to Paris, as Lord Baltimore had not been able to give them the most recent information concerning those they must seek.

It seemed that the two men who George Washington had asked Cecilius to find, Comte Victor de Lameth, and his brother, Charles Lameth, having been accused of treason, had escaped, fled the country but were now prisoners of the Austrians. So it seemed they were moderately safe, for the time being, and they need not seek for them.

Cecilius spies had discovered what had happened to most of the other families who those in America wished to help, along with others, known friends of them. It seemed that they would be unable to help one family which particularly Daniel Carroll had wanted to help. This was Guillaume, Comte de Malesherbes Lamoignon, for after acting, unsuccessfully, for the defense in the trial of King Louis XVI, had be declared a traitor, imprisoned with most of his family. Then they had all been guillotined, along with many of his grandchildren. However one granddaughter, Manon Lamoignon, nineteen years of age had escaped along with two of the Comte's illegitimate children by one of his mistresses, the wife of the Marquis de Condorcet, whose family had, already, met the same fate.

These were twenty one year old Jean Condorcet and his eighteen year old sister, Antoinette Condorcet These three persons owed their life to the bravery and resourcefulness of one of the Comte's servant girls, Jeanne Cristal, only twenty three years of age. The three men found from the

American Embassy that all four of them now were hidden with a sympathetic family, in one of the 'safe houses' in Paris, but feared discovery every day.

Finally they discovered they would be unable to help one woman, Cecilius Calvert had especially asked them to help. She was Madame Louise de Lambelle, the personal friend of Queen Marie Antoinette. After she refused to take the oath against the monarchy she was turned over to the fury of the mob. These men raped her many times, cut off her breasts, beheaded her and mutilated her genitalia. The raping of every women with an aristocratic birth, was now the norm and Jean had, had to witness the raping of his sister, Antoinette, several times before Jeanne Cristal had appeared and enable them to escape. Poor Antoinette now feared she might have conceived their child.

However, quite independently, two of Madame de Lambelle's children had escaped. Her son Jacques Lambelle, twenty seven years of age and his sister Louise Lambelle, twenty two, had been rescued and, now, had been given sanctuary in another 'safe house'. Finally, although another man George Washington, wished to help for his assistance during the last war, an engineer Jacques Le Raye, had been executed, he had managed to get his twenty two year old son, Francois Le Raye, and his nineteen year old daughter, Charlotte Le Raye, to the American Embassy, were they now rested.

This was then, the information they received as soon as they entered Paris and called at the American Embassy. Four persons in one 'safe house'. Two in another and two, actually in the Embassy. Their task, therefore, was to find some way of either helping them to escape separately from France, or altogether, and which way would seem to be the safest. Also, in which direction should they flee from Paris. To which port, and where could they arrange for a ship to take them to Britain, even if they arrived, safely, at that port.

After meeting Francois Le Raye and his sister, at the Embassy, who they found was anxious to go with them, where ever they wished, the three men's next task was for them to visit everyone, calling at each of the 'safe houses'. This had to be done with some discretion, so as not to alert anyone who might question three Englishmen visiting a French house. The embassy staff were able to alert them of their coming and they visited the two houses on alternate nights, during darkness, and with caution.

They quickly discovered the state of desperation of all of them. Explaining how difficult would be their means of escape, telling them of the others they wished to help, not yet deciding, whether it was to be a combined operation, or in two parties, and for which port they should try to make it. They found that, in their haste, all six of them were destitute and without any funds. However the three men were able to tell them, that if they reached Britain, they would be ensured of a happy future. They left them reassured that, now, they might escape their fate, which until that time, they felt impossible. At least with Francois, the three men had three more men to help them, if needed.

After several more visits, and after long discussions with the embassy, it was agreed, it was better if they attempted a single escape of all seven of them. It seemed so many of the original émigrés had escaped through Calais, Boulogne or Le Harve, that these ports were now, guarded very carefully. It would be very dangerous to take, what was the quickest route to the sea. However there was a chance, but with the risk of discovery, in a longer overland journey.

It seemed a Royalist rebellion had occurred in the Vendee. They might be able to get a ship from Saint Nazaire All agreed this gave them the best chance of an escape. They must act quickly before France sent regiments to quell the uprising, though in fact the chaos might prove a blessing for them. David, Jack and Stuart made a quick journey to Saint Nazaire, via Tours and Nantes arriving in three and half days. A journey of over two hundred and eighty miles.

9

They were fortunate to find an English ship in the port, involved in the, now, very lucrative employment of smuggling. It seemed for the appropriate sum of money, this would include the smuggling of persons to Britain, but, if so, as they disposed of their quantities of cognac and wines in Bristol, so it was this port and not Dublin, which would have to be their destination. It seemed that they now made the journey from Bristol to Saint Nazaire once a week, always arriving on a Thursday. Finally, depositing a sum of money as a deposit, the ship owner agreed to look for them in three or four weeks time. So the three men returned to plan the escape.

The journey had been useful for many reasons, besides ensuring that if they arrived at the port on a Thursday, they could be certain of boarding the ship, secretively during darkness. All three knew they dare not make the journey, as they had done, in a coach, which they had used. Their journey had been beset by suspicion and been stopped many times and searched. Only their English papers enabled them to proceed.

Also, though they had slept overnight in various inns, they discovered it would be unwise to use them on their escape journey, as not only did they have to register, but also, had to show all their papers to ensure they were not French aristocrats. So it seemed that they must all sleep rough, in the countryside. On their return journey they made detours to find suitable places, away from any habitation, for this purpose. Again it would be better if they used two very large covered farm carts, large enough to hold ten persons, as well as food for their long journey. It was unlikely they could make more than fifty miles each day, so their journey would be at least six days, or more.

Finally, they were disgusted with the complete depravity throughout the country. The Sans Colette now ruled the countryside, not just the streets of Paris. Licentiousship and fornication was ripe. No woman, whether a loyalist or a monarchist, was safe. Men now possessed, without their consent, any woman they could capture and frequently raped them. It seemed to the three men, they must persuade all six men to act and dress as Sans Colette, and it seemed that the four women would have to appear as if their were their captives. In this way they would avoid suspicion, as far as it was possible. However it might mean, that at times, they had to appear so, and really act the part.

When they returned they went to everyone to explain what would be required of them. David was the spokesman. "Dear ladies, it seems we must expose you to humiliating consequences. You will often be bound with your hands tied behind your backs, as if you are our captives. We may even have to take liberties with you, perhaps, to demonstrate this by applying our hands to your bust – or even elsewhere. We may need to fight others who would like to take you from us, and demonstrate you really belong to us, by even forcing your dresses over your shoulders. – Would you be prepared for this?"

Antoinette and Louise replied for the others women. Antoinette said, "I have been raped several times. I still do not know if I've conceived. I can assure you, whatever you had to do to me, could not be any worse. In fact I believe we should appear to even want to enjoy this. For it is not only our lives who are in danger, but all of you who are so willing to help. We must, all, give you the liberty of doing anything that is necessary, to give everyone the appearance we are completely in your control."

Louise, though not quite so forward said, after she learned what happened to her mother, no indignity they caused her, was as bad as her mother had suffered. So their escape was planned with the full assistance of the embassy. Firstly a very small and dilapidated house on a small farm holding, south of the city was purchased and two large wagons, but in very good repair was settled there. Then supplies of none perishable food were gathered for their journey. They decided to allocate eight days for their journey, fearing, at times they might need to make detours.

So their journey would start at night on a Tuesday, to give them a chance of arriving in time for the ship to sail on a Thursday. They all agreed they should spend as little time as possible at the port, and would, adjust their journey, as they neared the port, to arrive in the dark. Probably the most difficult task was to secretly move the persons from the 'safe houses', and the embassy to the farm. Deciding to do this in stages. This took nearly a fortnight. In fact since the convention had altered the names of the week, they had to be careful to ensure what Tuesday now meant on the new calendar. At last the time for departure had arrived.

All dressed appropriately for their knew role and the five women's hands were tied behind their backs. Even gags were tied over their mouths to prevent them screaming, as they had seen this happened nightly in the Paris streets. With ample supplies of food, wine and water, they set out late at night. It was a hazardous journey. They were stopped many times but it was sufficient to show they were well armed, and their women, their own captives, to prevent any brawl. Only once did anyone try to rush them, David had no option and shot the man dead as he approached. His colleagues quickly dispersed as both Jack and Stuart, along with Francois showed their own weapons.

Each day they rested during daylight in the spots they had chosen on their return journey. This was the only time the girls hands were free, though in fact, they had been loosely tied, and could have released themselves, if necessary to defend themselves. Each carried a short knife in their tied hands, to use if forced. They avoided passing through the big towns in daylight and would discuss the happenings at the end of each day. Already there was a sign of companionship, even friendliness between the men and the women.

Perhaps to relieve their tensions, the girls would jokingly ask them if they were not going to molest them before they untied the knots. All six men realized how courageous were the five girls accompanying them. It was a journey which was to bring them together. One, - none of them - would, ever, forget.

In spite of their many problems, their journey became more safe as they entered the Vendee. Since this land was still loyal to the king. It was time to relinquish and change their dress, to those the peasants wore in that area. At last the girls hands were free. Now their one concern was of French soldiers, who were arriving to help quell the rebellion. Fortunately Saint Nazaire was to the north of the Vendee and away from the main trouble.

They were only fifty miles from the port on the Tuesday, a week after they had left Paris. Finding suitable places to hide their wagons, eventually, they were only twenty miles from their objective. Now the three men left the five girls in the care of the other three and went, as Englishmen, into the town. They waited until they saw their ship enter and tie up at the quay. Then going on board they arranged to bring everyone into the port and board the ship before midnight, which was the time the ship, normally left for Britain.

Though they still feared they might be stopped, their perils were much less than a few days ago. In fact it went without any stoppage, and a hour before midnight all ten were safely on board and could sit, even if crowded, in the large hold next to the crates of brandy. At last they felt they were safe. It was the girls who showed their appreciation. In turn they all came and kissed David, Jack and Stuart on the lips, telling them, not only had they saved their lives, but after what poor Antoinette had suffered, and Louse's mother, her mutilation., they even considered they had been saved from a fate worse than death.

There only disappointment was that Antoinette was now long overdue. She feared she carried one of her raper's child. She was a fallen woman. Perhaps it was because Stuart was nearer her age than the other men, that it was he who tried to console her as she broke down sobbing. She always remembered his kind words. "Dear Antoinette, to me you will always be as pure as any woman I have known. I shall ensure you have a happy future." Although the others smiled, Antoinette felt deeply moved at his kind consideration, stopped crying and gently kissed the side of his face.

They had a stormy crossing and all were sick several times but at last they sailed into the large port of Bristol and alighted at the quay. The three men had sufficient money to house them all in a local hotel. They could stay there for sometime at their expense. Meantime the three men had to return to Ireland to report their success and the failure of those already executed.

Lord Baltimore was delighted at their report. He asked them if they wanted to return to France and try to free more people but they told them they now intended to use the money he had given them to go to America, which they said was the very reason they had accepted his project. It seemed that during their long journey these three had explained their intention to go to America if they were successful. As none of the eight others had any means of support when they arrived in Britain, they had all told them, if possible they would like to go with them to Maryland. However they had no means to do this and even the three men would not have sufficient funds for this.

Now they told Cecilius Calvert what the eight exiles had said. When they told him they would be pleased if the eight could come with them, Cecilius, just smiled. Then said, "In that case I will pay for their passage. I'm certain either Daniel Carroll or George Washington, or others there will see to their future. You can tell them I will deposit letters of credit in a Bristol bank. If they do wish to go with you, then you can draw on these and pay for their passages on the same boat on which you sail."

It was a very happy David, Jack and Stuart who returned to Bristol and informed them of Lord Baltimore's generous offer. There was no doubt the relief on five girls and three men's faces. America would give them a future, for in Britain they had none. They all, gladly, agreed to join them and sail to Annapolis on the first ship leaving for that port.

They had written to Michelle Carroll, a very long letter in French, a combined effort, telling them of their success in obtaining the release of the eight exiles and that they would now, all, be coming to Maryland, naming the ship, bringing with them the eight persons, whose life they had saved, and whose passage Lord Baltimore had paid. Somehow they felt sure Michelle would find a home for all of them.

10

It seemed that madness was sweeping over the whole of Europe. France was at war with Austria, Britain had, just, declared war on France. To the east, Russia had invaded and now annexed Poland. This in turn must lead to Prussia becoming involved and the low countries were the areas most effected. Worse, poor harvests meant that starvation was facing most ordinary people and soon some were dying. This new country which called itself the United States of America, seemed to he a haven of peace. Anyone who had sufficient means to pay for a passage on a ship, now wanted to escape from Europe and go to live there. It seemed a country of opportunity.

America appeared to be the only place which, at present, was at peace, and the place that most wanted to escape. So it seemed the population of America would increase even greater than during the religious persecutions of the past. It was, also, the haven to which four persons fleeing from Austria, four from Lancashire and now eleven from Bristol, would make their escape.

Louisa Modena and Anton Albrecht had, already, made their escape. After sailing from Trieste to Cartegena and saying with Anton's cousins, they married in the Catholic Cathedral and spent a short honeymoon near the sea. Then they obtained the advice of their friends concerning Spanish plantations in Florida. Maps showed the vicinity and tracks still available for purchase. Each had a hacienda already established on the land. They, deliberately chose and purchased one near to where some of their Spanish relatives had gone to live sometime before.

All this took sometime, yet only then did they learn that the Austrian court were making inquiries concerning them and another couple. It was time for them to leave. They obtained passage on a ship sailing to Miami, the southern port in Florida. They stayed until their friends' relatives came with coaches to collect them and then drove in style to their plantation near to a small, but growing town of Sarasota, In fact their plantation was very large, over two thousand acres, covering mainly flat land, so different from the land in Europe. In the middle was this elegant mansion, and they had Negro servants to serve them and tend the land. It was already being worked, as previously it had belonged to a Spanish family, but who had left to live in New Orleans, in the north.

They were rich and could live a life of ease, though not as great as in Austria, it was a land of Spanish nobility where they could entertain and be entertained. More important to them, Louisa was now seven months pregnant and required to rest. There would be qualified doctors and nurses to attend her during the delivery. However it meant that when their baby was born she could keep it, impossible if she had stayed in Europe. Also she knew she had a husband, who was completely in love with her as she was with him

Meanwhile Roy Marshall and Fay Bradbury had gone with Hugh and Lynda Foyle to the Liverpool docks to find a ship to carry them to America. Several sailed from there to New York, though with Britain, once again at war with France, they were warned that the French Navy might intercept them, and take them as prizes back to a French port. It was a risk they must take and their desire to get to America demanded they took this risk. The first ship was sailing the next day and it would be several days before another left.

Unfortunately only two cabins remained unsold. Of course Fay did not mind sharing it with Roy, she had slept in the same room in the inn the previous night. Linda felt she could not sleep in the same cabin as her brother, for he had never seen her naked body since she had been a child, and knew it must happen if they shared a cabin. It was Fay who came to her rescue, and suggested that Roy and Hugh occupied one cabin and Fay share the other with Linda. It was agreed and so after purchasing a supply of extra food and wine, in case their passage, expected to be about three to four weeks, was prolonged, and to prevent them being short of both food and water, they returned for a final night in the inn.

That evening they discussed how they could make the journey from New York to Philadelphia, but decided they must wait until they arrived to find a way. Hugh was able to enlarge on what he knew of the proprietor who had asked his father to come and offer his invention in the mill he was erected for this purpose. Hugh felt sure the same man would be willing to offer Roy employment, even suggesting he might help him to set up his father's invention and make it work.

Roy could not help thinking of his fate. He had gone to Grimshaw's mill to help destroy this mechanical means of weaving, now it seemed he must spend his life erecting the machinery in another mill in America for exactly the same purpose. He would be using Grimshaw's money to get there and do this thing. However he had to live and this was an opportunity. Perhaps this would be they way all cotton was woven in future. In any case he had promised to look after Fay and her unborn baby. He had no alternative. The next day they boarded the ship and sailed away in the afternoon. The four of them were escaping from a dangerous life in Britain.

~

Anna Alexandra and Andrew Reeves had arrived at Bristol and Andrew took her immediately to meet his family at Wookey. They were delighted to discover he had escaped possible death in Austria and made Anna very welcome. In fact they were overwhelmed to find their son had brought with him, one of the Austrian nobility and were not sure how to address her. Anna had smiled at them telling her, she was little different to them, and she knew she must accept this, if she was to remain with Andrew, who she confessed she loved and was the father of her unborn child.

Anna told them she wanted to marry Andrew as soon as possible, even though she felt it would not be a proper wedding, as he had told her it would be in a protestant church. In spite of this she felt she was already married to Andrew and begged to be allowed to sleep with him, whilst she stayed with them. His mother had smiled and then told her she approved.

Andrew had told them he knew they dare not stay in England, as the Hapsburg's might discover them and use their powers to take Anna, and possibly him back to Austria for trial. He told them of his plan, after their marriage, to take them to West Virginia, to set up a home, with the money from the sale of Ann's jewels. The whole family knew well of his uncle Neil Reeves, who more than twenty years before had left their farm at Wookey, gone to America, and settled there.

Neil had written to them some time later, telling them of a small holding he had purchased in West Virginia, beset with difficulties, as it was covered in hardwood trees. It seemed he had found a girl called Claire, but never told them much about her. It seemed he had not married her, or possibly, the small holding had not been successful, for the last letter they received, a few years later, told them he was living with another woman called Sophia, who it seemed was very rich. He had told them he had fallen in love with her.

But that was the last they had heard of him. They had not received any further letters, so, now, had no idea where he lived, or even if he was still alive. Andrew's mother begged him to try and discover what had been Neil's fate when the arrived in America, and then let them know. This time his mother demanded, however busy he might be, he must write frequently and tell them what was happening. It was Anna who now smiled and promised she would write to them and keep them informed, telling them of the difficulties, as well as their success.

So Anna and Andrew spent a happy three weeks at the farm. They married in the local protestant church and Anna became Mrs. Andrew Reeves, though she still felt she was living in sin, but Andrew promised he would marry her again, in a Roman Catholic Church in Maryland. There was no time for a honeymoon, nor did they want it. They had sold their jewels in Bristol, amazed at the money they received. On advice they converted a large portion of it into diamonds, as this was preferable than to convert it into American Dollars, though they did convert some for use when they arrived.

Andrew's entire family came Bristol to see them board the ship destined for Annapolis in Maryland. It was an American ship, preferable as Britain was now at war with France. They had purchased a cabin and now they waited for it to sail. Before they left Bristol they had inquired from agents about available land in America. Though land could not be purchased in England, they were told there were still several tracks of land available in West Virginia, at a price they felt they could afford. This then would be their new home.

They were not to know of this, but a little over two weeks after they sailed from Bristol, eleven other persons were leaving on another American ship sailing to Annapolis in Maryland. Again like the two of them, these eleven new passengers were escaping from Europe. Each for different reasons, but all with one resolve to try and establish a new life for all of them in this new country, as none of them had any real future if they had remained in Britain. They were not to know it, but chance meetings were, in the future, were to effect all their lives, as were those other six people, who had, already, left Europe.

PART 2

AFFILIATIONS

ACQUISITION

It seemed the danger from attack by French ships, was even greater than they had been told. The last ship which left Liverpool, bound for America had been captured. Because of this their ship had the unique help of two British naval ships, but this would be only for a small part of their journey. It did however make Fay, Linda, Roy and Hugh feel a little safer. In any case both Hugh and Roy knew they had no choice. For two different reasons, they knew they must leave Britain.

They left Liverpool under escort and entered the Irish Sea, sailed northwards and journeyed through the North Channel into the Atlantic. It was October, and they knew they might encounter a very stormy passage. However, at present, though with a heavy sea, it was calm enough for them to spend most days on deck, even enjoying the blustering weather. Only once or twice were they sea sick and soon they found they were able to overcome this. It did give Hugh the opportunity to tell Roy of this man in Philadelphia, who intended to set up this mill.

It seemed he was a man aged thirty one, called Jansen Carroll, though his mother, Anna, was one of the important Van Buren families, Dutch Platoons, who help found New York, then called New Amsterdam in the seventeenth century, and who were very rich, and owned a large part of Manhattan island. His father, was Edgar Carroll, who defied his father Lord Carroll, renouncing his Roman Catholic faith, becoming a protestant and married into the Van Buren family.

All Hugh knew was that, during the last war his family had needed to leave New York and with other Dutch families, and went, either, to Philadelphia or West Virginia, as they supported the American cause. Rich as Jansen's family were, he had been bored with his indolent life on an estate near Berkeley, on the River Potomac, believing the future of America, was not in agriculture but in industrial development. Hearing of what was happening in

England he had decided to copy what was happening and with his relatives in Philadelphia, had decided to mechanise cotton weaving and establish a mill near Philadelphia for this purpose.

However to make this new machinery efficient he needed the Foyle's 'flying shuttle', and learning this was Hugh's father's invention, had asked him to come to America, promising him a partnership in his new endeavor. Hugh told Roy he knew exactly how this worked, and felt confident he could fulfill his father's task and install it successfully. Finding Roy, with his knowledge of hand weaving felt he, too, could add to all their knowledge, perhaps improve on what had been developed in Lancashire. So it seemed Roy would be certain of employment when they arrived there.

Hugh had smiled, "You know I believe it was fortunate that we met you at the inn. Although I know all about the shuttle, I know very little about weaving. I'm certain you can help me in this way. I have no doubt but that I will be able to persuade Jansen Carroll to employ you. – Frankly I need you – I've been afraid my lack of knowledge of weaving might turn this man against me. With you there to help, it won't occur."

Now he questioned Roy. "You said you knew this man Grimshaw, who set up this mill in Manchester, which the mob destroyed. Do you know anything about his machinery?" Roy smiled, "I've visited his mill many times. I wanted him to employ me but he disliked my father from something that happened in the past, so he refused. – Yes, I've seen it in operation. It is essentially simple, the real important trick is the use of steam power to drive the looms. I think, with time, I could draw diagrams of how these should be constructed – I will do rough sketches whilst we are on this ship. Then show them to this man, Jansen." It seemed that Hugh needed Roy, just as much as Roy needed Hugh.

With Hugh and Roy engrossed in their conversations, it had given Fay and Linda a chance to talk of more personal matters. Before they had left the inn, Roy and Fay had, between them, devised an elaborated on the fictional story Roy had given the Foyle's. As their apparent wealth had actually come from his stealing the money from the mill, Roy emphasized, they must not appear to have taken part in the mill's destruction. So when asked by Linda if Fay was in love with Roy and were engaged to be married, for Linda, now, knew Fay was pregnant.

Fay had told her the story they had agreed upon should the Foyle's inquire. "No! Roy is just a very good friend who has agreed to look after me. I was engaged to be married to a wonderful man, Trevor Reynolds – we loved each other so much – I'm afraid I let it go too far. So now I carry his child. However my family and his could not sell our wares and both our parents died of starvation. – In fact Trevor died in an epidemic in the area, himself weakened by starvation. We had intended to marry this very week."

Now Fay, though her story was incorrect, could only think of the lovely man she had lost and broke down crying on Linda's shoulder, who tried to comfort her. Eventually Fay was able to continue. "Our families had been friends of the Marshal family, who lived in Gorton in Manchester. Roy's parents died in the epidemic and he was their only child. Discovering what had happen to me, he came to see if he could help. When I confessed my condition to him, he amazed me by telling me as he had intended to look for work in Liverpool – or elsewhere – as he had, now, the money his family had acquired, he offered to take me with him. "

Now placing her own interpretation of the events she confessed. "I was amazed that he should even consider me. I feared, knowing my condition, he would demand intercourse with him. – I had no one to look after me – I had no future. – Even this was better than the horrible alternatives. Then more amazingly he had smiled, promised he would never molest me, and would help me to look after my child when it was born. – With gratitude, I agreed to come with him."

Now she smiled at Linda. "You asked me if I loved Roy. – I'm not blind – I've seen your interest in Roy, so I suspect the reason for your question. -- I, honestly, do not know. – I know he is a wonderful man, to even think of me – but, you see, I'm still desperately in love with Trevor. We had been friends since we were young children. – But you know Roy and I shared the same bedrooms at the inn. He made no demands on me – though naturally he saw most parts of my body. – I did not mind. – I felt, I owed this to him, it was the least I could give him."

Then she laughed, "Linda, I warn you, if you think you can take Roy away from me – I will fight you. – I may not love him – I may not ever find another man like Trevor. But I do believe Roy is a wonderfully kind man. – At present he represents security to me – otherwise I have none. – He tells me he will provide for my baby. – If only because of this – If he wants me, I will agree to go and live with him, married or not. I realise you can try to win him from me. – But please tell me why you may feel this way. Hugh told us at the inn you were engaged to marry another man. Why, now, do you consider a future life with Roy?"

Fay could see Linda was embarrassed and that she had guessed the reason for her questions, but Linda felt she must try to correct Fay's impressions. "Really Fay, I don't know where you get those ideas. – I admit I find Roy a very attractive man – but I'm not looking for any one else. – Yes! I am engaged to another wonderful man Peter Knowles, two years older than me. We planned to marry next summer. – But we had to leave, so quickly, I could not let him know where we were going. – I know I still love him, but I fear I will never see him again – not, now we are going to America. – I won't fight you – You can keep your man." Now angry she walked away and during the rest of the voyage she refused to say more and avoided Fay, as much as possible, considering they shared the same cabin.

Actually, now, their passage across the Atlantic became a very stormy one and they had few opportunities to converse on deck. The British Naval ships left them to sail south along the Irish coasts. They were left alone. Then a week later it seemed their fears might be proven. They saw a large naval ship heading straight for them. They were defenseless. They had no means of fighting any attack. The captain hove to, their ship and waited to be boarded.

However as the ship grew nearer they saw on it the flag of the United States. It was an American naval vessel. They were boarded but once they found it was an English ship and was bound for New York, they agreed to accompany them for some distance. It seemed they had been in a fight and sunk a French ship only a day before they found them. By doing so they may, well, have saved them from such a fate. They were less than a hundred miles from New York when the Americans left them to sweep down the eastern coast of America, protecting American vessels from the French who, it seemed, did not respect America's neutrality.

Now they were in far safer waters, and in fact completed their journey up the Hudson River and docked a New York, just under four weeks since they had left Liverpool. Now the four of them disembarked with the little luggage they had brought. Took accommodation in one of the many inns. Rather then inquire, how they might journey to the city of Philadelphia, Roy suggested to Hugh, that he should write to Jenson Carroll, informing him of their arrival, and ask him how they might meet him there. Hugh readily agreed.

2

At least Anna Alexandra, now Mrs. Andrew Reeves, felt she was appropriately dressed for the long voyage across the Atlantic. Before she had left Austria, knowing a little of her future life, she had been careful in the choice of the few clothes, she was able to take with her when she made her escape with Andrew. She only took two of the more elaborate dresses. The first the long dress in white in which she had married Andrew in that protestant church. The second she chose, as it was her favorite. She always felt in emphasized her good figure and knew Andrew loved to see her wearing it. She would keep this, just in case a time might arose, when it would be suitable to wear it. However the rest were ones designed to be worn of long journeys, warm and suitable for outdoor wear.

Anna now needed to use two of these on that cold sea voyage. However both were extremely serviceable, yet were still quite attractive, and so knew it appeared to make her, a woman of some social standing. Nor was she wrong. The owners of the cabins were of a mixed social class. Some men and women, often with children, who had scrapped enough money for their passage, wanting to start a new life in America, but were now had insufficient resources to purchase anything special, and the women's clothes told everyone the state of their finances.

On the other hand Anna saw a number of women and their male escorts were far better dressed and felt sure they came from a high social state. Both Anna and Andrew's ability to converse in several languages enabled them, when the weather permitted, to socialize with them on deck and during meals. One family Adele and Charles Dupont seemed to be in that category, and finding they were French, both Anna and Andrew pleased them by speaking to them in their own language, a relief for them as, at times they had found it difficult on an America ship.

They had with them their five children. They told them they had escaped from France, just as the terror had begun. Being jewellers, they realised the dangers if they had stayed in France and were fortunate to make their way to England, in time. Now, with sufficient resources and they were going to America. They had intended to travel to New York, which was the center of the jewelry trade but as most ships from Bristol went either to the Caribbean or Maryland, they had decided to go there first, and possibly travel overland to New York. Of course they were quite rich and carried in the ships hold a fortune in diamonds, far greater than their own in that vault.

Before they left England both Anna and Andrew had devised a suitable story to cover their actual ones, as they had no intention of telling anyone of Anna's nobility and give the Austrian court a lead to try to find them. They told the Dupon's, like them, they had left Europe, because of the uncertainty, and with the war between France and Austria, they had decided to come to America. Stating their reasons were similar to them. They quickly formed a friendship with them, hoping to continue this when they arrived in America.

However both Anna and Andrew were especially pleased to meet an older couple, Kenneth Bacon and his wife Sheila, when they found that they were returning to Maryland It seemed having made this journey at their age, since they were about sixty years old, virtually, as a penance, to set right what seemed had been a serious family feud. It seemed they had come to try to reestablish the relationship with Sheila and her seventy seven year old mother, Lady Christina Percy, this was for the Bacon's siding with the American cause in the last war.

It seemed her mother had married Sir Clifford Percy, a relative of the Duke of Norfolk, who held an important position in Antigua, in the Caribbean. So Sheila had been a Percy before she married Kenneth. So her mother and father had been disgusted when they had sided with the Americans against Britain, and during the war her mother had refused to communicate with her. Her parents had retired to England during the war and Sheila's father had died. However Sheila had been desperate to try to heal the breach with her mother. That was the reason for their visit. Now it seemed a reconciliation had been achieved, so at last Sheila felt she had been forgiven.

The Bacon's had explained that one of the most serious consequences of the war had been that many families had been torn apart. Some favouring the Americans and others favouring the British. It had been a civil war as much as a war between the United State and Britain. As the Bacon family had been living in Maryland for nearly two hundred years, and owned large estates there, they had felt obliged to support the United States, for they knew, if not, their lands would have been confiscated, when the United States won.

There had been another reason. They were staunch Roman Catholics and as Maryland accepted religious freedom, they feared the power of the New England section would have forced everyone to become protestants. If

United States won and they appeared to have supported Britain, it might have forced them to become protestants. Of course Anna, as a Roman Catholic understood. She told them that her husband was a protestant, but wished her to retain her faith, even though he would not change. In fact they had decided to try to settle in West Virginia, as there they could worship as they choose.

Sheila Bacon confirmed this telling them her own daughter Isabel had married a protestant, Eric Casimar, however as they had married in both a protestant and a Roman Catholic church, they could still continue to worship as they pleased. In fact she told them they had, themselves, settled in a magnificent mansion beyond Fort Cumberland, set in a estate covered in hardwood trees, in West Virginia. Sheila felt sure they would enjoy living in West Virginia, though much of the land was being purchased by families from abroad, and they must be careful to choose the best area from those remaining.

Having explained their own position, and their reason for their quick flight from Europe, Anna confessed that she had only been married in a protestant church, though Andrew had promised to marry her again, in a Roman Catholic church, when they arrived in America. It seemed Sheila was delighted at her news. The Bacon family had seen they were well educated and saw they could converse in French with the Dupon's. To their delight Sheila invited them to come and stay with them in Annapolis as soon as they landed there.

They could stay for a short time until they purchased their own land and her husband would help them to choose the land most suitable. Whilst they stayed with them they would arrange for them to married in their own Roman Catholic church in Annapolis. As Sheila said, "It was imperative that Anna, you did not continue to live in sin.". Only when married, need they travel on and occupy the land they had bought.

It was a wonderful opportunity for both them. Not only could Andrew keep his promise to Anna, but they would not need to waste they limited money on an hotel, and could stay with the Bacon's, perhaps even meet some of their friends, for at present they had none in America. Of course they agreed to stay with them and thanked them, but the Bacon's told them their wedding would be at their expense. As Sheila said, "I am only doing God's work and ensuring, you, Anna did not become a heathen." Anna understood but smiled to herself. She wanted this wedding, if only to ease her sin, but she neither considered her husband, nor herself were heathens.

Of course after that they spent as much time as possible in their company. They were to learn of the history of Maryland. How Lord Baltimore, had become a Roman Catholic receiving his barony in Ireland and the whole of the land of Maryland, which the Virginians considered belonged to them, becoming its governor. How the Bacon's, Mowbray's and the Roman Catholic Carroll's had come to America at that time. So all three families had a long history of life in the old colony, even accepting a fair degree of freedom of religious worship, so unusual at that time. It had been necessary for the economic prosperity of the old colony, as most of its inhabitants had been protestants.

They even learned how a protestant branch of the Carroll family who held lands in Somerset had come there. In time, one of them had become Governor, a man called David Carroll, who though a strong protestant, had placed his life in danger, risking this, to persuade King William III, to continue the right of religious freedom. It seemed a descendent of Sir David, a Daniel Carroll had done much to keep peace in Maryland, after the war had began. When it had become impossible, he had done much to save and ensure they were able to retained their own lands.

Sheila had told Anna, "You will love living in America. It may not be possible, as they live far from us, but whilst you stay with us, I hope I can arrange for you to meet our friends, particularly Anton Tencin, who it seems is an illegitimate son of King Luis XIV and Claudine Tencin, - also his French step-sister Julie Scarron. If so you will have a chance to use your French language with them. There a number of Frenchmen and women living there, who came to live here, long before, the last war.

Now Anna was looking forward to the introduction of her life in this new country. She regretted that she felt she dare not acquaint them of her ancestry. To do so would put her future life in jeopardy. However she did confess to Sheila that she was, already, carrying Andrew's unborn child. Again, Sheila felt her wedding in their church must be as quick as possible. So she was very happy to spend as much time with Sheila, learning about their past.

3

Both Anna and Andrew had been amazed at the size of money they had received from selling her jewels in Bristol. Expecting to have to live a very fugal life in America, almost in poverty, they, now, knew from the agent in Bristol they would have sufficient wealth to purchase at least two Negro slaves to take with them to live on the land they purchased. As from Sheila they learned that any land still available was likely to be covered in hardwood trees, it would be unsuitable for agriculture.

In any case they had discussed during their flight from Trieste how they could exist in this new land. Neither of them were used to physical labour and knew nothing about farming, yet they had to find the means by which to live, feed themselves and see to their unborn baby. It had been Anna who had suggested a way. They were both well educated. They could set up small school and earn a living by teaching the children of the many families, on the lands surrounding their own. Now learning their land would not be suitable for any other use, they both agreed, this would be the way they lived.

At least the abundance of trees ensured they could use them to build a home and next to it a small school building. Sheila had told them they could hire, very quickly, men, now, well used to doing such work and their money would allow for this, helped by their Negro slaves. Speed was essential, firstly to have a place where their baby could be born, but, also, to quickly establish an income on which to live. So, in any case, their stay with the Bacon's must be short. However Anna said, this must not happen until they were married in a Roman Catholic church, and Andrew agreed.

Apart from the storms which still; caused them sea sickness, being on an American ship meant they were never attacked, even when two French Naval ships approached and boarded them, looking for contraband. So they were delighted when they docked at Annapolis, for the Bacon's to arrange for them to be driven in their coaches, waiting for them on the quay, to the Bacon mansion not far away.

They spent a very happy, if busy fortnight at their home. Kenneth Bacon took Andrew to the office on the quay and advised them on the most suitable land, still available, as he had informed Kenneth of their future plans. From the sites still available, they, eventually, decided on a small tract to the east of the Monongahela river a little over twenty miles from Fort Pitt. Since the end of the war, the area surrounding the fort had become a small town, so they could easily take their wagon, they were advised to purchase, to the fort for food and any other necessities. Kenneth sold them, at a very cheap price, two of his Negro slaves, a man and his wife, to make their life less arduous.

Meantime Sheila was busy with Anna making the arrangements for their wedding in the Roman Catholic church. It seemed Anna's heavily decorated white dress she had decided to bring with her from Austria would be very suitable but Sheila insisted on providing an paying for an, equally elaborate wedding veil, and Kenneth supplied Andrew with a suitable suit as her bridegroom. Only ten days later after they had arrived, the Bacon's provided them a small but wonderful bridal party. One of Sheila's younger daughters was Anna's bridesmaid and a son was Andrew's Best Man.

During that time Sheila had done her best to try to get either the Tencin's or Scarron's to join them but it seemed they were both occupied in making arrangements for the landing of some French exiles they had managed, with Daniel Carroll's help, to escape from Europe. Not wishing to indulge in a honeymoon. After all they had celebrated this in England, they said goodbye to the Bacon's, anxious to set off to their new home, with the men to build their home, and their two servants, if only to establish a basis by which they could earn enough money on which to .live.

The Bacon's promised to invite them in the future, and after they had settled on their land, to come and stay with them as their guests. They told them how much they appreciated all they had done for them, since they met on the ship, but added they must first ensure they had a suitable income, so it might be sometime before they could accept their offer. The Bacon's understood. However they did more.

It seemed Sheila was particularly anxious to go and meet her married daughter, in the wilderness, to tell her of their success in re-establishing good relationships with their family in England. So they insisted they should accompany them part of the way, and to introduce them to her daughter who now lived on a magnificent estate, only ten miles from where they had purchased their own land. They would travel that far in the Bacon's own coaches with the Reeve's Negro servants driving their wagon and its contents for future use.

On the way Sheila told them, as they past through Berkeley, they would introduce them to both the Tencin's and the Scarron's. However when they arrived there they were disappointed, as it seemed they had left going in the opposite direction to Annapolis to meet the exiles coming from Britain. However they did meet a Donald and Kate Wilson, and discovered the adventurous life they had endured since they arrived over thirty years before in America. Once again they heard of this mysterious Daniel Carroll and his wife, Michelle, who it seemed had done much in helping them to achieve happiness.

Sheila and Kenneth Bacon, during their stay with them had, explained, a little of how their Roman Catholic daughter and come to know and fallen in love with a protestant, called Eric Casimir. Sheila had admitted she still did not fully approved of their wedding, but it had been necessary, as the United States now demanded full religious freedom. It seemed the Casimir family were very rich and had come from Poland many years ago. Their daughter's friend, Hilary Mowbray had, likewise fallen in love with Eric's friend, John Holstein, a member of an equally rich Swedish family. Again Hilary was a Catholic and John was a protestant. It seemed after their joint marriages the two couples had decided to live on the large Casimir/Holstein estate near Fort Necessity. They now lived in a very large logged mansion of their own, Really two mansions, joined together by central rooms, for entertaining.

Nearby was another large mansion which was one of the homes of the men's parents. It would be there that they would stay, at Isabel's invitation, quite large enough to house many people at the same time. It was here Anna and Andrew stayed with the Bacon family, and were soon introduced to the two married couples, each now with a young child and quite, obviously, both pregnant again for the second time. The two girls made them very welcome, even more delighted when they told them they soon intended to set up a school for children on their land, promising as soon as they were old enough to send their children to them to be educated.

Both Isabel and Hilary were certain the school would be a success, for their were many families in the vicinity with young children, wanting their children to at least learn to read and write. They insisted they stay with them until, at least, their home was erected, removing Anna's fear of having to sleep in their wagon. Even more helpful, the two families sent some of their Negro slaves with their own and the builders to fell the necessary hardwood trees and help to build their home.

Whilst the two girls conversed with Isabel's mother, telling them of her success with Isabel's grandmother in England, Eric and John took Anna and Andrew to meet some special friends of theirs who worked a, now, very prosperous arable estate, only a little to the north. These were Kylie and Adrian Scott, and introduced to their children, Esther, now twenty eight, though married to a local boy and with two young children aged seven and four and her unmarried sister, Sarah, two years younger than Esther, though courting, were not yet married. Kylie had three more children, two sons, Alan, now fifteen, and Clive, just twelve and a final daughter, Elsie, aged eight. It seemed that Kylie was now too old to conceive again.

Like the Casimir's and Holstein's, they were delighted to know Anna and Andrew intended to set up a school, promising they would be pleased to send all their children of school age to attend. It seemed they would soon have a number of children to teach, providing them with an income, especially as Kylie knew of other families nearby, who would, also, want their children to receive basic education. However their greatest surprise was when they had been introduced as Mr. and Mrs. Reeves, learning that Andrew's original home had been in Somerset, where they had first married.

As they sat enjoying their refreshments, Kylie had asked Andrew, if he was in any way related to a Neil Reeves, who they had known. Of course Andrew told them Neil was his uncle, and asked how well they knew him, telling them his family had lost all trace of him. Kylie had looked at Adrian, then considering the difficulties concerning him, Kylie had said, they had known him very well and had lived with them for a time. She told them they knew he had died about four years before. As it was a long story they promised to inform Andrew of everything at a later date. Andrew, though anxious to know the fate of his uncle, realised they were hiding something, perhaps some crime he had committed, and wished to inform him in private, when Eric and John were absent, so he decided not to press them into an explanation.

After a very enjoyable time, and now knowing they might have the basis of some pupils to start their school, they returned to the other estate where they waited, enjoying their hospitality, until their house was erected. By then the Bacon's had returned to Annapolis. After venturing several times to their own land, realising how beautiful it was and seeing their buildings gradually arise, eventually everything was ready, even the school house was partially completed, and soon be available for them to start work.

So bidding farewell to the hosts, they went to set up their new home. Anna and Andrew realised how fortunate they were to meet Sheila and Kenneth on the ship. Up to now their only expenses had been for the purchase of their land, the two slaves, and to pay the builders for erecting their home and the school house. Since they left the ship they had not needed to use very much of their small wealth they had acquired by selling Anna's jewels. They felt sure they now had a future in this land. Anna was now five months pregnant and as they had been taken to the Fort Pitt during their stay, they had booked an appointment to take Anna, there to deliver her child with a doctor's attention.

4

James Downey and Paul Eliot were very disappointed when they arrived at Fort Washington in late May. There seemed to be little preparation for an excursion against the marauding indians. In fact they were, virtually, the first of the militia bands to arrive, and it would be weeks before they achieved their desired strength. Although they received their small payment for their appearance, it seemed their period of service had not yet begun, so ensuring they would have to remain for more than the three months they had expected

At least they had been paid at Fort Cumberland for the sale of their four horses and, having pocketed a small amount of the proceeds, they had ample resources to enjoy their enforced stay. Having, at least received reasonable training as infantry cavalry, able to give a reasonable account of themselves, if not as well as the Regular Army, they were disgusted at the lack of preparation for the military preparation. It seemed that the Governor of the Northwest Territories St. Clair had appointed General Harman in overall control. Harman was in no haste to start the campaign. To the two men, it seemed he underestimated the ability of these indian tribes to give serious threat to them, having successively dealt with them in the past, establishing with them the Treaty of Fort Mcintosh in 1785.

Although they wondered how they might fair in the coming conflict, it was still for them, a great adventure. As little was required of them at this time, they decided to explore the lands to the north, where in future they would have to give battle. The country was very different to their own hilly but rather bare countryside. It seemed here it was a country of small hills and river valleys with many areas covered with trees. They were equally astonished at the increasing number of homesteads and small estates being populated by emigrants for all parts of war torn Europe. They were many squatters. In fact they were really stealing this land from the indians, land granted to them by the treaty of 1785.

The Miami Indians were a very proud race who long ago held lands close to the Iroquois tribes but driven westward during the late seventeenth century now occupied the lands along the Maumee and upper Wabash rivers. They were the major tribe but there were also Shawnee, Delaware and Ottawa indians. Since the Americans did not appear to abide by their treaties, the indians felt no compunction in raiding and killing the settlers. This was happening every day and was the reason for the militia and the army incursions to remove the dangers.

Both James and Paul soon realised the fear in which thee settlers lived. But they were, equally, determined to stay. Life even here was better than what the had endured in Europe. At least the were not persecuted. They could see their enemy and use their hands to fight him, whereas in the past they had to submit to others. The men admitted the countryside was quite breath taking. If only they could be free of indian attack the settlers would form a settlement which in time could lead to riches.

Both James and Paul had learned from their parents how settlers in Maryland, Virginia and other parts of the wilderness, in the past had to face the same indian problems. Many had perished but most had survived to produce the prosperity now enjoyed there. They felt sure, in time this would happen in this new wilderness.

They called on many homesteads, explaining they were part of a force sent to protect them and to drive away the indian threat. They were made very welcome. Their only difficult was language, for many came from Germany, Sweden, Poland and even Russia, though most still came from France and England. The further north they travelled they found the influx was mainly from Germany. Members of the Mennonite Sect, persecuted for so long by the Roman Catholics particularly in Bavaria. Some families had acquired some wealth in Germany but eventually after several of their sect were murdered, they followed the lead of others of the sect over fifty years before and used the little they had, to purchase passage to America.

Most had expected to go to live in Pennsylvania were the earlier members of their sect had settled. However land was no longer available to them there, except at a price they could not afford. So they had travelled westward through the Ohio Country into what was now being called the Indiana Territory. Here land was available free for the taking, but with the dangers from the indians was the price they must pay.

Eventually on their travels James and Paul had come to a small settlement which was called Anderson on the White River, arriving at a small celebration following the wedding of one of their settlers. They were invited to take part. It was a Mennonite Group and only a few could speak any English. Even then it was very little. However the were attracted to two young attractive girls. The first, whose name the discovered by sign language was called Lilie Gartner who was nineteen years old and who James found quite attractive. The other was Helga Feld, a year younger, who it seemed to like Paul, and who was equally attracted.

The result was they were invited to the nearby homesteads which in fact were neighbours. The all agreed to meet the next day at the Gartner's home and were in fact made very welcome by their parents. Having explained with difficulty why they had come to Anderson, they were invited to stay with them, as they were so delighted that, at last, they might be free from indian attack. It seemed raids had occurred the previous year and two families further north had been murdered.

Disappointed at the lack of military action so far, and the adventure they had sort, at least now, it seemed their other reason for coming to Fort Washington was maturing. This was their desire to meet prospective females for amorous pleasures. There was no doubt but that these two flaxen haired, and very pretty young girls, stirred their manly desires. They wasted no time in trying to obtain their sexual favours.

The two girls were equally delighted to meet such handsome young men. Both were intrigued by their lack of ability to converse easily with each other. They would all laugh when they found it difficult to make each other understand. James and Paul would take each of them sitting behind them on their horses into the lovely countryside, sitting with the men's arms around them on the banks of the White River.

Now James and Paul experience in lovemaking, with the girls they knew in the Potomac valley, began to make advances, as they would have done at home, gently kissing first the side of their girlfriends faces and then daring to place kisses on their lips. However they already found progress was much slower than it would have been at home.

James and Paul discussed this in bed at night, and decided that they girls were shy and they must make the first moves. They attempted this as they sat near the river on the third day. As they would have done at home they took the girls into their arms kissing their lips. They felt their bodies tense, but ignoring it, continued. Then their hands strayed to clasp their covered breasts. Suddenly the two girls screamed as if they had been hit. They broke away slapping the boys cheeks very firmly, shouting "Nein! Nein". Then they broke away and collapsed on the grass sobbing violently.

Unfortunately neither could understand each other fully but it seemed to James and Paul they had committed a terrible offence. The girls appeared terrified and attempted to run away. It was obvious they had committed a terrible sin. They followed the girls who were unable to escape. However once they cornered they were at last able to assure them they would make not further advance on them and persuaded them to mount the horse and took them home.

The girls ran to their parents, who to James and Paul's horror ordered them to leave at once, indicating they felt they had actually raped their daughters. They had no option and left without seeing either Lilie or Helga again. Very disappointed they returned to Fort Washington. Preparations were proceeding but very slowly. However they found they could discuss matters with Major John Hamtramck. He laughed at their discomfort, telling them that the Mennonite Sect were very strong puritans. It seemed that no girl would let a man actually touch her upper body until at least she was engaged to be married. It would seem to Lilie and Helga that they had truly tried to rape them.

However they found Major Hamtramck was very distrustful of their Commander General Harmar and said, frankly that he was too over confident, and feared a disaster. Hamtramck had been ordered to make an attack from Fort Vincennes when Harmar made his attack further east. Both James and Paul liked him and so gladly accompanied him a further 150 miles to the west.

Most the militia gathering there came from Kentucky but all three of them could see they were a very poor lot, including men sent from their prisons. However it was arranged that when General Harmar attacked from Fort Washington on September 30th. Major Hamtramck took James, Paul and the militia along the lower Wabash River as Harmer attacked to the upper reaches. They were to meet there.

Hamtramck's 'legion' as it was called was relatively successful and occupied, burnt indian camps and sent many indian bands away to the north east. Then the Kentucky brigade rebelled, refused to go further saying their three months of service had expired. Hamtramck had no option but to return to Fort Vincennes and disband his 300 Regulars being too small to do the job. He did appreciate the assistance which James and Paul had given him , even appointed Paul a Lieutenant, like James.

There they soon learned of the disaster besetting General Harmer's brigade of 320 Regulars and 1400 Militia. It was a combination of Harmers inefficiency as commander, the hopelessly inadequate training of the militia and the brilliance of Chief Little Turtle of the Miami Indians. Turtle killed a large part of the militia and were only saved from complete rout, but for the devotion and heroism of the regulars. At least Harmar was able to retreat with most of his men to Fort Washington.

The campaign was over. It was a complete failure leaving the poor settlers, even more at the mercy of the indians. Major Hamtramck at Fort Vincennes knew this and told James and Paul to return to West Virginia, demobbing them but vigorously shaking their hands. Telling them he would be pleased to have them with him, in the future.

So both James and Paul made their return slowly enjoying the beauty of the land. The adventure had not been what they had expected. Militarily it was a disaster. However, so was their desire to meet and enjoy new feminine company. Yes, and to sublimate their carnal desires.

They still could not rid their minds of Lilie and Helga. They knew, even in that short time, that they would have wanted it to progress much further than just a flirtation. They were the type of girls they had always wanted. Now it was impossible, though they both admitted that someday they might want to retrace their steps to Anderson. Perhaps if they learned German they might be able to gain forgiveness for what they had done, quite innocently, that day by the river.

5

Eleven persons, five women and six men boarded the ship at Bristol, eight exiles from France and the three men from Ireland. It was an American ship. As a result they had an uneventful journey, though the weather was very rough. They had taken five cabins, two sharing and only one in a cabin, with difficulty, housing three. They were, all, often sea sick and they had little opportunity to extend their friendship, begun in France, during the voyage. However it was a good ship and they arrived at the quay at Annapolis only a little over four weeks.

As the ship grew near and tied to the quay they could see several people on the land looking expectantly at them. David, Jack and Stuart hoped that amongst these was this mysterious Michelle Carroll, who had so kindly helped them, in the past, hoping she was one of them. Yet it was in some trepidation they walked down the gangway onto the quay, along with many other passengers. They still had a little money left from what Lord Baltimore had given them, so they had sufficient to spend a night or two in an inn. However without future help, they would soon become penniless.

To there relief they heard a man, extremely well dressed, calling out, "Are any of you exiles from France? If so please come to me. We wish to help you." The three men left the others and did as been asked. They saw a woman, still lovely but possibly about sixty years of age was standing next to this man. It was David, who usually took the initiative, spoke to her in French, "Are you possibly the wonderful Michelle Carroll, who has helped all of us so much, and is the main reason we have come from Britain to meet you."

A broad smile now covered her face as she replied, "Yes I am Michelle Carroll and this is my husband Daniel. We have come today, with others, who want to help all of you." Now very relieved they beckoned the other eight persons to come to them and introduced them to the Carroll's. Only then did this man bring forward several other persons, who it seemed were, equally, anxious to meet them. Daniel then introduced each of them to their new arrivals.

First to be introduced were Julie and Louis Scarron, again both about sixty years of age, asking to be introduced to the children of the Come de Malesherbes Then when Manon Lamoignon, and Jean and Antoinette Condorcet came forward, Louis, now, introduced them to Marie and Henri Colbert and another woman called Catherine Lespinasse and her husband Jacques. To their amazement Marie and Catherine came and hugged all three of them saying openly they had been intimate friends of the Comte, implying but not stating that they might have born children to the Comte.

Now Louis Scarron wished to meet the children of Madame de Lamballe and Jacques and Louise Lamballe came forward. Also they wished to know and meet Francois and Charlotte Le Raye. This, now, only left Jeanne Cristal to be introduced. It was a very old lady who now came and asked to be introduced to Jeanne. Infirm as she was, she was able with the aid of her son, who was called Francois, to embrace a bemused Jeanne.

She then explained, "I am Ruth Tencin, the widow of Anton Tencin. I lost my husband five years ago. He was a wonderful man. Jeanne, dear, though Anton had the King of France's blood in his veins, he could still take pity and come to love me, a convicted felon, and give me a wonderfully happy life. Jeanne, dear, I am no better than you, just a fortunate old woman. You must come and stay with me, not as my servant, but as my guest, for as long as you wish. I will promise you a happy life in future."

So at last all were introduced and Michelle took charge of the three men from Ireland. "We are all going to Berkeley first, and stay for a time. However afterwards, I want the three of you to come and stay with Daniel and me on our large estate at Racoonsville. In time you will find I am no better than Ruth. I owe so many wonderful years of happiness, because my dear husband, Daniel, found he could love me. It is a long story which, in due course, you will learn."

Now they were all lead to the coaches waiting for them and drove along the Cumberland Road, past the large tobacco estates of the lowlands, then into the Cumberland gorge until they all came to a large estate by the side of the River Potomac, which they were told was the home of Julie and Louis Scarron. There they would all stay for a time, though later, they might be invited to join other estates in the area.

It seemed Daniel Carroll was in charge of arrangements, though his own estate was many miles to the south-west. "All of you are our guests. We are delighted and fortunate that you have escaped from the chaos in France. You need, never, fear for your future. We shall ensure you are happy here living with one of our families until you find more permanent homes of your own. We are all very rich and will provide, adequately for all of you. You will find, in the past, we have all suffered, often in danger of our lives. That is why we are so pleased that you have survived the terror in France."

Nothing more was said and they were lead, each, to their allotted rooms. Negress servants, came to attend to them, bathe them, and offer them new clothes suitable to come down to dinner. Though tired, after their journey, they could hardly believe what had happened since they had walked onto that quay. It seemed they were assured of a happy future. So they could at last sit down, around an enormous table, to eat, waited upon by Negro servants. Apart from pleasantries, nothing more was explained over dinner. After a few, after dinner drinks, they were all pleased to be allowed to retire for the night.

The next morning they all came downstairs at different times, dressed again in clothes given to them and suitable for daytime wear. Only late in the morning after all had arrived, were they led outside to a covered patio, for though the sun was shining, the weather, outside, was cold. Now it was Louis Scarron who took charge.

He smiled kindly, at all of them, "I believe you should know – though we all have helped – the reason you are all able to join us today, is entirely due to Daniel's wife Michelle. It was Michelle who during the last war corresponded with David, Jack and Stuart. If she had not, encouraged them, to learn to write and converse in French, we could never have found you and brought you here."

He paused and then smiled again. "Because of this, these three men were able to go to France and risk their lives to find and bring you to Britain. Without their courage we could not have helped you. We shall, all, ensure they receive an adequate reward, for we were desperate to help the many friends – no relatives – in so much danger. Yet, here, we were powerless. Sometime you will learn why and how we, in similar difficult circumstances, met each other – actually as enemies – yet eventually to become friends. That is why we know we must help, all of you, to settle here, and have, as wonderful life, as we now enjoy."

Again he paused. "In due course you will meet several other of our friends. Again some we only met, recently,, and came to love, some in the last but one war, we call the 'Seven Years' war. The others in the last war. It is a remarkable story. I'm afraid, it is so complicated, it may take you weeks, even months, to come to understand "this.""

Now to her surprise he spoke directly to Jeanne Cristal. "Again we all know that but for your own courageous stand, neither Manon, Antoinette, nor Jean would be here with us told. Jeanne, you must never again, consider you are, in anyway, inferior to us. You see many of our friends, and I include dear, Ruth, in this, are , again, no better than you. All with a past – yes – even Michelle, yet you are probably far more worthy than the rest of us, who were born into nobility. It is America which has made us one. We have lost our past and, now, proud to be citizens of this new United States. You too must lose your past. Forget you were born in France or Ireland. You too will now become American citizens and I know our president, George Washington, will, quickly ensure, you are given papers announcing you members of this New Country"

Now he concluded. "We cannot bring back your parents who were murdered. But here you are safe, and we promise you will have a happy future. David, Jack and Stuart, have needed to leave their loving families. Again we shall see you are all happy here. – If not I know Michelle would kill me. We may, all be old and Ruth is our oldest and longest friend. However you will meet many persons, both men and women, much younger. You might even find a future husband or wife, from one of them – who can tell. Tomorrow you begin a new life here. Different from the past, but we hope, even more rewarding."

6

They all stayed together for two more days so that they could all get to know their hosts and hostesses. During that time Jacques and Louise Lamballe decided they would like to come and live with Julie and Louis Scarron, as Julie had known her mother, before she had to flee from France, many years before. Though Julie's three eldest children had married and now live close by, but her daughter, Danielle, named after her life long intimate friend, Daniel Carroll and her son, Michael, called after Michelle, were still living with them. Both were of similar ages to Jacques and Louise, which provided another reason for wishing to stay with Julie and her family. Because of this, as Louise Lambelle and Francois le Raye had certainly showed interest in Francois and his sister, Charlotte, were pleased to stay with Madeline and Jean Dumas.

Manon, Antoinette and Jean came to know Marie Colbert and Catherine Lespinasse very well, especially when Marie introduced them to her two children, Louise and Guillaume, whose father was the Comte, born so many years before. This also applied to Catherine and her son, Antoine, also by the Comte. Louise and Guillaume were already married but Antoine, though now twenty seven had not married. They were given the choice of going to live with Marie and Henri Colbert or going to live with Catherine and her husband.

There were two reasons whilst they decided they wished to go to live on the Racoonsville estate with Catherine. Firstly, because Michelle had spoken, in private, with Antoinette about her pregnancy, advising her to abort her child, which she would pay for. But also, since his outburst on the ship, coming to England, Antoinette and Stuart had become firm friends. This had developed as they had crossed the Atlantic. Antoinette knew that David, Jack and Stuart were going to live with Michelle, and by going to Racoonsville she would be living quite near him. Perhaps Stuart had suggested this. As a result Manon and Jean, wanting to remain near

Antoinette, particularly as she had decided to accept her abortion, so they accepted Catherine's invitation to stay with her and her husband.

Ruth had spent several hours talking with Jeanne Cristal, telling her, everything about her past life. Her conviction as a felon, her years as an indentured servant to two evil men. How Anton, having met her on the ship coming to America had come to find her after being captured and torture by Indians, then eventually asking her to marry him, in spite of her past. How now she missed Anton, who had given her such a wonderful life.

Ruth had taken Jeanne's hand, "So you see you have no need to feel ashamed that you once were a servant in the Lamoignon household. You are a very courageous woman. You saved Manon, Jean and Antoinette's lives. If not, neither David, Jack or Stuart could have freed all of you. My husband left me a rich woman. I will set a large dowry in trust for you, to become yours when you marry – or find a man you want to live with permanently. I accepted that position, willingly, a long time before Anton, then asked me to marry him, and not until I had born Francois. In Maryland, there is no shame in a woman living with a man, even if not married."

Now Ruth smiled at her. "So I want you to come and live with me, become my protégée. I have no doubt, with so many men living here, all close by, in time you will meet a man with whom you would like to spend your life. Your past, means nothing here. I will make you a woman of quality – just as great of those you once served. – By doing so, I feel I will have been able to give another woman a chance of happiness, which but for, dear, Anton, I would never have enjoyed." Jeanne placed her arms around Ruth and thanked her, telling her she would very much like to come and live with her. Then she had smiled, "In one way I want to remain a servant. I want to serve you. I want to look after you, see to your needs. It is something I really want to do." Ruth kissed and thanked her.

So after three days they all went to live in the households they had chosen, hardly believing that by coming to America, they now could live a life, virtually the same as they had enjoyed in France when they were children. Then Daniel, Michelle and Catherine took the three Irish men and the three exiles by coach on the long journey to Racoonsville. Though Jean and Manon when to live with Catherine and her husband, Antoinette went with David, Jack and Stuart, to live with Michelle. This was so Michelle could, quickly, arrange for her abortion.

This happened in the mansion a week later and three days later she had recovered. But Antoinette was very pleased that as she had convalesced, Stuart had been a frequent visitor to her bedroom, comforting her, even holding her hands. She now knew he must think, highly, of her. Perhaps he might, even, be falling in love with her. She liked the idea. Though still a little traumatised by her raping and her ordeal since leaving France, even she now felt her feelings for Stuart, were much stronger than friendship. She might, even, be falling in love with him, as he was only two years older than her.

Although Michelle had enjoyed speaking with the three Irish men whilst on the Potomac, she now had many more opportunities to converse with them. The three men had told her how much they owed to her, for what she had done in the past. How her actions had intrigued them, as they spent her money in receiving an education. They had begged her to tell them why she had done this. Michelle had smiled, then during the early days as they stayed at Racoonsville, she had told them the story of her life, and its tribulations.

Confessing she had born Jack Wilson, a smuggler, a child, his murder and that of her child, her raping by the custom men and the birth of her daughter, Sophia. Her rescue by his brother Donald, who they had met at Berkley, now married to Kate. Her ten years living as a wife with Donald, but preventing herself baring him children. Then her courtship by Daniel. Her foolishness in, nearly, refusing him and the many years of happiness she had enjoyed with him.

She then had to explain about Daniel's ancestry. His grandfather marrying Amelia Eliot, a convicted felon, and him bringing many of her family to live in America. Then how this man, now Sir David Carroll, a Knight of the Bath, and his son Sir Robert had continued corresponding with all Amelia's descendents, just as Daniel had continued to do. Why, with Daniel away from her during the last war, she had decided to take his place. So this is how she had come to know and wanted to help all of them.

They felt bond to ask her, why had she chosen to write to them, and help to educate them, and not others of their family. Michelle could not be sure. Perhaps it was Jack, who still bore the name of Eliot, then learning from him that David and Stuart were his constant friends. Michelle had laughed that she still could not really remember how she had come to choose them. "Frankly, I was bored. Daniel was away from me for so long. At that time, I had quarrelled with my daughter, Sophia, who having lost the husband she adored, had began a life style, I disapproved."

Then she smiled at them. "You know, I may have been testing you. Writing to you in French - it's still my favourite language. Perhaps I thought you would never try to learn the language, though I admit I hoped you would. The way you, quickly, managed to try to write to me in French, made me think you were all very intelligent men. – You have proved this. – After this, knowing how fortunate I had been, I felt obliged to continue and to ensure you had a good education. For I knew your parents could not afford to give you one. --- Well, you have, more, than repaid me for my trouble. Now I want you to find a happy life here. Meet some women. See if you could come to like them. Remember, I still have two unmarried daughters. You've met them. Every mother wants her daughters to meet men of which she would approve. – We shall see."

That is where the conversation ended. Afterwards all three agreed, if only to please Michelle, they would try to gain the acquaintance of these daughters, but Stuart knew by now, he was far more interested in developing an acquaintance with Antoinette Condorcet. He knew he liked her and felt she did care a little about him. He, just hoped, it might mature. Strangely he knew, even if she had kept her child, he would still have wanted to be with her. He even thought, he might have had a better chance of improving his position if she had done so, and become an unmarried mother.

As for the other two. They had already met Catherine and Michelle's daughters, but they had realised that a number of the daughters they had met during their short stay at Berkeley were 'interesting'. Since it seemed all these families appeared to have a close relationships, as time past, they felt sure they would meet them again. It seemed to all three of them, apart from now being given a chance to have a profitable future, there were many other rewards awaiting them by coming to America. Rewards, with their poor wealth, they could never have enjoyed in Ireland.

7

Neither Hugh nor Roy had to wait long at the inn before a letter arrived from Jenson Carroll, telling them that he would send his coach to collect all of them and bring them to Philadelphia. It arrived three days later and so, in style they completed their journey to the city, though the roads were still well used and causing a somewhat unpleasant drive. The coach took them to the Carroll mansion outside Philadelphia. A Negro Butler and other servants met them, taking care of their little luggage, then led them into the large withdrawing room.

Jenson Carroll came to meet them, shaking hands with the four of them, as Hugh provided the introductions. Then Jenson led them to a beautiful lady sitting in a chair, but engrossed in playing with a one year old boy who was trying to walk. Then as she looked up Jenson introduced her as his wife, Mechia. All of them were astounded at her beauty. Probably in her mid twenties, with long jet black hair which streamed over her shoulders, and as she smiled she, also, greeted them with piecing dark eyes. So different from the women they had encountered since they arrived in America.

There was no doubt but that Mechia could not help but notice how entranced were her visitors at her appearance. She gave a little laugh, "It seems you are surprised at my appearance. It is the result of my parentage. Though my father is French, my mother Zoreia, is of indian birth, who met my father in the Ohio country when the French were fighting the British."

It seemed that Jenson was very pleased that they, so obviously, were attracted to his wife. He smiled, "So you can see what a very fortunate man I am to win the affection of such a lovely woman It would never have happened if my father had not come here from New York during the last war. However I can tell you I had to stave off, the many other suitors for her hand in marriage. Louis, named after her father, is our most recent child. Mechia has given me two other daughters since our wedding."

Now they all sat down whilst they were given refreshments. Then leaving Fay and Linda with Mechia, Jenson took Roy and Hugh to another room to talk business. It was for Hugh to explain why he had brought Roy with him. "I understand the shuttle perfectly and will make sure it works as well as my father would have done. I told you how he was murdered in Rochdale and why we had to flee to America to save our own lives. However I know little about machine weaving, only having seen it in operation."

Of course Jenson was a little disappointed but Hugh smiled, "It is fortunate I met Roy Marshall, who intended to come to America, in any case. However he was well acquainted with Grimshaw's mill in Manchester, which the mob destroyed. He can see to the introduction of all the machinery, if you are willing to include him in your offer to me. – Roy, please explain."

Roy, very quickly gave Jenson the rough sketches he had made on the ship. "I shall need to compile more accurate designs than theses, so that engineers could build the frames." Then he gave him two more sketches. "These, are probably the most important. They show you how the looms are connected to the Steam Work Horse which provided the power to work the looms. I can assure you, provided Hugh makes the shuttle work, you could have a series of looms working within twelve months and the first a few months earlier. – However it will be very expensive and you will not receive profits for two years, at least. However it will then destroy all Hand loom weaving, except for the most intricate designs.. As in England, you will become very rich.

He waited as Jenson devoured his rough sketches then Roy decided it was time to assert himself. "You have offered Hugh a partnership in your new company. Without my expertise it will not work. In fact, Hugh and I decided on the ship coming over, unless you make us both partners, we shall look elsewhere for others interested in this new form of weaving. " Now he lied a little, "Though not rich, we have adequate resources to live on until we find such a partner."

Jenson just smiled as he handed back the rough sketches, and showed his business acumen "But it is I who must provide the means by which this factory could be built. – However as Hugh Foyle has the patent rights to the shuttle, yet does not know much about weaving. As you are needed to perform this task. I admit, I like the way you have drawn your sketches. Though not an expert, I'm certain, you can do that job. – Please tell me then what you would expect of me? – Remember, if it fails, I am the looser not either of you."

Now it was Roy's turn to smile. He had persuaded Hugh, whilst in New York, on how they should confront Jenson, so he continued, "You have a valid point. As it will take two years before you could hope to show a profit. It is only fair that you reap some benefits from your investment. So for four years you will pay us an equal salary, as we set up and operate the factory. However, before we begin, you must agree that the assets of the factory, after the first four years will belong to the three of us. One half will be in your control and we each shall then receive a quarter of those assets. – We shall become partners." Hugh had felt they were asking far too much, but Roy had insisted.

Jenson was quick to reply, "And supposing after four years, or sooner, the idea is not successful?"

Again Roy smiled. He could not but admire this man. He seemed to be one he could trust. "The factory, until then, is yours. You can close it at any time. You will lose your investment. We shall lose our salary. But that is my point, we have an incentive to make it work. Our salary is only to repay us for the work we do – nothing more. However, from what I've seen in Lancashire, I've little doubt but it will be extremely profitable. This is a new and growing country. The demand for woven goods will multiply. It could become a gold mine. – If this is because of the expertise we have put into it. I believe we shall, then, have earned that partnership."

Now Jenson broke down in uncontrollable laughing. "It seems – you – English – are good business men. – However I like – the way you work. " At last he regained control. " I must admit your proposal seems fair. – I make an investment – You provide your knowledge – if successful, we should all benefit from it. – I will ask my lawyers to draw up a contract covering these points. Then, satisfied, we can all sign. - One further point. – Your contract will ensure you receive what you deserve. However, during those four years you must instruct me in all it mysteries. I want to know, in future when you suggest alternatives. – Meantime you can, all, stay here as my guests, until we find you, alternative accommodation I hope if, in time, if we are to become partners, our families may, even, become friends. – Finally, let us discuss your salaried for the first five years."

Both Hugh and Roy were very satisfied with the results. Neither argued at the sum offered by Jenson. To Roy it represented more in a month than his whole family had earned as Hand-loom workers in a year, even when they considered themselves prosperous. He knew that not only could Fay and he live in some comfort, but he would have sufficient to keep his promise to look after her unborn child.

It was three happy and satisfied men who returned to the ladies, before they all retired to dress for dinner, and Fay and Linda were delighted, they were to stay with the Carroll's for a time. It had been necessary for Roy to explain poor Fay's anomalous position, her pregnancy, and that he was not its father, but had promised to look after.

Mechia had surprised them by asking Fay, "Do you live with Roy? " Fay had blushed but told her she did. It did not seem to make Mechia think less of her and she added, "You have no need to feel ashamed. It often happens in America even when not married. We both hope we can enjoy your stay with us. We shall consider you two are married. – In fact I believe you are fortunate to find a man like Roy, willing to look after you and your child."

When at last Fay and Roy were shown to their single bedroom and they undressed, she came to him and kissed the side of his face. "You know Roy, Mechia is right. I am fortunate to find a man like you to look after me. You have, already, given me so much – yet I have given you so little. We have even slept together, yet you have respected me, and not demanded intimacy. Roy I have failed you. – That is wrong. – Dearest, I think you're wonderful – but I cannot, honestly say, I love you. – If you should want me. – If you find me sufficiently attractive. - I release you from your promise to not molest me."

Now Fay smiled, as she kissed him again, "Actually, after what Mechia has told me about her life and that of her mother – I will tell you about that tomorrow – I actually, hope, you will break your promise. Dearest, I know – that for a time – I would like to live with you – as a wife should do. It will not be to repay you. – I feel I may never fall in love the same as I did with Trevor. – To me – he is still there. – But we both have lives to live. Please, dear, I need you – I believe you need me."

At last Roy took her into his arms, naked as they both were, and buried his lips on hers as she responded to his embrace. Then he laughed a little. "Dear Fay. I've wanted this for sometime. Many times I've wondered if I dare ask it, of you. But my promise – and like you – though I think you wonderful – at present I cannot promise it is love. However, if you really want this – it will make me a very happy man."

Fay smiled, took his hand, and led him to the bed. He was patient and took his time. She was ready when he wanted intimacy. She found she could yield her lovely, but pregnant, body to him. In fact it was very late before, exhausted, they eventually fell asleep. In the morning they smiled lovingly at each other, kissing gently, but without passion. Both knew this arrangement would continue – at least until Fay bore her child.

8

They were awakened by a Negress servant when she came into their bedroom carrying a tray of morning tea. Then she calmly asked them to ring for her so that she could bath and dress both of them before coming down for breakfast. Roy was amazed that this young black woman intended to both wash his naked body and help him to dress. Only later did he discover this had, long, been the practice in the old colonies. Even Fay had smiled at his predicament, and was not surprised when he told her they would wish to see to this, themselves.

After she left Fay said, "It seems whilst we are here, you could have a female to massage you – perhaps – see to your needs – if you asked. Someone –besides me."

Roy had turned over in bed and gently kissed the side of her face. "Tell me truthfully. Do you regret –er – what we did last night?" Fay kissed him back, "No! Dear. You were wonderful – my only sadness was that it was not Trevor who was doing those things to me. – Come let us bathe together. We can clean each other others bodies – as a wife and husband should do. Now I know I want this to continue."

They arose and as they bathed away the rigours of the previous night and then helped each other to dress, Fay told Roy what Mechia had told her and Linda of her past history, as the two men had talked with Jenson. It was a long and very complicated story. "You should know Mechia's father never married her mother who was called, Zoreia. It seems that he treated her as if she was his wife and had lived with him before he married the woman, he had met in France and then lost to him, but eventually reunited."

Fay explained that Louis Scarron, born into French aristocracy, had come to New France, now called Canada, after his teenage girl friend, Julie Tencin, had flown to Holland, to avoid imprisonment, as she, though a Roman Catholic, was a Jensenist. Sent to man a fort then called Fort Duquesne, now renamed, Fort Pitt.

Here he had been obliged to enter into an indian marriage with fifteen year old, Zoreia, to cement good relationships with the local Chickasaw indian tribe, on the same day as his friend Jean Dumas had, likewise, married another indian girl, Aleia. It seemed that this enforced liaison had led to both coming to love their indian wives. So when at last the two men rediscovered the two girls they loved and married them, their new wives accepted their two indian 'wives' as part of their family and lived happily together. This was all Mechia had been able to tell them before Roy and Hugh returned. It seemed to be an intriguing situation, only possible in America.

Promising to discover more they dressed and joined the others at breakfast. During the days that followed Jenson had taken Roy and Hugh to the large building he had purchased to house their expected factory. Together they devised the layout and after Roy drew accurate diagrams, set engineers and builders to carryout the task. It would take several weeks, and for the time being they all lived with the Carroll's. It did give Fay and Linda a chance to come to know Mechia better and now learned the whole history of her parents lives and that of their friends.

It seemed Louis' superior, though the same age as him, Jean Dumas, had also lost the girl he loved in France, Madeline Colette, sentenced to six years as an indentured servant for aborting Jean's illegitimate child, whilst Jean was fighting in Austria. How both Louis and Jean had eventually found the girls they loved – it had taken ten years - and then been able to marry them, was also a story on its own. Meantime both men had come to love, deeply, their indian companions.

At the end of the Seven Years war, with the future of New France lost, it was probably, the fact, that though both were still willing to die for their country in Fort Duquesne, they knew, if so, their two wives would die with them. Both had then born them four children, born in the wilderness, without medical aid. Perhaps, even more than the promise, that at last, they could meet their girlfriends again, they could not sacrifice the lives of these two women, who had served them as well as any wife should do. It was this which had made them surrender the fort to George Washington.

Though prisoners, they were allowed to be united with both Julie and Madeleine. In fact they were never sent to a prisoners camp and were able to marry them. Also their new wives agreed to their indian wives acting as second wives to their husbands, bearing them further children. Mechia, was one of these born in 1767. So Louis and Jean each had enlarged families. Mechia had told them this was not, uncommon, in America, and why she saw nothing wrong in Fay living with Roy, although not married. It seemed it had happened many times between women and men, who though, not necessarily in love, but wanted security.

Naturally, Fay had asked Mechia about the rest of her family. Zoreia had born Louis four children in the wilderness and five more as they had lived with

Julie. It seemed that Aleia, who was Zoreia 's step-sister, had born Jean a similar number of children. Though each had lived in comfort in the Potomac valley, in a large mansion, all treated the same as Julie and Madeleine's own children, even Zoreia and Aleia had wanted to visit their old tribe at times, and taken their older children born in the wilderness to meet their relatives. Aleia's brother, Tonsac had become chief of the Chickasaw's. The tribe had settled on land given to them to the north-west of Fort Pitt, as a gift from George Washington. They had become very prosperous, raising horses, in great demand.

It seemed when Zoreia's eldest son, by Louis, Tartun, had visited and taken a young indian girl as his wife, the call of the wild to several of the children born in the wilderness, had led two Zoreia's eldest two daughters, Zoeca and Artor, deciding to stay and marry an indian husband. It was the same as Aleia's two eldest daughter, Alia and Dumei. Each had preferred the open range on which they had been reared, to the confines of a prosaic life near Berkeley. This was not the life which Mechia preferred.

On the contrary, Mechia had fallen in love with Jenson, as he had been overwhelmed by her beauty, so they had married in 1785, and had now born him three children. Mechia admitted she preferred to live in comfort having boyfriends before marrying Jenson. However she had, fully, approved his move to Philadelphia, and wished to help him in his work.

This then was the long story both Fay and Linda absorbed as they lived together, becoming great friends. Now both girls realised that a life in this new country would be very different from what they had lived in England. In fact both were a little sad when, at last two separate houses were purchased, in which to live. As they parted, Linda had been even more surprised when Mechia had spoken to Linda in private.

"Linda you are now going to live in the same house as your brother. You've told me how much you miss the ardent felicitations of your boy-friend, Peter Knowles. You are nearly nineteen years of age. At your age, I was no longer a virgin, in America we are rarely that way when we marry. Neither is it uncommon for girls to have intimate relationships with their close relatives. My step-mother Julie, lived for ten years with her much older step-brother, Anton Tencin, as though they were married. Julie even conceived his child, though they both agreed to an abortion. In fact Julie was the daughter of her mother Claudine Tencin, with her own son."

Now Mechia really, shocked Linda, "So if you feel those urges, we all suffer, Hugh is a handsome man. I'm certain, he could relieve you of these." For a moment it repelled Linda. The idea of intimacy with her own brother. However as the weeks passed as the lived together and Linda, still did not find any man who interested her, except Roy, who because of Fay, was not available to her, even Linda wondered if she might, yet, adopt the American way of life.

9

Louisa Modena Albrecht gave birth to a daughter, Antonia, in December 1793, in the presences of a mid-wife and doctor. It was an easy birth considering in was her first. As she fondled and held her tiny daughter to her bosom, she marvelled at her joy of holding this dear baby in her arms. She knew if she had stayed in Austria, she would now have been condemned to a life in a convent and her daughter would have been torn from her. Perhaps her beloved husband would have been killed for his crime.

Life here, in Florida, was, if anything, much easier than when she had lived in Europe. She was now a free woman, able to live her own life, with Negro servants to attend on her. Only the country was so different to Austria. There were no mountains as a backcloth. It was, virtually, flat. The weather was always warm, often very sunny, although beset by violent thunderstorms. Though still rich from the money they had brought from Europe, their extensive tobacco plantation provided further riches and more than covered the upkeep of their estate.

Their only concern was that their tobacco crop was not of the same quality as that grown in Virginia and Maryland, not as good as that grown in Cuba. Even there, the land was being cultivated in other ways, growing sugar canes and cotton. Perhaps, in time, they must pay a visit to both these lands, perhaps start alternative crops or import strains of the better tobacco. However, there was not any need to hurry. It could wait, as she recovered from her birth and again enjoyed the social life provided by their many rich neighbours.

They had found that their Spanish friends who had helped them purchase, and settle, on their estate, were involved in the Spanish administration of Florida, responsible to the main head quarters situated in New Orleans in southern Louisiana. Many of the male Spanish neighbours had to travel to New Orleans from time to time. Of course neither Louisa nor Anton were involved this way, but Anton enjoying discussing matters with his Spanish friends.

It seemed they had no fear of France, although after the revolution, it was, greatly, affecting life in the French Caribbean. Equality meant the planters there were told they must free their slaves and then employ them with wages, but this was, fiercely, resisted. Their only concern was the growing threat from this new country the United States, which had occupied part of Florida during their recent war with Britain. They knew that the United States would like to possess, not only the whole of Florida but the vast lands to the west, known as Louisiana. This area, was still only partially occupied and American settlers in the Ohio country would, dearly, like to press westward into the Spanish territories.

In the summer of 1794 Louisa and Anton learned that the United States Congress had requested to send a delegation of Congress men, to New Orleans, to discuss these matters with the Spanish. Of course their Spanish friends, responsible for administration in Florida, must attend. As Louisa had now weaned her baby, they suggested that Louisa and Anton, might like to accompany them. First to see the beauty of this City of New Orleans, but also to take part in the many social occasions which the Spanish authorities would host, as a welcome to their American visitors. They both agreed. It would seem like a holiday. Their overseer could attend to matters, whilst they were away.

It was a relatively short and safe passage by sea from Florida to New Orleans. Both Louisa and Anton marvelled at the elegance of the city, as great as any in Europe, yet so different. Their hotel accommodation was as good as any in the old country, except that all servants were black. Yet they were often entertained by them with their melancholy singing, they called Soul Music. It was an experience they would never forget. As expected, they received invitations to the several social receptions provided to entertain their American guests, who both Louisa and Anton, soon came to meet and even know.

It was a large delegation from Congress, but after many introductions, they became, particularly interested in the Senator for Virginia, Robert Carroll, in the United States Congress, and his wife Hedwig, as his family was involved, like them, in growing tobacco, but, of course, of a superior quality to there own. Naturally Anton spent time with him asking if they could purchase strains of the Virginian variety, and were told that his family had shares in the company which cross-bred these good strains, promising to send him more information, when he returned home.

Meanwhile Louisa was happy to talk with his wife, Hedwig. Louisa was surprised when Hedwig told her she had been born in Poland and only came to America with her family nearly twenty five years before, explaining her father, Michael Casimir had been an important aristocrat at the Polish court, but realising Russia would invade and take Poland for the Russian

Crown, had sold his vast estates and come to settle in West Virginia. Then emphasising that her husband's family had for over a century been important persons in Maryland and Virginia. Robert's great grandfather, Sir David Carroll had been Governor of Maryland for many years.

Of course Louisa was intrigued, and realised these two people were really aristocrats in their own country. She dare not confess her true status but did inform Hedwig that both she and her husband came from a similar lineage in Austria, surprising Hedwig by explaining she was Austrian and not Spanish.

The result was that both Hedwig and Robert, quickly introduced them to other members of the delegation, who were also their friends. Firstly the Representative for West Virginia, Francois Tencin and his wife, Anne. Of course the name Tencin was a notorious one in Europe, as Claudine had been the mistress of King Louis XIV for many years bearing him numerous, illegitimate children, so carefully they asked if he was any relation of the French Tencin's.. They were even shocked at his reply. "My father, Anton, was one of her sons by the king and Anne's mother was the offspring of Claudine. You see we still have strong ties with France – but the old France, not the present murderers."

Again as Roman Catholics they were surprised that in protestant America, though a Senator of that country, Francois and Anne were firm Roman Catholics. Louisa asked, "Are you allowed to worship as you please?" Francois had laughed, telling her this was the right of every United States citizen, and surprised them more. He called over another man and his wife to introduce them.

Taking hold of the man's hand he said, "My I introduce, Eric Casimir, the Senator for West Virginia, who is the elder brother of Robert Carroll's wife, Hedwig, and like them is a staunch protestant, coming from originally from Poland. But now I am delighted to introduce his extremely beautiful wife, Isabel, who was a Bacon before she married. Isabel, as is her family, is an equally staunch Roman Catholic who still worships, differently to her husband. You see in America we do believe in religious freedom of worship."

All Louisa could do was to laugh, calling Anton over to introduce everyone. After that Louisa and Anton monopolised an equally delighted group of people at every future function. Before it was time for the delegation to return, they had become firm friends, even if their talks with the Spanish authorities had been abortive, leading to no concessions on either side. It had, however, provided a measure of understanding, which might prevent serious consequences in the near future.

The one salient result of these meetings was to establish a firm friendship between Louisa, Anton and their new American friends. Although Francois and Robert's estate were deep inside Virginia and West Virginia, as were Eric Casimir's'. However Eric, who was the oldest of their new friends, invited them to come, someday, to Maryland, to land at Annapolis, where he and his wife shared a large town house with their own childhood friends John Holstein, of Swedish birth and his wife. It seemed Hilary, herself a Mowbray, before marriage, was still a Roman Catholic, as her husband was a protestant.

If so they would come to meet them, then take them to stay on all the other estates of the friends they had now come to know. Louisa and Anton were delighted, but explained how first they must see to the prosperity of their own estate, expecting to have to visit Spanish Cuba, to see if they should introduce new stocks or, even, new alternative crops of sugar cane or cotton. They did promise to available themselves of this invitation within the next five years.

Their short, but rewarding holiday, came to an end and they sailed back to Florida. However it seemed to them that the United States, was not only a new country, with a President, instead of a king. However, it seemed it allowed a remarkable degree of religious freedom. Even though staunch Roman Catholics, both had to admit that, if they had stayed in Austria, Louisa would now be a virtually prisoner in a Covent and not allowed to keep and bring up her own child, simply because it was born out of wedlock. Yet two couples were legally married in America, though still of different faiths, bringing up their own children to understand both, until they were old enough to decided for themselves. Surely this could not be wrong for all of them were Christians, only wanting to worship in slightly different ways.

10

Although there was work waiting to be dealt with when they returned, they did correspond with their new American friends and were delighted to receive replies. This was possible as American ships called frequently at Miami through which all their correspondence was routed. They, also, received a letter from Robert Carroll informing them that he had asked the cross-breeding company of which he was a large shareholder to contact them about their tobacco crops.

The letter arrived from a Richard Marsh of the Marsh Tobacco Holdings, explaining that Robert had asked him to contact them. He, gave details of the varieties available and the prices of their products, explaining how they could be obtained. Anton was pleased to receive this, but decided to wait until he went with his neighbours on their projected visit to their neighbours, Spanish relatives in Cuba, for Anton was, equally interested, in obtaining information about growing sugar cane and cotton, wondering I these might be more profitable.

It was impossible to arrange this visit until the following year. Again, as Louisa had not yet wanted to conceive again, when a date was fixed, he decided to leave baby Antonia with their nursemaid and take Louisa with him, for another short holiday. Louisa was delighted to at last travel to part of the Caribbean, of which she had learned so much. They would be the guests of their Spanish relatives in Cuba. Although they knew that the war between France and Britain and the socialist attitudes of the French Government was creating strife in the Caribbean islands, particularly in Guadalupe and Martinique, this was well to the east of Cuba. For further safety they decided to travel in an American ship, as the United States were still neutral in the European conflict. In any case the voyage, was relatively short.

They arrived in Cuba in the early spring and were well received by their hosts, who were delighted to meet Austrian friends in a place, almost exclusively Spanish. Though Anton was extremely busy trying to ascertain whether new alternative crops were desirable, and not being particularly keen on the different tobacco varieties, as he was, now, more interested in those grown in Virginia, Louisa spent the days with the many Spanish ladies. She learned two things. First that the Spanish in Cuba were far more virulent Roman Catholics that those in Florida or those she knew in Europe. Since her last birth she had followed the practice of their Spanish friends ladies in wearing preventatives, as she did not want to conceive too quickly.

She discovered this was frowned upon in Cuba. Women were expected to do their duty to their husbands and bare their children very quickly. Their daughters were chaperoned when in the presence of any men, even their brothers and hoped to marry before they were seventeen. To Louisa's horror, she learned that these poor women often endured miscarriages, infants dying early and sometimes taking the life of their mother. Even in Austria, a woman was not expected to conceive so frequently.

She also found that the Spanish in Cuba hated the British, who had been their enemy in the Caribbean since the time of Queen Elizabeth and King Philip II of Spain. Although they disliked the new form of government in France, especially as France were trying to free all slaves in their colonies, the Spanish in Cuba still preferred the French to the British. Louisa decided she much preferred her life in Florida to that in Cuba, though she was made very welcome.

Another thing which annoyed Louisa was the dominant way the men treated their women. Even in Florida, the men were certainly the master of the household, but this was not very different to the way it operated in Europe. Here in Cuba, it seemed that women were merely the chattels of men, born to serve them, and provide them with a large family. Ever since she had come to know and fall in love with Anton, he had treated her very differently. She would acknowledge he was the head of the household, but he did not order her to obey. He would discuss everything with her, even his business affairs. He welcomed her advice. It was a truly happy relationship, which she valued.

He only laughed when she brought the attitude of men in Cuba to their women to his attention. He had replied, "You see I have no difficulties that way, as I have such a wonderfully understanding wife to look after me. In one case, I do fully agree with you. I have always considered it should be the wife, because of the dangers to herself, who should decide when she wanted children, and not her husband. Thankfully we have found in Florida a way of achieving this, not easily available in Europe. Dearest, I may ask you for a baby, but if you did not, at that time want it, I would accept your decision." This only confirmed her love for Anton. He gave her a love life she could never have hoped to enjoy in Austria.

At last it was time to return. Again they all decided to wait for an American ship. In the event, their Spanish neighbours had to leave before them on a Spanish ship travelling directly to New Orleans, so they had to wait for the American ship to call. It was a regular shipping route from Caribbean ports of call to Florida, then New Orleans and back via Florida to the American eastern seaboard, Charleston, Annapolis and to New England. The normal trade route.

They boarded the ship to sail to Miami, in good weather. Then on the second day A French privateer appeared and ordered them to stop with a shot across their bows, when they tried to run to escape. The French were only interested in their cargo and had no means of sailing their ship. Having transferred all the crew and passengers onto the privateer, as well as the enormous number of precious goods, the privateer sunk their ship. Then telling them they would take everyone to Martinique for ransom, they set sail eastward. Poor Louisa and Anton were their captives. They had no choice.

By chance two days later as they sailed north of Cuba and south of the Bahamas the privateer was attacked by a large Untied States frigate which outgunned them two to one. The privateer had no chance to escape and after a very brief encounter was dismastered and the Americans came aboard. The Frenchmen were taken prisoners and put in chains. As from the other passengers they learned that they had fired upon and sunk an American ship, and that America was supposed to be a neutral country., it meant that the Frenchmen would be brought to trial in American on a charge of piracy.

Naturally as Miami was only two hundred miles to the north-west, Louisa and Anton begged to be landed there, which would have been their original destination. However it seemed relationships between Spain and the United States were a little strained, at the moment, and the Port of Miami would not welcome an American ship of war, even if it did its merchant ships. As the frigate which had rescued them was assigned to sail the eastern seaboard, to prevent exactly what had happened to them, and was now bound for their base at New York, all they could offer them was land them at any American port on the way.

Both Anton and Louisa realised the only place where they might meet friends was in Maryland, having impressed the captain by explaining their friendship with the two Senators Robert Carroll and Eric Casimir, there was no difficulty in him agreeing to land both of them at Annapolis, though most of the Spanish, who had sailed with them from Cuba, asked to be landed at Charleston, where they could obtain a ship to Florida or New Orleans.

So in the summer of 1795 both Anton and Louisa made, an unexpected, visit to Maryland, alighting from the frigate on the quay at Annapolis. Fortunately they were not destitute and had sufficient money with them to pay for rooms in an hotel there. So due to circumstances beyond their control the Albrecht's like Anna and Andrew Reeves had followed them to the United States, though at this time neither knew of each others existence. However the Albrecht's hoped it would only be of short duration as Louisa wanted to be reunited with her young daughter again.

PART 3

CONNECTIONS

CONNECTIONS

As their journey to Maryland had been so unexpected, they had not been able to acquaint Eric Casimir and his wife, Isabel, of their arrival. Even though they knew the address of his town house in Annapolis, they felt sure he would not be there, knowing of his estate near Fort Pitt, which Eric had described to them when at New Orleans, was his chief home. However he had told them that Isabel's family, the Bacons had an estate near Annapolis. So they made inquiries as to is whereabouts.

Discovering it, they both hired a coach and called at the house. Shown in by a Negro Butler they met Sheila Bacon, Isabel's mother. Of course she had heard of persons being landed from an American Naval ship, who had been passengers on a merchant ship sunk by the French. It seemed this happened several times recently. They explained fully what had happened to them and how they had come to meet and become the friends of her daughter and her husband. How they had been invited to visit them, but never expected it might happen this way. They proved this by giving Sheila an address of her daughter's town house in Annapolis.

After this, Sheila Bacon had, no doubts, about what they had said. Immediately she invited them to leave their hotel and come to stay with her. It seemed her son-in-law, Eric, was attending Congress at the moment and Isabel was living with him. However Sheila promised to acquaint her daughter of their arrival and the strange reasons and why they had been forced to come to Maryland. She even sent her coachman to their hotel to collect their few belongings, even paying their hotel bill.

Louisa had been ashamed that circumstances meant they had little money with them but assured them they owned a prosperous tobacco estate in Spanish Florida, and would be pleased to recompense them for any expense whilst they stayed with them. That evening they met her husband Kenneth. Although he realized they would wish to return to Florida as quickly as possible, so Louisa could be with her young baby, he did suggest they stayed, a little time in Maryland, so as to meet their friends. Suggesting they sent letters to Florida, which he would ensure were dispatched as quickly as possible, through the diplomatic postal system, of which his son-in-law had access. So everyone in Florida would know they were safe. Because of this and their kindness, both Louisa and Anton, agreed to spend, at least a week or two with them.

It seemed that Sheila, now sixty years of age, delighted in writing letters, if only to pass the time. On her own device she sent letters, not only to Isabel but also to Robert Carroll and his wife, who were with Eric, attending meetings of Congress. She also enjoyed conversations with Louisa, concerning her past life. Of course Louisa had to tell them she and her husband were born in Austria, ensuring she knew Louisa's family were rich landowners in Europe, but refrained from telling her of her relationship and that of her husband to the Austrian Court.

Louisa received a surprise, as Sheila then told her of their meeting on a ship coming from Bristol of another Austrian couple, who they had befriended. Again these seemed to be of good breeding and very well educated. It seemed only the wife was Austrian and her husband was English. They had now gone to live on land purchased near Fort Pitt and set up a school. Louisa admitted to Anton it intrigued her. How could a Austrian woman of good breeding come to meet an Englishman. Anton had laughed replying that not all Austrian women received the same strict chaperoning as she had to endure.

They enjoyed staying with the Bacons but it was not long before Eric Casimir and Isabel, Robert Carroll and Hedwig, came to see them. Eric and Isabel insisted they came to stay in their own town house and Robert and Hedwig agreed to join them. After thanking Sheila and Kenneth Bacon, promising to visit them again, they went to live at Eric's home. Since Robert knew of Anton's interest in Virginian tobacco and that he had received information from Richard Marsh, concerning tobacco crops Robert took Anton to meet Richard. This gave Louisa a chance to talk with both Isabel and Hedwig.

Louisa and Anton felt they could trust their new friends. In any case their positions in Congress might mean they were knowledgeable about the scandal at the Austrian court. The name of Albrecht was well known. Their friends might, already, have some suspicions about them. They decided they should confess their true identity. So after dinner one night, with the other four, as they sat drinking, Anton made his confessions.

"Louisa and I feel you have the right to now the truth of why we had to come to live in Florida. Louisa is a princess of the Austrian court, and of Tuscany, I am a prince of Savoy. We became lovers and dear Louisa conceived my child. Not only would we not have been allowed to marry, but for her crime Louisa would have been sent to a Convent and when her baby was born it would be taken from her and adopted. I, probably., would have been executed. So we fled first to Spain and then to Florida, to prevent us being returned to Austria for punishment."

Now he smiled, "By telling you this we place our lives in your hands. If the court came to know of it, pressure would be brought on the United States to return us both to Austria for punishment. Fortunately we both had sufficient wealth to escape and buy this estate in Florida, though not rich, we have adequate resources. We feel certain we can trust you and did not want to continue to live a lie."

It was Eric how replied but his words were confirmed by everyone. "Thank you for telling us this. You need never fear that we would betray your confidences. Further more, our positions in Congress, would mean we could, possibly, stop any chance of extradition proceedings being brought against you. – However, I should add, this would be much easier if you were landowners in the United States, as well as in Florida. You know why we came to New Orleans to discuss matters with the Spanish authorities. Secretary of State, Pinckney is at present in the process of concluding a treaty with the Spanish to ensure peace between our country and Spain."

Now Eric smiled, "But this is only the beginning. It is only a temporary peace. Eventually, the whole of Florida, perhaps even part of Louisiana will become part of this new country. Settlers are pouring into these spaces and are already demanding our protection. I am not suggesting you sell your Florida estate. In time your land will, inevitably become part of the Untied States, however, since you have resources I would suggest you, also, purchase, at a pittance, a little land in the west. You do not even need to work it. However you could then apply to become a citizen of the United States. No longer would you have to fear going back to Austria. You know, even in Spanish Florida, you are not, completely, safe."

Neither Anton nor Louisa had thought of this before, but where they lived did, at present, belong to Spain. If their true position was discovered Spain might be forced to arrest them and return them to Austria. After that evening they both discussed Eric's proposal. Anton had sufficient Letters of Credit of European Bank, to buy a small holding in this country. When Eric assured him that by a series of transactions this money could be accessed without anyone knowing it had come from Anton in America they agreed to follow his advice.

As they had no intention of working the land, Eric had suggested one of the many small landholdings in the wilderness, still left because it was so heavily wooded, and so useless for agriculture, until it was cleared. Eric explained how his family had long since bought a large estate, for this reason, reaping great financial rewards from selling its hardwood trees. He could arrange for their own trees to be felled and sold in the same way. It was merely an investment. However it would give them the right to apply for citizenship. Within days, all this was arranged.

Though Eric and Robert must soon return to Congress, he had written to his friend John Holstein and his wife, Hilary to come to stay in Annapolis. When they arrived they were told of the difficulties both couples had experienced before they were allowed to marry, yet all kept worshipping as they pleased. Now John and Hilary suggested they should take them to stay for a short time on their own estate which they shared with Eric and which was close to the small holding they had purchased.

In spite of Louisa's desire to be united with her baby daughter, Anton, fascinated at what he had heard of this area, persuaded her to accompany John and Hilary into what they called 'the wilderness'. All traveled in coaches supplied by the Holstein's. Arriving, they were both captivated by the beauty of the wooded estate. They slept in an enormous wooden mansion. Actually two joined together with common reception rooms, their wing was on the right whilst the Casimir's owned the left wing. It seemed their families had been bosom friends for many years.

They were introduced to their neighbours as they stayed, marveling at the vastness of the area, and to their personal friends, Kylie and Adrian Scott and their families who worked a successful arable farm close by. They were able to view the land they had bought, seeing how densely wooded it was. John Holstein volunteered to have much of it cleared and the hardwood sold for profit. However it was only a means to an end. For now, before they left, they could apply for American citizenship, the only reason for its purchase.

However when they were taken to the local school where the Scott's and other children went to learn to read and write, they were introduced to the schoolmaster, and schoolmistress, Mr. and Mrs. Andrew Reeves being informed that his wife Anna, was born like them in Austria. It was the couple Sheila had told them about who she had met on the ship.

When they returned to the estate Louisa was anxious to speak with Anton. "I know it's very improbable – but I could swear I've seen Anna Reeves at the court in Vienna. It was only a little time before we had to flee from Austria. If she is not – then she is a remarkable double." Of course Anton felt sure she was wrong, and they did not explore the possibility.

At last Louisa was able to persuade Anton they must return to Florida. So they persuaded John and Hilary to take them back to Annapolis. After once again staying with Sheila and Kenneth Bacon, and thanking them for helping them in their time of need, they boarded an American merchant ship to take them back to Miami and then hired a coach to take them to their estate. They had been away over four months and baby Antonia was now trying to learn to walk. Louisa had enjoyed her enforced say in Maryland and the wilderness, much more than their stay in Cuba. However she was happy to once more be with her baby daughter. Still she still could not get over the idea she had seen and met Anna Reeves at the Hapsburg court.

2

That night after the visit from Louisa and Anton Albrecht, poor Anna Reeves was a very worried woman. She poured out her troubles to Andrew. "You know I feel sure I knew that Louisa Albrecht and I'm sure she recognised me. – You know the Albrecht family is an important family at the court in Vienna. – They come from Savoy. I dare not question the woman. – You know she might have come from Austria on a visit. – If she did recognise me – she might let the authorities in Austria know we are here."

Andrew tried to reassure her. "I believe you are wrong. In any case they have not come here today on a visit from Austria. John Holstein told me they own a large tobacco estate in Spanish Florida. They may, even, be Spanish. Please do not worry. Even if they make inquiries or others from Austria try to do so, we are now American citizens, I'm sure the Holstein's, Casimir's or Bacon's will stand by us. It's very different here to the European countries – even Britain. The United States are not likely to stand for any intrusion by a European country on any of their citizens."

Anna tried to be comforted. "Oh! Andrew! I hope so. I've been so happy since we came here. You still keep blaming yourself for us having to flee here. But just being with you is wonderful. Knowing and feeling you love for me. I don't mind the work – even the hardships. My so called life of easy in Europe was really a prison. In spite of the work, I'm very happy here, just looking after you - and baby, Philip, he's already one and a half. Look how well he walks. – Oh! Please God, let us continue to live here."

Andrew took her in his arms and hugged her. "You don't regret me causing you to give up your easy life in Austria?"

Anna just kissed him. "Regret – Why, you given me a life I could never have enjoyed if I had stayed, being married off to some noble, to increase the status of my family. I should, just, have had to submit to him, whether I wanted to, or not. – Andrew I'm free. I choose to work here – not just to get money. It means we can have a true family – one of our own. – and Andrew

– I –er– will soon want to increase our family. So we must work hard to earn enough to keep all our children. The love you give me is ample reward for what I have to do."

Then she laughed. "During the summer, after the school goes on holiday, I think we could afford to go down to Annapolis – accept, kind Sheila Bacon's invitation and stay with them for a few days. Isabel Casimir reminding me that her mother hoped we'd come, only a few days ago. - You know really, we are quite rich. Besides our now quite large earnings from the school, we still have the larger part of the money we got by selling my jewels. We need a few luxuries – some better clothes. We could afford a few days in the town – perhaps meet Sheila's other friends – the ones she wanted to introduce us to, when we arrived." Andrew kissed her again telling her they must do this.

Meanwhile in the year and a half since they had arrived in America the French exiles and the three Irish men were enjoying their new life. As both had hoped, the affair between Antoinette Condorcet and Stuart Brady had developed into a love affair and even become intimate, up to a point. If it continued Michelle, hoped it might become a permanent arrangement. Whilst Jack Eliot was enjoying flirting with the feminine company offered so close to Racoonsville. She had spoken to Daniel, getting his promising to help any of the exiles, financially, if it became necessary. She emphasised they were rich enough for this, and it was because of their intervention, that they had arrived here.

Manon and Jean had enjoyed flirting with Michelle's and Catherine's children, but so far, no serious affairs had developed. However they had, also, come to know Sophia Chalmers and her second husband, Colin. Besides her children by her first husband Keith Brookes, Sophia had presented Colin with four more children, living on the combined Goochland/Brooke estate a little distance away. It seemed that by now all had become accustomed to their new life.

Those who had chosen to stay in the Potomac valley had, also, enjoyed their new lives. Jacques and Louise were enjoying staying with Julie and Louis Scarron. Here there were many eligible men and women living close by. Already an number of assignations had developed, some somewhat intimate, but as yet, it had not become serious. Again both Julie and Louis had told them they need not worry about financial problems, should it become permanent.

However perhaps the happiest of any of them was Jeanne Cristal. Used to working as a servant from an early age, she now found that most of her time was her own. However, true to her promise, she ensured that Ruth

Tencin enjoyed an equally full and happy life to herself. Jeanne knew she now loved Ruth. She was more a mother to her than ever her true mother had been, sold into service at an early age. But it was a mutual arrangement. Jeanne marvelled at the way Ruth had survived those terrible years before she first became Anton's mistress, and later his wife.

Ruth told her of her own downfall and the wicked man who made her pregnant and then deserted her, How, having an abortion, was discovered and her sentence for five years as an indentured servant. Then Jeanne was to learn of another girl who had suffered because of what that same man had done to her mother. Her name was Clare Wycks, now married to a rich man, Philip Wycks, and become his second wife. In confidence Ruth had told her how Clare's mother had conceived by the same evil man who had made her pregnant. Her mother bore Clare and became a prostitute.

Ruth had continued telling her, in time Clare had to become one herself. How she met a man in the Bristol brothel, who brought her to America providing she lived with him as his wife, though he told her he would never marry. Her terribly hard and unhappy life with him until discovered by Michael Casimir who had adopted her, providing her with a dowry.

In time Clare and Philip had become friends as Clare managed to convince Philip that he was not responsible for his first wife's death, in childbirth, having nearly died herself, when carrying the other man's baby, yet telling him she would still have tried to conceive, even if she had known what would happen. It seemed Philip had fallen in love with her. Yet when she confessed her past life to him he still wanted to marry her, eventually persuading her she did love him. For Clare had never allowed herself to fall in love before.

When she had finished Ruth told Jeanne, she would see, and ensure, she enjoyed a happy life, one as happy as she and now Clare had found. She said, "You see it seems we women must suffer in many ways before we can hope to achieve happiness, - Please believe me, Jeanne, you will find a man who loves you just as Anton loved me and Philip loves Clare."

To try to convince Jeanne she took Jeanne to where both Clare and Philip lived on their large estate and when Philip was away, Ruth asked Clare to tell Jeanne about her earlier life before she met Philip. Clare was happy to oblige. "It is no longer a secret. My mother suffered from the same evil man as Ruth. Became a prostitute to keep me, for I am that evil man's daughter. Eventually, when fourteen I had to help my mother and became a prostitute with her in Bristol. A man called Neil Reeves came and used me in the brothel. He was going to America. He offered to take me with him, so long as I acted as his wife. Even then he told me he would never marry me. I did not mind. Anything was better than living in the brothel."

Now tears came into her eyes, "Well after several years I conceived and then lost his child - I nearly died. A very kind man Michael Casimir saved me, took me into his home and gave me a dowry. It was a miracle that I met Philip. He was suffering so much from the loss of his wife, he told me later, it was I who prevented him committing suicide. He fell in love with me, even wanting me after knowing my past. Well, I finally realised what love meant. I married dear Philip who has given me a wonderful life. – Dear Jeanne, forget your past. It means nothing in America. I know you will find a man, like Philip, who will love you – You just need to be patient."

By now Jeanne was beginning to believe it would happen to her, yet she had, so far, made no attempt to meet other men. In any case, she knew she would never leave Ruth while she still lived. For Ruth was now her true mother. She hoped by helping her, Jeanne might enable Ruth to live a little longer. This to Jeanne was far more important than any thought of finding a man to marry.

3

It was now over three years since James Downey and Paul Eliot's abortive journey to Fort Washington, as part of the militia to accompany the Regular Army under General Harmar, to help pacify the Miami Indians. It had proved a disaster for both of them in everyway. It had never achieved that degree of adventure which had made them volunteer for it. However they had both appreciated the friendship shown to them by their own commanding officer, Major John Hamtramck. It had, also, failed to provide the amorous adventures, and the women they might enjoy. Perhaps the real and main reason for them joining.

They had returned very disillusioned men. However neither of them could forget those three days at Anderson and their flirtation with the two girls, Lilie Gartner and Helga Feld. They both cursed themselves for being so hasty in assuming the girls wanted amorous pleasures as much as they desired them. Foolish, yet could they really blame themselves. Their lovemaking had only proceeded at the rate any girl in West Virginia would have expected, even losing interest in them, if they had failed to make such progress. It had never occurred to them that the religious beliefs of these women would make them to react, and be shocked, at what the boys felt was a harmless expression of the admiration of the female body.

For long afterwards they both admitted to themselves that their attraction to these two girls was a little stronger than a mere flirtation. After all they had gone to Fort Washington, with the idea that they might find a girl who might possibly become a partner for life, as they had failed to find any near home. Both knew they would have wished to explore the possibilities with these girls. It was their haste, which had destroyed any chance of it happening.

In these last three years both men had failed to find women who they would consider as partners for life. Because they still felt so strongly about Lilie and Helga and might, in the future, return and try to undo the wrong they had done, perhaps begin again the courtship they desired, they even began to learn German, much to the amusement of their families..

The following year they heard of the decision of President Washington to send another army under the generalship of General Arthur St. Clair, Governor of the North West Territories. It was to be a large force of 850 Regular Army and about 1400 Militia, for which volunteers were requested. However after the last foray, James and Paul had no interest in repeating the mistakes of the past.

Perhaps it was a wise decision for this resulted in the worse defeat of any United States army by indians. The defeat at the Battle of the Wabash was far worse than General Custer's defeat, at the battle of the Little Big Horn. The America Confederacy under Chief Little Turtle and Chief Blue Jacket routed the American army, killing or capturing over 600 men and wounding a further 250, whilst the loss to themselves as ridiculously small with only 60 killed. St. Clair's remaining force raced back to Fort Jefferson and then to Fort Washington.

However this defeat meant that the whole of the settlers in Northern Indiana and Ohio were now at the mercy of the victorious and blood seeking indians. There was nothing to halt them. Of course James and Paul heard about this and now feared for the lives of the two women they had known for such a short time. It seemed the settlement at Anderson, had been overrun. However they knew there would have been little they could have done to save them, even if they had joined St. Clair's forces.

Soon they heard that well over two hundred homesteads had been attacked and the families on them murdered, though as usual, after an indian attack, many women's lives, particularly the younger ones, were saved, to become the sexual sport and slaves of the victorious warriors. Both James and Paul felt sure that Lilie and Helga would probably now be the concubines of some indian brave.

Of course they knew that President Washington was sending another Army to attempt to subjugate the confederation. He called on a compatriot of the war, a hero, General 'Mad' Anthony Wayne, for this purpose, and the President had forced Congress to greatly increase the Standing Army and a probable 2000 sized Militia. At the end of 1793 both James and Paul were astonished to receive a letter from Major John Hamtramck, to whom they had given their address when the parted three years before.

Hamtramck asked them to join him, now a Lieutenant-Colonel to take charge of the cavalry company, telling them what a strong general was Anthony Wayne, and was now certain of eventually victory. Perhaps the fact that he added that they knew a large number of captured white women were being held near to Fort Miami, which the British stilled held near Lake Erie, though supposed to be given to America in the Treaty of Paris. In fact they knew the British has been arming the indians and giving them support.

By now James' brother, twenty year old Stuart Downy, had been trained in the militia, so he was delighted to join them, when James and Paul decided to accept Hamtramck's offer and again taking extra horses as requested, all three of them made their way again the Fort Washington in the September of 1793. A smallpox epidemic delayed any action until October but then General Wayne proceeded north to Fort Jefferson. Sensibly, after wintering there, he moved slowly during 1794, establishing Fort Greene Ville and Fort Recovery, at the site of St. Clair's defeat.

Wayne moved forward methodically, after Little Turtle attacked his supply train with over 1500 Miami, Delaware and Shawnee indian warriors, he built another Fort Defiance. Little Turtle realising they were now dealing with a different and resolute type of men, refused in August to commit his force against him and was, immediately removed from command by Chief Blue Jacket. This was what Wayne was expecting.

He moved his force along the Maumee river, destroying indian villages on the way. This forced the indians to attack at a place called 'Fallen Timbers', where a number of trees had fallen during a small hurricane. Cleverly, knowing the indians always fasted before attack to limit the dangers of stomach wounds becoming diseased, Wayne attacked on August 20th. a day late. James cavalry, in some real danger, drove the indians from the trees which were their protection, then Wayne's infantry routed them with few losses to themselves.

The indians retreated to Fort Miami hoping the British would support them. In fact they refused, but, also, refused to surrender the fort to the Americans. What was to become known as the Battle of the Fallen Timbers ended that day with an American victory. Instead Wayne returned to Fort Greene Ville. Starving, Blue Jacket knew he had no option but to end the war and negotiate. All fighting ceased and a year later in August 1795 the Treaty of Greeneville was signed and the whole of the North West Territories became almost free from indian attack and settlers poured into it, replacing the many killed in the previous three years.

However August and September 1794 were important months from James, Paul and Stuart. They were to enjoy the spoils of their victory. They received the warmest congratulations from Colonel Hamtramck, for without their courageous charge through the forest, in great danger, the indians would have remained, leading to heavy causalities on both sides. But now they had the opportunity to seek out the women who had been spared death on the homesteads, only to become the sexual slaves of the indians.

They knew it was unlikely, but there was just the possibility that Lilie and Helga had survived the massacre at Anderson which they knew had resulted in the extermination of the entirely community, which they had enjoyed visiting almost four years before. They now explained to Hamtramck, the real reason, why they had accepted his invitation. As he remembered very well their predicament those years before when, despondingly, they had returned to Fort Washington, and when he had explained the reason for the girl's refusal of their advances. Now he understood how strong were the feelings of these two men for these women.

He immediately wrote out an order, giving all three of them permission to enter any encampment, as well as any camp set up to house any captured and now free women. Further more if they were to discover the women they sort, then they would be given complete possession of these women and allowed to take any women, willing to accept their offer, to any place they chose, being given all means of transport, and, finally, the release of the three of them from further military service.

He had smiled at them before saying, "I valued very much your help, at and after Fort Vincennes, that was why I wrote asking you to join me. However yesterday and the day before you made victory certain, at no small risk to yourselves. You saved many lives. Frankly your work here is done. There are others who can finish the job. – I do hope you find the women you are seeking – and that they are still alive. --- But please, remember what they must have suffered, and pity them, - try to help them, for they will now, probably, consider they are now unfit to live a civilized life."

James had told the others, he feared what mental state these two girls would be in, even if they found them alive. Colonel Hamtramck had only confirmed their fears. However they would try to find and help them.

4

James, Paul and Stuart found several branches of the militia invading the indian villages and pillaging them. This also included the usual crime of a victorious army, of enjoying the bodies of several unprotected indian women, but in addition, were also discovering, many white women captured in the past years and forced to become squaws of their indian captors. They saw several of these unfortunate females, of all ages, being helped into covered wagons to be sent to a central staging area, where their position could be ascertained and where help would be available to them.

The three men first went to view the two centres already provided. It was a sorry sight. In the first were over twenty women huddled together, still in fear, holding one, two or even three children, whose fathers were the indian brave who had captured them, having killed the rest of their family and taken them for their pleasure. It seemed that some had been captives for over five years, though some, for a mere eighteen months. It seemed that the older ones had more quickly come to terms with their position. Often, already married with children, they could more easily accept rape, and sexual cruelty than the young ones, often virgins, with no sexual experience, before their capture. However each had no chance of avoiding conceiving a baby by their captor.

They noticed the older ones, in spite of still managing their young children, were trying to give succour to the younger girls. At once they realised what this must mean to both Lilie and Helga, if they were still alive. Both would have been twenty or twenty one when they had been taken. However unlike the women at home, who by then, were either married or in an intimate relationship with a boy friend, these two girls, because of their religious abstinence were not only virgins, but had never known or enjoyed any intimacy with men. Suddenly taken and raped by a savage, not knowing if they would die, their experience would have been terrible, enough to even drive them mad.

At least it seemed, unlike the tales they had heard of white women being tortured, often to death, these women had not had to endure torture.

However they were treated even worse than an indian squaw. Beaten frequently, when the transgressed against a rule they did not know existed, learning by suffering, their duties, apart from sexual ones, expected of them. Further more life was exceedingly hard for them.

They quickly discovered that none of the twenty odd females already brought there were either Lilie nor Helga. Mostly, they were older women, mainly German or Polish though one or two were English. A least the men's efforts to learn German now proved rewarding. Even the Polish women, with help from a nearby German woman, could understand their questions. However, as expected, none of them had heard the names of the two women they searched. A woman of thirty five, with three offspring's from her captivity, explained it was unlikely any would know of them unless they were very close to their own abode, as they were never allowed to wander from the camp.

So the three of them made their way to he second centre, where nearly thirty women, with their children, had arrived. Again these were mostly German women, with some Polish and English females. At least it seemed that some of the younger mothers, especially about twenty, were more composed than the ones in the previous centre. However they showed their despair, fearing what future they had, knowing that few men would even considered them as mistresses after being used so frequently by indian men. James did his best to allay this, explaining they were looking for two girls about their ages, who, if still alive, and if they found them, would ensure they had a happy future. He stated many men would be willing to look after them, though in fact, he feared he might be lying.

Having ensured neither Lilie nor Helga were present and saw that in each of the centres, women were being brought in fairly regularly, they decide to comb the surrounding area, particularly the three large indian villages, now being ruthlessly raided, and raped by the militia.

As they entered the first village they were disgusted at what they saw. Several soldiers were at that moment forcing, young Indian girls to the ground, ripping away their few clothes, and were lying on top of them raping they defenceless bodies. They realised these men were worse then the indian men who had taken the white women as captors. At least they had treated them as squaws, their rapings had been far less brutal, only the taking of the women without her consent was their crime.

Fearfully they made their way, to several other villages, stepping over the soldiers enjoying their intimacy. Then, at last, they came to a number of wagons. It seemed most of the soldiers had not sunk so low as their colleagues, they were entering the toupees, finding white women huddled inside, in abject fear, not knowing that their indian masters had been defeated. Seeing soldiers raping indian girls, many feared this would be their fate.

In fact many had to be dragged out before they could be forced to mount the waiting wagons. Since most were German or Polish, the soldiers found it difficult to make them understand they had come to help them. At least James, Paul and Stuart were now able to assist, explaining in German they would be taken for safety to a camp where they would meet other white women and the children, and where, in due course, arrangements would be made to take them back to civilization. They were rewarded by the sincere thanks they received from them, now anxious to climb into the wagons, taking their children with them.

The three walked further into the village. Suddenly they saw some soldiers were finding it difficult to deal with two white girls. It seemed the soldiers were desperately endeavouring to get them to leave their tent but even when they did this, they were refusing to board without them also being able to take with them a very beautiful young indian girl, who was completely naked and sobbing. A quick look at her lower body showed the spots of white liquid adhering to pubic hairs. This girl had been raped several times recently.

To their utter surprise and delight, they saw the two girls struggling with the soldiers were in fact Lilie Gartner and Helga Feld. As fortunately they could now understand her language, they knew they were shouting, "We will not come with you unless you also take this indian girl. She is our friend, who had helped us for so long. Now three of your evil soldiers have just taken and raped her repeatedly. She would have died if we had not taken her in and hidden her. You must leave us here, unless you take her with us."

Of course the poor soldiers did not understand a word she had said, and replied by telling them it was impossible and they must come alone – but of course the two girls did not know what they said. James at once took command, thankful now that he had learned the language.

He turned to the soldiers who saw at once he was a officer, "These two women are trying to tell you they will not come with you and will stay here unless you take the indian girl with them. It seems that some of your fellow soldiers, deserve to be taken out and shot. If I discover them I shall ensure this happens. It seems they have brutally raped this young woman. You are no better, nay worse, than the indians. You will accede to the two women's request and let the indian girl enter the wagon with them, after another of you will search around and find some cover for her nakedness. That is an order and I will accompany you on the wagon down to the centre to ensure this woman is treated properly. – Now do as I have ordered."

The two girls had listened as he had spoken to the soldiers. Although they did not really understand was he was saying they knew it concerned them and their indian girl friend and seemed to be giving them orders. Now at last he turned to them and spoke to them in German but with a very strong English accent. Still they could understand what he said.

"Dear Ladies, since it is what you wanted, I have ordered these men to take both you and your indian girl, in the wagon to one of the centres we have established for women such as yourselves, who have been captives of the Miami tribe. I will travel with you to ensure your indian girl arrives safely for it is forbidden for them to take them and is why they refused, until I gave orders to them. – Please tell me – have you any children? – Please bring them if so – you will find many other women like yourself there with their own children."

James saw both girls blush very much. He was not surprised, so he added, "My dear women, you do not need to be ashamed. We are only too delighted to find out both of you are still alive. " It was Lilie who replied, "Yes! We both have a daughter about eight months old – You must guess they are by and indian brave – we had no choice. We are fallen women."

Now James came and took one of her hands and kissed it before replying, "As I said you do not need to be ashamed. Please believe me when I say it is a small price to stay alive. I hope we can, soon, prove that to you." James was tempted then to inform them he knew who they were and remind them of their previous meetings, but decided to wait till they arrived at the centre, when he could arrange to speak to them in private. Now with Paul and Stuart, he helped them, to gather their children and their few possessions, and climbed into the wagon.

They then waited until a soldier returned, having obtained an indian dress for the indian girl, James asking Lilie to explain to the girl that she was coming with them and would be safe. Then she joined them in the wagon. In fact the soldiers had found two other white women and their children who were glad to board the wagon. It set off and the girls saw the three men, two of whom were officers rode their horses close to the wagon.

At last Lilie and Helga were able to talk to each other in German so none of the soldiers could understand.. It was Helga who spoke first, "Please tell me. Is it my imagination. Have we not seen two of these men before." Lilie confirmed her suspicions, "I'm glad you think so. I thought I knew the officer as he gave orders before speaking to me. Then I saw that other man, also a officer with him. I'm sure we've met them before. You must remember. They both look to like those two men who called on us at Andersen and stayed with my parents. We both liked them at the time – that was until they took those terrible liberties with us, thinking we were loose women, willing to bestow our favours on them. We had to make them leave us, though, afterwards, I wondered if we had misjudged them."

Helga agreed, "I felt the same. At the time, I did like the one, I think he said his was called Paul. – But they cannot be the same men, they could not speak our language, whilst this officer spoke quite good, though not perfect German. However I still feel they are so like the others. What were their full names."

Both girls tried very hard to remember but could not quite do so, though they felt they should have remembered. Now the two girls began to consider what they should do after they arrived at the centre. What future did they have. They feared, particularly with their indian daughters, that few men would want to know them. How could they live. Where could they get food, perhaps the soldiers would give them some, but for how long. They were only trained to work in the fields. Some homestead might befriend them.

Then suddenly to their horror they knew, if not, their only alternative was to sell their bodies, join a brothel. Far worse than the horrors of doing this and yielding their bodies to men, was the fact that their souls would be damned, they would fall into hell when they died. Very real tears were running down their face as they arrived at the centre and there were men to help them alight. At least those three men who had helped them were still there. To their surprise they alighted from their horses, giving them to soldiers to look after them, then they accompanied them into the centre, insisting the indian girl was allowed to come with them.

Then for a few moments the older officer left them, although the other two stayed with them, almost chaperoning them. After speaking with others and demanding something with great authority, even showing a piece of paper. When having got what he had demanded, returned to them and spoke. "I do not want us to stay here. We have been given an office next door where we can go, as I want to speak to you all in private. Please be willing to come with me. We do wish to help you. Please trust us."

Almost in a dream they all followed him outside and to a small hut a little distance away. He opened the door and leading them inside, then asked both the two girls and the indian girl to sit down whilst the three men stood explaining that very soon some food and drink would be brought to them. Still in a dream. Believing they were receiving some special treatment, quite different from that given to the other women who had been in the wagon with them. Happy that, at least someone wanted to help them. Then the man smiled kindly.

He was speaking in German, "Dear Lilie and Helga, both Paul and I are so pleased, not only to find you alive, but be able to discover you. We had nearly given up hope. We had been to the centres and then to the various villages. We had seen the terrible things happening there. It was a miracle you caught our attention, arguing to take our dear indian girl with you. We realise how wickedly she has been treated and has suffered. So we shall include her when we ask you to come to live with us, - and our families – they will make you very welcome - in West Virginia. Perhaps you may even remember Paul and me – I'm called James. – We once stayed with you for a few days when you lived in Andersen. – It seemed we did something which offended you. – I'm sorry – Then we could not speak your language, so could not explain. We did not know your strict religious teachings. – If you come with us we promise there will be no repetition of our past behaviour."

Both Lilie and Helga could not believe their ears. They looked at each other then held hands and laughed, happy at the miracle that had just happened. It was Helga who replied, "But now you can speak our language. In the wagon we felt sure you were those men, but however much we tried we could not remember your names. Yes! We remember the past. Now having lived in this terrible cruel world we realise we misjudged you at that time. – We never gave you a chance to explain – or even tell you what was your crime."

Now Lilie continued, "Now you see us as fallen women. With babies born out of wedlock – the squaws of indian men, several who have violated us, resulting in our children. Yet now, knowing this, you want us to come an live with your family, and bring our babies. But why do you do this. You say you were looking for us. It was not, then, an accident that you discovered us at the village. Please tell us how this has happened."

Briefly both James and Paul told them how they had discovered why they had been suddenly expelled that day in Andersen. The disaster which had occurred afterwards but the friendship with Colonel Hamtramck. How they had thought long about them and had intended to someday come to Anderson, and so had learned German to be able to speak with them. The knowledge of the attack on Anderson, but actually prayed that the indians would spare them, in spite of what must happen to them. Then the invitation to lead the cavalry division , and realising this might just give them the chance to see if they were still alive. Finally how that had happened that day.

James now repeated his offer. "Please we want you both, along with your indian friend, come with us in a wagon, away from here tomorrow, and come to stay on our estate, where we raise horses? Our family will make you all welcome. If so we can come to know you better as we travel this long journey back to West Virginia. "

Just an hour ago both Lilie and Helga wondered if they had any future except that of prostitution. Now amazingly they were being offered a refuge, not only for them but for their daughters, to go and live with a family, by two men they had only known for three days many years before. It really was a miracle. Of course they feared they might have to reward them for this deliverance However the girls could not resist it. Not only did they agree to come with them but stood up and kissed both of them in turn on the lips. Then added, "This kiss forgives you for any wrong we thought you might have done. Now truly we believe, it was we who committed a sin."

5

Throughout he whole of 1794 the affair between Antoinette Condorcet, now nineteen years of age, and Stuart Brady, two years her senior, had developed. Antoinette had never forgotten that impetuous outburst from Stuart on the ship as the escaped from France. His pledge to look after her when it had been confirmed she had conceived her child, the result of her raping in Paris. However as the months passed the two of them were drawn closer together. Antoinette had been especially pleased at the considerate way Stuart had come and commiserated with her as she recovered from her abortion. He seemed to understand that she had wanted to keep her child, only agreeing to the abortion, to avoid being an unmarried mother.

It was after she had recovered that she allowed Stuart, more intimate privileges with her. Brought up at the Court of Versailles, Antoinette had grown up to expect to yield her body to a man before she was married. Again she found Stuart very kind and considerate, showing restrain and ensuring she enjoyed the occasions. Again, perhaps the loss of her child, had made her long to conceive another. Only the fact that neither she nor Stuart had very much money, prevented them doing more, as it meant it would be difficult to raise a child.

Both had discussed the problem for, at last Stuart had proposed marriage to her, and she told him she would liked to accept and that she did love him. Also she had smiled when she added that she had known for some time that he had been in love with her. However they both agreed they could not go on for ever, living with Michelle and accepting her generosity in seeing to their needs. Certainly not to increase the expenditure by adding the cost of a child.

Stuart had an idea, but if so it would mean Antoinette relinquished her easy and privileged life, which she had enjoyed, since she was born. He, as well as Jack Eliot, and particularly David Downey, knew well the profits of horse breeding. David's family had made a very successful life that way.

Only the size of the family, the same as Stuart's and Jack's had recently put such a strain on all of them, financially.

Stuart had heard as they stayed at the Carroll's, about another part of the amazing Amelia Eliot's family who had come from Ireland, some years before. How Daniel Carroll had financed them and helped them to settle on land, virtually given to them by George Washington, to raise horses. Also how profitable this had become. Perhaps if they married, Daniel might do the same for them. Stuart knew he could make it a success. However he warned Antoinette, it might be a hard life, certainly one very different from what she had enjoyed date.

To his surprise she told him, not only would she not mind this, but events in France, even her own raping, had told her, her family had done little for their country. This was why the ordinary people had revolted. If they had appreciated these dangers in time, she would never needed had to flee from France. It was the same here in America.

She held Stuart to her and kissed him. "You know since we all came here with the three of you, we have followed the same privileged position as in the past. Our friends have been very generous to us. But as they said when we arrived. This is America not France. It is time we all did something to repay them for first saving our lives but then giving us a place to live. I know the life you are suggesting will be hard. But I shall have to learn to endure it. I know you will help me and understand I shall have to learn – But dear Stuart - I do love you – I want to marry you – yes and have a family – if possible a large one. So we must work together to achieve the wealth for it to happen. – Let's talk to Michelle and Daniel. I'm sure they will understand."

Stuart merely took her in his arms, hugged her to him and smothered her face with kisses. It was sometime before he replied. Then he said, "Dear, dear Antoinette, I do love you. I've loved you from the first moment when we hid at the farm near Paris. I could never hope that you, coming from such a noble family would ever consider me as a partner. – I could not resist what I said on the boat. I loved you then, and was so sorry for you. – Now I have found, not only that you could love me, but would be willing to forgo the life of ease, just to be with me. Dearest, I will not fail you. I will make you the happiest woman in this world. Together we will come rich. – Yes! Let's go and see them. I think we should first speak to Michelle – I'm certain she will understand."

Of course Michelle was delighted, particularly when they first told her they loved each other and wanted to get married. However she was surprised when they explained how they wished to arrange their future. She smiled at them. "You know you can stay here as long as you want."

However Antoinette replied very firmly, "But I want children, many of them. Neither Stuart nor I, would consider letting the expense fall on you.

- No! We both feel all of us who escaped from France should find someway of looking after ourselves. It would be wrong that we continue to live here in America, forever as your guests. It was perhaps right that you first helped us when we arrived. None of us had any wealth. However, now we are Americans. This is a new country. But it is our country - It's time we all now tried to repay all of you and this country which has sheltered us. "

However Michelle inquired how well Stuart understood horse breeding. Stuart replied that all three who had come from Ireland knew what was involved, though David Downey was the expert, as his family's wealth had depended on it. Stuart felt sure that David would ensure he would know how to cope. In any case they wanted to try, but for it to happen Daniel would have to loan them money to buy land and of course, purchase the stock for breeding. He realised this would be expensive.

Seeing they were determined and had thought through the problems she waited until Daniel returned, and explained what Stuart had asked. Naturally he was surprised, but joined Michelle in speaking to both Stuart and Antoinette ensuring they both realised what would be involved. However Antoinette was able to convince him that, although she would need help, she felt certain she could endure such hardships. Finally again stating she wanted a large family and she knew Stuart wanted it as well. In fact Daniel was delighted that they had considered a life of their own.

Now he explained the problems. "Firstly there is little land now available in West Virginia suitable for horse breeding, like the land they had purchased for the Downey's and Eliot's in the Allegheny Mountains. They would need to go into the lands further west, Kentucky, Ohio or what was now called Indiana Territory. Here there was still danger of indian attack .

Also he still wondered if Stuart really understood what was required to be successful in horse breeding. Here he made a suggestion. He would take them to the Downey/Eliot estate and they could work on their land for a time. Only when these families assured them that they were proficient in the task would he consider buying land and a stock of horses for them. To his delight both Stuart and Antoinette agreed and in fact considered it wise.

This agreed Michelle now stepped in. "Since it seems you have a future we must first ensure you go there as husband and wife. It's been sometime since we had a wedding at Racoonsville, yet it was a regular occurrence in the past. I shall ensure your nuptials will be a least as grand as any held here before. All your friends from France, all our friends in Virginia and in the Potomac valley will attend." Then turning to Antoinette she stated, "And you my dear will be wed in white – you are as pure as any bride who came to the marriage alter. – The question I must ask. Is it to be in a Roman Catholic or Protestant Church – or both. What will be your religions when you marry?"

It seems neither of them had considered this. Of course Antoinette was born a Roman Catholic and Stuart a Protestant. It was Antoinette who answered for both of them but first asked Michelle a question. "Michelle you were a Roman Catholic when you came here from France. Yet you told us you first lived with Donald. However you also told me you married Daniel in a Protestant Church. Had you changed?"

Michelle smiled, "Yes! Long before I came to know Daniel. But here we do not need to change. You can both retain your present beliefs and marry twice in each church." Now Antoinette looked lovingly at Stuart, then replied, "I owe so much to Stuart. One of the three men who saved my life but who stood by me when I knew I had conceived. – Michelle, I want to make a good wife to Stuart. I will begin by accepting his beliefs in god are the same as mine. I shall copy your example."

So it was all arranged. All the party who had come from France were delighted at the news. Michelle was determined it would be a magnificent affair. A very elaborate white wedding gown and veil were commissioned. It was agreed that they should spend a fortnight's honeymoon at the Tencin Beach house by the Potomac, which had been the venue for many honeymooners in he past. The long list of wedding guests were invited, and all accepted. This even included a few people like Clare and Philip Wycks who they had never met, but were long-time friends of both Michelle and Daniel.

However it seemed that there may have to be changes in the arrangements, already in an advance stage of preparation. Three weeks before the date set for the wedding, Monica Carroll, Michelle's fourth child by Daniel, now twenty five years of age, had come with David Downey in some trepidation. It seemed that unknown to her parents, Monica had forsaken the two beaus who had for some three years attempted to win her hand in marriage. It seemed Monica had completely fallen in love with David, almost as soon as he had arrived at Racoonsville.

Their romance had been a secret, as they had persuaded Catherine and Jacques Lespinasse to allow them to come and live in their nearby mansion. Catherine had always liked Monica, and came to know her as a girl during the last war when she and Jacques had run the estate in the Carroll's absence. It seems it quickly had become intimate and they usually slept together at the mansion. There was now doubt that it soon changed from infatuation to love. Whether by design, as Monica at twenty five wanted children, or because accidents did happen and were not infrequent.

Now Monica came with David to tell her parents she was over a month pregnant with David's child. Even before they asked, Monica told them she would not abort her child. She loved David and David loved her. It was so different from her love affairs in the past, which of course both Daniel and

Michelle were well acquainted. However like Stuart, David had little wealth. Still they came to ask their permission to marry.

Of course David knew of Stuart and Antoinette's plan to learn how to breed horses, for Stuart had come to him for advice. Now to Michelle and Daniel's surprise the lovers hoped they could join the other two when they went to the Downey/Eliot estate. After all David was related to another branch of Pamela and Simon Downey's family of the past. Also David had been involved in horse breeding in Ireland.

Both her parents had to smile and asked if Monica, who had to date, enjoyed a life of luxury at Racoonsville, at least, if not better, at least as equal, to Antoinette, could she endure a hard life which David now offered her. Her reply surprised them. "I've talked at length with Antoinette, though she did not know my condition. I realised if she could endure this than so could I. In any case the real reason for both of us, is that we both want a family of our own."

After that there was nothing anyone could say. However it meant a hurried change in the planned wedding. Fortunately both Antoinette and Stuart agreed to have a joint wedding, even a joint honeymoon on the Potomac. Of course a knew set of invitations need to be addressed and distributed, and even more quickly, a similar, but different Wedding Gown and veil for Monica.

The Wedding of Antoinette Condorcet and Stuart Brady and Monica Carroll and David Downey, at the church at Racoons Ferry extended some years before in view of the magnificent and large weddings at Racoonsville, was now planned for the coming summer, with a place selected for their joint honeymoon.

6

Fay Bradbury was delivered of a seven pound daughter at the home she now shared with Roy Marshall, in April 1794. Fay named her Terry after the baby's father and Fay's lover, Trevor Reynolds, who had died at the mill in Manchester. However she bore Fay's surname of Bradbury. Long before that, Fay had been glad to share an intimate life with Roy. Neither found as yet they could love each other, but, now, happily shared their bed with each other, glad to act as if married.

Even before Terry was born they had discussed what they should do after Fay gave birth. Certainly, now and for some time, Fay did not want more children, and Roy understood. However Mechia had shown both Fay and Linda the way women in America limited the number of children they conceived. Although it was not fool proof and conceptions did occur, abortion was easily available to save any woman who could pay, from bearing a living child.

With this in mind, and now enjoying their sexual pleasures with each other, they had decided to continue their liaison after Terry was born. Fay was very pleased that Roy stayed with her during her painful eight hours of labour as did Linda. Nether Fay nor Roy could be sure, but they did think that Linda may have taken Mechia's advice, and as it seemed, close relationships were not a reason for denying sexual pleasures. A times they felt both Hugh and Linda were somewhat uneasy when they met them, particularly when they spent an evening together. Certainly Linda seemed far more cheerful and now rarely talked of the boy she had loved so dearly in England.

Both Roy and Hugh had carried out their task in establishing the cotton weaving machinery with diligence. They had impressed Jansen with the effort they engendered in planning the mill he had bought for this purpose. Jansen soon realised that Roy Marshall was probably the most valuable acquisition. Using Jansen's money he had transformed the accurate drawings, made from the sketches drawn on the ship, into working machinery. Roy admitted he had even surprised himself, as it seemed, unknowingly, he was a capable, if untrained, engineer.

The actual mechanical looms created no difficulties. As a Hand Loom expert he understood the principles of weaving. Also he remembered very vividly those looms in Grimshaw's mill. The ones he hated for the damage it did to his family. If he closed his eyes he could see these monsters, which now, he must create to bring future wealth to himself. The Steam engine was a different matter. Fortunately there were several different types used in the Philadelphia area, mainly for water pumping, and as Steam hammers.

Roy experimented with two types which seemed similar to the ones used in the Manchester Mill. Once satisfied they had sufficient power he devised his own way of revolving belts to connect them to the looms, using a series of leather belts to add the motive power, discovering by connecting them in series he could control the speeds at which the moving parts of the looms operated. This was essential when, working with Hugh, he had to incorporate the horizontal movement, back and forth of his Flying Shuttle.

Soon after Fay's birth they were able to demonstrate to a fascinated Jansen Carroll the first of what would be many cotton looms using mechanical power. They had achieved this under nine months. They had kept their promise. Jansen admitted he was surprised at their progress. However Roy just smiled and replied, "We hope that we can prove the mill's profitability very quickly – If so you might consider that we have kept to our part of the bargain and you might make us partners earlier than the five years stipulated in our contract with you."

Jansen left them in no doubt that he would gladly consider this if the profits came more quickly. Already there was a genuine friendship developing between all three of them, far more than an employer, employee, relationship. Now they were invited for evenings at his house, especially as Mechia and he entertained guests.

Soon they were introduced to members of his family who came to visit them from their homes in the Potomac valley. Once they met his father, Edgar Carroll, and his mother Anna, who had been a member of the illustrious Van Buren family of New York, each over fifty years of age. During dinner Jansen was proud to inform them that actually his father could claim the British title of Lord Carroll given to his forbearers in the time of Charles I of England. However now a citizen of the United States he never considered using this title.

His father was able to tell them that there were two branches of the Carroll family. His own who came to live in Maryland when Lord Baltimore was given the colony by Charles I. All at that time strong Roman Catholics. However there was another protestant branch of the family who had held lands in Gloucester and Somerset, but who had supported Cromwell and then lost most of their lands when Charles II came to the throne. However one of these sons had come to America to escape persecution and eventually after his father helped to place King William III on the throne, had become the actual Governor of Maryland.

It seemed that Edgar Carroll was pleased to know of this man, who was knighted as Sir David Carroll, and that it was his ancestor, also called Edgar Carroll who had brought David to America. Proud because this David Carroll, though a staunch protestant had placed his life in danger by refusing the King's demand to force all Catholics in Maryland to become Protestants, winning for that colony the right of every member to worship in either faith.

Now Edgar Carroll laughed. "I too was raised as a Roman Catholic, but met my wonderful wife, Anna, a staunch protestant. After meeting her. It was no contest. I became a protestant and was disinherited by my father. Only the victory of the United States, eventually, enable me to re-establish friendship with my father before he died."

Of course the four from England were fascinated by this information. All strong protestants, whose only knowledge of religious strife was whether they should worship as Methodists – a very strong movement in Lancashire, or as Anglicans in the English Church. In fact they admitted they had not strong religious feelings. It had been a very interesting evening.

Another time and for a longer period, they were introduced to younger members of the family and not just Jansen's but also Mechia's. Jansen's younger twenty one year old brother, Edwin Carroll came with his very attractive eighteen year old sister, Electra Carroll but they had brought with them Mechia's twenty two year old indian brother, Torus Scarron, as well as a cousin, Ellia Dumas. Ellia was the daughter of Aleia Dumas, who was the step-sister of Mechia's mother, Zoreia. Ellia had the same dark but very beautiful indian characteristics which had enchanted them when they first arrived from England .

The four of them came to stay for over a month and Fay, Roy, Linda and Hugh came to know then very well. In fact they could hardly fail to notice that Hugh showed and equal interest in both Electra Carroll and Ellia Dumas. Roy and Fay also saw that Linda was quite smitten by the very handsome Edwin Carroll two years her senior

Although his interest was not nearly as strong as Hugh's, Fay could not fail to see that Roy, also, was attracted to the two new girls. It seemed that the introduction of these four people might in time produce problems, especially for the relationship of Fay with Roy. However both knew their relationship was more of sexual friendship than a permanent arrangement.

In any case the four visitors returned to their homes in the Potomac after a months stay. For Hugh and Roy there was much work to keep them occupied, as they endeavoured to get the first ten power looms operative. On advice from them, Jansen had purchased from England a large consignment of Egyptian cotton. In spite of this they had decided to send for, and purchased cotton now being harvested in Georgia and South Carolina. Charleston, was the port from which the cotton was shipped. If this product was found to be as good as the cotton from Egypt, not only would it cheapen the cost of manufacture but also act a stimulus for the growing cotton industry of the south.

As its success depended on the cheap labour of slaves, it was in the future to lead to the Civil war between the industrial north, in which Philadelphia lay, and the agricultural south. However at this time this was not a problem to the Marshall's, Foyle's or Carroll's. At the beginning of 1795 the new Cotton factory in Philadelphia commenced producing woven cotton, on its power looms installed with the knowledge brought from England by Roy Marshall and Hugh Foyle. It soon became evident it would become a very profitable venture for both of them, but especially for their benefactor, Jansen Carroll.

7

With Europe tearing itself to pieces in the war with France it was difficult for the United States to maintain their neutrality. The trouble lay in the Atlantic where both French and British naval ships consistently boarded American merchant ships, searching for contraband, but also the British often took American sailors, claiming they were deserters from their navy. John Jay's Treaty with Britain in 1794 removed most of these problems, as well as, at last, getting the British to exit the forts on the frontier with Canada, as stipulated in the Peace Treaty of 1783.

However it also seemed to give the British far more than the Americans received. In any case the country was divided, the north mainly supporting the British but the south with strong French sympathies. The division was amplified by the arrival of the French Revolutionary Governments Ambassador, Edward Charles Genet. In fact calling himself Citizen Genet, he came with the sole purpose of promoting American support for France in the war.

Amazingly instead of landing and immediately going to Philadelphia, the capital, to present his credentials, he purposely landed at Charleston in South Carolina. Here he was warmly received and welcomed as there was strong French support in that area. Then he began to financially arrange for American ships to act as privateers to pray on British ships. Not content with this he began to raise and organise militia's to go south and attack Spanish Florida, as Spain was then at war with France. He claimed that the United States Government was in error for not invading and taking Florida, as it should belong to them.

Of course once it became known, it caused great concern in Congress. Both Eric Casimir and John Holstein were concerned for the friends they had come to know, living in Spanish Florida, using their powers they demanded that both Alexander Hamilton and Thomas Jefferson combine for once, instead of being rivals, and help President Washington to force Citizen Gent to stop his actions and report to Philadelphia.

They also sent letters, using the diplomatic bag, to Louisa and Anton Albrecht warning them that American insurgents might attack them, but they did not have the support or any authority of the U.S. Government. Also if they should attack their estate, they should try to speak to them. Although it had not yet been approved they should claim they were actually American citizens and demand their property was respected, as they were not Spanish.

In fact, apart from attacks by American privateers on a few British ships, which quickly ceased when financial support from Citizen Genet was withdrawn, and he was at last forced to come to Philadelphia, and desist from any further attempts to get support for the French. Very soon this embarrassing situation ended in a farce. It seemed Citizen Genet was a Girondist, who had now been eliminated by the Jacobins. If he returned to France he would be guillotined. So he asked for asylum, which was granted. He moved to New York and married a daughter of the Clinton family.

This episode showed clearly the divided loyalties to Britain and France, which continued for many years.

At least with the Jay Treaty and the British evacuating the northern forts, the indians were denied the support they had enjoyed for so long. Although there were still a few cases of small indian raids, the Ohio region, Indiana territory became much safer places to settle and the lands of Tennessee and Kentucky became ideal areas for new settlers to occupy.

Now James and Stuart Downey with Paul Eliot sat down with the three girls, to a fine meal which James had ordered. As they ate, James asked first to be introduced to the indian girl, who sat terrified and traumatised by her recent raping, now brought to this strange place, wondering what the future held for her.

They were told her name was Pohanna and was probably about eighteen years old. Both Lilie and Helga told them this young girl had helped them many times, even explaining how they could avoid beatings from their indian masters. Now they had been forced to witness her being taken by three soldiers in succession and viscously raped, without them being able to help her. James took hold of Pohanna's hand, though he saw the fear in her eyes. Then he gently kissed them before releasing them.

Now he said, "Please can you tell her, she is now safe with us. Can you explain that we want her to come with both of you to where we live and will not be harmed but treated tenderly." Lilie smiled and with Helga's help, as they had learned a little of the native tongue, and by using their hands, indicated they were all going away from here, a very long way, and they all wanted her to come with them. They would make her happy. At last a little understanding seemed to surface on her face and the terrible fear of a moment ago had vanished.

It was now with a little embarrassment that the girls told them it was time for them to suckle their young daughters. Then men smiled and understood. Again James spoke for all of them. "Dear Ladies we will not embarrass you. We will leave you for a hour. However after that we will return. We will then take you to the store, where all three of you can be fitted with our type of clothes and your present ones burnt. Then we shall have three mattresses brought into this hut. We shall leave you to sleep here on them tonight, alone, again so as not to embarrass you. Rise early in the morning for I shall send three baths of warm water and you can bathe in privacy. You see I would like all of us to leave together quite early after breakfast. Would this meet with your approval."

Lilie and Helga could not help themselves they each took hold of one of James' hands, "We still cannot understand why you wish to help us. Can I say we now trust you implicitly. We will all gladly come with you, for there is no future for us here." Then the man left, but returned later having given the two girls the time to feed their daughters without embarrassment. As planed they were taken to receive a dual set of clothes for all three of them. Very basic and not very attractive but clean. Their indian clothes were taken away and destroyed.

It was now dark so the men left them to rest and found accommodation for themselves. Whilst the girls had been occupied earlier, using the letters given to them by Colonel Hamtramck, they had requisitioned two good wagons and filled it with sufficient food for several days. Also flagons of water for their journey, though, of course they would be able to renew supplies on their journey. So everything was ready for then next day.

8

The next morning the men returned to the hut but now, arrived, driving their two wagons. They brought breakfast for all six of them, which as requested they ate hurriedly. Then with their soldier's horses attached to the back of the wagons James asked Lilie to sit with him as he drove the first coach, and persuaded Pohanna to sit inside but near the front, so she could see where they were going. Paul had asked Helga to sit with him on the second wagon and Stuart was his passenger inside. Then they set off in a southerly direction. There was little chance for any conversation at first. There was so much activity with soldiers and wagons going about their business. Not until they stopped four hours later for a late lunch, was it possible to discuss anything.

As they sat eating James was able to explain his intentions. "Dear Ladies, we are not going to either Fort Wayne or Fort Washington. I intend to travel almost due south into Kentucky. I must ask you to accept this diversion, to where we live, though possibly it might be quicker than the route from Fort Washington. The three of us have a reason. Our family in West Virginia have become very wealthy by raising and breeding horses. Unfortunately there is no further land available to buy near us."

Now he smiled at them, for they could not understand why he even troubled to tell them the route he had chosen, "My brother and I and Paul here wish to set up our own business doing the same as our family. As we have been in the army waiting to set you free, I have spoken to a number of men from Kentucky. You may not know but Kentucky was accepted as State of the Union in 1792 and now has its own government. Well it seems that there is still lots of lands to be purchased in that state and one area I have been informed they refer to as the Blue Grass area."

Now he explained , "On our way home I want to explore this area around two towns they call Lexington and Winchester, though I believe there is more land available near the later. If the grass there is as plentiful as they say.

I know this would be an excellent place to rise horses, and we are all experts in this task. So that is the diversion I ask you to accept."

The two girls simply put up their hands showing they were puzzled. It was Helga who replied, "Dear men. It is sufficient that you are kind enough to take us to your home. Until you came to us yesterday, we had no future. Yet you tell us you even joined the battle so that you might find us. Now we know we have a future. Please, we understand, choose the way you want to travel. We are grateful that we now know we have a future"

Nothing more was said. However once when riding again on the wagon, Lilie felt she must question James on his intentions. "Forgive me if I now hurt or displease you. Last night Helga and I had to ask ourselves what were your true intentions concerning ourselves. We knew in coming with you, ostensibly to a better life at your home, we knew we would be travelled with three men travelling through lands without any people. We would therefore be placing ourselves at your mercy."

Seeing he was about to interrupt, she quickly continued, "Please if this is your intentions, we shall not mind, providing you take us kindly and not brutally. Frankly it is your right. We refused your attentions years before, even sent you away. For some reason you have come to find us, even possibly offering us a home. We are fallen women the harlots of indian braves. Whatever you do to us will be no worse. We decided we will not fight you. If afterwards you want us as your mistresses, we shall be pleased, if you do not discard us, particularly if we then carry your child. All we ask is that you be frank with us. Helga and I are yours for the taking. We shall understand."

To her surprise James held up his hand so Paul following could see he intended to stop. Then having done so turned to look at Lilie, "Dear Lilie, you wrong us to think of us in that way. However I suppose its our fault. Everything has happened so quickly. Frankly we have not had the time to explain everything to you. You see we did in fact commit a crime in taking Pohanna with us. We are supposed to punish her and her native race for what they have done to the settlers. She should have been tried and punished. That was the reason for our haste."

Now he took hold of both her hands. "I will be frank with you and if you ask Paul he will tell you the same. Our feelings for the two of you are not entirely honest. When we came to Anderson we had come to Indiana to try and find a woman, who with time, might want to become our partners. We had not found any we could consider a future with at home. It is true we took an immediate liking to both of you. It seemed, with time, you might come to like us and we might all consider a future together. You must believe us our more intimate approach to you is what we knew the women in West Virginia would expect of a man. Even losing interest if not. We had no intention of insulting you."

Now he laughed a little cynically, "Well we soon realised we had made a terrible transgression. Only later did we understand your religious views. It hurt our pride, yet as the years past and we still failed to find girls who might interest us. We then had to admit that meeting you and those three days together, meant far more to us, than it had seemed at the time. So we decided to learn to speak your language and intended to come again to Anderson, this time to court you. Then we heard of the armies defeat and knew you were either an indian's squaw or dead. – Well you now know why we came to find you."

It was now Lilie's turn to smile and once again, as yesterday kissed his hands. "And what now, do you think of us. It is unlikely you can still have those same thoughts about us after you know and have seen what has happened to us, with an indian's daughters born out of wedlock." In fact at that moment she really did not want to hear his reply, fearing it would be quite unpleasant.

Instead he now returned the kiss on her hands. "You are very wrong. Frankly we have known each other, for so short a time. It is only right both of us should see if we might have a future together. I will try to court you, if you will allow me. Neither Paul nor I see anything wrong in the life you were forced to endure since your capture. Should it progress we hope you would let us adopt your daughters as our own."

Now at last he concluded, "Actually the real reason why I told you we had decided to travel home by Winchester in Kentucky, is that we want the two of you to see the place. – For if in time we might want to make our relationship permanent we might ask you both to come with us, as husband and wife, and settle here and help to provided a prosperous future where we could raise a family."

Even to Lilie his last words were too amazing to contemplate. "What marry you. You would still want to wed us, not just ask us to become your mistresses? Please tell me are you serious. " His answer was just to pull her close to him and this time kiss her on the lips. "Lilie I hope this may be our decision after we have had time to really know each other. – and if you could consider a life in Kentucky. Let us say no more. Until we arrive home, neither Paul or I will; make any demands on you. You three girls will sleep in one wagon whilst we sleep in the other."

At this moment Paul exasperated as to why James had haltered and could hear them taking, drew his wagon alongside the other. James simply called out to him. "Lilie will have something to tell Helga tonight. Then tomorrow Helga will probably tell you what she has said. You will, just, have to wait for that."

As James had said the three girls always slept together in one wagon, whilst the men slept separately in the other for the whole of the journey. However there was a growing degree of intimacy. No longer did the two girls ask the man to leave as they fed their children and quite often they would be able to see a beautiful pair of feminine breasts.

In fact though they bathed separately in streams or lakes, when they were available they bathed completely naked and at times both their bodies were on view for a minute or two. So the journey continued. They managed to discover the small township of Winchester. They found in it an office with land for sale. Together they went to view what was on offer. Eventually they found a delightful spot of several acres. Large enough to raise a large herd of horses, with large expansions of luscious green grass, ideal for feeding horses, surrounded by a selection of trees providing a beautiful picture.

They had not the means to purchase it outright, but they had sufficient to place a holding on it for twelve months. If not then completed, their deposit would be lost, but everyone, and particularly Lilie and Helga thought the area delightful. This finished they now travelled eastwards again. It was a hard drive along the slopes of the Allegheny Mountains. Winter was coming in earnest and they had to force the wagons through thick snow.

However at last they arrived safely but exhausted, in early December 1794, at their homestead receiving a rapturous reception. They were able to introduce both Lilie and Helga with their two daughters. However their family were surprised to find they had brought with them this young indian girl, Pohanna. During the journey they had managed to teach her a few English words and she could now make herself understood. It was noticed by everyone that it was Stuart who spent most of the time trying to talk with her.

Pohanna was still terrified, not understanding her new way of life, yet her original fear that she might die – or again be subjected to a sexual attack had gone. Furthermore she now seemed to trust Stuart more than the rest. Even James and Paul had to admit she was very attractive. In European clothes she did not have too many indian characteristics. In fact her dark hair and piercing green eyes made her quite beautiful. The other two men wondered if Stuart was developing a sexual interest in her.

Of course their mother's and father's were so relieved and delighted that their sons were still alive and in good health. James had told his father of his plans to start another business similarly to theirs in Kentucky. Even having placed a deposit on part of it. His father approved, though one he knew his mother opposed. The idea of further separation from her ones appalled her, as she did not want to lose her sons again so soon.

However their parents made the three girls very welcome. Even sympathising with Pohanna, as it seemed she had conceived the soldiers child. Though it was difficult, with Lilie and Helga's help they were able to assure her she would be looked after during and after her pregnancy as well as any child she bore. Though, if she would agree, they could abort her child, something no indian girls knew was possible. So ended the excursions in Ohio and the Indiana Territory. The saga began four years before had eventually led to a happy ending. It had, also, developed connections between so many diverse families. Yet it also forebode another equally adventurous future, not only for those who had just arrived, as well as those resident there for many years, but a future for other families still to join them.

———————

PART 4

EXPANSION

EXPANSION

"Ellia, I'm not fool, when you returned from your visit to Philadelphia, it was obvious you had your eyes on Hugh Foyle." Aleia Dumas was addressing her twenty-two year old daughter, Ellia Dumas, by Jean Dumas, with whom she had lived as a wife, ever since he had to accept her. For as a French serving officer, he must accept her in an indian marriage, to ensure her tribe of Chickasaw Indians, supported the French army in the Ohio country in the 1750's.

It was early January and the weather was fine but quite cold. They sat with Jean's French guest, rescued from France, twenty one year old, Charlotte Le Raye, who had chosen with her brother, Francois, to live as the guests of Jean and Madeleine Dumas, since they had arrived in America. Ellia Dumas had returned a week a two ago, from a month long visit to her cousin's, Jenson Carroll.

Aleia continued, "You know I thought when you returned you had become love sick, did you indulge in intimacy with Hugh, and did he reciprocate?"

Ellia retorted, "Don't be silly mother. I accept, I found him very attractive and he was very kind to me whenever it was necessary – but that was all. You see he has a very attractive younger sister, Linda, with whom he lives, and has done so every since they arrived from England. – In any case, I doubt if I would have much chance in opportuning Hugh, if I wanted to. The intimate way he embraced his sister and the revealing clothes she wore, makes me believe that they may share an intimate life. It seemed they both had to flee from England in danger of their lives. Linda had to leave her boy friend – perhaps she has need of Hugh to satisfy her feminine desires."

They were conversing in French which was the language they preferred, though they could easily have spoken in English. This was in deference to the presence of Charlotte Le Raye. It was Charlotte who interposed. "Ellia, simply because Hugh and Linda live together in the same house, does not mean they have an intimate relationship. – In any case – what do you mean by intimate. I love my brother Francois, I always will. We have both seen each other completely naked many times, but we have never indulged in sexual pleasures of any kind. We both love each other, but only as brother and sister I would willingly live alone with Francois in some isolate house far from anyone, without any fear of attack. As now, we would never worry about each seeing our naked bodies – but would be as far as it went. – Ellia, I believe it is the same between Hugh and Linda, an understanding of a life together."

Ellia threw up her hands, "It may be as you say. I do not know. Anyway Hugh is in Philadelphia and I'm here at Berkeley, miles apart. Unless we meet again, I fail to see how I could start an affair with Hugh. – Though, mother, I admit I would like it."

Her mother changed the subject. "Are you likely to want to come with me when I go to my brother Tonsac, and call on your sisters, married into his tribe. – You know if you come, it will be very different to what you saw some five years ago. – No longer living in tents. Tonsac had transformed the 'Reservation' granted to his tribe, virtually into an American village. All the tribe now live in wood cabins. In fact Tonsac and his three wives now live in what you might call a wooden mansion. We all owe a lot to the generosity of dear, Michael Casimir. He sent the same team which built further mansions on his land near Fort Necessity, to show and help them to build this village."

Ellia replied that she did not think she would come. "I like my sisters but I think they were foolish to go back and marry in the tribe, when they could have, easily found partners here." Now he mother smiled, "That is because, unlike them you have never had the wonderful life of living in the open, sleeping under the stars. – It took me a long time to learn to live here with you at Berkeley. – I owe so much, to both Jean and Madeleine for helping me to become accustomed to this type of life. – No Ellia, you would not enjoy life with the tribe – but I must tell you, you do not know what you are missing, if only you could overcome the love of luxury you at present enjoy."

Now Aleia concluded, "Well then, I will travel, just, with Jean, as Madeleine wishes to remain here." Now Charlotte inquired, "Has Jean mentioned to you the request Francois has made to him to let both of us accompany you when you go to see Tonsac?" Aleia looked surprised, "No! At least I do not remember, But why should both of you wish to visit an indian encampment?"

Charlotte smiled, "Neither Francois nor I can forget our training in engineering and chemistry, which our dear and wonderful father installed in us. I'm sure Jean has told you of the excellent assistance my father Jacques

Le Raye, gave George Washington during the last war. Well he was just as wonderful to us. We both have high qualifications in both engineering and metalwork. It mattered not to father, that I was a woman. He instilled in me the importance of figures. I did most of the calculations concerning the various stresses in any bridge he was building. He made Francois design it and told me to test if it was strong enough. I loved doing it. Then he would check it and punish us if we did it wrong."

Aleia was amazed. "Why I can't even check the change given to me when I purchase things at a store. – But why do you want to go to Tonsac. I don't think he will want anyone to build him any bridges. " Charlotte shook her head. "No it's not for that. However it seems Jean has fascinated Francois when he told him that during his stay at Fort Pitt, when it was then called Fort Duquesne, and Jean was in command of the fort, he saw outcrops of coal, which they used to heat their fires, and Francois believes Jean's description of what we both call iron pyrites."

Aleia was even more puzzled. "So what. Of what use is that. It's not like silver or gold – or even copper, which Jean tells me is useful." Charlotte could understand her disbelief. "Because put coal and iron ore together and you can first get iron or even steel, and this country is very much in need of steel. When Ellia returned from Philadelphia we learned of the difficulty Jenson, Hugh and Roy had had in obtaining steel for the machinery for their mill. The trouble was the lack of steel for making it. It seems demands are so great we have to import it from abroad. Now with Europe at war it is even more difficult."

Now smilingly she took hold of a perplexed Aleia's hand and kissed them. "Both Francois and I know just how valuable it would be for the United States if we were able to confirm that both coal and iron ore, are present in the land around Fort Pitt. Why it could make it into one of the most important spots in the country. It could provide great wealth, provided Francois and I could get people like the Van Rensselaer's, the Wycks or the Jenson Carroll's to invest in mining and smelting it. – All we want to do at present is to confirm it is there. That is why we want to come with you to meet your tribe."

Still Aleia was puzzled. "But why are you and Francois wanting to do this? You know Jean will provide for you here for the rest of your life. You can live in comfort – Yes! Even if you marry. Jean, Louis and the others all promised this when we brought you here from France."

Now Charlotte laughed then kissed Aleia's hands which she was holding. "We both know that. You are very generous. However we both feel it is wrong to live such an idle life. Perhaps unlike the others that came with us from France, our father taught us to make use of our lives. He certainly wanted Francois to follow him in his engineering business, and he included me in his plans. He even taught me to draw to scale and I even designed a bridge for him. Although he changed and improved it, he made me proud when he told me if he had built it, it would have worked."

Squeezing Aleia's hands, she continued. "We love living with you but we want to play a part in helping to develop this new country which has given us hospitality and security. If possible we want to become independent, particularly if, in time we both find partners with whom we wish to live and start a family, We are both grateful for your generosity. We know if we fail, you would still be willing to help us. However if coal and iron ore is present near Fort Pitt. Perhaps this might be the start for Francois and I, to start a business of our own, perhaps make our poor father proud of us."

Now Aleia gathered a little understanding of what Charlotte was saying. "Dearest if you both want to come with Jean and I to Tonsac, we shall be delighted. In fact we had hoped that Louis and Zoreia, or just Zoreia, would join us. However it seems that both of them and Julie have other plans which prevents this. I know Jean will be as please as I, if you and Francois join us."

Throughout this exchange, Ellia had sat perplexed and not understanding. She could not understand why any woman, like Charlotte, would want to leave the comfort of this mansion. Yes, and even considering exhausting themselves in attempting to discover such unimportant things iron ore and coal. Was Charlotte a normal woman. Did she not want a man of her own and find one with whom she could raise a family. Had she not the same desires as herself. It seemed strange that she could calmly tell her a little time ago, that although she had many times seen her brother naked, and let him see her that way. Yet it seemed that had not affected her, as Ellia felt a woman should be affected.

However in spite of what she had told her mother, Ellia knew that Hugh Foyle had stirred her innermost feelings, in a way few men had effected her that way. She still feared, even if she had the opportunity to enjoy his presence again, his own sister might be a rival for his affections. Ellia knew, given the chance she would ensure she made some progress. After all she was already twenty-two years old, and knew she wanted a baby.

2

Jean Condorcet now happily established in the home of Catherine and Jacques Lespinasse was delighted that his sister, Antoinette had found happiness, and wanted to marry Stuart Brady. He had felt so sorry, yet helpless after Antoinette had conceived after her cruel raping in France, and then had to suffer a painful abortion. Now he was pleased that Stuart had declared his love for her, and wanted her as his wife. However Jean could not understand his sister's desire to leave the comfort of their new life in Virginia, and risk the discomforts of a working life in the wilds, rearing horses.

Not that he had been idle since the Lespinasse's had provided them with a home. Jean had very quickly become friendly with six year older Antoine Malesherbes, the illegitimate son of Catherine and his own father, the Comte de Lamoignon, who like his mother had been at one time the mistress of his father. Antoine had welcomed Jean's offer to help him in overseeing the tobacco crop which brought the considerable wealth to the Carroll family. Jean was not lazy and was delighted to be of some assistance, but he would never have considered trying to find a life in the wilderness.

The ghost of his father was everywhere in the homes of many now living in Virginia or West Virginia . Besides Catherine's son by his father, on the Potomac in the home of Marie and Henri Colbert, were Louise and Guillaume Malesherbes, the illegitimate daughter and son of Marie Colbert, born to his father when Marie was already married to Henri, providing the resources by which that family could escape from France, after the chaos following the Seven Years War with Britain.

Perhaps at first these illegitimate children of her father had caused Manon Lamoignon, the only legitimate offspring of her father still alive, some embarrassment. Though Manon knew and her mother had informed her when quite young of the infidelity of her father with so many mistresses. Yet Manon had loved her father who had, always been attentive to her needs.

Soon Manon was able to converse, first with Catherine and then when she called, with Marie Colbert, about their affairs with her father.

Though both confirmed they had yielded their bodies to him and conceived his children for the generous wealth he bestowed on them, which at the court of Louis Fifteenth, was the accepted way of life, knowing if called, they would have to yield their bodies, unreservedly to their King, and suffer the consequences. Yet Manon had found that both Catherine and Marie had been able to obtain sexual pleasure during the unions with her father. Evidently he had been very considerate of their needs, and was particularly kind to them during their pregnancies, always being present as they delivered his child. Afterwards amply repaying them for their suffering during labour.

It seemed that for many years after they came to America the Comte still sent considerable letters of credit to help pay for his offspring. Neither Catherine nor Marie felt any ill of her father. It was this nearness with ensured Manon enjoyed a happy life since she had settled with Catherine. Both jokingly claimed they were really her substitute mothers. Manon had always been an active girl even when she lived in splendour in France. She had devoured the many volumes of books in their library and this had led to her desire to write. Although those books were now lost to her, she still retained her excellent command of both France and English and had settle down to write again.

However from being a young girl Manon had blossomed as an artist. Just before the revolution had torn France apart, she had created some excellent water and oil paintings, and displayed them in an art shop in Paris, even selling one or two of them. So now having settled comfortably into this new life in America Manon had recommenced imbibing in her ability to paint and write. She loved to paint the human form and being from a young girl, brought up in an atmosphere where partial or full nudity were accepted, Manon had no inhibitions in painting the nude bodies of Catherine and her daughters, though her water colours were beautiful vistas of the delight countryside in which she lived. Unlike her nude studies these had already found there way in the art shops in Annapolis, and even were returning a reasonable some of money from their sale.

Her writing was a different matter. Intrigued as to why so many France people had come to settle in a British domain, long before their had been any attempt for independence. This at a time Britain and France were at war, first on the continent of Europe, and then here in America, Manon was determined to ascertain exactly what had led to this unusual situation, and then commit the reasons to paper. She was determined to research it in detail. Though it may never be published she was determined to become the author of a factual historical account which might in future be invaluable to others researching this period. So Manon had not been very idle even if she lived here in comfort.

Both Manon and Jean had known that Catherine's son by the Comte, Antoine, had married Ruth and Anton Tencin's daughter, Rosine, Ruth's final child at the age of forty eight. They had soon learned that both Anton Tencin and his step-sister, Julie, now married to Louis Scarron, were the illegitimate children of the notorious Claudine Tencin, mistress of both Louis Fourteenth and Louis the Fifteenth. They knew Anton's father was King Louis the Fourteenth, though it seemed Julie's father may have been Claudine's own son.

They were even more intrigued to discover that Anton's wife, Ruth, had been sent to America as an indentured servant for six years, as her crime was aborting the child of an elder man who had seduced her. Her life story was an adventure in itself and the miracle that Anton, so proud of his ancestry, had discovered his love for Ruth and eventually married her.

Manon soon realized that the events during the Seven Years War between France and Britain, as they clashed for power in America, had resulted in some very strange outcomes with couples torn apart for years, yet eventually finding happiness together. It seemed Manon would be extremely busy in researching the reasons for all this. However she did have Catherine's blessing in her travail, and soon realized how much the present happiness of these couples was, in no small way due to the intervention of Daniel Carroll, many times at the risk of his life. No wonder that both Michelle and Daniel were considered to be possibly the most important family they had met.

Although Manon had not yet developed any real attachment for any of the many sons in the several families in her vicinity, she was a French woman, brought up in the licentious court of Versailles, and had indulged in amorous affairs since she reached puberty. She found she could enjoy the apparent interest of Jack Eliot, four years her senior, though she had needed to play the role of the seducer, for Jack's approach had lacked the ardour of her boy friends in France. Never-the-less, though it was nothing more than a flirtation, it did give Manon the pleasure of more intimate desires.

Meanwhile Jean Condorcet had become a very frequent visitor to the nearby tobacco estate of Goochland, belonging to Sophia and Colin Chalmers. His reason was his interest in Sophia's daughter by her previous marriage to Keith Brookes, Kitty Brookes, who was the same age as Jean. It seemed that his interest was not disliked by Kitty. Also, due to the often flagrant life her mother Sophia, had engendered after the death of her husband Keith who she had adored, it seemed this had effected Kitty's own way of life.

So it was not long before a more intimate relationship developed between

Jean Condorcet and Kitty Brookes. It was through Kitty that Jean learned how, after the sudden and unexpected death of Keith Brookes, which devastated Sophia, being so madly in love with her husband., she had taken many lovers, unable to accept her unhappiness. How she had stolen a young man from England, Neil Reeves, then living with his common law wife, Claire Collins. Completely dominated him and made him subservient to her needs.

Later discovering her own wickedness and discovering Neil was madly in love with her, and refused to accept Sophia did not love him, even attempting to kill her before joining the militia and sacrificing his life to save his fellow soldiers, ensuring Sophia, herself, suffered, as she learned of his sacrifice. Indicating he did not wish to live if she had no longer any use for her. How it had taken the considerable efforts of Colin Chalmers to restore Sophia's wish to live, and eventually marrying her and combining their two large estates into one.

Even as Jean was to learn a little of this episode in Sophia's life it seemed some other person was also trying to discover what had happened to Neil Reeves. Someone who only recently had settled in America. However it seemed that neither Jean Condorcet nor Manon Lamoignon would be leaving the comfortable lifestyle at the Lespinasse's unlike Jean's sister, Antoinette, soon to become the wife of Stuart Brady. Then to begin a much harder life trying to earn a living breeding horses. Never-the-less both had found a pleasant way of occupying their time and in Manon's case, it might lead to a profitable source of income by selling her very acceptable landscapes. Also, perhaps she might pay a service to new adopted country by placing on record a factual account of how it had provided for both French and British emigrants to find happiness.

3

It was Andrew Reeves and his Austrian wife, Anna, who wished to learn more about the life of Neil Reeves, Andrew's uncle. Ever since the first time when they had called upon Adrian and Kylie Scott, Andrew had pressed them for information about his uncle. However, try as they did, they could discover little more than that Neil Reeves had brought with him Claire Collins, a prostitute from a Bristol brothel, when he traveled on the same boat bringing Adrian, Kylie and her two daughters.

How they had formed a friendship on the ship, then purchased two adjacent small holdings in the wilderness. Finding to their dismay that their lands were covered in hardwood trees and unsuitable for agriculture, which was the reason they had come here, realizing only by combining their efforts could they hope to stay alive, and cut down sufficient trees to provide ground for vegetables, to keep them in food. How together the four of them eked out an existence in deplorable conditions until by chance they had met a rich émigré from Poland, Michael Casimir who it seemed discovered that Clair was the image of his first girl friend in Poland, who had committed suicide when Michael's parents had forbidden them marrying.

Because of this Michael had sent his own loggers from his nearby estate to help clear their land and make it suitable for farming. From that moment their fortunes had changed. Again due to Michael's assistance they prospered with a share of the money from selling their trees, and helped several times with his slaves set to help them, even inviting them to his estate on the Potomac for a well earned rest.

They were happy to tell Andrew that Neil had lived with Claire as if married, and that she had even conceived his child, but that she had miscarried, nearly losing her life. After that the information Adrian and Kylie were willing to tell them was little and obviously they were hiding something, perhaps a crime. It seemed after her miscarriage, Michael had taken pity on Claire, separated her from Neil, bringing her to live on his estate and made her a ward, placing a dowry on her so that eventually Claire found love with a rich widower, Philip Wycks whose first wife had died in childbirth, breaking his heart. It seemed Clair and Philip had married even though she had informed him of her early life as a prostitute in Bristol

As regards Neil, all the Scott's would tell them is that after Michael forcibly separated Clare from him, Neil had found a new life with a rich widow, Sophia Brookes and gone to live with her on her estate in Virginia. Later for some reason he had left and joined the militia towards the end of the American war of Independence, and been killed trying to save a number of his fellow officers.

Either Adrian and Kylie did not know what happened after he separated from Claire, or did not want to inform them, for some reason of their own. Andrew did feel that the Scott's had been very disappointed in Neil's treatment of Claire and yet did not wish to blacken his name too strongly, as the four of them had lived together on this combined estate for many years, which was now theirs, fighting it and desperately earning barely enough to stay alive until that chance meeting with Michael Casimir. At least they knew Neil had lost his life somewhere near Williamsburg in Virginia. However Andrew wished to know what had happened to Neil after he had gone to live with this Sophia Brookes on her estate in that area.

As the term at the school was ending and the summer vacation was coming, Anna had written to Sheila and Kenneth Bacon, asking if they might avail themselves of their promise to let them come and visit them to meet the other persons who were not available when they had stayed with them, whist Sheila had arranged their second wedding in a Roman Catholic Church. She received an immediate reply inviting them to spend at least a fortnight with them, even suggesting she might then arrange for them to stay longer with other of their friends.

So as soon as the school finished, leaving their now two Negro slaves to attend to their land, Andrew and Anna had traveled down the Cumberland road to Annapolis and to the Bacon's mansion, receiving a magnificent welcome. Sheila consider she had saved poor Anna from a life of sin, having only been married in a Protestant church, and arranging for her second marriage in her own Catholic Church. In fact both Andrew and Anna were extremely grateful to Sheila and Kenneth in helping them to obtain their land near Fort Pitt and establish their school which was now providing them with some wealth.

They were entertained almost every evening and met Louis and Julie Scarron and a dear old lady, Ruth Tencin, who came to visit them, also meeting her young protégé, Jeanne Cristal, who it seemed had escaped from the terror in France after first, as a serving girl, helping to save the lives of some aristocratic young men and women. There was no doubt of the devotion of Jeanne to her sponsor, but it was genuine friendship, for it seemed that Ruth Tencin admitted to being a woman with a past, who found love with a thirteen year older man Anton Tencin, an illegitimate son of King Louis of France. If anything Ruth was proud of her past, and was now ensuring that Jeanne was no longer considered a servant, but a protégé of Ruth.

How Anna would have liked to inform these important persons, exiles from the French court many years before that, she also had aristocratic blood in her veins, a princess of the Hapsburg court, but knew only too well she must keep her past a secret. In any case both Anna and Andrew were now very proud to be given American citizenship.

As Congress had adjourned for the summer Eric and Isabel had returned to the townhouse in Annapolis, and Robert and his wife, Hedwig had come to stay with them for a time before going home to their mansion of the Racoonsville estate. Naturally they visited the Bacon's every day so soon came to know both Anna and Andrew, though Eric and Isabel remembered their meeting in the wilderness many months before.

It was almost by accident that Andrew during one of their visits to the Bacons had mentioned to Robert Carroll of a Sophia Brooke whose name had been given to them by Adrian and Kylie Scott, who they would like to meet. To their amazement Robert was able to explain that this Sophia Brook was now remarried after her first husband had died and now was Sophia Chalmers married to Colin Chalmers now living on their combined estate only a relatively short distance to the south of the Racoonsville estate.

Robert smiled as he added, "In fact I suppose Sophia is really my step-sister though she is old enough to be my aunt. You see Sophia is my mother's daughter conceived in France, many years before she met my father. My mother came to America with Donald Wilson after he gave up his life as a smuggler and Sophia had conceived by either Donald's brother, Jack, or the raping by French custom men, who killed Jack and their baby on a terrible night."

He smiled even more as he added. "It seemed it took my father a long time to win my mother's approval, for she evidently lived with Donald as his wife for about ten years. Fortunately, after an adventurous life, which even today astounds me, they came together, married, otherwise I would not have been born. I can tell you my mother and father have lead a very adventurous life. It is one which makes me very proud of them."

Discovering that Andrew and Anna need not return to their school for a further three weeks, Robert and Hedwig invited them to come to stay with them at Racoonsville where they could easily take them to meet Sophia and Colin Chalmers's and inquire of his uncle Neil. In fact Robert told them, "It seemed my mother and father have arranged a joint wedding of my sister, Monica and two exiles from France and Antoinette Condorcet to Stuart

Brady. You will both be welcome to attend the wedding, which of course Hedwig and I must attend. I feel certain Sophia and Colin will come to the wedding. It may not be necessary for me to take you to them."

So after thanking both Sheila and Kenneth for delightful fortnights holiday, then traveling in their coach, following Robert and Hedwig to their magnificent mansion on the Raccoon River to stay for a time, first to attend this large wedding party and then later to try to ascertain more information about Andrew's uncle, Neil Reeves, when they visited Sophia and Colin Chalmers, or they might meet them even earlier if they had decided to attend this joint wedding. So a chance remark had enabled them to at last make some progress in this mystery.

4

The joint wedding was a magnificent event. Almost everyone who had endured that fearful escape from France and come to America attended. Then after an enormous wedding breakfast the two couples went to spend their combined honeymoon in the Blue Mountains in a large wooden mansion Daniel, Michelle and his elder brother Anthony and his wife Esther had built, alongside the head waters of the Shenandoah River. They would enjoy a fortnight's holiday there with Negro servants sent from Racoonsville to attend to their needs.

The guests stayed on at Racoonsville for two more days still celebrating, before returning to their homes. It was during this time that Andrew and Anna were able to speak with Sophia in private. They had been introduced, even before the wedding, but considered they should not raise the subject until it was over. Purposely waiting until they found Sophia alone, Andrew at last confronted her.

"Sophia, I am the nephew of Neil Reeves who I am told you knew some time ago. I have come to America with my wife, who is Austrian by birth, I come from Wookey, in Somerset, where my family lives. They asked me to try to discover what happened to my uncle, who they knew went to America, taking with him a girlfriend he met in Bristol. My family received several letters from Neil, telling us of the very hard life he was living and that he was living with the girlfriend, Claire Collins as if they were married. It was in this way we learned of the friendship, forged on the ship traveling to America, with Adrian and Kylie Scott. How together they tried to develop a stretch of land in the wilderness, covered in trees. Then suddenly his letters ceased and my family has asked me to discover what happened later."

As he was speaking both of them saw a look of apprehension appearing on Sophia's face. It confirmed what they had suspected, that there was some real suspicion concerning Neil later life. However Andrew continued. "Well, by chance we purchased a small strip of land near Fort Pitt and now run a school for the children in the area. We soon discovered the now highly successful farm belonging to the Scott family, and indeed teach some of their children in our school".

He paused but Sophia said nothing, so he continued. "Naturally we have questioned the Scots about Neil who have told us of his life with them in the early days on their combined holdings. We know of his life with Claire Collins. Neither Adrian nor Kylie say anything derogative about Neil, but it seems they disapprove of his treatment to Claire. I'm certain they know more but tell me they do not know what happened to him after he left Claire, after she miscarried his child. They have told me he did at one time know a Sophia Brookes and that he died later in Virginia, serving in the militia in the last war."

Now he laughed. "It seems whilst staying with Sheila and Kenneth Bacon, Robert Carroll and his wife visited, and a chance remark enable Robert to tell me that you were that Sophia Brooke but who after the death of your first husband, married again to Collin,. That is why Robert invited us to come and stay with him so we could meet you. – Please can you give us any more information about Neil after he broke off his association with Claire?"

By now they could see that Sophia was very unhappy. It was obvious she had a secret. Finally she turned and sat down asking them to sit facing her. "It seems I must make a confession to you, and one of which I am not very proud . It seems, it is one for which I must still be punished. You see I feel I destroyed Neil Reeves life, probably drove him to his death."

Sophia explained of the sudden death of her first husband, Keith Brookes, who she adored. She had felt her life had ended. "My mother suffered similarly after her Jack, probably my father, was murdered in France. However she refused to consider marrying again enjoying a sexual life with his brother, Donald Wilson. – This attitude lasted for ten years until at last Daniel Carroll eventually persuaded her to marry him. Mother was indeed a lucky woman to find Daniel. Now you've met him, you can see just what a wonderful man he is. I have always regarded him as my true father, never knowing my actual one."

Tears flowed down her face. "I felt the same as mother - when Keith died, - but I took a different, and selfish way, out of my misery. I decide to 'play the field'. I had no intention of settling down. I suddenly wanted to use my wealth to dominate men. It was then that I seduced Neil Reeves away from Claire – It was a terrible thing to do – but I know Neil never loved Claire, merely enjoyed her body. To him she was still the prostitute he took from the Bristol Brothel."

She stooped for a moment as she tried to control her emotions, "Now you can see what a wicked woman I had become. I brought him here to Virginia,. I gave him a life he had never experienced before, I smothered him in riches, whilst I used him to assuage my very intense feminine needs, whilst I dominated him, but did not love him."

Now still sobbing she looked at Andrew. "Too late I discovered that he was madly in love with me, not my money, not even the use of my body. He had fallen for me, and now saw I thought no more of him, but the other two men I had now come to know. – After I had spent a night with another man, he suddenly turned on me seized a knife intending to kill me, saying he would never allow me to go to live with another man. – It was a miracle that my boyfriend of the night was near enough to stop him and overpower him."

She gasped, "We had no alternative, I stuffed his hands with a great deal of money. I told him he must leave and never return. Yet I knew then I deserved that attack. He had every right to harm me for merely using him for my pleasure. – Well, I suppose he gained his revenge though I still believe he meant what he said in his final letter. – It seemed he no longer wanted to live. He joined a nearby militia, distinguished himself as a soldier, finally sacrificing his life to save the lives of many of his fellow soldiers. It was because of this that his final letter was brought to me – Wait my mother still hold this in her archives. I will go and get it and show you it."

She got up and left them and was away for some time, eventually returning with the letter in its original envelope. She opened it and gave the letter to Andrew who read it with some sorrow.

It said, '*Dearest Sophia, I so love you. I always will. Try to forgive me for my past. It was my love for you which made me behave so abominably. I could not bear to loose you – for you are my life – and always will be. I knew then I could not go on living without you – there was no purpose. Once I realised the British were so near to you and might injure you, I joined the militia. If I should die, please do not blame yourself. – At least it may show you, I did love you, and wanted to protect you. Your devoted and loving Neil Reeves. P.S.. I bless you, for the many happy hours you have given, me.*"

Now Sophia spoke gently. "So you see I was really responsible for your uncle's death – just as much as if I had plunged a knife into him. I can never forgive myself, though, - surprisingly I feel a little better now I have confessed this to his family." However it was Anna who came and threw her arms around Sophia. "No dear Sophia, your blame is little. It seems to me that Neil, himself, deserve some punishment. I believe Adrian and Kylie Scott are right. Now I know the whole story I will ensure Andrew's family know the truth. It seemed, even if he did not love Claire. He was responsible for bringing her to America. He used her body, just as you used his. He never gave her any real love. He even gave her a child, which she miscarried. No Sophia, what ever was your crime you have already suffered the punishment. – I shall ensure Andrew informs his family in a way, that will in no way place the blame on you."

Now Andrew came and gently kissed the side of Sophia tear wet face. "I agree with my wife. What ever was the result – for a time you gave him a life he could never have believed. That was repayment enough for your use of him. The fact he fell in love with you when you did not reciprocate, is no different from him enjoying Claire's body for so long. We both thank you for telling us this and would both be honoured if you could still consider us your friends."

It was a very relieved Sophia who gladly assented. Now she was more practical. "I understand you have come from England with little wealth, and you must run your school to stay alive. Both Collin and I are emensely rich. Please, if I failed one member of the Reeves family, please let me help his nephew and his wife. In the future please let us help if you should have any financial difficulties. Also I would be extremely grateful if you could come and stay with us next summer holidays, instead of the Bacons."

So it was two very happy people who after thanking Robert and Hedwig for giving them a home, now returned to their school to start a new term in a new year. However before then together, Andrew and Anna had written to his family in England, telling them all they knew of the life of Neil Reeves. They did not maligned Neil, not did they praise him. It was a truthful description of his sexual lives with Claire Collins and Sophia Chalmers and he fact that he died a hero saving other men's lives. They had carried out their promise to his mother before they left Somerset. Now they had a life of their own to live.

5

As soon as Daniel Carroll had promised, in the future, to give the two wedding couples, money to purchase land on which to settle and raise horses, he had also realised that this might be a very profitable investment. There was no doubt how profitable had been the decision several years before to settle Simon and Jessie Downey and Elsie and Peter Eliot on their land in the Allegheny hills to breed horses. The situation now was even more advantageous, with hundreds of emigrants pouring into the United States and settling in the new lands of Ohio, Indiana and Kentucky. There was an ever growing demand for horses, for riding, driving coaches and ploughing the land.

Instead of giving the two couples a small stretch of new land in the wilderness, it would be financially profitable to invest in larger stretches for this purpose. However it would place a strain even on the Carroll's riches. In any case it would take a time before he could expect any returns on his money. So he considered setting up a partnership and approached his friends to try to interest them in his proposal. He knew he could count on Louis Scarron, now even richer, as his parents and Julie, his wife's father, had transferred large amounts of assets to them as France lapsed into chaos.

However once he approached Michael Casimir and William Holstein, both now over sixty years of age, they also realised the potential of Daniel's project. So, even before the wedding, the four of them established a joint company, trading under the name of 'Equine Development'. Now after the newly married couples returned from their honeymoon, it was time for Daniel to put his project into action.

Firstly he must take them to the Downey/Elliot Breeding grounds and persuade them to accept them to help and train them further in horse breeding. Of course both David Downey and Stuart Brady, had already been involved in this in Ireland. Once he was informed they were capable, his new firm would purchase land in the wilderness and buy stock from the Allegheny farm from which they could breed their own stock. This would take some time.

In any case his daughter Monica was now six months pregnant with David's child. It would be sensible for them to stay in Alleghenies until she was delivered of her child, rather than it occurred in the wilderness. Now Daniel made it clear that he was investing in their future. It was a business venture, and after the first year his firm would expect ten per cent of any profits. They all considered this very fair. So he now took them all to meet both Jessie and Simon Downy and Peter and Elsie Eliot.

Since James, Paul and Stuart had arrived back at the Alleghenies, with Lilie Gartner, Helga Feld and their young indian babies, along with the young indian girl, Pohanna, their family had made them very welcome. In some ways it was a strange situation. There was no hiding, how both Lilie and Helga were so extremely grateful to the men, for being taken out of their hellish life as white squaws, and being brought here to live with their parents. Even more surprised that these men had not made any sexual demands on them, even though they had admitted their interest in them, as possible future partners.

Poor Pohanna had quickly discovered she had conceived by her raping with the soldiers. She was still terrified of her new life however much she was welcomed by these kind people. Her fears were eased by the solicitations of Stuart Downey who was trying to teach her to speak in English. Whether through fear, even possibly by her own manipulations, three weeks after she arrived she miscarried her child. Though she was never in danger, it was a very unpleasant time for Pohanna, and once again she could not fail to notice the kindness Stuart bestowed on her at this time. She felt, of all the persons around her, she could trust this man, so unlike the dominant indian men of her tribe.

Neither Lilie nor Helga could hide the fact that it seemed that James was more interested in Lilie whilst Paul preferred Helga, and neither the important fact, that the two girls, also, had similar preferences. Yet after the initial few weeks as the two girls, with their babies settled into their new life, it seemed that their men friends, though very attentive to them, made no further approaches. The two girls felt it was time they qualified the situation.

On the pretext of both of them being taken to see the extent of the estate and the wild horses being reared, the two girls, at last, managed to get James and Paul alone. As they had previously agreed between them, Lilie raised the subject. "James and Paul surely you both know how grateful we are for you finding us and bringing us here. You must know, in spite of the difficulties on the journey, we greatly enjoyed your company. Frankly after the episode many years ago at Anderson, where we now realise, we were in the wrong, in complaining about your more intimate attention to us. – Then you admitted you joined the militia in order to try and find both of us. That in itself must forever make us indebted to you."

She continued, "We now both admit that when you found us, and told us you would bring us here, we had decided that you would require payment for doing so. By then our attitude to intimacy was very different from the days we lived at Anderson. We had suffered rape, invaded by several men, conceived their child, we were fallen women, even if it was not our fault. So if you had wished on the long journey, if both of you would have wished to take your pleasure of our bodies – I tell you now – we would willingly have yielded to you – yes, perhaps in doing so conceived your child. It was your right."

Now she smiled and they both took hold of their men folks hands, "That you did not take advantage of us amazed, but naturally pleased us. Then on the journey you both told us you wanted us all to get to know each other, even admitting you might consider us as a partner, if not a wife. Yet since we arrived here, though you have been very kind to us, it does not seem as if you want to, even flirt, with us. Please tell us, are you having second thoughts of us as possible future partners. If so, is it that we have born our indian babies. We will understand, but we should tell you, no matter how it happened, we both love and wish to keep our children. – But please be frank with us."

As had happened on the journey, it was James that replied for both of them. Firstly to their delight they both took both their hands gripping them and raised them to their lips, kissing them, "No dear, Lilie and Helga, that is not the case – well – I suppose it is difficult for us to explain. You told us on that journey you expected us to take advantage of you. Of course we knew you were grateful for not doing so. Since we arrived, we realised that should we make any advances to you, we felt certain you would have accepted them, even some intimacy, merely to repay us for bringing you here. – We both agreed we must give you sometime to see if you might find a genuine interest in us, not based on any idea of repayment. – Since you have now broached the subject, we can both say, that our feeling for you are now far stronger, than even when we came try to find you. – The truth is we know now, we both love you."

This was the moment for both Lilie and Helga to take the initiative. They both pulled their men folk to them and pressed their lips on their mouths. It was a long and passionate kiss. Again Lilie spoke for both them. "Dear, dear men, haven't you seen ever since we arrived here the adoration we both have for you. Both of us had fallen, completely, in love for you on that long journey – but us had said, then. You hoped by coming here we might better come to know each other. This meant you were not sure of your feelings towards us, understandable as we were fallen women, with illegitimate children. Dear James, and I know Helga feels the same about Paul, we both love you and believe it would be wonderful, if we could spend our lives with you. We both understand if you feel you cannot marry us. We still want to live and behave as wives with you – if you will have us."

It seemed incredulous to James and Paul that their women were offering themselves to them. They hugged them to them, now smothering their lips with their kisses. It continued for some time. Then even more incredulous to the two girls, their men dropped on one knee and proposed marriage to them, telling them they wanted them as wives not mistresses, and if they would agree they would wish to adopt their children as their own and give them their own surname.

It was four delighted persons who now raced back to the house to tell everyone they were engaged to marry. They were delighted that it seemed their parents not only agreed with their decision, but were as delighted at the outcome, just as much as they were. Now the only question was when and where the weddings should occur.

Even more so when their women told them how much they wanted to travel with them to Kentucky and set up a home for them there. The only question was could they afford to pay the larger balance of the purchase of the land, on which they had placed a deposit. Their parents would help, but even this would be a large financial burden on their accumulated wealth. However they all felt it was the right thing to do. If they established in Kentucky, the same profitable working they had here, it would not be long before they could have repaid their investment.

It was at this very moment when Daniel Carroll appeared bringing with him Stuart and Antoinette Brady and David and Monica Downey, intending to see if they could stay with them and be trained more efficiently in the matter of horse breeding.

It was quite an astonishing first meeting for David and Stuart, for like Simon and Peter, as they were all descendents of Simon and Pamela Downy, again Pamela was the elder sister of the amazing Amelia Eliot who had married David Carroll before he became Governor of Maryland. Pamela and her husband had not wished to join her sister in America, when David had taken several members of his wife's family, she preferred to stay in Ireland. Now they were to meet still more descendents of Pamela, finding they were in fact close relatives.

6

The greetings over, Daniel was to discover a situation, which if anything added to the plan, he had devised for the newly married couples. Of course Daniel knew most of the offspring of the Downey's and Eliot's, for Daniel and Michelle had often visited their Equine Establishment. However now they were introduced to Lilie Gartner, Helga Feld and the young indian girl, Pohanna, and how they had been saved from a life as white squaws of the Miami tribe, being brought here with their illegitimate young babies as a result of the adventurous excursions of James and Stuart Downey and Paul Eliot.

It was necessary to explain their early association with the two girls at Anderson in Indiana Territory, for them to understand why the three of them joined the militia, with the one idea of trying to discover their whereabouts, knowing they had been attacked an possibly captured, when the indians destroyed Anderson. Even Daniel was surprised by their efforts, even their certainty that the girls were still alive.

After a short description of the battle their discovery of the two girls and then bringing them, with Pohanna to their home. Now if seemed their relationship had grown and that soon Lilie Gartner would be marrying James Downey, and Paul Eliot would be marrying Helga Feld. It sounded like a happy ending after the difficulties of the last three years.

The explanations completed Daniel now explained the purpose of their visit. "We have come to ask you to help train David and Stuart in becoming efficient horse breeders. They were brought up in Ireland and learned the basis of this from their families, but I want them to fully understand what is involved. If you would kindly do this, I would gladly recompense you for your trouble. Then in due course I intend to purchase suitable land in wilderness where they can set up a equine establishment of their own. "

Now he smiled, "You see David has married my younger daughter, Monica, who is now six months pregnant, whilst Stuart Brady has fallen in love and married Antoinette Condorcet, one of the two of they, rescued from France at the height of the Terror. – I seems though both Monica and Antoinette have previously lived a life of ease, they are now both determined to immerse themselves in the work of the husbands, not caring the hard demands on their constitutions. – Only time will tell us if this will be possible. However if they survive your training here, I have promised them land of their own, for this purpose."

It was James Downey who replied, "Daniel my family know we owe so much to you and Michelle for helping our parents during the last war and ensuring we had a successful future. We will all be delighted to help David, Monica, Stuart and Antoinette. Since it seemed we all come the same stock in Ireland, and David and Stuart were raised in this work, I have little doubt that we can ensure they become experts very quickly. – May I inquire where you are considering buying suitable land on which they could settle."

Daniel laughed, a little embarrassed. "Frankly, I have not given any great thought to that – but there is so much new land now available in Ohio, Indiana, Kentucky or Tennessee. Along with my friends the Scarron's, Holstein's and Casimir's we have set up an investment company trading under the name of "Equine Development", entirely for this purpose. We intend to invest in several projects like the one we are offering our newly weds. It is entirely a business proposition. After the first year, once we are sure they are able, we shall expect ten percent of their profit annually, to repay us. "

Daniel was surprised by James reply. "If I were to tell you that I have placed a small deposit on a beautiful stretch of grassland in Kentucky, which I shall forfeit if I do not complete the contract within a year. We discovered this land near the town of Winchester. It is quite large, and at present their are other stretches of similar land close by, for sale. You must see the land for yourself, it is covered with blue grass, a product of Kentucky, unlike any I have seen elsewhere. Land especially suitable for horse breeding and rearing. Mr. Carroll would you be interested in investing in this land I have mortgaged. If so you might consider, also, buying one of the other several tracks close by on which David and Stuart could settle."

Daniel immediately retorted, saying he would consider this offer. He told James that he respected his knowledge of horse breeding and knew he would never have tried to purchase land unsuitable for this purpose. "James, I will of course have to consult my partners but I believe they will be willing to agree to your proposition In any case I think I would, alone, make this investment.. Also, if the land for David and Stuart could be close by, I'm certain you would help them to overcome the early difficulties. Since in your case you have already made a part investment, we would not expect the full ten per cent return for the first few years. If you agree, we will discuss the details tomorrow, after we have all rested."

Nothing more was said that day and they all enjoyed a large joint dinner. The next day rested, Daniel and James spent considerable time together. Daniel asked James if he would make a quick journey to Kentucky to place another deposit on a stretch of land on which David and Stuart could settle in a short time. James gladly agreed. He now admitted that without his offer he knew his family would have found it difficult to offer him the remaining part of the contract on the land. Now Daniel's investment made it so much easier and Daniel told him he would return with letters of credit in less than a week, after which James promised to act.

It seemed that the future of both the newly weds and James and Paul, also soon to be married, were now assured. To Daniel it seemed that now, though over sixty years of age, he was still helping to develop and expand this new country, as in his youth he had helped to develop the Ohio country., even when it belonged to the French. He knew his late uncle, Sir Robert Carroll, would be even more proud of him. Daniel knew his and Michelle's prosperity and happiness was because of the enormous gift of the land of Racoonsville, from his uncle. He felt he was still investing in the country's future as he knew his uncle, and grandfather, Sir David, had done in the past, but also investing in his grandmother, Amelia's descendents.

Within a week Daniel had returned with sufficient Letters of Credit, to pay the remainder of the land James had mortgaged and sufficient to purchase an area, at least as large again, having consulted and got the approval of all partners in "Equine Development". James then took Paul with him and made a quick return journey to Winchester in Kentucky. When they returned the land was now their own for development, as soon as they could go to live there.

However there were still a number matters needing resolving, before this could happen. The first was the marriage of James Downey to Lilie Gartner, and that of Paul Eliot to Helga Feld. Michelle insisted that it occurred at Racoonsville. Also as by then her daughter Monica would be eight months pregnant, she also insisted Monica returned home to bear her child under the correct supervision. As usual Michelle got her way.

However like the recent marriage of David, Monica, Stuart and Antoinette, there was a complication. It seemed that twenty two year old Stuart Downey had fallen in love with Pohanna. Ever since her miscarriage Stuart had spent most of the time with her, teaching her to speak English, even beginning to teach her to read and write. Pohanna, quickly responded. She realised she could trust him. She was never afraid when he was with her, and gradually he was succeeding in making her believe she was safe here and would not be discarded. She liked the feel of his strong arms around her, even surprised that he did not take the liberties, male members of her tribe would have taken on these occasions.

Eventually he would draw her close to him and gently kiss her lips. Pohanna was pleased to respond. When alone he told her about the coming marriages of James and Lilie and Paul and Helga. Pohanna only knew of the indian marriage which would be arranged by her father, and Stuart had to explain how much more complicated an English marriage was. It puzzled poor Pohanna. Now her English was good enough to ask questions.

"Stuart, I have no father, so he cannot arrange for me to marry. It seems I can never have a husband of my own." This enabled Stuart to question her, "Would you like to have a husband?" She smiled, "Very much. I would like one just like you, one who could give me babies, for I lost my last one and want another very soon."

Stuart knew he had been in love with Pohanna, almost from the moment he first met her in Indiana but even then he had recalled at the idea of having an indian woman as his wife. Gradually that had changed. Perhaps the way she so relied on him for her security. He was the only one with whom she showed no fear. He also came to realise what a very beautiful woman Pohanna was, now dressed the European ways. Slowly he came to understand that Pohanna was little different from other girls, except for her jet black hair and lovely but piercing eyes.

Now the questioning had reached the point of no return. Stuart, now knew he was desperately in love with her, and she had just admitted he was 'the type of man she would have wanted as a husband'. It was now or never. His emotions won. Quickly he asked, "Pohanna would you really like me as your husband? Would you like me to give you those babies?" Her answer was very quick.

"Oh! Yes! Stuart. I would have hoped my father might choose you. You are strong. You would give me strong babies." Now Stuart hugged her body to his and for a moment saw fear in Pohanna's eyes, but his lips kissing first those eyes and then her lips and his hands gently massaging her back, removed that fear and she responded.

He partially eased his body from hers. Then quietly he said. "Pohanna here in this home, it is you and not your father who makes the decision of who you should marry. Dearest, I love you, I've loved you since I first met you. I would want to marry you just as the other two are marrying and make you my wife. – However", he now broke apart but took hold of both her hands before adding, "However, for this to happen you would have to tell me and others you really did want to marry me. You have that decision. No one else, not your father or any of my family. Pohanna you would have to say you wanted me as your husband."

A look of amazement came over her face. She could not understand. Then she gasped, "You – you really want me. – Oh! Stuart I would so want you as my husband. If this is possible let us go now so I can tell everyone – If it is my decision then Stuart I do, really want you. – I will be a very obedient wife as an indian girl should be."

After that they went and confessed their desire to marry. His parents were surprised, as they still considered her as just an indian girl, but both Lilie and Helga, spoke up for her, telling everyone what a courageous girl she was and how she had helped them in the past. After that it was agreed and Michelle, once again had to change her wedding plans.

In March 1795 there were three weddings on the Racoonsville Estate, though their honeymoons were only a week on the estate. Then at the beginning of April Monica Downey gave birth to a seven pound daughter, Maureen. By then the training of David and Stuart was virtually complete. It would not be long now before all the pairs of families would buy stock from their parents and drive them, in the late spring across the hills into Kentucky to settle there and begin a new life there.

7

Jean and Aleia Dumas were delighted that Francois and Charlotte Le Raye wished to accompany them on their journey to Aleia's family. They all traveled in a Surrey keeping to the Cumberland Road, now so well used by emigrants making their way into the wilderness, but it had long since been improved and metalled. Gone were the ruts caused by so many wagons for so many roads. It was a very pleasant journey up the gap to Fort Cumberland, now a small and prosperous town, built around the original fort.

Having rested there in a small hotel they now took the road again through the wooded areas, for so long fought over in the Seven Years war. Francois and Charlotte saw nearly all of the land on either side was settled. Originally covered in hardwood trees, most had been removed to make it suitable for arable farming and herding. They were fascinated when Aleia and Jean, explained when Jean was an officer in the French Army, it had then, only been populated by indian tribes, who often fought each other. Yet this was less than fifty years before.

They could see how the influx of so many families fleeing from war torn Europe and oppression, had made the whole area into a very populated community. They passed a very large estate on which they saw several log mansions of some size had been built. They were told this land belonged to two families, who were their friends. The Casimir's who had come here from Poland and the Holstein's who had come from Sweden. Both had been very rich, selling their lands in the old country and coming to live here before the last war. Now they did stop at a smaller land holding just to the north, where they were introduced to Adrian and Kylie Scott and their family.

It was necessary explain that this family along with another two families nearby, the Reid's and the Hobbs' were very special friends of both Daniel and Michelle Carroll, as well as the Casimir's and Holstein's who had helped them to settle and overcome the difficulties when they first settled on this land, helping to clear the trees to enable them to farm. The Scott's made them very welcome.

Some time before, Francois and Charlotte had been introduced to Philip and Claire Wycks when they had called on Jean and Madeleine. Now they were to learn from the Scott's, of Claire's earlier life when she lived with Neil Reeves. How Claire had been forced into prostitution in Bristol. How she met Neil who brought her to America providing she lived with him as if married, though he told her he would never marry her. How due to Michael Casimir, Claire had been given a new life when Neil found another woman and went to live with her. How this led to her marrying Philip a widower, who lost his first wife in childbirth. How he fell in love with her, even knowing her past,. Now they lived very happily on one of the estates they had passed on their journey.

Again the two of them saw how this new country provided an opportunity quite impossible in Europe, where the past meant little, provided they were willing to accept hardships. It made both of them more resolved to try to repay this land for the future it had given them. After a stay of two days when they were introduced to Andrew Reeves, evidently a nephew of Neil Reeves, and his Austrian wife Anna. They were the local school master and school madam who now educated many of the local children. Charlotte had always been a very observant woman. She told her brother she felt Anna came from aristocratic stock. Her mannerisms and the way she conducted herself seemed to imply she was born into a higher state in society than her husband. Yet they seemed to be a devoted couple.

Now the four of them traveled on to Fort Pitt. This was very much larger than Fort Cumberland. In fact the old fort was almost lost in the very large town which had grown up around it. Jean explained that he had once been officer in charge of the fort when it was called Fort Duquesne, a French fort built to stop the English invading the lands of Ohio, which then formed part of New France. How Aleia had lived with him for nearly ten years as his indian wife. Both admitted the indian marriage was forced on Jean to ensure the friendship of her tribe, but how this had turned to love and they knew Jean loved Aleia, just as much as he loved his Madeleine.

How it had been his misfortune to eventually have to surrender the fort to George Washington, to save further bloodshed, when the war was lost,. However Jean hugged Aleia to him and explained, "I confess I did this to save dear Aleia's life for if we had fought on and I had been killed I knew Aleia would have followed the indian tradition. She would have killed herself. I could not let the woman I love do this, even for the honour of France. Well the British when they occupied the fort renamed it Fort Pitt in honour of the British Prime Minister of that time, William Pitt, the elder."

Jean and Aleia could not refrain from asking the military to let them see inside the fort again. He was able to show the commanding officer his name and that of Major Louis Scarron inscribed in the walls of one of the rooms in the fort, impressing on him his importance when he once commanded the fort. Francois and Charlotte were allowed to accompany them.

This did give the two of them a chance to ask them to show, where Jean had told them he has seen iron ore and coal. The fort had been so altered, this proved impossible but Jean promised, as they stayed with Tonsac, he would take them outside, about two miles from the fort, where he had also seen it. So without staying there they made their way to where Aleia's indian tribe now lived. All receiving an exceedingly warm welcome.

Her two married daughters, Alia and Dumei, embraced their mother who they had not seen for over three years. Then Francois and Charlotte were introduced to their two husbands, finding as was the custom, that they, also, had married two other indian wives, and like Tonsac who was married to three woman. When they commented on this Aleia had merely smiled and replied, "Is this how I lived with Jean, who also is married to Madeleine. I can tell you in the wilder lands where fur trappers still trade, these men normally have more than one wife, if only to ensure the friendship, and possible avoid being killed, by the tribe to which they belong."

Still seeing they were not convinced she continued. "In the past it was a necessity, and necessary if a indian woman was able to marry and conceive the children she wanted. The constant warring between the various tribes, greatly reduced the number of available men. Females were often twice, or more times, as many as males. Only by a man taking more than one woman could that woman achieve her longing for children. It was not any intention to make the woman inferior, but a necessity if a woman was to achieve her desire." At last it seemed the two of them began to understand.

The habitation was not what they had expected. In fact, although the houses were all really log cabins, they were quite spacious and well equipped. The Chickasaw tribe had prospered greatly under Tonsac's leadership. Although most still wore Indian attire. It was well made and of good quality, and it fact was far more serviceable than European clothes. The inside of the houses were well lit with many oil lamps and the kitchens were as well appointed as those in the Potomac valley. In fact the tribe had become very civilized, which was a tribute to their leader.

Charlotte enjoyed talking with both Alia and Dumei, finding just how happy they were, and how pleased they were that they had made the decision to come and live here. The whole of the childhood had been spent in the wilderness, and wherever Jean was sent to command. Even the two years they had endured at Berkeley seemed to be a prison to them. Now they were extremely happy both with a husband, who loved them deeply. They would never consider returning, though they admitted they would like to visit, particularly their mother, from time to time.

Meanwhile Jean had kept his promise and took Francois to were he had found the iron and coal. It only took both of them about an hour to confirm Jean's assertion.. Using only a spade they quickly uncovered rock containing iron pyrites though Francois consider some deposits were of hematite ore. They also found a layer of what seemed to be good quality coal, though it would have needed much digging to confirm they extent of their find. Still it was promising and Francois felt it might be the answer to America's present shortage of these materials as it expanded so quickly. It was sufficient for him to see if he could interest investment, as he felt, eventually, the returns would far exceed the expenditure.

However as they had journeyed from the fort to the indian encampment and now as they had explored the area again, Francois marveled at the number of families traveling in their wagons, with their children, almost in a continuous line, all heading west to settle and colonize the lands now becoming available, as the Miami and other indian tribes had been defeated and where land was considered relatively safe. Francois could hardly fail to see that after Fort Pitt the quality of the road west was overused and in bad weather would soon become impassable.

Again as an engineer Francois saw it would be essential, like the Cumberland Road, to build a virtual; highway to the west. It seemed to him this was a priority in which the government itself, should be involved. Only they would have the resources to build an adequate highway, as returns to investors would be small, even if they erected toll gates. He knew how much he would like to be involved in its construction and would enjoy planning with Charlotte the many bridges, which would be necessary.

However if the quality of the road made communication difficult, Francois could hardly fail to see that many would be settlers desperate to travel west were building rafts of wood to place on the River Monongahela, which would join the Ohio River and take them to the new western lands. A few managed to buy a boat, but they were very few to purchase and very dear. Francois, who had helped his father in building small boats, saw this as an alternative and profitable business until he could interest others in building a new road.

Now he would discuss what he had found with Charlotte. When they returned the two of them must bring their finds to the attention of the many prosperous and rich landowners in the valley, as well as those in Philadelphia. It seemed that still; using Jean and Aleia's home as a base, they would need to travel far to see if they could interest many and even the government in their proposals. Perhaps, even provide funds to establish a small boat building business on that river. However it would be a task they would enjoy.

So their visit to Tonsac and his tribe had proved very profitable, apart from their enjoyment in meeting so many new people. They stayed there for over a month and took the opportunity to view the wonderful vistas the country offered them. It was a delightful place to settle. Perhaps in years to come, both of them, either together or singularly, this might make this land, their home. Their visit over, they gladly returned with Jean and Aleia calling again on the Scott's as the returned and this time meet the Reid and Hobbs' families and discovering again that their wives had once been indentured servants, even purchased by the men now their husbands, but how this had turned to love, and a settled and happy future.

Again Francois and Charlotte realised how this new country appeared to provided for so many people, who were at one time in great difficulty. It provided a haven just as it had done for them. Now they were determined to help pay back for the security now offered to them and made them determined to explore further the areas still offering sanctuary to those escaping from the war in Europe.

8

Louisa and Anton Albrecht were very troubled persons. It seemed that their true lives in Austria may soon be discovered. Spain had very recently signed with France the Treaty of San Ildefonso, which made them the allies of France and the enemy of Britain on whom they had, now, declared war. This in itself would have had little effect on their own lives being so far from Spain, but for the fact it, also, made Austria an enemy of Spain.

Although Spanish Florida was many thousand of miles from Madrid and always enjoyed a considerable degree of independence, their government in New Orleans had received a directive demanding that the names of all British and Austrian persons living in Florida should be registered, as aliens. Although this did not in anyway restrict their movements, nor were they in Florida, considered to be a danger, it meant that the name of Albrecht was now known and registered to the Spanish administration in New Orleans.

Of course all their Spanish neighbours and particularly those who had arranged the purchase of their estate where they had stayed, after their escape, to Spain, knew little of their past. Unlike their friends there, the Spaniards in Florida had no idea of their true identity, or their relationship to the court in Austria. The name of Albrecht, though, not a very common name, was be no means unique. However both Louisa and Anton realised that should New Orleans send a list of all aliens to Madrid, it was possible that the grouping of the names of Louisa and Anton with that of Albrecht, might lead to their true positions.

Of course, even then, since Austria was now an enemy of Spain, nothing may result, even if it was discovered. However the two of them had another reason for fearing discovery. Anton had recently learned that his account in Europe from which he had arranged the letters of credit to purchase that strip of land in America, to be able to apply for United States citizenship, had suddenly received enormous increases in investment. Anton had suddenly become a very wealth man.

Of course when the two had flown from Austria to Spain, Anton had not informed his family of what he had done, fearing it would lead to their discovery. The reason was that unknown to him, his bank deposit had grown so quickly was because his father, desperate to know what had happened to his son, fearing for sometime that he was dead, possibly killed as he fled with Louisa, had been in touch with the bankers who he knew dealt with his son's accounts.

When money had been withdrawn to purchase the land, his bankers had cautiously, informed his father. Even though the careful way the transactions had been made though intermediaries, so that the location of his son was still unknown, it did tell his father that somewhere in the world his son was still alive. Now from those bankers, again through intermediaries, Anton had received a letter from his father, begging him to inform him where he was.

Anton would have wanted to do this, if only to set his families minds at ease, but knew he did not dare do so. Yet he feared his father, desperate to hear from him, might alert the Austrian court to his whereabouts. Now with his and Louisa name registered in Florida, there was a double chance of being discovered. In spite of the war, even because of it, Spain might be willing to do a deal with the Austrian court and force their return to Vienna.

As these two events brought such fear to the two of them, they were delighted to receive from Eric Casimir an embellished parchment declaring the two of them as citizens of the United States of America. This might, in itself, make their position more secure, especially after Minister, Thomas Pinckney, had negotiated the recent Treaty with Spain concerning not only Spanish Florida but the whole of the Spanish land of Louisiana and the right of passage up and down the Mississippi River which was the present boundary between the Spanish and American possessions.

This created very good relations between the two countries and might, just, prevent them exporting the Albrecht's back to Austria, now being Americans as well as Austrians. However, dare they take the risk. Anton decided to write to Eric and tell him of the dire position, their registration as aliens and his fathers attempt to reach him, asking his advice. At least he could add that because of the generosity of his father he was now a very wealthy man. It was the beginning of summer when he wrote.

To their delight he received an immediate reply, endorsed by Robert Carroll, suggesting, that the two them with Antonia, travel from Florida, leaving his overseer to attend to his, now, prosperous estate, and sail immediately to Annapolis, where Eric and John Holstein would meet them and take them, once again, to stay on their large estate near Fort Necessity. They would then place a proposal to them which might remove, for ever, their fear of discovery.

Glad to receive this offer of help and looking forward to another holiday in West Virginia, they persuaded their Spanish neighbours, to look after their assets, whilst they were away, offering them a small percentage of any profits. It was a business arrangement, as they were uncertain as to the length of their visit. Then traveling as a family to Miami, with a coach load of many clothes, they cautiously waited and boarded an American ship to sail to Annapolis, where Eric and John and their family were waiting to meet them and in a series of coaches, and took everyone to the estate in West Virginia.

It was then that Eric and John suggested a solution to their problem. They should not consider returning to Florida. They advised them to still retain, for the time being, their estate there, worked as at present. However on the small strip of land they had purchased, they should build a mansion, now they had sufficient wealth. They could stay with them until it was completed, but this strip should then be their permanent home. They might, occasionally, return, temporary, to Florida. At present they should not dispose of it, as Eric felt sure that in a few years the whole of Florida would become part of the United States, when their home, there, would be invaluable.

Eric and John would introduce them to their fathers, Michael Casimir and William Holstein who would be delighted to advise them on investing their wealth in many profitable ventures, particular in real estate in the growing new lands. Let their money do their work whilst the lived in comfort at present on their small estate which was very picturesque and reminded both of them of the homes in Austria. It seemed that the money from the sale of the trees which they had agreed for sale on their last visit, would now provide the assets to pay for their new mansion in the cleared area.

Eric and John emphasised to them, that by agreeing to these proposals they would now be completely free from any attempt to return them to Austria. If they stayed for a year, even if they returned to Florida, if only to visit, their American citizenship would prevent Spain, or Austria demanding their return. Further more they could now acquaint both their parents of where they now lived, knowing the information would be useless to the Austrian court.

Once good relations had been re-established with their families, Anton knew his father was so rich he might be willing to accept his son's advice and invest his money in America, a far less dangerous investment that anywhere in war torn Europe. So from living in fear, especially for the last few months, the Albrecht family could now live in peace with even less travail than looking after their tobacco estate in Florida.

There was another reason why this proposal appealed so much to Louisa.

She had told Anton, some months previous, she wanted him to give her another baby and Antonia was now three years old. Anton had wished to give her, her wish, but had to refused when their very existence was threatened. Now agreeing to live a new and settled life in the United States, even before their new mansion could be built, there was no reason why the Albrecht's should not increase the numbers in their family.

9

By late summer 1795 Jansen's new Cotton Mill was fully operative and woven cotton articles were being produced in quantity. There was no doubt that Jansen was impressed by the energetic way both Roy Marshall and Hugh Foyle had ensured it came into production so quickly. It was less than two years since they had arrived at Philadelphia, now profits from his investment were beginning to appear. Though it would be some time before these were substantial enough to repay Jansen for his investment, he knew that within a year or two it would be adding greatly to his own wealth.

The contract with Roy and Hugh stipulated, if successful he must offer them a junior partnership in the firm after five years. Until then they were, merely, his employees and received an annual salary. However for two reasons, since he was so delighted at the progress made, Jansen decided to offer the two of them an immediate junior partnership.

Jansen had quickly realised that the most valuable acquisition was Roy Marshall. It had been he who had devised the layout and purchased the machinery coupling it in his own way to the steam motive power. Hugh, though useful, his greatest asset was the 'flying shuttle' whose copyright he held. Without this Roy's work would have been useless. So the first reason for so quickly making both of them his partners was the knowledge that if not, there was now nothing to prevent them selling their expertise to another investor to start up a rival company.

However it went far more than this. Jansen had come to like them both, particularly they way they had carried out their tasks. He knew his wife considered them both, and particularly their women, Linda and Fay, as her personal friends. They would meet frequently during the day when the men were at work. The truth was that Mechia, though she loved, deeply, her husband, she still missed the large family of Scarron's living in Berkeley, where she had been brought up. Linda and Fay were the first two women she could trust and call them her friends, since she had come to Philadelphia.

So both Jansen and Mechia now considered Roy and Hugh as well as Fay and Linda, as their friends, no longer employees.

So at the end of the summer Jansen had called both Roy and Hugh to his office in which they discovered was Jansen's lawyer. He had with him the original contract which stipulated their two salaries and the promise of the partnership, if successful, after five years. Now Jansen told them he would offer them each a quarter share in the company, operative in three weeks time, and after only two years instead of five. Of course both Roy and Hugh were delighted and told him so.

Roy as he shook hands with Jansen said, "We shall ensure that in time we shall all become very rich. I'm certain the demand for our goods will mean, either an extension of the present factory, or the building of an extra one. First we must ensure your original investment is repaid. As partners we pledge to receive a lesser share until that has happened. Only then will we progress together. You will not regret your decision today."

Jansen smiled and gripped both their hands firmly. "I have no doubt of that. I should add that Mechia, from the moment you arrived, had great faith in you both. It was she who persuaded me to trust both of you, and I admit I was impressed by both of you when you first stayed with us. Now we are partners. However I believe that firstly we are friends, who can trust each other. That, to me, is more important."

Now he smiled, "Mechia is home sick and wants to return for a visit to her family in Berkeley. I have agreed to us spending a full month there. You have already met several members of our family. I think the factory can continue to run under the two experienced foremen you have appointed. My accountant can see to the financial side. Mechia and I are inviting you, Roy and Fay and you Hugh and Linda, to accompany us and spend a months, well earned, holiday in West Virginia."

Naturally the two of them, gladly, agreed, planning to leave together in a fortnight's time. It would be the first time either of them had seen any other part of the country, excepting the area around Philadelphia. The only other view of this new country had been the coach drive from the port to first meet Jansen.

The two men returned to their house and to the two woman with whom they lived, to tell them the good news that they were now partners in the company and would soon be taken on a holiday to West Virginia. When Roy informed Fay, it was sufficient for both of them to go upstairs and celebrate, enjoying almost three hours of intimacy. Neither, now felt any difficulty in acting as if they were husband and wife.

Roy lay naked next to an equally naked Fay. Their bodies showed the results of their recent passionate endevours. Each were, now, tired but each were completely satisfied. At last they could talk sensibly to each other.

Fay, smiling, stroked Roy's long hair, soothingly. "So we are all going to Berkeley. – Roy, you know I saw the way you looked at both Electra Carroll and Ellia Dumas when they stayed with Jansen. – I know you found them both interesting. – Well you will soon have the opportunity to meet them again."

Seeing he was about the remonstrate with her, Fay put her finger on his mouth and continued, "No! Roy! There is no need to apologise to me. – You owe me nothing. – You made it clear from the start that you, merely, wanted to help me – and you have in every way. – You saved my life in Manchester, took me to Liverpool, paid to bring me to America. – You made no demands on me – yet I knew you had the right to use me. – Why it took months before we both agreed that it was foolish not to enjoy each others bodies."

Now she kissed him but not passionately, "You owe me nothing. – I feel certain you do not love me – though I know you like me and want me to be happy. – Frankly – I do not even know my own mind. – Each time I look back and realise what you have done for me since Manchester, - for a few moments I've often felt, I might be falling in love with you. – Since we started our intimate moments – I have sometimes felt the same – just as I do now. – Yet for most of the time – well – I just don't feel that way. – However I do know I want to be near you. – It's that I cannot sever my intense love for Trevor. – perhaps I may never be able to completely love a man again."

Now as she paused, Roy kissed her back, he smiled, "Dear Fay – It's the same for me. To begin with, I know my only feelings for you were pity. - I wanted to help. – I admit I enjoyed seeing the naked body which you so generously gave me from the very first night. – I admit I desired you, but you were so helpless and so trusting in me, I could not take liberties with you. – Then on the boat I knew from what you said you would have agreed then to give me intimate pleasure. – However, I knew it was only because you felt I deserved it. – At that time you would have given it me but I felt you did not want it."

Now he laughed, "Well we arrived here and received such a welcome from Mechia. Perhaps it was her lack of inhabitation – her free talk of her relations with Jansen – it effected me but I saw it also effected you. – Then when we got this house of our own, I believe it was this which broke down the barriers between us. – Life in America was so different from life in Britain. - We saw how foolish it was to live together in the same house, and yet not get the pleasure we could offer each other. – you know – We both agreed to this at the same moment. – It was not either of us who caused it."

He looked straight at her and took hold of her hands. "Fay, dear, I have enjoyed every precious moment you have given me by yielding your body – and I believe you have enjoyed it the same. – Fay, I have felt for some time I have been falling in love with you - Even more so after Terry was born, for I love your son, just as much as if he was mine. – Then those others came to stay. – You are right I discovered my attraction to both Electra and Ellia – I'm not even sure who I liked the most. – Fay, I still want you – but it seemed I have inherited my father's faults. You see he hurt my mother by having an affair with her sister, my aunt. I know she conceived his child but miscarried. I was old enough to remember this."

Fay could see the guilt on his face as he continued. "I now know one woman will never be enough for me. – I doubt if I am the man to make you happy. Perhaps I can never be faithful to one woman. – You can see my selfishness – I confess to you – now – I do not want to lose you – yet I know when we go to Berkeley I shall probably try hard to seduced one of those two girls. – After what I've said – Do you want to finish our intimacy? – We can still live together in this house."

Fay smiled and pulled his head down to her and kissed his lips passionately. "No, Roy, not unless it is your wish. Let us continue as we have now done for months. We obviously like each other – I enjoy what you do to me and know you feel I give you your reward. – let us accept, that neither of us have a monopoly on our emotions. At Berkeley feel free to trifle with you wenches affections. I may discover a man who may interest me. – let us enjoy our holiday."

⁓

At the same time in their own house, Linda Foyle had just arisen from her bed on which still lay her brother Hugh. Linda needed to go to remove the result of her recent endevours and the sexual satisfaction her brother had given her. However she first turned, bent down and kissed her naked brother on his lips.

Then she said, "You know we cannot enjoy this whilst we are at Berkeley. – Brother, I shall miss it. I thank heaven that Mechia convinced me that it is not unusual for men and women, near relatives, to enjoy the pleasures of intercourse. - Of course I would never had dared doing this, but for the wonderful things Mechia gave me which limits the dangers of me giving you a child. Much as I love you and now what you do to me, I don't want to give you a child."

Now Hugh in turn kissed her. "Yes! I doubt if we shall have much chance of indulging our pleasures in West Virginia. – however, you never know, things here are so different to Britain. – Well no! - But you do know I found both Electra and Ellia exciting, particularly Ellia. – But then I saw just how much both Edwin and Torus interested you. I feel certain we shall both find other partners with whom we shall enjoy intimate moments."

Linda agreed, "You are right, particularly about Edwin. Hugh, I can tell you I would be very willing to go to bed with Edwin. Further more, it seems he is very rich. – But then their whole family appears to extremely rich. – Perhaps none of them will consider we are of sufficient station to warrant any interest in us." Then she laughed before concluding, "But brother this is America, not Europe. Even since we arrived here we have seen how its borders are expanding and the thousands making it so. – Brother we shall both try very hard at Berkeley to expand both our own fortunes."

PART 5

ENABLEMENT

ENABLEMENT

George Washington, whilst he was president, had done everything possible to prevent political parties being formed amongst the members of Congress. Just as George, until it became impossible had tried to avoid the war with Britain and the Declaration of Independence. He had always believed that Britain needed America just as much as America needed Britain. Together they could form a commonwealth greater than any in the world. He blamed the party system in Britain for causing the war. The Whig Party would have discussed sensible terms with the United States, but they were in the minority and the Tory party ruled Parliament.

For this reason George had tried to prevent it. However it was a hopeless wish. The actual enmity between Thomas Jefferson and Alexandra Hamilton had ensured the formation of a party system, with Jefferson leading the Republicans and Hamilton the Federalists. George still managed to use the undoubted abilities of both men, but knew there would be open warfare in Congress after he retired. Many others realised what would happen and was why they endeavoured to persuade Washington to retain the Presidency for a third time. However he was tired and longed to retire with his wife to their home in Mount Vernon.

Congress had to decided who should succeed him. It was a compromise. When Washington stood down in 1796, John Adams, a Federalist became President, whilst Thomas Jefferson, a Republican, became Vice President, which in fact lead to perpetual quarrels in Congress for the next four years. It even split the loyalties of both members of the Senate as well as the House of Representatives. They would support one for a time, and then oppose him, and support the other.

This happened to Senator Robert Carroll and Senator Eric Casimir, as well as Representative Francois Tencin. As Jefferson came from Virginia and in many ways supported what they wanted for their areas, so had supported him. However, all three having been trained from their youth in high finance, were forced, at times to support Alexandra Hamilton, whose Federalist ideas on the economy were making the country rich again, and removing the heavy debt caused by the war. It did make heavy demands on them all, and could hardly miss any vote when Congress was in session.

The other problem was that Thomas Jefferson still promoted friendship with France and gave them support against Britain, whilst Hamilton, realising the chaos in France, and needed trade with Britain, supported the British cause. On this matter the three of them supported Hamilton, if only because of their father's loyalty, though Francois did it to support his aged mother. There was still strong family affiliation in the liking for Britain. So the years between !795 and 1798 passed very quickly, yet in those three years the population explosion and expansion had continued even more so.

At least the quasi naval war with France, with the French navy boarding American merchant vessels and often stealing their goods proclaiming them as contraband, even though it did occur to a lesser extent with Britain, before Jay's Treaty was signed. By 1797 it had given a sharp rise in anti-French hysteria, which supported the measures President Adams placed before Congress. Though the following year Thomas Jefferson and James Madison drafted a protest against the government usurping the power of the Federal States, and carried through some measures to prevent this.

In fact Robert, Eric and Francois were delighted when each term of Congress ended and they were able to return home and discover what had happened in their absence. Of course this applied even more to their wives who, usually, accompanied them the whole time they attended Congress. Though they benefited from growing friendship with the wives of other Senators and Representatives from other states.

Conditions in France had improved during these years. The Terror had ended on the 27th. July 1794 when a more moderate, but equally demanding power, took charge and arrested and then guillotined Robespierre and in 1795 set up a five member Directory, which by almost annual coups, gradually established a degree of dictatorship. It was still weak government and this gave increasing power to General Napoleon Bonaparte, whose many military victories against combinations of European nations increased his authority.

America could only watch as the war between France, Holland and now Spain tried to defeat Britain, succeeding to some extent in Europe but without a similar extent at sea. Under great pressure Britain's naval was still safely defending its shores, even blockading the coast of both France and Spain, though their was constant naval war in the Caribbean. Since this was the area where America depended on trade, it often lead to American ships being boarded and even sunk. Yet somehow President Adams was able to establish a measure of neutrality

It was the terrible conditions in war torn Europe which was creating the influx of so many Europeans, able to raise enough money for a sea passage, to sail into American ports, especially New York and Annapolis then to make their way up the Hudson and through the Mohawk Gap into Ohio or further west,. Whilst from Annapolis they had the benefit of the Cumberland Road, as far at Fort Pitt, then beginning a more difficult journey through Ohio, into Indiana, or southwards to Kentucky and Tennessee. But still they kept coming, even overcoming the very real dangers of the Atlantic, from storms or enemy fire.

But this expanding country was benefiting from this influx. Each new family which arrived required food, horses, land to grow crops, and implements to plough the land. This greatly added to the economy of the new country., and gave established Americans, such as Daniel Carroll, Michael Casimir, William Holstein, the Scarron's and since the end of 1795, the new citizens from Florida, the Albrecht's. a chance to invest their wealth and profit considerably from its results.

Both Louisa and Anton Albrecht now settled on their small holding in West Virginia, had quickly taken Eric and John's advice and spoken to Michael and William. With Daniel's approval they had invested in "Equine Development" and soon were to invest in other investment holdings the other men were establishing to profit from the new settlements in the wilderness.

Anton's wealth had been assured, once he discovered his father had placed so much in his European account. However, now convinced that there was no danger of Austria being able to force their return to Vienna, Anton had written to his father telling him where he now lived, and now married to Louisa. How they had escaped from Europe to Spain and then to Spanish Florida and the tobacco estate they owned there.

How they had obtained United States citizenship and owned another smaller estate in West Virginia. Where they intended to live for some time. Thanking his father for his gifts of money, and which he was using for profitable investment in America, joining with a number of friends he had made. It enabled him to expect a very successful financial venture He now, invited his father to join him and invest some of his large wealth in this new country, emphasizing this would be a far safer investment than any similar investment in Europe.

Like so many of the people who had escaped from Europe, including those exiles from France, the Albrecht's now regarded themselves as Americans and would help to make this new country a prosperous one for everyone, yet at the same time profit by it for themselves. These three years were to alter the lives of everyone.

2

It had been the injection of money from "Equine Development" which had enabled the expansion of horse breeding from the slopes of the Appalachians Mountains to these new area in Kentucky. Although David and Stuart were now considered proficient in these skills, and even their women partners had learned enough to be able to assist their men as their wives, it was, correctly decided, that the men folk should first travel to their new landholdings in Kentucky, to build suitable accommodation to house their families, especially as Monica would be suckling baby, Maureen.

The five men left their wives in the autumn of 1795 and travelled to Winchester. It was the first time that David Downy and Stuart Brady had seen the land purchased for them in the spring by James Downy. They were amazed at its size, but extremely pleased to find their land was adjacent to that James had purchased a year previously. Though as each was an area of over forty acres, their houses would, still, be a distance apart.

As winter was coming it was imperative that they completed one large house in which to live when beset by snow and inclement weather. However this must eventually form part of the whole habitation. They decided that the house for James and Lilie should be he one planned and built for this purpose. All five men working together, were able to quickly build a three bedroom house with a kitchen and withdrawing room, in wood from the trees which grew in abundance on their property.

They complete this before winter set in. In fact they had time to build a similar house on David and Stuart's estate, which would be the one Stuart and Antoinette were to live in, doing this before the bad weather came. However they made James house as their centre. In fact only a few times did the weather prevent them working outside. And they completed the third house for Paul and Helga, only a short distance away from James' house before the second week of December.

They had decided, before they left to come to Kentucky, to return to their wives and enjoy, together, both Christmas and New Year. The third house completed, they closed up and made their way through the snow to the families. Riding on horse back, they found it was a far easier journey than the one they had endured with two wagons the previous winter. Of course they all received a rapturous reception, hardly surprising, for except for Monica all the other four wives were either six and a half or seven months pregnant by their husbands.

This had been a combined decision by all their wives, even before their wedding day. They all knew it would probably be a year before they could set up their new homes on their land in Kentucky. None of them, as yet wished to risk a delivery of their baby in what was still a wilderness, though there might be medical attention in the neighbourhood. Their women, desperate to begin a family with the man they loved, sensibly considered they should deliver their first child near to excellent medical facilities. This then was the reason why they had done their best to conceive as soon as possible after they married.

James and Paul had admitted that they were surprised that Lilie and Helga had wanted another pregnancy so soon. In fact their two wives had laughed, both saying, that, whilst they appreciated the fact that their daughters by the indian had been adopted by their husband and bore their surname, they considered it their duty to bear a child of their own as soon as possible.

Of course Antoinette had wanted her baby to replace the one she had needed to abort, and had for some months wanted to conceive David's child. She had told David she would not be protected on the bridal night.   In the case of Pohanna, it was what she would have expected to do if, on her father's orders, she had married and indian brave. It seemed poor Stuart had no chance.

As soon as he had taken her to his family and she had, publicly proclaimed her wish to marry Stuart, she had then appraised him of the procedures which would have followed any indian marriage. Even though she knew she must marry him, like the others, in a church, she insisted he agreed to follow the strict ceremony which her tribe would expect of them, and this before the European wedding.

Instead of it occurring in a toupee, it happened, in private in Stuart's own room.. She came to him dressed in her indian clothes, stood before him and asked if she might undress him, which she did. Then she bent down, took hold of his penis, kissed it, in doing so signalling that she accepted his manhood, and gave him the right to use it on her, so she could conceive his child. Then she stood up and then bowed to him, asking if he would now remove all her clothes. This he did. She had warned him what must follow, and obtained his promise he would do so.

As soon as Stuart removed the three pieces of clothing she wore and stood naked as he was, he had to place his hand on her pudenda, thrust his fingers inside her vagina, and prove she was still a virgin. – Of course this was impossible as she had been raped by the soldiers at the camp. Because of this poor Stuart had to learn six indian words, and now recite. She told him that this meant that, although he had discovered she was not a virgin, he still wished to make her his wife. The final part of the indian wedding was one which, at first, he had told her he must refuse. However, though she told him how much she wanted to marry him, she could not do so, in church, unless he completed the ceremony.

Though it was against his beliefs, he must now take hold of her naked body, lie on the floor and proceed to have full intercourse with her, knowing by doing so he might be making her conceive. However realising this meant so much to her, he did his best to make her happy. After that, two weeks later, Pohanna accepted the normal wedding and left the church as Mrs. Pohanna Downy, as it seemed, already the mother of his child, and a very happy woman.

So all five men where able to resume and enjoy intimacy with their wives, with only Monica using preventatives. The entire enlarged family enjoyed a very happy Christmas and New Year, before the men returned to Kentucky again to finish and build the other two houses. As the weather improved they were able to complete their tasks and now had sufficient time to visit nearby Winchester, really for the first time, though they had visited, from time to time, simply for provisions.

They found it was a rapidly growing community. Already their were many settlers occupying the surrounding lands, though only a few appeared to be involved in horse rearing, the majority had established themselves as arable farmers. Already Winchester was becoming a town, with its saloons, banks, estate agents, and stores, of every kind. Soon it would grow, even larger, as new settlers came to settle on the large, if somewhat expensive land.

Naturally the five men enjoyed what the saloons had to offer them. However , although they flirted with the salon women, they refused their offers of intimacy, though, to avoid dislike, paid them the usual fee for their services, which was much appreciated. Here they learned about the growing town of Paris to the north of Winchester. It seemed this had been, mainly, settled by Whisky drovers from Pennsylvania, driven out from the home made distilleries, during the Whiskey War of 1794, when the government had imposed an impossible tax, causing a savage uprising.

Although the army had won the day, and though afterward the impossible tax had been removed, many people had been killed including the soldiers. Now several had become fugitives and fled from Pennsylvania, escaping to Kentucky and begun to set up illicit stills around this town of Paris.

For so long American whiskey, corn liquor, due to s shortage of rye, it had needed to find substitutes. It could, in no way rival Scotch Whiskey, losing the smoky flavour as it was fermented on peat fires. Further more it had a very high alcohol content, which made it seem like 'fire water', enjoyed by many hardworking men, but not the drink of men liking a more civilized way of life. Still Paris was providing adequate supplies of American whiskey. It seemed that a local scientist, Dr. James Crow, was experimenting in blending various things such as wheat, rye and malt barley.

Unfortunately he was a very impoverished man. The locals in Winchester told them if only Dr. Crow could receive financial assistance he might well produce a whiskey, different, but just as desirable as genuine Scotch Whiskey., but there were few people in this new state of Kentucky with sufficient means to help the doctor in his work.

The five houses complete, their work done, the five men returned as quickly as possible in February to try to be present when their wives delivered their babies.. Fortunately they all arrived in time. The first to go into labour was eighteen year old Mrs. Pohanna Downey, watched by a terrified Stuart. However he marvelled at the strength of his young wife, who, although in pain uttered no squeals. She told him later that no indian woman would have dared to show any weakness in front of her husband, who later would have severely punished her. To both their joy she bore him a seven pound daughter, Stuart named Pearl, who seemed to have the same beauty as her mother.

Antoinette then bore Stuart Brady an eight pound son, they called Trevor, whilst the next day Lilie bore James a son, they christened Leslie. Finally, a week later, Helga presented Paul with a seven pound daughter, they called Hester. So now all five couples who had married the year before now had begun a family, and there was no doubt that this would be added to and expanded, in the future, particularly if their plans to establish a fortune in horse breeding, on the new estate in Kentucky was successful..

Their wives were pleased when their husbands could tell them that two doctors had, already, established a clinic in Winchester. So it seemed any future births would have the attention of a qualified medical practitioner. There were no reason, now, to delay them all travelling to Kentucky. Before Easter all five families had selected good breeding horses to become the basis for their future herds, knowing that it necessary more could be obtained in the future. Slowly, there was no need for haste, they all drove their flock across the mountains then down onto the Kentucky plain and eventually on to their lands near Winchester. Now each family with a house of their own, but knowing that their two estates, though separate, would, really be one large horse breeding and rearing establishment. They were ready to begin their new lives. They decided to call the entire ranch 'Camargo'

3

Roy Marshall and Fay Bradbury, Hugh and Linda Foyle had driven in one of Jenson Carroll's coaches, accompanying Jenson and Mechia to his father's large estate near Berkeley. His father was an exceedingly rich man. Besides his own large fortune, his marriage over thirty years before to Anna Van Buren, had included an enormous dowry from the Dutch Van Buren families. It had been a loving marriage of two persons so strongly attracted to each other. It had been sufficient for Edgar Carroll, brought up a staunch Roman Catholic, to risk disinheritance from his father by becoming a protestant and marrying in the Dutch Reform Church in New York. Anna had born him seven children Now in their sixties, they were still as strongly in love, as when they married

Their guests were each allocated a suite of rooms, with Negro servants to attend them, and made very welcome. However dinners had been arranged to entertain them and where they met several other important and rich families, mainly of Dutch extraction who had come to settle near Berkeley in the middle of the last war, to escape from New York when it was occupied by British soldiers, for as Dutch, they had, always disliked the British. After all, they had settled New York as New Amsterdam which was invaded over a century before by the British and renamed New York. It was natural that they supported the American cause.

There were two main families, the Van Rensselaer and the Wycks, though their families had intermarried and married other rich persons in the vicinity. So the three families had now proliferated with many children, many married and living in several mansions on the various estates. It was essentially a Dutch community in the Potomac valley. Several of the children were in the same age range as their English guests. Once again providing an opportunity for all four of them to meet and begin light flirtations.

Having seen Hugh Foyle's reaction when Electra Carroll and Ellia Dumas had visited Jansen and Mechia in Philadelphia it was hardly surprising that Hugh, once again tried to interest them in a little flirtation. However they were surprised that Electra did not seem keen to want to develop his friendship. In fact Fay could hardly fail to see that Electra showed far greater interest in Roy than Hugh, yet to her surprise it seemed that a man, three years her senior, who introduced himself as Karl Wycks, appeared to try to monopolise her attention. It was a new experience for Fay. In fact she had to admit to herself that her entire knowledge of men were her dead lover, Trevor, Roy and to a smaller extent, Hugh Foyle. In fact poor Fay felt at a loss as how to respond, though his attention flattered her.

So unsure of her own reactions Fay had adopted a more informal response. Though this had surprised Karl, so used to his girl friends more intimate approach. If anything her attitude intrigued Karl. He was not sure if she was rejecting him, yet she was smiling at him and still wished to engage him in conversation. As he knew she had come that night with a man introduced to him as Roy Marshall, yet was obviously not his wife, there did seem to be a close affinity between them. Perhaps she was his mistress. If so he could not fail to see her man was being opportuned by Electra Carroll, and that he was responding and already flirting with her. The situation was one he had not encountered in the past and he decided he would try to develop it, to his advantage. Poor Fay, still confused, decided she might as well see if his attention could lead to a more interesting relationship for herself.

If Hugh was disappointed at Electra's response to his advances, he was quickly recompensed by the equally intimate response from Ellia Dumas, who in a few minutes reminded him of their enjoyable relationship a few months earlier. It seemed to Hugh that, though he had missed any chance of advancing his relationship with Electra, Ellia Dumas might provided an equally interesting time together. He made sure he let Ellia know he was pleased at renew their acquaintance. Meantime his sister Linda was doing her best to make progress with Edwin Carroll who she had enjoyed his attention in Philadelphia. So all four of them were quickly introduced to a much more informal and perhaps more intimate relationship.

Although these occasions portended very enjoyable sessions in future, as they stayed at Berkeley, both Roy and Hugh were questioned by Jenson's father, of their new cotton mill and of a possible profitable future. They knew, that Edgar Carroll had invested heavily in his son's idea, to the extent of fifty per cent of its cost, so naturally he wanted to know if his investment would have been worth while. Roy took considerable trouble in explaining what had, already, been achieved. Roy even told him that in only two more years it would make Edgar, as well as himself, since he was now a partner, very rich.

Roy explained, "It won't be long before we shall have to decided whether to extend the factory or start a new and bigger one on another site. – We must do this before anyone else realises its potential and sets up in opposition to us. – I have seen, and suffered, from its success in Manchester. Soon, except for specialised work, hand-looming will be obliterated. The ever growing population of this country, will ensure great demands are made on cotton for clothing, increasing demand – and increasing our profitability."

Like his son, Edgar was quick to realise the ability of Roy Marshall. He was far more essential than Hugh Foyle. Only the fact that Hugh owned the copyright of his 'flying shuttle' made it necessary to include him. Still Jensen told his father that Hugh, though taking orders, had helped Roy very much in setting up the mill and making it work. Completely satisfied Edgar had told his son he would be happy to invest further if they decided to expand.

However it was whilst they were enjoying their stay in the household that Francois and Charlotte Le Raye came with Aleia Dumas to be introduced to Edgar Carroll to see if he or one of his Dutch friends might consider investing in one of the three projects they hoped they could develop. The result of their visit to Fort Pitt and the countryside around. As they admitted these were engineering matters, Edgar asked Roy Marshall to join him, having proved his engineering capabilities Edgar thought he might understand what they were proposing better than himself.

Francois began by telling them of his discovery of what must be large deposits of both coal and iron ore, around the Fort Pitt area, which showed its potential as a possible site for iron and steel manufacture. Francois was gratified in receiving Roy Marshal's approval, when he explained to Edgar Carroll the shortage of raw steel in the country, which had delayed his buying of the machinery for the mill. However he added that to start steel production would be a very costly investment, and it would be a few years before it could show a profit.

Francois had agreed but added that the collection of the coal would be much easier as, to begin with, it would not be necessary to mine it and it could be obtained by open cast, digging in the ground. This could be obtained and easily transported to the industrial areas of New England and Pennsylvania for cheap fuel. The mining of iron or could come later.

Now Francois explained the necessity of building a metalled road like the Cumberland Road, from Fort Pitt to the west, describing the hopeless facilities which at present existed, yet was the only ones available for the multitudes travelling west to Ohio, Indiana and beyond. Francois admitted that besides private investment the majority investment would have to come from the government. He hoped that the rich business men of this area would lobby government, to act on this as soon as possible.

Now he had smiled and told them his chief reason for approaching them. Since road communications to the west were negligible, families were risking their lives on wooden rafts to sail on the rivers as small boats were not available or ridiculously expensive. Francois swore a quick investment in Small Boat Building facilities, of which his father had trained him, would provide a very quick profit, as with wood available, they could be constructed and sold, at a fair and reasonable price.

In the end Edgar promised to consider his proposals and speak to other families about investing, but admitted at once, that the boat build enterprise interested him. It was then that Roy suggested he might be able to help Francois set up a small factory for this. "You will produce the boats more quickly, and with less labour, if your factory use steam power for cutting and shaping the local wood, cutting the cost." He offered to show Francois how this could be done. When he left, Francois considered his visit had been worthwhile. More so, when he explained this to Charlotte, she told him they must cultivate this man Roy Marshall. He had, already, demonstrated his ability and engineering capabilities in setting up this Cotton Mill and using Steam power, something about which they admitted they knew very little. Francois could hardly fail to notice that Charlotte volunteered to approach this man, to see how he might help them. It made Francois smile to himself.

However for Roy and Fay, Hugh an Linda, this visit to Berkeley was essentially a holiday, a gift from Jensen. The were delighted with the progress they had made so soon, in meeting so many other men and women of their own ages, who it seemed were used to idolatry lives, and to spend their lives in pleasant and intimate activities.

4

Fay and Roy were lying together, naked, in bed, in their luxurious suite allocated to them when they arrived. A little tired after the pleasures they had both enjoyed in the intimate use of their bodies. Now content to just stroke each others bodies and a times give each other a light kiss. At last they had a chance to talk, after so many very hectic days of enjoyment.

Roy began the conversation, "It seems that we both appear to have attracted the attention of several of the opposite sex. I admit, I was surprised to find the open way, Electra opportuned me. At Philadelphia, I thought she had shown a great interest in Hugh. Here she has completely ignored him and made a bee line for me. I must say I feel flattered with the attention of a very beautiful twenty year old girl.".

Then he laughed, "It seems I may have made another conquest in Charlotte le Raye, the French girl. I'm not a fool, although she told me she came to enlist my help in the project to build small boats near Fort Pitt, I felt she was willing to use her feminine wiles to ensure I helped them, to connect the Steam engines to give them motive power for their machinery. – In fact I must say how fascinated I am at the knowledge of that young woman. Her proficiency in mathematics, quite exceeds my own. - She proudly told me she had helped her father to design bridges, ensuring the forces in the members would not cause failures. – Fay – I must say, I feel pleased of the interest this, obviously intelligent girl, takes in me, it is refreshing as to the idle rich attention of Miss Electra Carroll. – It might prove interesting."

He kissed Fay, "Now tell me, I saw the great interest Karl Wycks showed in you. I thought he seemed very anxious to possess you. What is your opinion of him?"

Fay turned away, then turned to him again. "Roy, I don't know. I feel afraid. Really I do not know what to do – You know only too well, I'm not very equipped to understand how a girl should react to a man's advances. – With Trevor – we just grew together over the years – that's how it became intimate – and my downfall. – Because of your kindness, it took months before I could submit myself to you – and Roy, I want you to know, whatever happens in the future, I've wanted it and enjoyed every moment with you – just like this evening. – But how should I respond to Karl."

Roy understood but wanted to help, "Treat him as you treated me. Don't be over anxious to go to bed with him – but you still must learn how to keep him interested. It may only be a flirtation, but I do believe he is interested in you - perhaps even more, since you have done little to respond to him. – In fact this may have intrigued him, as it seems he will have very easy conquests with the aristocratic women around Berkeley."

Poor Fay shook her head, "I do not know what my feelings are for him. It pleases me that a man has shown interest in me – again – like you, I believe he thinks I would be an easy conquest. – Roy – Do you think me evil – I think I would like to become intimate with him. – Yes – I suppose, as a woman, I'm looking to find a man to live with and start a family – but I know this may be impossible – especially having baby Terry for a man to see to. Would any man consider me as a partner after he knew about Terry?"

Now Roy held her close and kissed her lips firmly, "Fay, dear take things slowly, let your affairs develop – don't rush them – you have no need to think you have to find a husband or a father for your babies, very quickly. – Together we have learned to enjoy each other – only possible because of the means we found of avoiding pregnancy. – I believe you must sample again, others, in the same way, but – play hard to get – then let them believe he has seduced you. – Don't think of him as a permanent partner."

He now pressed his hands on her pudenda, which pleased her, behaving as if he was her husband, saying, "You're only twenty one and already have a fine son, to be proud of. You don't need more – not just yet. - Fay – I may not love you – but after the months of happiness you have given me, you need never fear for your future, nor for Terry. – I know soon I will become rich – Even more so than that man, Grimshaw – I've promised you a share of my partnership with Jenson. It is yours by right – for months you have been my wife, if not in name."

Now he held her close again and gave her a passionate kiss. "Even if you do not find a suitable partner, I promise, even if I marry, I shall see to both you and Terry's future. – So, please 'play the field' – See just how far, how interested Karl is of you. He wants to use you, as no doubt he has used other women here. – well use him – Only yield to him when you feel he can give you pleasure. Ironically he may feel more strongly about you because you do this. Play with him but do not completely frustrate him – or you will lose him."

Fay returned Roy's kiss and thanked him. Then said, "Even if we go our separate ways in the future – I still hope we shall still have many more wonderful times as we had last night." However Fay felt more relieved. She would take his advice and no longer felt an unsure girl, even if not an innocent one..

Roy was right, having failed to make progress at after the dinners, Karl Wycks came calling on Fay and offered to take her into the beautiful countryside and show her the historical sites which she gladly accepted. However it did not take long before, as they picnicked by the river, Karl began to take liberties placing his arms around Fay, whilst his hand rested on her covered breast, even giving it a gentle squeeze.

Now more sure of herself after the confidence Roy had imbued in her. She quickly divested herself of his embrace saying, "It seems you consider me a woman of low esteem. You may be able to quickly win the favours of many idle women who seem to live here. I assure you, I am very particular as to sensual approaches of any man. You would have to prove yourself to be a man I might desire for those purposes before I would let you take liberties with me."

Fay wondered if Karl had ever received such a rebuff before. He spluttered, "I'm sorry, I thought you would appreciate my attentions. You see I know you live with Roy Marshall but are not married to him and that you have a young baby son. I believed you would enjoy a little liaison with me."

Now she showed anger. "It seems you do believe I am a woman of low repute – one you could manipulate. I think you must take me home, immediately. – Yes I live with Roy, and we satisfy our mutual pleasures, but I am not a whore, but a woman who is sure of herself and thinks carefully before she bestows her favours on any man – Certainly not on one who she has only met twice." Karl had no option and took her home. Fay feared he would not attend on her again.

However she was wrong. The next day she received an enormous bouquet of flowers with a note. "Dearest Fay. I apologise for my behaviour yesterday, it was inexcusable. – I assure you I did not consider you to be a woman with whom I might take liberties. However, having failed to attract your attention when we talked after dinner, I was trying, in my way, and the way we act here in Berkeley, to show that I was extremely attracted to you.- I would consider you were a very generous woman, if you could excuse my appalling behaviour and let me call on you again, promising their would be no repetition of my previous conduct – Your obedient servant, Karl Wycks."

Fay was amused and when she showed the note to Roy explaining what had happened, he complimented her and told her it was now safe, if not imperative to accept his apologies and let their affair develop more slowly, which she did, even enjoying, now his solicitations to her, accepting some passionate kisses. Within a few days of courtship, Fay now let it become a little more intimate, which pleased both of them.

Meantime Hugh, now realising he had no future with Electra, had readily acquiesced to Ellia readily offered charms. Especially when Ellia could not resist asking Hugh what was his true relationship with his sister, Linda. The question amused Hugh. He had no intention of compromising his sister's honour. He very sternly told her the untruth that Linda was his sister, and they merely shared the house together. To Hugh's delight this answer seemed to please Ellia, who allowed him, now, far more intimate pleasures. She even took him to meet her mother, Aleia, and her father Jean Dumas, both of whom made him very welcome. There was no doubt but that Hugh wanted this affair to develop much further, even after he returned to Philadelphia.

Similarly, his sister, Linda, had resumed her friendship with Edwin Carroll begun in Philadelphia, but was disappointed that he seemed loath to take liberties with her, which was what she had hoped for, though he was very attentive and called on her frequently. Still Linda had hopes that with time, an affair might develop.

Now Roy had the happy problem of satisfying the attentions of two quite beautiful woman, twenty year old Electra Carroll, and twenty two year old Charlotte Le Raye. Also he realised they both knew they were each contenders for his attention. Roy was never a cruel man and did not want to bring sadness to either of them, so he appeared to give equal attention to both of them, trying hard not to raise jealousy between them. Somehow he managed to keep this assertions apart, spending almost equal time with each woman. They were both direct, knowing that he lived with Fay Bradbury. He saw no sense in lying. They could easily discover from Jensen or Hugh the truth. So he was frank telling them he and Fay enjoyed a happy intimate life together, though at the moment, neither wished to marry and make it a permanent arrangement. It seemed this did nothing to detract from their interest in him.

Electra had told him, she was intrigued with his English accent, so different from the other Englishmen she knew. He replied but telling them, every part of Britain spoke with a different dialect. This was different from the south and even more different from how it was spoken in Scotland. In return he told her he considered she betrayed a German accent in her speech. Electra now willingly allowed more intimate relations with Roy, telling him she approved of his life with Fay, which was, now, quite common in America.

At the same time Roy told Charlotte that there was no mistaking her French upbringing. She had smiled, and replied, that this was why she could see nothing wrong in his relationship with Fay. Being brought up at the French court, intercourse was very common between an unmarried man and a woman. Roy was bold enough to ask her if she lived intimately with Francois.

She had smiled, "I have lived with Francois since we were little. Frequently we have seen each other naked. Once or twice we have occupied the same bed, yet I assure you neither of us have had any intimacy, nor want it, though I love Francois, with my life, but it is merely as brother and sister."

Roy, actually found he enjoyed his liaison with Charlotte more than with Electra, though each offered him complete sexual relief, as they knew how to protect each other, and had long since lost their virginity. Charlotte was such an intelligent woman. He knew he wanted both these relationships to continue, perhaps even, eventually becoming more permanent. However Roy knew he would enjoy renewing his association with Charlotte when he kept his promise to her to help with assembling the steam power. Meantime he enjoyed some very intimate and satisfying interludes with both of them.

Perhaps the most gratifying result of their visit was when Jenson's father, Edgar, wanted him to come and speak at length with him. Firstly Edgar told him that he still felt very strongly devoted to Britain. His father had allied himself with Britain during the war and had to pay a heavy penalty afterwards. He admitted it was only his over powering love for his wife, and her dislike of the Dutch treatment in New York which had made him a rebel.

Now Edgar thanked Roy personally for helping to ensure his son's mill became operative and would be profitable. "Roy, I'm so pleased that Jensen has made you a partner. I can see Jenson would never have succeeded without your help. Jenson, was and is very headstrong. He wanted to be as financially successful as I have been, but on his own. I loaned him the money but feared it would fail. – Now I know it would have done but for the fact you came from England to help."

He now put his hand on Roy's shoulder. "Jensen tells me you and Fay live together as if wed but are not married, nor, at present intend to do so. I think I'm a little sorry, for I think I like Fay very much, and she is good for you. – However, I would be blind if I failed to see the way my daughter, Electra, throws herself at you. I can tell you, I admire you so much, that if your relationship became a partnership or even a marriage. It would have my full approval – and I would ensure you had the means to both live an good life.- All I ask, is that you continue to help my son, as you have, so readily done for so long."

Roy told Fay everything Edgar had said, and admitted he was very moved by his trust in him. Fay had smiled, "And so now, you know the offer of this easy life with Electra, do you wish to relinquish our own partnership."

Roy replied by taking Fay in his arms and kissing her passionately. "No my dear, certainly not. I admit having these intimate affairs with both

Electra and Charlotte. Yet, I can't say, I would want to take either of them, at the moment, as my wife. – Yes! Now I know marriage to Electra would be financially advantageous, but I wonder what a life with Electra would be like. – She is so shallow, and admits she gives her favours freely for her pleasure. "

He surprised Fay be kissing her again. "I really feel far more at home with Charlotte. She is so intelligent, she makes me feel insecure. I admit I will enjoy spending time with her at Fort Pitt over the Steam engine. " Now he hugged Fay to him, "However my dear, dear Fay. If you can forgive me for taking other women into my bed, I mean it when I say, I would hope you would forgive me enough to let me still continue to sleep with you. – Oh! How I wish I could fall in love with you – However you should know, neither have I, as yet, fallen in love with either Electra or Charlotte. Darling is there a chance."

A few moment ago Fay felt she had lost Roy. She understood, like him she could not feel she really loved him. However she knew she would miss the wonderful hours of intimacy she had enjoyed with him. Now he had asked her to continue. She responded equally to his embrace burying her lips even more firmly in his, "Oh! Yes! Please. Dear Roy. I want that as much as you."

So after almost a month Fay and Roy, Linda and Hugh returned with Jenson and Mechia to Philadelphia to ensure that their cotton mill became even more profitable, as this was essential for any life they might chose in the future, and with any of the women they had enjoyed at Berkeley. The holiday was over.

5

When Anna and Andrew Reeves returned to their home near Fort Pitt, they had a very busy time preparing for the beginning of the new term at the school. However they were very pleased with the large influx of children wanting to receive basic education. It seemed that neither of the two of them need fear any real shortage of money. Though they had to spend so much time in the schoolroom, they now had three Negro slaves to assist them in everyway, even preparing and cooking their meals.

However as soon as the immediate chaos had been quelled, they were anxious to visit Kylie and Adrian Scott, to tell them of how they had learned about Neil. They were still teaching two of their children. In fact their son, Clive, now fourteen years of age was very intelligent. They felt he would benefit by a short finishing course in the Upper school in Annapolis and might even obtain entry to University.

At last in October Anna and Andrew found time at the weekend to call on the Scott's, pleased to find both Erin and Craig Reid and Mary and Brian Hobbs had, also, come to visit them. Again they had six of their two families children attending their school, so they had met them several times in the past.

They at once informed everyone the success of their visit to Racoonsville during the summer. It was Andrew who explained. "Adrian and Kylie we now understand your reticence in telling us all about my uncle. You obviously disapproved of Neil's behaviour when he left Claire, after she miscarried his child and went to live with Sophia Brookes. Perhaps you are right because of the way he treated Claire, but to be fair he had told her, before they left England, he would never marry her."

He smiled, "We had very long talks with Sophia, who is now married again to a Colin Chalmers. It does seem that Neil did fall completely in love with Sophia, and she admits it was not for her money, also, that she had never loved him. She confessed, she used him as she could not face life after

Keith, the husband she loved, who died suddenly at an early age. She is still not proud of what she did, even punishing herself for it. However, now I know all about Claire, I accept Neil, also disseveред some punishment."

Now Anna intervened, "I now understand why you felt you could not tell us all about Neil. I believe you were very fair. Although you deplored the way he left Claire you had no wish to speak ill of him when he could not defend himself – Adrian and Kylie, we know, now, we would like to know more about Claire. We know she was a prostitute when Neil found her and brought her here, yet eventually if seems she has found happiness with another man. Please tell us about her."

Now it was Erin, Mary and Kylie who explained. "We all came to love Claire, she was such a courageous woman." Erin said, "You may not know but both Mary and I were indentured servants to a very cruel man at the fort. Even then when we met Claire in his shop she stood up for us, even more so when Craig and Brian purchased us as their servants. – Yes! We lived with them – and they used us – for some years before we all fell in love and have now enjoyed so many happy years of marriage. All the time Claire helped us."

Kylie now said, "You must judge for yourself. We will arrange a visit and take you to see Claire, she lives on an estate between Fort Necessity and Fort Cumberland with her very rich husband Philip Wycks. She is not ashamed of her past. She will tell you everything. How Michael Casimir took pity on her, gave her a home and how she came to meet Philip who, after his first wife died in childbirth, fell in love and married her. We will arrange it for next weekend."

So one week later Adrian and Kylie took Anna and Andrew to the Wycks estate. They were introduced to both Philip and Claire, both about forty five years of age. It was obvious that Claire was probably five or six months pregnant. She proudly told them this was her fifth child by Philip, adding with a smile, "It was necessary. I was thirty three years of age when I married Philip. I only had born Amanda who was then already fourteen years of age. Come, please sit down, I want to tell you everything about me. Philip knew this before he proposed to me. He hopes you will excuse him, as he has several tasks to perform. He, also, feels it will help me to confess better, if he is not here."

After she ordered drinks and Philip left, Claire, as promised told them, in detail the whole of her life story. The misuse and abandonment of her money Sarah, but Joseph Parry, who was, also, responsible for the fate of another women Ruth Tencin, who they had heard of but never met. Her mother's prostitution, and then her own from the age of fourteen. The reason for Amanda, conceived in the brothel, her meeting with Neil and him bringing her to America. Their difficulties on the forested land with Adrian and Kylie.

Now a few tears came into her eyes, "I never know if I loved Neil. I was grateful for taking me out of that hell. I know, even if he had never married me, I would have lived with him as a wife, - yes! – and bore him children – for I wanted them – I needed them. However it seemed he could never feel any love and bonding with me. Of course it hurt me when he went away with Sophia, - yes, I missed his intimacies with me - yet I had to admit, I had no right to demand any more from him."

Now she smiled and dried her tears. "A miracle happened. Accidentally meeting Michael Casimir in a store at Fort Pitt, without knowing it then, I became his ward. Years later he told me he saw in me the reincarnation of his first love, his girl friend in Poland, Carla, who committed suicide when Michael having proposed to her but was forbidden to marry her by his parents. – It is just possible that he is right – It seemed I was born almost at the same time as his Carla, killed herself. "

Smiling even more, "Well after Neil left me, Michael insisted I came to live with him and his wife, Ulrika. He gave me a dowry for when I married. Well it is another amazing story for I was to meet dear Philip, who had just lost his wife in childbirth and had to leave New York, as British soldiers entered it. How we came to fall in love is equally amazing. Yet, he is such a wonderful a man, and has given me over fifteen years of heaven, yet still wanted to marry when I told him, completely, of my past. – So you can see what a fortunate woman I am. – I cannot blame Neil, for I would never have met Philip, if had not taken me from that brothel."

Anna and Andrew, thanked her profusely for her tale. It was Anna who replied for the two of them. "Dear Claire, as a woman I can understand what you had to endure. You are truly a courageous woman to withstand those years in the brothel, then your life with Neil, who you gave pleasure, yet he could never return your love for him. – You see having now heard everything about you from Adrian, Kylie, - yes, even from Sophia. – I believe you did love Neil, but never dare admit it to yourself. Misused for so long – you did not know what love was. – I cannot tell you the truth about Andrew and me. It is our secret. Yet, for a few months, whilst pregnant it seemed that Andrew would be executed, I would be sent to a convent for life and my baby taken from me. – So I can understand a little of what you had to suffer."

There was no doubt but that Claire was first pleased to learn of Anna's remarks about her past, but then startled by her later admission. She saw almost fear in Anna's face. Claire could not help herself,. she arose came down and sat besides Anna on the couch. Placed her arms around her. "Those few words tells me that in the past both you and Andrew's life were in real danger. I miscarried a baby, so know what it is like to lose something precious. – It seemed for some reason, some people had the power to tear both you and Andrew apart. I will not press you more. However some day, I hope you can tell me your secrets as I have told you mine."

Soon afterward Philip returned and a beautiful late lunch was served. As they all sat together afterwards, enjoying after meal drinks. Andrew felt he must say. "We are grateful for what Claire has today us today. Neil Reeves was my uncle, but I believe he did deserve his own untimely end. It was right that he should suffer for the suffering he had caused Claire. – May I add, that though she feels you are such a wonderful man to accept her after her past. – Actually, Anna agrees with me, I believe you too, are a very fortunate man."

Philip smiled and took hold of Claire's hands, "I know that only too well. She may not have told you, but, long before I proposed to her, she did, save my life, for but for her persuasion, I believed I had killed my first wife, and was contemplating suicide. She used herself to convince me I was wrong. – I too agree with you that your uncle did not treat Claire, as he should have done. – Yet, but for that, I would not have had the last fifteen years of happiness with her."

They had asked both Anna and Andrew of their present circumstances. They quickly realised how hard they must work to make their school successful. Again in reply they inferred that this was much more preferable to the alternative which awaited them, if they had not come to America. Remembering Anna's earlier confession that day, Claire offered, "It seems your secret made it necessary for you to leave your homes and come here. Perhaps someday you may feel free to tell me about this. Now you have a hard life whilst I enjoy both security and comfort."

She now turned to her husband. "Philip, if only because Andrew is Neil's nephew. Since he blames his uncle more than me. I feel I owe Andrew a little for not condemning me, would you agree Philip, that should circumstances in he future demand it, we would be very willing to help them, were it necessary." Her husband readily agreed. "Feel no shame. If you need help, please call on both of us. I would gladly help you, for if Neil; had not brought Claire here, I could never have met her – yes and might now be dead."

They left that afternoon a very happy couple and thanked Adrian and Kylie for making it possible. They both hoped they might never need to call on Claire and Philip for help, but it was reassuring that help was available if necessary.

Andrew did take Anna to task for so dangerously exposing their secret. However she said she could not suppress it, as she felt so overcome with Claire's confessions, which had alerted her own mind to her dangers in the past. However both Anna and Andrew felt they had far more to fear from, discovery by the family from Spanish Florida, who they had been told were Austrians and not Spanish, who had bought that small heavily wooded strip of land, near theirs, and had come to live on the Casimir/Holstein estate, whilst a large mansion was being erected on their land. It seemed they intended to come and live there for some time.

Anna was convinced, in spite of what Andrew said, that she had seen the Austrian woman at the court in Vienna. She felt sure the woman had recognised her the only time she had called on them. However foolish it might be, they realised they must be extremely careful, less this family were to inform the authorities in Austria of their own existence.

6

The Albrecht's now happily settled on the heavily wooded estate but living comfortably in the new and extensive Mansions specially built for them, had now felt assured of a settled future. So Anton was happy to give Louisa her wish and in the middle of 1796, Louisa conceived again by Anton. Knowing they were now extremely rich they wished to invest their wealth in further projects than just "Equine development". In fact Anton knew it was imperative that his money must multiply by making suitable investments. However, grateful for the security this new country had given them, both Anton and Louisa would like to reward it by investing in its future.

They had approached the Casimir's again, for this purpose. As both Michael and William's second eldest sons had married into the rich Dutch families in the Potomac, Olaf Casimir had married Juliana Wicks, the daughter of Charles and Elizabeth Wicks and sister of Philip. Also Stephen Holstein had married Jeanne Van Rensselaer, daughter of Albert and Wilhelmina Van Rensselaer, along with their financial interests in the Bank of Manhattan. So they took them to meet these rich Dutch Platoons with the idea of forming joint investment companies, to support the future development of the newly acquired lands to the west.

They arrived at an opportune time, for they found the equally rich Edgar Carroll had recently approached the same families with his idea of investing in the Le Raye's proposals of mining outcrop coal deposits near Fort Pitt, but even more in establishing a small boat building enterprise there for families of settlers travelling west, who preferred to purchase a boat and risk the rigours of the river, rather than the hopelessly rotten road, at times completely impassable, as their means of communication.

Roy Marshall had convinced Edgar of both possibilities as a worthwhile investment and promised to help the Le Raye's with both projects, but particularly the introduction of steam power into the boat building factory. Edgar had made it clear to his son, Jenson, before he left, how very great importance, he considered Roy Marshall was, to his company, obtaining his promise to release Roy from obligations at the factory, for a time, so he could go and help the Le Raye's. He told Jenson before that, now partners, Roy should instruct both Jenson and Hugh sufficiently to enable the factory to work successfully during his absence.

It did not take long for the Casimir's, Holsteins, and the Albrecht's, as well as the Wycks and Van Rensselaer's that Edgar Carroll had found projects worth their investment. However they realised that these two projects would not be the only ones worth investing their money. Together they set up a new investment company named "Western Development" for this purpose. Though they realised the proposed building of a new metalled road from Fort Pitt or even from Fort Cumberland on the same basis as the existing Cumberland Road would become essential, financial returns from the road would be difficult to accrue.

However once built they realised the potential for investment in the new lands. It opened this for both farming and industrial development. It would be almost unlimited. Together they agreed to try to persuade Eric Casimir, Robert Carroll and Francois Tencin, to use their talents in trying to interest Congress, the President and the whole Government of the United States in building such a road. This could only be constructed by public investment. Everyone realised it would take some time and even the exertion of economic pressure from business men like them, for the government to invest in such an expensive road. Yet if the West was to be populated it must be done.

Now satisfied that they may soon have a number of projects, like the two now agreed, in which to invest their money and gain its rewards, Anton could spare the time to correspond more fully with his father in Austria, again suggesting his father might wish to invest in America more than in Europe. However he first asked his father to inform him of what happened after he and Louisa, had decided to flee first to Spain, and then Florida, asking exactly what had happened.

His father had told him of the scale of the scandal their disappearance had caused. It seemed his father was arrested and placed in jail in Vienna whilst he and other members of his and Louisa's family were questioned to ascertain if they had any complicity in helping them escape. Anton was now very pleased that he had purposely not made contact, nor allowed Louisa to do the same with any members of their families. How sensible this had been was proven when his father said, that after a considerable investigation, they could all prove their innocence.

By now, in spite of the war between Austria and France, the execution of Marie Antoinette and Britain entering the war, every method was used to try and trace their whereabouts. For the first time Anton learned that this intense searching and attempt to discover their whereabouts was not limited to their own escape. It seemed that, almost at the same time, a similar, if not more serious scandal had occurred. A Princes of Lorraine, Anna Alexandra had eloped with a commoner, her language and education English tutor, believing that Anna had conceived by this man. The shame was so great, that far greater efforts were made to discover their whereabouts, than even those of Anton and Louisa.

In the latter case they had eventually discovered they had escaped to England from Trieste. However when diplomatic pressure was placed on the British Government to find and return them, all investigations had proven negative. The only clue that they had reached England was when valuable jewellery belonging to the Court of Lorraine appeared in London for sale. It was traced, that this had originally been sold to jewellers in Bristol. This was as far as their search stretched.

In Anton and Louisa's case, over a year later it was discovered that they had first flown to Spain. It could not be proved but it was assumed that they had gone to stay with Anton's Spanish friends in Cartegena. However their was no evidence to prove this and of course these Spaniards had denied any knowledge of them, though they admitted their friendship to them. So once again the path was lost. It seemed both couples had managed to allude their searchers.

Although his father realised Anton must still be alive, somewhere in the world once money had been withdrawn from his account in Europe, which had enabled his father to invest far greater sums into his account, should he need it, wherever he was. Not until Anton had written to him telling him he and Louisa were now Citizens of the United States and lived in West Virginia, did either his father or anyone know where they were.

Since Anton had told his father to tell everyone where they were, he had gone to the Emperor. As Eric had told Anton, there were no extradition treaties between the United States and Austria. In any case the United States would never extradite any of its citizens to any country, the Emperor had no means of demanding their return. In fact Anton had been especially amused when his father wrote to tell him that the Emperor had said, in any case, he would never lower himself to correspond or speak to a commoner, who called himself the President of the United States, a man elected by people and not one chosen by god to rule. In any case the emperor blamed America for causing the trouble in France which led to them turning against their king. He believed the existence of the United States would be very brief.

So at last, both Anton and Louisa came to know what had happened after they made their escape from Austria, and were now assured that, unless they were foolish enough to land in Europe, the Austrian court could never bring them back for punishment. However both Anton and Louisa were intrigued at learning of the second scandal where evidently a pregnant Princess of

Loraine had eloped to England with a commoner, her English tutor, no doubt responsible for her condition. Yet since they could not be found in England, the two of them must have left to travel to another country.

They both mused at the possibility of places they might have flown to. With Britain at war with France and with Holland supporting France, followed by Spain, it was most unlikely that the two of them had gone to anywhere in Europe. This only left Canada or the United States. It was as, they were considering these places that Louisa suddenly placed her hand to her mouth and almost shouted at Anton.

"The Schoolteacher – You know the one we were introduced to over a year ago after our enforced landing at Annapolis. We were told she was an Austrian by birth, although her husband was British. When we returned I told you I thought I had seen her before at the court in Vienna. You told me I was foolish, but I said then, if not she had a very exact double."

Louisa took Anton's hands. "Anton the school is only a little distance from here. We must go an discover if we are right. An Austrian wife with a English husband and a baby almost the same age as ours. I do believe we have found the missing Princess of Lorraine. Let us go and accuse them."

Anton kissed her hands, "Louisa we must not accuse them. Remember if so they are in the same state and danger we were in before we met Eric and became American citizens. If they have not done the same as us, it is still possible Austria might be able to force them to return. Neither you nor I would want this. – Look – we have been fortunate to gain such wonderful American friends. Perhaps they cannot afford the cost of asking for citizenship – or even that they may not know it is possible. – Louisa – we are rich –many people have helped us to come and live here in peace. It is our duty to help them."

He smiled and kissed her hands again. "Let us go an visit them, telling them, we are inquiring about the possibility of placing Antonia in their school and ask them how soon they take young children. Let it seem to be an innocent inquiry. Only after we have won their confidence need we make any approaches as to their past life." Louisa smiled and agreed, "Yes! I must remember this poor woman would have had to face the same horrors which I faced, until you took me away and brought me to America. Her fate could have been mine. A convent for life, her baby taken and adopted and her lover executed. We must help this couple, if they are who we think."

7

Michelle lay naked in bed with Donald, both just awakening after a fully satisfying intimacy the previous evening. Pleased as Donald had once again commenced to stroke the parts of her body she liked to be massaged, almost hoping he might consider intercourse with her again. This is something which happened either, here, at Berkeley, or Racoonsville roughly every three to four months.

After all Michelle had lived with Donald Wilson, as his wife for ten years before she fell in love and married Daniel Carroll. Even after the marriage, it had been the custom for both Michelle and Kate to share their pregnancies by their husbands, simply, so they could safely indulge in swapping partners without either suffering an unwanted result. It had been Kate who had persuaded Donald to continue to enjoy Michelle's lovely body, after they married, being pleased to offer herself to Daniel in exchange.

Both Kate and Daniel had agreed to this, as it was evident that, married or not, Donald and Michelle could not forget their ten years of partnership. Very soon after they indulged in intimacy, on the ship coming to America, after Donald had rescued her from France, after the custom men had killed her lover, his brother Jack, and their baby daughter, before raping Michelle several times, so that she conceived. Since she had been intimate with Jack before the custom men came, she never knew if Sophia was Jack or the custom men's child, though Daniel insisted she was Jack's child.

Michelle and Donald never loved each other. Michelle felt Donald was not like his brother Jack, but each respected each other and, since they must live together, if only for security, they agreed to live as husband and wife, though Michelle tried not to conceive again. The agreement after each married had turned out to be an admirable arrangement, as both Daniel and Kate found they, too, could enjoy each others bodies. Now both women were too old to conceive so it was safe to swap more frequently.

Both Michelle and Donald knew that Daniel and Kate would probably be awakening after an exhausting, but enjoyable night together before, again, going to sleep. Actually Daniel had insisted on her coming to Berkeley for her arrangements for the recent two sets of marriages at Racoonsville, had exhausted Michelle, now sixty eight years of age. She need a rest and a holiday, and Donald was just the man to restore her normal desire to recover.

Michelle sighed as Donald's hands stroked and then squeezed her large, but still firm breasts, reviving those delicious feeling inside her, but listened carefully as he spoke, "You know Kate and I are delighted that that French woman, Jeanne Cristal, has come to live with Ruth Tencin. We told you that we had real fears about Henry, after his affair with Fredericka Carroll ended, so abruptly when she fell for Martin Der Donk. We feared he had taken it so badly he might injure or kill himself. You know they had been living together for over two years. He had taken to drink."

Michelle interrupted, " But why - Jeanne Cristal, Louis and Jean told me Jeanne is now so devoted to Ruth for adopting her, giving her a home and placing a dory in her name, that Jeanne has sworn to look after Ruth for the rest of her days. She loves her. It is not a duty, it is a labour of love. However they tell me she won't look at any man."

Donald smiled, "Yes, we thought that was the case. It still may be, but Jeanne has severely reproached Henry, in a way neither Kate nor I dare do. Telling him to stop drinking, and not make a fool of himself. – It all stated when Jeanne had taken the surrey out to obtain some goods early one morning. She found Henry sprawled across the road, unconscious, dead drunk. How she managed it I don't know, but she either picked him up, or more probably, aroused him sufficiently to get him into the surrey and took him home to Ruth. Together, as he had vomited, over his clothes and urinated in his trousers, they completely undressed him, cleaned him, then let him sleep it off."

Now Donald laughed, "It seemed Henry awoke in bed, as Jeanne brought some hot broth to him. Realising he was naked, he almost shouted at her, asking how dare she undress him and see him like that. – It seemed she shouted back at him, telling him not to be so stupid, as a servant in France, she had many times had to undress and bathe naked men, in the same state as he had been. – She then told him angrily, what a foolish man he was, and why did he behave that way. Well eventually she managed to get him to confess of his failed love for Fredericka, telling her he had no wish to go on living."

Still continuing, "It was her reaction which brought him to his senses. She told him it was so foolish for any man to behave like he did, simply because his girl friend had preferred another man. She told him in France, if that happened then he would take one of the serving girls, whether she desired it or not, to sublimate his desires."

"Of course Henry had reacted quickly, asking bluntly, if she might play that part and help him to overcome his sadness. – Surprisingly she did not seem to be disgusted. – She was truthful, her words were, 'In France as a serving girl, I had to submit in that way. So I'm not a virgin and men have known me. – Now however, due to Ruth Tencin's kindness, I no long need to do this. – Henry Wilson, You are a fool. I've seen your body, it is a strong masculine one. Many women would enjoy uniting with you but not me. Not after the state you were in last night. You are a disgusting and drunken stupor of a man.' – Michelle Henry was so amazed at what she had said, he remembered every word. When he came home he told both Kate and I exactly as I have told you."

Donald smiled again, "Well Henry became a changed man. No woman had ever dared to speak to him like that. He returned to Jeanne, fortunate to find Ruth was resting, so he was able to speak to her in private. First, he apologised for the last time asking her to submit to him, telling her he considered her more an angel, than anything else. Then he begged her to befriend him. He said he knew she had promised to look after Ruth, until she died. Henry told her he respected her for this, but then added, but if she would let him, he would like to make her own life more pleasant. He did not expect intimacy, but would like to establish a lasting and mutual friendship."

Michelle asked, "And did she agree?"

Donald replied, "That is the wonderful surprise. She did not rebut him. She even said she liked him but until he could prove he could change, give up drinking, become the man he should have been, born with privileges, ones she had never had, until now. Then, even more surprisingly, and certainly to Henry's amazement, after she had berated him for long, she told him to come to her each day, and prove he was sober. Then she took hold of his hands, kissed them, saying if he could prove himself to her, she would be pleased, even honoured, to become his friend – but at present, it was all she would offer him."

Donald concluded, "Well Henry is a changed man. Obediently he calls on Jeanne each day. Except for a glass of wine at dinner, he hardly ever drinks. It seems Jeanne feels he is behaving better. She now lets him take her around the countryside and even goes sailing with him on the Potomac. The only intimacy she allow him, is to hold his hands whenever possible and occasionally let him briefly kiss her. It seems Henry is quite content with this for the time being. There is no doubt but that now he is a happy man again. – This means a lot to Kate, for, of course she called Henry after the brother she adored but who was killed in England by the Press Gang, in the Inn in Bristol, where the two of them had just eaten."

Now both Donald and Michelle bathed together, as was their custom. After they had slept together, dressed and gone down to breakfast finding Daniel and Kate had proceeded them and were sitting enjoying their breakfast.

As they joined them Daniel asked Michelle if she had enjoyed her night, telling her how grateful he was to Kate, for being so kind to him, understanding the way he liked to act. Unabashed, she replied, that he must try to improve his times with her, for Donald had greatly surpassed him, in his love making last night. It was the type of bandier which normally occurred after these nights together.

It did give Michelle a chance to tell Kate that Donald had told her of the good news about Henry, which had been a worry the last time they had swapped partners. There was no doubt but that Kate was very pleased. That day Daniel was able to tell both Donald and Kate about his investment in "Equine Development", and how they set up five families on new estates in Kentucky, breeding horses, feeling sure that it would bring him good rewards in the future. He then learned of this other consortium of the families in Potomac, and the company they had created for similar projects in the developing west.

Daniel was a little disappointed as he thought Michael Casimir would have told him of this, as Robert was married to his daughter. He would call on Michael before he returned, to inquire exactly what had happened, and if he too could join this new consortium. Meantime it was a beautiful day and they went down to the river and enjoyed sailing in one of the many available boats. This truly was to be a holiday for Michelle, essential, as Daniel had feared she had exhausted herself. Daniel wanted to be certain she recovered her strength, for he knew he could not contemplate life without her.

Before they returned to Racoonsville Daniel decided he must speak to Michael about this new investment company, so he took Michelle with him and drove up the gap to Michael's estate, met and made very welcome by Ulrika, as Michael was away visiting north of Fort Necessity, but it seemed not visiting his own estate there.

Eventually, as they waited, he returned, and when Daniel tackled him on this new investment, he just smiled and replied, "I'm sorry, it all happened so quickly. Firstly you must blame Edgar Carroll, who approached us all, over two projects he wished to support near Fort Pitt, a coalmining and small boat building promotions."

Now he laughed and said, "However we have a new and quite rich family who have settled near my estate. They are Austrian, in fact the wife is a Austrian Princess, a member of the Hapsburg and her husband is a Prince of Savoy. They had their reasons for leaving Austria very quickly. They are fascinating people. I've just come from there, but I will take both of your to meet them tomorrow and Ulrika can come too."

8

Louisa and Anton decided they should confront the Reeve family as soon as possible, taking their three year old daughter, Antonia, with them they drove in the afternoon to the school house, whilst classes were in operation and waited until they ended. Then they were met first, by Andrew Reeve, and then his wife Anna, leading a three year son, by the hand. Louisa could hardly miss the startled look on Anna's face but said nothing.

Anton commented that their son seemed to be about the same age as their daughter, and explained they had come to discover how soon they would accept Antonia for tuition.. Andrew told them they would accept them very soon though most parents waited until their children were four years old. Now he offered them afternoon English Tea, telling them he was English and came from Bristol in England, but added that his wife, Anna, was Austrian, who he had met whilst teaching in Europe and married before coming to America.

Now as arranged Louisa intervened. "I'm so delighted to find, Mrs Reeves, you were born and come from Austria. You see both Anton and I are Austrian by birth. In fact we had to come to America, though we first settled in Florida, as the two of us caused a scandal. You see Anton, is a prince of Savoy, whilst I am a Hapsburg, born a Princess. However my family have always hated the families from Savoy. – Well Anton and I fell in love – it seems I was not very careful – I found I had conceived his child. It was therefore imperative with left the court in Austria as quickly as possible."

Now Anton took up the storey, "Mrs. Reeves, since you are a Roman Catholic, though your husband tells us he is a protestant, you will know the attitude of our Church to the sin of Louisa conceiving before marriage. – In fact because of the dislike of our two families, it was worse. Mr. Reeves you may not believe this but it is true. – if we had stayed, not only would I probably have been executed for bringing disgrace on Louisa, but she would have been sent into a convent, for life, and our baby, once born, would have been taken away from her and adopted. So we had no option but to escape. We first went to Spain, but realising the court might force the Spanish government to return us, forcibly, for punishment, so we crossed the Atlantic, purchased an estate in Spanish Florida and settled there."

All this time Anna had been listening, hardly believing that these two Austrians would dare to confess to them what they had done, apparently not caring that their presence, even in West Virginia, might be discovered and still forced to return to Austria. Now she could not control herself, "But are you not both afraid that the Austrian court will discover you are here, and demand that the United States return you to them?"

This was just the question they had hoped would be asked. Again as agreed in advance, Anton replied, "Oh! No! That is impossible. In fact I have written to my father telling him where we are living, about our estate in Florida, and our new small holding near here. You see we have both taken United States citizenship. We have been assured by our friends who are members of Congress, that our government would never agree to sending us back, for technically, we are no longer Austrian citizens."

Anna could still not believe what they had said. "You've told them where you are and being American citizens make it impossible for them to demand your return. "- As they hoped, Anna suddenly realising that this might apply to her, forgot her predicament and unwisely asked, "But both Andrew and I have become citizens of the United States. – Does this mean they cannot demand I and Andrew return to Austria? – Oh! My God! – What am I saying.---" She looked at Andrew now speechless and seeing his reproving look at her making this confession.

Events had occurred just as they had hoped, Anna had made her confession. Now it was time for Louisa to come and place her arms around Anna, as tears of disgrace ran down her face. Louisa gently kissed the side of her face. "Dear Anna – I thought many months ago when last me met I knew you. I told Anton, I was sure I had seen you at court. – Anton's father wrote to us telling us there was another scandal at court, almost at the same time as our occurred. – A Princess of Lorraine who conceived by her English Tutor and, like us had to flee. Admit it – you are that Princess and Andrew is the tutor who caused the scandal."

Before she could reply, Louisa continued. "However, you will be pleased to know that no one in Austria has yet discovered where you have gone. They traced you to England, even Bristol, due to the royal jewels you sold there. However, after demanding Britain to make a search, nothing more was found. – Once we learned of this, we guessed, with the war, neither of you would have returned to Europe, so you must have come to either

Canada or the United States. – After our previous meeting, I was convinced you were this pair. Please now admit it, for you have nothing to fear."

At last Anna stopped sobbing and smiled whilst Andrew took hold of her hands, as she replied, "Yes! We are those two who escaped, first to Andrew's family, at Wookey in England, where we married in a protestant church. Then to Annapolis where we were befriended and I married again in a Roman Catholic church, before I bore Andrew our son, Philip. Yet, until to day, we have told no one of this. We are still afraid we shall be discovered and sent back to Austria, for exactly the same fate, which awaited you, if you had stayed there."

Louisa now hugged Anna lovingly whilst Anton came and offered his hand to Andrew, who gladly accepted and shook it. Anton explained, "We felt sure you were these persons, yet it seemed when we last met you that you feared discovery. We came today, hoping we could get you to confess – as poor Anna, did in fact. We were going to inform you that as you owned land you could get United States citizenship, after which you never need fear again that anyone could force you to return. – Now you've told us you are already United States citizens. – I can assure both of you that you never need fear of that happening whilst you live here."

After that the Reeves demanded they stayed for dinner, continuing to thank them for giving them this wonderful news. However Anton was more practical. "It is obvious that neither of you have the wealth which we now enjoy. My parents have placed a fortune in banks in Europe in my name. It seems you have established a very fine school, here, which is needed and you are successful. However three of us are Austrian, severely mistreated by our court in Vienna. Louisa and I have joined a consortium to invest money in projects which may in time make this country very prosperous. However by doing so, we know we shall, reap very substantial financial rewards, as well."

Now he came an put his hands on Andrew's shoulders, "Adversity has brought us together. But for the events which happened in Austria, we might never have met. I want to assure you, that we think your school is one of the ways we can all add to the future prosperity of this land. You can rest assured that we shall be very pleased to invest in your school, knowing you will accept all our children, when they are old enough. However from today, I hope we shall become friends. To help cement this friendship, since you have not seen our small holding, perhaps you would come as our guests, next weekend, when you might meet other of our friends."

Andrew and Anna, readily agreed though it seemed that they already had met and knew many of them – Eric and Isabel Casimir, John and Hillary Holstein, and of course their benefactors when they first arrived in America,

Sheila and Kenneth Bacon. Though they confessed they had not told them of their previous life in Austria. Never-the-less they were delighted to accept their invitation.

As it happened they arrived on the same day that Daniel and Michelle Carroll and Ulrika and Michael Casimir visited, to introduce Daniel and Michelle to Louisa and Anton. It was then their surprise to discover, that not only had Anna and Andrew, met them before, but actually stayed at Racoonsville and attended a wedding there.

However it was now possible to let all their friends know of their Austrian court connections, which explained also their high social behaviour. Michael was delighted to meet the nephew of Neil Reeves, though it did not stop him telling Andrew, how much he deplored his uncle's behaviour. Then being even more surprised when Andrew told him they had both met Sophia Brookes, now Sophia Chalmers. Also the long discussions with Claire Wycks, and her adventurous and at time unhappy life. Michael seemed pleased when Andrew admitted that he felt his uncle had not treated Claire as he should have done.

In the company attending Louisa and Anton's party that day, there was no doubt but that Anna and Andrew were nothing like as rich as the others. However as their hosts today had said to them at their school, Michael Casimir, who had taken a liking to the forthright way, Andrew had endeavoured to find the truth about his uncle and respected the opinion he had gathered, now would help them.

In typical fashion as he had done so many years ago in that store at Fort Pitt, he said to Andrew, "I believe God, in giving me not only a wonderful life with a fantastic wife, but also bestowing on me considerable wealth. – I have always thought God was testing me to see if I could use that wealth to give happiness to others.- That is why I helped, not only Claire – for she has told you my belief about her birth – but others such as Adrian and Kylie Scott and later Brian and Craig and their wonderful indentured servants."

Placing an arm around Andrew he said, "I still have more work to do. I believe at this moment you are contributing to this country more than any of us here today. I would like to see, in time your school become a college, employing other teachers, and taking them to higher levels of attainment in education. – I shall be delighted to invest heavily in such a project, should you decide to implement it in the future. – please let me know when this happens. "

It was a very happy Anna and Andrew who returned home that evening. A week ago their fears of discovery and returning for punishment were removed, now others where willing to invest in their future. It seemed they might not need to draw on that nest egg from the sale of Anna's jewels, even though their expenditure would soon rise, for like Louisa, Anna was again pregnant by her beloved Andrew.

It seemed that this last two years had seen further development following the expansion which had earlier taken place. It seemed it had also provided a period of entrenchment, an enablement, a time which enabled investment, which in due course would add greatly to the economic success, of this new and the enlargement of this rapidly growing country.

———————————

PART 6

ACHIEVEMENT

ACHIEVEMENT

1797 and 1798 were very dangerous years for the United States. It was only the brilliant statesmanship of President John Adams which prevented his country declaring war on France. What was later to be referred to as the XYZ Affair erupted in March 1797. It began a few weeks earlier. Adams sent Charles Pinckney, the author of the successful treaty with Spanish Florida, to France as part of a commission of three, including John Marshall and Elbridge Gerry., but Talleyrand of France refused to meet him as a Minister to France claiming, that Jay's treaty with Britain was an act of war against France.

Perceiving this as an Anglo-American alliance, French ships seized, no less than three hundred American ships bound for British Ports, from the Mediterranean and the Caribbean, as the United States, virtually, had no navy. However even worse events occurred, for when the three Americans tried to negotiate, it seemed three French agents, Jean Hottinguer, Pierre Bellamy and Lucien Hauteval demanded fifty thousand Pounds sterling and a Ten million Dollar loan to France, before they would consider introducing them to any ministers. As for a time these names were not released, they were referred to as XYZ, hence the name of the affair.

When President Adams released the report of what had happened, anti-France sentiment became so strong, that only by Adams diplomacy, was war averted. However, as up to then both Thomas Jefferson and James Madison had been actively campaigning for an alliance with France, Adams used this situation to get Congress to pass the Alien and Sedition Acts to at least, temporary, destroy their attempts to form the Republican Party and to remove all Federalists from Congress.

It was so successful that Jefferson and Madison were forced to make a plea to Congress, now known as the Virginia Resolution, virtually begging, Hoping to avoid the most serious clauses of the act, as being anti-democratic and against the constitution. It did go a long way to limiting the worse effects of the act. So throughout 1797 and 1798 there were real dangers of a war with France. In fact there was a quasi-war from 1797 up to 1800 where French ships continued to take American merchant ships, enabling, at last, for Adams to start building a navy.

Throughout all this time Senators Carroll and Casimir and Francois Tencin, though they supported the Virginian Resolution, had thrown their full support behind President Adams and the Federalist Party. These difficulties had ensured that the three of them were away from their homes for long periods. Yet in spite of the seriousness, very few Americans, certainly not the thousands still streaming west had any idea how close war had become.

This certainly was the case of the five families, who at last had settled on the new estates in Kentucky, having driven the stocks of horse for breeding from West Virginia. They had their own war to win. A chance to establish a rich financial future in horse breeding and rearing, as their parents had done in the Allegheny Mountains.

It certainly had been a hard time for Monica and Antoinette, used to comfort for most of their lives. However they were helped, greatly, by both Lilie and Helga, used to a hard life, even before their capture by the indians. There was no doubt that everyone, including Stuart Brady, were surprised at the ability Pohanna showed in rearing horses. When they mentioned this, she just laughed, telling them since a young girl, her task, as like many of her kind, had been to look after the horses of the indian braves.

They had arrived in sufficient time to prepare themselves for the rigours of the coming winter, and were very grateful for the strong and well equipped houses the five men had constructed for them earlier that year. In fact, soon, they were so well organised that there were times when they could relax, especially at weekends and go into Winchester for entertainment. Naturally they had needed to make many visits before this, just for food and implements, but now these visit were, essentially, for pleasure.

At these times the men folk would enjoy themselves in the local saloons, whilst their women, after doing their shopping for essential clothes for all of them, including their babies. Then after refreshments in a small local hotel, they would have to wait until their men appeared, somewhat inebriated and worse for wear. Unfortunately, excepting the two Irishmen, all the others had grown up to enjoy the corn whiskey from Pennsylvania. This unlike Scotch Whiskey had an exceptionally high content of alcohol. It was really 'firewater', which quickly effected those drinking it.

Well the Whiskey rebellion of 1794 had driven many Pennsylvanians, several outlaws for having shot Federal soldiers, and who escaped down the Ohio River, eventually settling in northern Kentucky, and adding greatly to the tiny village of Paris, making it a town, as they settled on the adjoining land to raise corn. It seems that this county of Kentucky had been named Bourbon County during the War of independence as a tribute to the kings of France, who bore that name. As this was the basis for their whiskey they provided the local salons, including those in Winchester, with their own distillation, considerably adding to their own resources.

It was the absence of peat to heat the stills which did not add to the aroma, and a shortage of rye which made this product so much inferior to that produced in Scotland. It took an impoverished exile from Scotland, a chemist, Dr. James Crow, to alter this and eventually produce what today is called American Bourbon Whiskey, which though different, was in quality a very close rival of that made in Scotland. He overcame most of the problem of Rye shortage, by blending with many other cereals, and developed an aging process in charred oak casks, perfecting the sour-mash process.

Perhaps it was a fortunate coincidence that the five men on a visit to the Winchester saloons in late January 1797, calling in town for implements and leather reins for their horses, met this man Dr. James Crow, as they drank the local distil. He, upbraided them for drinking such poor quality liquor, boasting he had developed a whiskey far more superior, and would even rival that from Scotland, although still a little different, due to the absence of peat in Kentucky.

Naturally they disputed his claim, so he forced them outside to his wagon and handed them a bottle of his own concoction for each of them to sample. They were all converted. Perhaps Stuart Brady and David Downey, who had sampled scotch whiskey in Ireland, were the best judges, agreeing that it would easily complete with the latter. Obviously Dr Crow was delighted at their appreciation but when they asked, since he lived in Paris, the centre of Kentucky Whiskey manufacture, why had he not set up a distillery for making it.

He threw up his hands, "The reason – you want to know the reason. It is money, and I have little, my earning for my chemical work barely keeps me alive. Of course I have approached those from Pennsylvania, but they just laugh saying the sale of their product is so great, it is foolish to be involved in a more expensive product."

Now he smiled continuing a little cynically, "Of course they are right. Few here in Kentucky would pay the extra for my product. The answer for it lies in the rich families living on the Eastern seaboard, who can afford the exorbitant charge for Scotch whiskey. I'm certain they would gladly accept my own, as a cheaper, but in its way, equal to that from Scotland. However think of the cost of transport from Kentucky to the east. There is no way I could finance this or obtain any help from the banks in Kentucky."

It was James Downey who suggested that he might travel and settle in the east, but Dr Crow stated that his product depended on the type of corn, rye and other ingredients which grew in Kentucky and would be difficult to find in the east. Before they parted they obtained his address in Paris, and told him, in due course, they would call on him there and purchase a little of his brew.

However when they returned to their women and told them of their encounter, it was Monica Downey and Antoinette Brady who were more practical. Each had enjoyed for sometime in the past, partaking of the Scottish variety, which they enjoyed. They confirmed to their men folk that if Dr. Crow's variety could be transported east, it might provide a gold mine for everyone associated with it.

As Monica wrote regularly to her father, if only to convince him she was well and able to cope with her new hard life, just merely as a news item, she described her husband's conversations with this Dr. James Crow, and his product he called 'Bourbon Whiskey'. How good all the men thought it was, but without the resources to transport it east to the only market available for it, adding her own and Antoinette's opinion that if it were possible it might make many very rich, knowing how well it would sell there.

Perhaps it was fortunate that Monica's letter arrived soon after Daniel, her father, had arrived back from West Virginia, where they had just set up the investment company of 'Western Development'. He knew the company were urgently looking for new investments, might not this be a worthwhile project, however if so it would have to be researched to ensure its feasibility, which meant some persons would have to go to Kentucky for this purpose. Anyway he would bring this to the notice of the board.

2

Francois and Charlotte Le Raye as soon as they were assured of the necessary finance, had gone to Fort Pitt and taken a two bed roomed house in the town outside the fort, living together as brother and sister but without any intimacy. In fact they had little time, for they were anxious to put their plans into operation as soon as possible. With the money advanced to them besides the house, they had purchased some land adjacent to the river and had a large shed erected with a slip-way down which the boats they built, could be entered into the river.

By February they were ready to order the necessary sawing and planning machinery, which necessitated them travelling back to Philadelphia. They knew what they required but needed Roy Marshall's advice as to which type could be most easily be connected to steam power. They stayed with Roy and Fay whilst this was achieved. Roy and Fay marvelled that Francois and Charlotte slept in the same bed but without intimacy.

It had so surprised Fay that when she was alone with Charlotte, she could not refrain from asking her, if she ever had the sexual desires, which Fay admitted she had and why she lived with Roy as if married. Charlotte's answer even more surprise her. "Fay dear, whatever you may think I have the same desires as any woman."

She smiled at Fay then said, "I'm not a virgin. In fact I conceived a child whilst in France and paid for an abortion. I had three lovers whilst I worked and helped my father and was intimate with them, but never considered them as a partner for life. You must remember this was the life we all enjoyed, whilst connected with the court. However if I had to attend a ball, I was careful not to appear near the king, for he would normally choose one new girl for him to spend the night with. It seemed many conceived his child, but usually aborted."

Now Charlotte was very direct. "Oh! Yes! I have the same feminine desires as you." She now looked straight at Fay, "I warn you. – I am very attracted to Roy. – If I can, I will win him from you. Now do you want Francois and me to leave your house." However Fay's reply surprised her.

Fay even smiled. "I care very much for Roy, but though we like each other very much – yes and behave as husband and wife – but we do not love each other. I have no hold over Roy – neither has he any hold over me. It seems very likely we shall both, eventually, find a partner with whom we might want to settle. – However, even if this happens to both of us, I warn you – we shall still share intimacy with each other from time to time. I know Roy does think a lot of you, as he did of Electra at Berkeley. However until I find a man I like, I will do all in my power to stop you taking Roy away from me." Surprisingly this encounter did not cause the two of them to become enemies.

Now the correct machinery had been ordered, in addition to the steam powering machinery, and it would soon be delivered to their shed near Fort Pitt, so Francois and Charlotte wanted to return to their shed and prepare for its arrival. After they left Fay told Roy of her altercation with Charlotte, which both amused and pleased him. Fay said, "So it seems Charlotte will have several weeks with you, to seduce you, as you help them with their work. - There will be nothing I can do to stop her with you living there. – But Roy, I really will not mind. – I do want you to have a happy life. – you owe me very little and I'm grateful for these months we've spent together."

She turned away for she did not want to show him how sad this made her, but did not wish to tell him how she would miss him, and the things he did to her. To her amazement Roy turned her round and pulled her to him, placing a very passionate kiss on her lips, almost bruising them. "Fay, that will not be the case. You are coming with me to Fort Pitt and if you will allow me I would still wish to sleep with you. Let us see how Charlotte reacts to that. – at least she will have to win me from you. You know I found her a somewhat dominating woman at Berkeley and so sure of herself. She will have to learn to alter, if she really wants to win me. – Please Fay, come with me – I need you."

Fay just returned his kiss and clung to his arms. "Oh! Yes! Roy, I will be glad to come with you." Then she laughed, "You know I might find Francois very interesting. It seems like Charlotte, he has much experience with women whilst in France, so it is surprising that he has not continued that way since he came to America."

So after arranging matters with both Jenson and Hugh and ensuring they knew what was required of them whilst he was away, particularly as production had needed to be increased, as their sale of cotton goods was in great demand. Linda was delighted to look after Terry, now over two years old. So three weeks later, both Fay and Roy drove up the Cumberland Gap, passed Fort Cumberland and finally, to Fort Pitt to stay in the same house as Francois and Charlotte.

As most of the machinery had arrived, none of them had much time to themselves, and Francois was pleased that Fay, though their guest, helped them in every possible way, to assemble the various parts. Fay did see how competent was Charlotte, for when Roy had drawn some rough sketches to show how the steam power must be connected by wheels and pulleys to the sawing and planning machines, ensuring they could control, accurately the speeds of the machinery, Fay saw the scale drawings Charlotte produced, to make it easier for all of them to assemble the parts.

They all worked very hard for six weeks, by which time they were almost ready to start manufacturing the small boats. They still awaited the scale drawings of the boats which they had ordered whilst in Philadelphia as well as the various timbers, necessary, including softwoods, even and in spite of, their ample local supplies of hardwood. In fact Roy had attempted to devise from soft wood, floor boards to their boats, but consisting of flat planes of wood sawn from the trees and then two or even three glued together to give it strength. If this worked, it meant they could more quickly, and more cheaply, construct their boats for sale.

Whilst they waited, as it was a delightful late spring, they decided to allow themselves a holiday. All four of them went in their coaches into the countryside which had so fascinated both Francois and Charlotte as they had stayed with Tonsac. It was not long before both Fay and Roy were, equally, impressed. In fact they were really seeing America for the first time.

They picnicked by one of the several lakes, mainly surrounded by hardwood trees. In fact they had needed to leave their coaches some distance away, and carry their lunch boxes and carpets to sit on. It was a very warm day and all four felt the heat of their labours. Without saying anything Charlotte stripped every piece of clothing from her body and plunged into the cool waters of the lake, quickly followed by Francois. Though surprised Fay and Roy looked at each other, smiled, they admitted they felt very hot, so they, also, took off their clothes and followed them into the water, as naked as Francois and Charlotte.

They swam together for some time, then crawled out of the water an came to sit, still naked, on the surrounding grass, leaving the hot sun to dry their bodies. Though both Fay and Roy felt self conscious, exposing themselves to the other two, the others had no such inhibitions.

Francois said, "Fay, you really have an extremely beautiful body. I confess I've seen many as naked as you. In France we rarely covered ourselves when we bathed in the lakes surrounding the palaces. I admit it did sometimes lead to more amorous pursuits. I can say, that your own body, is to me, as lovely as any other women's body I have seen. Fay, you honour me by exposing yourself this way. I am very grateful to you."

His words made Fay blush so Francois quickly continued, "Please Fay, I did not wish to worry you. – You have no need to feel ashamed. Charlotte and I have never tried to hide our bodies from each other since we were children. – Now shall we unpack our bags and partake of our food and wine." They did so and still sat naked until they had finished. Only then did they dress and return to their coach, to explore further the beautiful countryside.

After their short break they resumed again their task of providing the means to construct their boats for sale. Roy was able to connect their steam power to both their sawing and planeing machinery, Francois even showed them where they could get men to dig away the near surface coal, to use to heat the water for their steam. Soon hardwood trees brought in by a felling team from the nearby forests, were being stripped, sawn into flat planks, then planed to the shape required, though the hardwood was mainly used for struts onto which the planks were moulded. In fact they soon realised it was better to use pinewood for the flat sides of their boats, as it made them lighter and easier to move.

Soon many were being assembled each week. They had already set up an office besides the shed in which Fay helped as their bookkeeper, and advertised the sizes and cost of each of their different types of boats. They found, with the steam power which had greatly reduced, the cost of manufacture, they needed much fewer men to operate the system. They could offer these for sale little more than twice the cost of a comparable coach. In fact, very quickly, there was a demand for them. Some preferred to buy the larger boats, on which they could also take their horses. Some, if the family was large, would buy a second boat for this purpose and even dissemble their coaches and put them on the boat, so when they arrived down river, they would have transport readily available. Fay, determined to play her part, saw to the accounts, as she had helped in their early days in Philadelphia.

Very soon the traffic on the Monongahela River had increased considerably, and was becoming the favourite means of travelling west to join the Ohio River and into the new lands, now mainly, but not completely, free from indian attack. However neither these dangers, nor the dangers of drowning on the rivers, a not infrequent occurrence, nor the hard labour deterred them, so many families wanting to settle these new territories and begin a new and more prosperous life, on land which they owned.

During these hectic first weeks as they began their production, Fay could hardly fail to notice the rather intimate way Francois, from time to time, as he came to help or talk to her, would as they walked side by side, had taken the liberty of placing his arm around her waist. Fay did nothing to dissuade him, in fact she was pleased, for it seemed Charlotte was doing everything possible to ensure Roy's attention to herself. Fay had to smile when she saw the way Charlotte tried so very hard to find ways of pressing her body to his, and saw Roy smile, showing her he had noticed it.

As they slept together in the adjacent room in which Francois and Charlotte rested, Fay and Roy would often laugh together as they discussed the days behaviour of the other two. Roy had said, "You know, if we stay here many more weeks, it won't be long before Charlotte becomes even more demonstrative – and I can see that Francois has a very similar interest in yourself. You know due to their French upbringing, they might even confront us together, to see if we might wish to swap partners for the night and sleep in different rooms." Fay said nothing, but had to admit that she might enjoy a night in Francois' bed as a change from sleeping with Roy.

3

Although the five families now settled in Kentucky and the thousand of 'would be settlers', making their way, either by the inadequate roads, or on the river to the new lands in Ohio, Kentucky and Indiana, knew little, or cared little that the United States might soon be at war with France. It did bring considerable apprehension to Daniel Carroll, Michael Casimir, William Holstein, but particularly to Louis Scarron and Jean Dumas. Because members of their families were also members of Congress, and they were kept fully informed of these dangers.

Perhaps it was worse for both Louis and Jean, born in France and for many years serving as officers in the French Army during the Seven Years war against Britain. Though the France they knew was long gone, it was still the land of their birth. However all five of them had faced similar problems as America fought for independence, from Britain. It seemed so foolish that the United States might be in conflict with any land in Europe. Why could not those old countries stop interfering with their own future.

However the dangers of war also placed their own economic future in jeopardy, including their recent business formation of 'Western Development'. They knew these next two years would be critical. It was imperative they called a board meeting of everyone involved on the Casimir estate near Fort Necessity.

By chance Michelle had, only a few days before, told Daniel of her letter from Monica, explaining about this impoverished scientist Dr. James Crow and the special distillation he had devised of a special blend of whisky, which both Monica and Antoinette had tasted, telling them they believed it was much superior to anything yet distilled in America, and, in fact, would rival Scotch Whiskey.

Monica had explained that everyone who had sampled it considered it very remarkable, and Antoinette added that it even rivalled the Cognac Brady from her native France. However it would have little future in

Kentucky or the new lands, being far more expensive than the normal corn liquor. However they felt it would sell very readily in Virginia, Maryland and probably New England, where the more rich families lived.

It could certainly compete both in price and taste, with imported Scotch Whiskey and might quickly become a goldmine. The trouble was that no one in Kentucky would consider investing in its future because of it being dearer than corn whiskey and the cost of transporting it to the east, where a ready market existed. Jokingly Monica had already christened this "Bourbon Whiskey", as it originated from the County of Bourbon in Kentucky. Monica's final plea in her letter said, "Mother, why don't you use your wealth and beat father, by investing in this and become even richer than him. – I just know it will be a success."

It had amused Michelle, first because she had always known Monica's preference to Scotch Whiskey than even cognac, or other liquors, but also because she knew Monica had a very discerning taste. If she had such faith in it, Monica, may well be right. Because of this Michelle had shown Monica's letter to Daniel. At the time he had not taken any particular notice of what she had written, and had told Michelle, even if Monica was right, it would take some time before there could be any return on its investment.

Suddenly, however, at Fort Necessity, the dangers of war with France made Monica's proposal, possibly, more feasible. If war did occur, the United States with only a small navy, would mean American cargo ships would be at the mercy of the French Navy. Certainly the French would do everything to prevent them exporting goods to Britain, or returning with goods they required. Certainly only the most essential goods could be brought from Europe. If so it would be most unlikely that the eastern states of America could, any longer enjoy their addiction for Scotch Whiskey.

Daniel thought, denied of this liquor, if Monica's Bourbon Whiskey was as good as she claimed there would be an open market ready to receive it. It would sell in multi barrel loads. They were meeting to decide, if for a time, they stopped investment in the west, because of the danger of war. - Yet here, was a possible investment, which if war occurred might provide a fortune for them, in a very short time. Almost as they has decided not to go further with the mining of coal and iron near Fort Pitt, and to wait for developments, Daniel suddenly put forward his proposal concerning Bourbon Whiskey, giving them the reasons why the war, if it happened, would greatly increase the value of their investment.

All were surprised at his intervention. Only a few minutes before, they had almost decided to halt all investments until the question of war was decided. Now he was putting forward a new proposal. At last they asked Daniel to explain. He told them it all depended on how accurate was his daughter's appreciation of this distillation. Whatever happened, before they should consider any investment, one of them who enjoyed the taste for whiskey, would have to go to Kentucky and test whether is really was worthwhile, and could be produced in great quantities.

If war did occur and they could transport this liquor to the east, then obviously, it would sell in considerable quantities, with Scotch being unobtainable. If not as so many American ships were, already, being attacked by the French, Scotch was becoming very expensive and might even cost more in the future. In any case if its quality could be proven, it was very likely that it would provide a worthwhile investment.

The consortium had been formed so as obtain good returns from investments in the west, only the fear of the consequences of war, had made them consider a curtailment. It really was the last thing they had wanted. Now Daniel had suggested one which might be highly successful, irrespective of whether hostilities occurred. His proposal was accepted in principle. The only question was how were they to discover if this whiskey was as good as Monica had stated, and it needed a person who was very discerning that way.

All the men partook of Scotch Whiskey from time to time. However with the exception of Anton Albrecht none could claim they were connoisseurs of this drink, mainly preferring brandy or French liquors. Fortunately, for both, Louisa and Anton, whiskey had been their preferred drink whilst at court, Anton's father had even invested in a distillery in Italy, which had tried to replicate a liquor very similar to Scotch. It seemed that it failed, mainly due to the absence of peat, which gave Scotch its malt flavour.

In fact Anton stated, he might have doubts of Monica's claim over Bourbon Whiskey, as it could not be distilled over peat. Still both of them could claim to be able to be discerning as to whether the liquor Dr Crow had produced might have a chance of competing with Scotch. It seemed they were the only ones, at all fitted to travel to Kentucky, to ascertain its value.

Although Louisa was still suckling their son, Franz, born in January, neither of them had any other commitments. In fact they admitted that, though they enjoyed their picturesque estate and luxurious accommodation they missed even the involvement of the daily need, to control their Florida estate, and had become bored with their continued life of comfort. Certainly they would liked to become involved in this project but Louisa would want to come with Anton.

Firstly, it would be six weeks before it was time to wean Franz, so they could not leave before then. However, it seemed impossible to risk the lives of baby Franz and Antonia in the wilds of Kentucky, not to mention the difficult journey over land with few accepted roads. In fact as neither were good navigators, it was possible they could not, even, find their way, either to Winchester or Paris. Yet both admitted they would enjoy the opportunity of seeing this new land.

Daniel suggested an answer to their last problem. Since his 'Equine Development' investment had enabled the five families to establish themselves in Kentucky, and as Monica felt strongly in favour of Bourbon Whiskey, he felt sure he could bring enough pressure on either her husband David, or James Downey to come to West Virginia, collect the Albrecht's, and take them to his home. A little pressure would ensure the other four men would assist fully in his absence.

Obviously Louisa would not wish to travel until she weaned baby Franz, but after this Michael Casimir, was certain that Claire Wycks, now delivered of her fifth child by Philip, and living as indolent life as Albrecht's, would be pleased to take both Antonia and Franz into her custody, as denied babies for so long, she now idolised any young child. Michael promised to take Louisa to meet Claire, who lived only a short distance away, near Fort Cumberland. There she could see if Louisa would be happy in leaving her children with her.

In any case it would take at least six weeks for them to arrange for either David or James Downy to leave their stock and travel the many miles to West Virginia, by which time Louisa would heave weaned her baby and could, if she still wished, leave her children with Claire and join her husband in Kentucky. Certainly she told them she hoped this would be possible.

Now it was necessary to calculate the possible size of their investment, if the quality of the product was proven. Knowing the abilities of James Downey, they felt sure he could help them ascertain the cost of setting up a distillery of sufficient size to produce the necessary quantities of liquor. Then there was the transport problem. Jean Dumas suggested a method of transport. Paris was only a short distance from the mighty Ohio River. The Monongahela River was one of its tributaries and ran next to Fort Pitt and the Cumberland Road.

At Fort Pitt they had already invested in the factory for building small boats, which was already operating efficiently thanks to the efforts of Francois and Charlotte Le Raye but particularly Roy Marshall and his introduction of steam power. It would be easy for them to construct one or two boats of sufficient size which could sail both rivers, pick up supplies of liquor, bring it to Fort Pitt after which it could easily be brought to market in the east via the Cumberland Road. It seemed that they might use horse power to ferry these boats though rowing would be essential sometimes. They must remember that the journey from Kentucky to Fort Pitt was contrary to the current in the river. Rowing a large boat might be very difficult.

Before the meeting of the board concluded, they had already calculated rough figures so the possible size of their investment, and probably the best way of getting the product to market. Now everything would depend on the critical report they would, in time, receive from the Albrecht's. The later when the arrived back at their estate, were very happy at its outcome. Louisa admitted she was very excited at the prospect of seeing so much more of this country, she now had come to love so well.

4

It seemed that the ghosts of the Carroll families could never be laid to rest. This time, another, a female member of that illustrious family, famous in England for six centuries, had been forced to land on American soil, though she had never intended to do this. Her name was Estelle Carroll, probably part of the fifth generation following David, later Sir David Carroll, who had landed there in 1688.

In fact two branches of the Carroll family had come to Maryland in America. Both originated from two older branches, which separated on marriage. One settling near Kipling in Yorkshire and the other holding lands in Gloucestershire and Somerset. In fact the Yorkshire branch came with their friends the Calvert's, when George Calvert, a Privy Councillor, to King Charles I, resigned his position as he recanted the change of his father, who had become a protestant in King Edward VI's time, returning to the Roman Catholic faith, which was the same as the Yorkshire Carroll's.

King Charles gave George Calvert lands in Ireland and a portion of Virginia to the east of the River Potomac, which George Calvert called Maryland after his king's wife. So when the Calvert's travelled to America, the Roman Catholic branch of the Carroll family followed them. In fact the Edgar Carroll living at Berkeley was the direct descendent of that family who had remained staunch Roman Catholics until Edgar married his wife and followed her protestant faith.

The Gloucestershire/Summerset Carroll branch remain staunch protestants and supported Cromwell and Parliament in the Civil War. Consequently losing their large Gloucestershire lands, when King Charles II came to the throne. Now left with only their lands near Wookey, in Somerset, although greatly extended when they helped to place King William III on the throne.

Then by chance in 1688 Edgar Carroll, the elder, a staunch Roman Catholic, after warning the Carroll's of King James' coming attack on them, persuaded a young son of Lord Carroll to come with him to Maryland

and take possession and work a large tobacco estate in Maryland, called Rockville. He was then David Carroll. The whole of his life and success in becoming Sir David Carroll after meeting and marrying a convicted felon, eventually becoming Governor of Maryland, is described in an earlier book "Maryland".

Sir David's eldest son was Sir Robert Carroll who married David's niece, Dina Hanson. Their eldest son, Sir Gerald was a great disappointment to them as he left Rockville and never returned, marrying the daughter of John Churchill, Duke of Marlborough, Charlotte Churchill, and like his eldest son, Hugh, despised the colonists in America. It was Hugh who took possession of Rockville after both Sir Robert and Dina had died, and who caused so much trouble during the American War of Independence with his ultra strong views on British support, evening hanging some tenants who joined the rebellion.

After Yorktown fell and the British left, Hugh failed to escape in time, and a mob of his tenants murdered him on the road to Annapolis. Rockville, due to Hugh Carroll's British support became Daniel Carroll of Racoonsville property. Daniel had been fortunate that Sir Robert's son, Sir Gerald had so disappointed him. Because he admired Daniel for risking his life to safe two women, as a matter of honour, Sir Robert gave Racoonsville to David and Michelle when they married, whereas it had been planned to be given to Gerald.

So after the war Daniel Carroll could have taken Rockville as his own. However he greatly respected his uncle and knew he would not have wanted that. So Daniel gave Rockville to the youngest surviving direct relative of Sir David Carroll still living in America, Andrew Carroll and his wife Angela. Andrew was Daniel's nephew. His father was Anthony Carroll, Daniel's brother and their father Paul Carroll was Sir David's second son. Now the only branch still in America.

So after the war Andrew had seen to the prosperity of Rockville which was, actually, the largest estate in the whole of Maryland, and therefore worth a fortune. However Andrew was a retiring man, as was his seventy year old father. He was very kind and used his riches to help many unfortunate families as well as spending to increase the facilities for ordinary people in Maryland. Daniel had tried to get him to stand for Congress but he had refused preferring a less public life.

However the size and value of his estate, did mean he had no option but to joint Maryland's State Legislature, eventually becoming its leader. This also caused him to become Mayor of Annapolis, though he was only a figure head and other men acted in his place, though he did attend meetings sometimes.

It was this reticence to be seen in public, even whilst he donated so much to the welfare of persons in Maryland, which had decided Daniel to not call on him, up till now. Daniel respected his desire for anonymity, so even during their struggles to bring the refugees from France, Andrew had not been approached. However unknown to either of them the arrival of Lady Estelle Carroll on American soil, was to destroy any chance of this continuing.

After Hugh Carroll had been killed by the mob and his father Sir Gerald died, the second son, Alistair Carroll had inherited the title as a Knight of the Bath, in 1783. He was already married a relative of Edward Burke, Christine Burke. Their eldest son, they called David, in recognition of his great, great, grandfather, as this branch of the Carroll's still felt that their family had been robbed of the very rich lands of Rockville, still regarding residents of the United States, as rebels who had fought against their king.

When Sir Alistair had died in 1791, his son became Sir David Carroll, bearing the illustrious name of his predecessor. He was already married to Audrey Hanson, who it seemed could claim the original Sir David's sister, Julia Hanson, who married Lord Hanson, was her own predecessor. Their eldest child born in 1776, was the said Lady Estelle Carroll, previously mentioned as arriving on American soil under unusual circumstances.

The truth was, with the loss of the Maryland estate of Rockville, and the equally rich dividends from the 'Cross-Cropping Business', established by Rupert Marsh when he came with Lady Amelia's sister, Elaine Elliot, whilst Sir David was governor, had impoverished Estelle's family. When her great grandfather, Sir Gerald had decided to stay in England and married Charlotte Churchill, his father Sir Robert still sent him the dividends due to him from both Rockville and 'Cross-Cropping'. So besides the large dowry which his wife brought to him on their marriage, they were quite rich.

This had continued whilst his son, Hugh, went to live at Rockville and used every means to increase the dividends accruing from the estate. In fact Hugh would probably have sold Rockville, once he had milk-it of its value, then returned to England. First Daniel Carroll, foiled him in this. Then came the war and his vigorous support of Britain, meant, not just his death, but the loss of the estate and any future dividends from America.

Although that was barely seventeen years before, the descendents of Sir Gerald had placed the present family of Sir David and Audrey Carroll, Lady Estelle's parents, in debt financially, and they hoped that she might be their saviour. Lady Carroll had been pleased to meet and become friendly with Lady Charlotte Murray, the younger wife of John Murray, Earl Dunmore, Governor of the Bahamas when she came on a grand tour of Europe, leaving her husband in the Bahamas.

She had been Lady Charlotte Stewart, daughter of a Scottish Earl, before she married the older Earl of Dunmore, also a Scottish earldom. She and her husband had enjoyed an adventurous life. Her husband was Governor of Virginia, but both fled with their lives when Virginia joined the revolution, Then he became Governor of New York. However after the end of the war he was given the Governorship of the Bahamas. In that time Charlotte was a prolific woman, bearing him twelve children of which ten survived.

Now in her fifties she had come to Europe to enjoy life bringing her daughter, Lady Augusta Murray, who in a scandal married George III's son, becoming his daughter-in-law.

However she also brought her eldest son, Viscount James Murray, who had just lost his wife in childbirth, her third child in under five years. It seemed that the Murray females had to endure many. and frequent, pregnancies. Well due to her mother's friendship with Lady Charlotte, Estelle had been introduced to James, who had fallen in love with her. Her parents had ensured this romance matured, for a marriage of Estelle to James would not only in time, make her the wife of an Earl, but save their diminished fortunes.

The fact was that Estelle had no choice in that matter. She did not love James and having enjoyed several enjoyable escapades in the past, was not pleased when James had told her, as she was obviously a strong woman, she would be able to bear, at least as many children as his mother had born. In spite of her objections, her parents forced her to agree to becoming engaged.

As James had needed to return to the Bahamas, it was left for Estelle to travel by sea to the Bahamas, with her mother, to make the elaborate arrangements for Estelle's coming marriage to James Murray, and her father would follow in a couple of months. That is how Lady Estelle Carroll came to land at Annapolis, in Maryland.

5

They had left Southampton in September 1797 in a fast sailing ship, 'The Renown'. In spite of the war with France. Most of the French Navy had been forced to stay in its harbours on the channel. Also it carried four six pound cannons, for protection. There was not any fear it would fail to arrive at its destination in the Bahamas. Perhaps it was pure chance that they were so unlucky.

Having crossed the Atlantic and were driving south along the New England coast, they were unfortunate to meet a very well armed French privateer sailing along the American coast, attempting to collect, yet another American prize. The action which was making Congress consider declaring war of France. Once the French ship saw the British flag, it did not consider taking it as a prize, but intended to destroy it as an enemy of France.

In spite of its six guns, 'The Renown' was not a match for the heavily armed privateer. They were dismastered in minutes and cannon balls were sweeping its decks, as well as crashing into its port side. The passengers had no hope, as not only the heavy metal balls, but terrible splinters of wood, flew everywhere. Estelle's mother, Audrey Carroll was cut down by a ball even as Estelle held her hand. She died immediately.

Now Estelle was resigned to her fate. Then to her amazement the shelling ceased as quickly as it had begun, yet they still could hear heavy gunfire. Again by chance one of the new seventy gun United States Naval ships which President Adams had forced Congress to build, for the protection of American ships, at least near their own shores had arrived. It saw the crippled and dismounted, and flagless 'Renown', had assumed it was an American ship, which was being attacked.

The danger was now on the other foot. In spite of its heavy armaments, the privateer was no match for a ship of a 'seventy-four'. Also, they had been so involved in trying to destroy the British ship, they had not even seen the approach of the American ship. Not even known of its existence, until the savage broadside had hit them , destroying their masts, and killing most on their exposed desks. The American ship never received any fire from the privateer, and in ten minutes the latter was on fire and very soon afterward it reached the magazine, and it blew up

The was no doubt that it had been a miracle that had saved the remaining survivors on 'The Renown'. A complete chance that this United States warship the 'Benjamin Franklin', who only a month before had joined the navy to search for such ships as the one they had destroyed. Of course they were soon to discover the ship they had saved was not American but British, but then, after Jay's Treaty, the United States behaved with complete neutrality with British ships. 'The Renown' was sinking and the carnage on the desks demanded that the 'Franklin' transferred all that remained alive to their own ship, including the many wounded.

There was no time for any to rescue their possessions. Estelle was still traumatised by the terrible events and her mother being killed as they stood together, holding hands. At that moment she cared little what might happen to her, thankful to still be alive. However she was very grateful for the kindness and understanding by all the sailors on the naval ship. As her dress was covered in some of her mother's blood, a very kind sailor gave her a complete change of men's clothing and provided privacy so she could change and destroy her dress.

The ship now continued on its journey, and all the survivors, after a good meal, were given places where they could rest. Realising with so many people on board, the ship could not continue on its marked path. The following morning the captain gathered everyone together and told them, that as they were less than seventy miles from Chesapeake Bay, the ship would turn into it, and land everyone on the quay at Annapolis. He guaranteed that when they arrived, there they would be well received and looked after.

He make all laugh in spite of their condition by saying, "I understand you were all travelling from Britain to either The Bahamas or Antigua. I believe they are both very pretty and civilized places. However I can promise you that when you land in America you will not be landing amongst savages. There are not longer any indians inhabiting Annapolis, or Maryland. We are all god fearing people who will be glad to help all of you, being in such distress."

The following morning the ship manoeuvred up to the large quay at Annapolis. Estelle could still not be reconciled of the fact that her mother was dead and she was now completely alone, with no possessions. However she knew very well her families history. From being a young girl she had been told of that day when her ancestor, then just named David Carroll, after a most terrifying voyage over the Atlantic, coming to America at the invitation of his Roman Catholic cousin, Edgar Carroll, to take possession and run a large tobacco estate called Rockville on the east bank of the River Potomac, had landed at this same quay.

How before this he had watched and met a felon, Amelia Eliot, convicted to conceive three more children after she bore the present one, conceived by being raped by a Calvert in Ireland., walked down the gangway, after he had hugged and kissed her, promising, somehow to try to get her time of punishment transferred, so she could come and live with him at Rockville.

Then she marvelled at the fairy story, which though completely true, was far more astonishing than the story of Cinderella. How David managed to get Amelia transferred to Rockville, fathered her next child, then married her. Eventually becoming Governor of this land of Maryland and giving Amelia a title when he became a Knight of the Bath, even risking refusing the orders of his king, so that people of Maryland could worship as the pleased.

As now Estelle walked down that gangway, she felt very proud of her great, great, great grandfather, Sir David Carroll, and his wife Amelia. Estelle realised as she, herself, walked down that gangway, she was repeating what Amelia had done, for like her she had no possessions. Then she smiled, she felt pleased that unlike Amelia, she did not carry an unborn baby inside her.

It seemed that somehow the authorities had been warned of their arrival, for there were many persons waiting to meet and help them. Ambulances were waiting to take all the injured to a hospital in Annapolis. They were first led into large port building and were seated, whilst refreshments were brought to them. Now several clerks came and sat beside them, writing down their particulars, following some very detailed questions. It seemed they were particularly interested in what should have been their final destinations. It was essential that they could assure them they were all subjects of Britain.

A very nice man in his late forties came to sit besides Estelle and commenced to ask her questions.. She told him, her destination was the Bahamas, adding that she was espoused to be married to Viscount James Murray, the son of the Governor. Only then did she add that her name was Lady Estelle Carroll, coming from the Carroll family home in Somerset. To her surprise, at this point the clerk dropped his pen and studied her with a belated look. His mouth dropped open. Estelle could only smile wondering why he was behaving that way.

At last he recovered himself and asked, "Are you by any chance related to the Carroll families in both Maryland and Virginia?" Now Estelle could smile, for the first time since her mother was killed. It seemed that the name of Carroll was very well known in this land. She decided to use this very much to her advantage.

She replied, "Indeed I am, my ancestor Sir David Carroll was once Governor of Maryland and until your government after the war, stole it from us, you have near here a very large estate called Rockville which rightly belongs to my father, pray tell me who is the usurper who now occupies that land?"

Even more bewildered the poor man, gasped out a reply, " Mr. Andrew Carroll, the head of the State Legislature and Mayor of Annapolis, they have lived there since 1781. He and his family are very well respected in this state, for he donated large sums of money for the benefit of many people here."

This only made Estelle more annoyed, thinking of her families parlous financial state, which was forcing her into a marriage she did not want. She quite forgot she had just arrived as a refuge. "In that case please inform Mr. Andrew Carroll that a close relative of his has landed here today, and demands that he collects her and brings her to Rockville, the estate which rightly belongs to my father, Sir David Carroll." Then seeing the consternation on the man's face, quickly added, "My father is the fourth generation of the Sir David Carroll you have known."

After that the poor man had no option, but to be asked to be excused and went to contact his superiors. He was away several minutes, then an elegantly dressed man arrived, again over forty years of age, along with the original man. He bowed to her then smiled saying, "Dear Lady Estelle Carroll, let me introduce myself. I am that Andrew Carroll, Mayor of this town of Annapolis, and – er – the Master of the Estate of Rockville, who you claim was stolen from your family."

Now it was Estelle's turn to be surprised. Especially as he now bent down took hold of one of hands, raised it to his lips and kissed it, "Dear lady, whatever you may think, we are not all brigands and barbarians. Let me prove this. Without referring to your accusation about my ownership, please let me lead you to my coach and let me take you to this disputed estate, so at least my wife and I can welcome you as our guest, and where you can stay, as long as you want, until you want to continue on your journey, which was interrupted."

Estelle could only rise and smile at him before adding, "That was very gracious of you, particularly after my accusation. I will, with pleasure, and might add, with some considerable relief, accept your generous offer. For I stand before you, penniless, still traumatised by the death of my mother as we stood together on the ship. I must ask you to accept that, as my excuse for my recent rudeness."

Again Andrew smiled and led her by the hand through the crowds of people in that hall to his waiting coach and then on the relatively short journey to his estate of Rockville.

6

Estelle Carroll's arrival at Rockville was to create much activity. On the coach Andrew Carroll said little as to how he had become Master of Rockville but delighted her by telling her, everything he knew about his great grandfather. He was delighted that it seemed she was just as well informed as he was.

Of course he made sure she knew that Sir David, was a younger son of Lord Robert and Lady Anita Carroll, of Wookey, so she through his son Sir Robert, was also a descended of the same pair. He asked how well she knew of the present Lord Carroll of Wookey, and his family. It seemed that although her forebear Sir Gerald, Sir Robert's son, knew them well due to previous close relationship with the then Sir Winston Churchill and his son John, as Gerald had married one of John Churchill's daughters.

However after Sir Gerald died, and Hugh had been killed, his second son Sir Alistair had not tried to keep a close relationship with those at Wookey. She admitted that her own father, Sir David, had tried to re-establish the previous friendship, but it seemed that the parlous state of the finances had made them very unwelcome. Estelle admitted she had only once, and when a young girl, been invited to Wookey Hall.

Just before they arrived at Rockville Andrew had smiled at her, "It seems your knowledge of the original family which really is responsible for both of us being here, is just as poor as my own. At least, in spite of your statements about me and my family, we do have a common ground, and both owe so much to Sir David coming to America and marrying Amelia. " A servant exited the mansion, and held the horses head whilst another helped both Estelle and then Andrew to alight, before Andrew took her by the hand and led her up that magnificent stone staircase to the entrance to the mansion.

Estelle used to magnificent mansions in England was still overcome, by both the size and the magnificence of the building, so different in form to those in England. How she wished this had belonged to her father, for then she would have been delighted to live in it. Of course her arrival was quite unexpected, yet his still attractive wife Angela, rose to the occasion and gave her a very kind and generous welcome.

Once her husband briefly told her why he had brought Estelle here, her near death and that of her mother, Angela did not wait, she took hold of Estelle and practically forced her upstairs to her bedroom calling on her Negress servant to come and see to Estelle. As the servant undressed and bathed Estelle, Angela sympathised with her. Then as she was dressed in a new suitable dress belonging to Angela, Angela ensured her welcome.

She smiled at Estelle as the servant saw to her cosmetics, "It seems you are more a Carroll than I. I only became one when I married Andrew. However, I do know a little about the Carroll history. – My, dear, I cannot bring back your mother, but you are welcome to stay here for as long as you like. As soon as you have rested, I will take you into Annapolis and buy you many new clothes, since you lost all your possessions on the ship. Please feel free to ask for anything that may make your stay here more comfortable. We will gladly pay for this."

Angela kept her promise. Amazed that Estelle had so well overcoming the trauma of her near death and that of her loved one. She was delighted the next day to take her into Annapolis, returning with the coach filled with numerous boxes. She ensured Estelle had suitable clothes for any time of the day, and a choice of them. Since by then Andrew had told her of Estelle's claim that Rockville had been stolen from her own family, she had retaliated.

On the coach returning she had gently kissed Estelle's face. "As you feel we have stolen all this from you, it is only right we make some amends by ensuring Rockville pays to ensure your present comfort." Estelle smiled, but did not reply, even feeling a little ashamed of what she had said in anger on the quay. However, she still thought her accusation was correct, and was, eventually, determined to discover on what grounds Rockville had been taken away from her family in England.

However Andrew had told her, she must wait to discover the reasons, for he was a little unsure of how he came to live here. Using the jetty and crossing the Potomac, Andrew used the coaches always held on the other bank and with Angela, took Estelle to meet his father and family at Gordonsville, being introduced to his father and mother, Anthony and Esther Carroll, now seventy years old, somewhat infirm but in good health.

Andrew explained that his father was the son of Paul Carroll and his wife, Paul was Sir David and Amelia's second son, after Sir Robert. He also explained that his uncle and his father's brother, Daniel Carroll was the man who decided that he should take possession of the Rockville estate after Hugh Carroll was killed, so she must wait until he took her to nearby Racoonsville, which Sir Robert gave to Daniel, for rescuing two women, he had never met, himself in great danger, during the Seven Years War. Sir Robert had been so disappointed in the son, Gerald, going to live in England and never even returning for a visit. So instead, Daniel received Racoonsville.

After staying for a few days and learning how Sir David had first bought the original small piece of land which now had become the Gordonsville estate, planning to escape from Rockville when the Calvert's tried to imprison him and force Amelia to return to conceive the evil Sir Nigel Calvert's child. Saved at the very last moment when King James was deposed in England and King William ascended the throne. This was a story of which Estelle had not learned before.

So with Robert, Sir David's first son inheriting Rockville and the title, his second son, Paul, had been given Gordonsville, which in turn had come to Anthony, Andrew's father. Now Andrew knew he must take Estelle to Racoonsville to meet this mysterious Daniel Carroll, evidently responsible for taking Rockville from her family. However when they arrived they discovered both Daniel and Michelle Carroll were not at home and were involved in some project in West Virginia.

However Jack Eliot, introduced to Estelle as another descendent of Amelia Eliot, but only recently come to America from Ireland, was living a somewhat indolent life, though he did help Antoine, Catherine Lespinasse's son, on the tobacco estate. He had, never-the-less, become the intimate lover of Manon Lamoignon and was enjoying staying with Catherine. He was visiting nearby Racoonsville when Andrew and Angela, brought Estelle to meet Daniel.

For sometime Jack had used his free time to visit all the many families they knew in the Potomac valley, travelling as far at Fort Cumberland. When he ventured beyond into the forested land he had been charmed by it beauty. On his return he had fascinated his lover Manon, as they lay together, telling her she would love to paint these views and she had agreed.

Now Jack could see the disappointment on the faces of their three visitors. So, probably to relieve his boredom, he suggested to Manon that he should take her to the Casimir estate near Fort Necessity where they knew Daniel and Michelle were staying. Besides informing them of Lady Estelle Carroll's arrival and her wish to meet him for him to explain why Rockville had been torn from her family. He promised Manon he would stay with her there whilst she painted many vistas.

His real reason for offering to do this was because he hoped his relationship with Manon might develop further. He had, already asked her to marry him, but she had laughed and told him he had no means of supporting her and that she earned more than he did. They were very pleased at his offer but asked Jack to try to get Daniel to come to Rockville, for they were now returning there to await his arrival. Jack had to warn them that even when he reached Daniel and informed him, as Catherine had told him, he was involved in a very important business transaction, it might be some time before Daniel would be able to meet them.

Then they arrived back at Rockville. Since Estelle had told them soon after she arrived of the reason for her mother and her, journey to the Bahamas, pending a wedding to her espoused fiancée, as it seemed it might be sometime before Daniel could call, they asked her how vital was the necessity for her resuming her journey for the nuptials. As she had not enlarged on it, they were startled at her reply.

Estelle came and sat besides Angela and took hold of her hands. Then she asked, "Dear Angela on my first day here you told me I could stay with you as long as I wanted. – Of course I realised this was to ensure me I was welcomed but you would not have envisaged a very long stay. – Now, I must ask, how long would you be willing to give me shelter here." She paused then kissed Angela's hands, "You see I do not want to go onto the Bahamas. I do not love, in even the slightest form, my fiancée, James Murray. My father and mother arranged this marriage due to my mother's friendship with James' mother, Lady Charlotte. "

Estelle could see their surprise. "It seems James first wife died in childbirth, her third delivery in under five years, hardly surprising as it seems the Lady Charlotte herself, had endured fifteen pregnancies. – In fact James, as he courted me, had the audacity to tell me he thought I would make him a good wife. – Much stronger than his last, and able to bear him many children. He seemed to consider me as a 'mother hen', to added considerable to the Dunmore flock, whether or not, was, it what I wanted."

Angela was very shocked at what she had just said. "If you objected to your father, why then did he go ahead and agree to your wedding. Estelle laughed and replied, "I do not really blame my parents. In fact I love them both, and why my mother's death on that ship has so embittered me. – There were two reason's. My family are heavily in debt – a fact mostly due to my grandfather's wasteful expenditure, which father, inherited. So if I married James, his family are very rich and would undoubtedly remove our debts. – However, the second reason, was prestige. James will soon inherit his father's title as Earl Dunmore. My father would have a daughter of greater importance than himself."

It seemed neither Angela nor Andrew were aware that such things could happen. It was Andrew who replied. "It seems women in America may, now, have more privileges than you. In colonial days, it was not uncommon for women to be sent from England, simply to add to the white population, knowing they must bear so many children, though not married. That, mainly ended when we became independent. No longer could Britain send women here for that purpose. I believe they now send them to Australia."

He continued, "It may not always be the case, but in all, what we call civilized areas, women here have these privileges. They decide who they marry, sometimes against their parents wishes. However, for the women, like Angela, they can decide when they wish to conceive our children, - that is unless it is an accident – for our preventatives are not perfect. – I very much doubt if they would be willing to accept what your parents demanded."

Now Angela kissed Estelle, "Dear Estelle you can stay with us for as long as you want. You have nothing to fear, even if you think we may have robbed you in the past. Neither Andrew nor I would want you to go to a life of what must be hell for you, in the Bahamas. – Of course in time we must let your fiancée know your decision. We must take Daniel's advice, for it is possible that your father in Britain, could demand either, your return, or dispatch you to the Bahamas to marry. Stay here till Daniel comes."

7

Daniel and Michelle were staying with Michael Casimir, in the mansion near Fort Necessary which Michael had built as a wedding gift when his daughter, Hedwig had married Daniel's son, Robert. They had written to the families in Kentucky using the many persons travelling to and fro to that state, imploring for one of them to agree to come to collect both Louisa and Anton Albrecht and take them to Kentucky.

As expected, though they soon received a reply, it would be nearly two months before arrangements could be made for anyone to be able to leave their work. It seemed by agreement, James Downey, as he had travelled most of this journey, four years before when going to Fort Washington and joining the militia, would perform this task. This length of time would ensure Louisa had weaned her baby and it could be left with her other child, with Claire Wycks.

Daniel had decided to put that time to good use and went with Michael to Fort Pitt to the boat building factory, the La Raye's and Roy Marshall and Fay Bradbury had set up. They found there a hive of activity, and small boats were being erected at an amazing pace, in a few days, due to Roy's mechanising the production using steam power. They certainly were impressed.

Now Daniel raised the question of larger boats, telling them for the first time about a possible project they had of investing in the production of a special whiskey, they called Bourbon Whiskey, and if so the need to transport it by river to Fort Pitt, and by carts to the eastern seaboard. Francois La Raye, saw no difficulty in building much larger boats, though, if so they would demand a much larger and further investment, to pay for it. Daniel was certain the consortium would agree to that.

However both Francois and Roy immediately reminded them that the transport of the goods would be against the flow of the river. They seriously doubted if the banks of these rivers were suitable to use horse power, as it occurred in the canals in both America and Europe. They consider, except for a very short distance it could not be sustained over such long distances and with such large boats. It was what the consortium had feared, but Daniel told them this must be overcome.

Once again, as Edgar Carroll had discovered when Roy came to Berkeley, Daniel was quick to appreciate the value of Roy Marshall. He had been informed of the brilliant way he had mechanised Jenson's cotton factory with steam power. Now Daniel could see how he had used and devised it to produce boats so very quickly. For it was Roy who supplied a possible solution.

"The only solution is Steam Power. Somehow it must be installed on these new large boats once constructed, to provide propulsion. I know in Britain it has been used on land to move large carts they now call Tractors. However we would need much smaller engines which could fit in a boat, and devise a means of turning that power to drive something, that can drive the boat as required."

Daniel was impressed, "And could you devise such an engine, and make it drive a boat?" Roy had just laughed, "No! I have not had the same training in engineering as either Francois nor Charlotte, yet they are not proficient in steam power. However, I do remember when I was looking for suitable Steam power for our looms in Philadelphia, reading about the work of a John Finch and his helper Harry Voight. It seems they had, somehow, built one small enough to fit in a large boat, and used it to turn rotating paddle wheels. Even installing it as a ferry on the Delaware River. - I believe, with some difficulties, - for it seems Benjamin Franklin, had objected, claiming copyright, and he had built something similar, yet eventually they had succeeded."

Roy told them, "I could return to Pennsylvania and inquire further. See if we could use their idea, though, if it is patentented, it will cost a lot for us to use it." Then he turned to Daniel. "I am not rich, even with my quarter share in Jansen's company. Were I to succeed in this, it would become a very profitable undertaking. It could be used to carry anything on these rivers. Even large ones could be used on the Mississippi River right down to New Orleans. Mr. Carroll, I would have set up my own company and you would have to pay me to use it."

It was a challenge, but Daniel was not annoyed, and he replied.. "And you would be entitled to this. I believe, as this is essential, if our project in Whiskey is approved. We should invest in your company and provide for it existence, accepting, say, five per cent of your profits, as repayment. I challenge you, Roy Marshall, build us one large boat and power it by steam and I will guarantee you funds to establish your own company to build many of them. I will give you today a document which will ensure we do not rob you, if you succeed."

Roy smiled, held out his hand and Daniel shook it. They both understood, but more important, respected each other. Satisfied Daniel and Michael returned to Robert's house to wait. Meanwhile as Francois, Charlotte and Fay had heard everything of the exchange between Roy and Daniel asked, "Can you do it. If so you will become a very rich man."

Now Roy surprised all of them. Without waiting, in turn, he took first, Charlotte and the Fay, in his arms hugged then, then kissed them passionately, finally releasing them and gripping Francois' hand very firmly. Then he smiled and said, "No! You are very wrong. – The truth is – we all will become very rich. Look I need all of you. Perhaps I know more about steam power than you, but I have not any training as a engineer. We shall all need each other in the future, if we are to make this a success."

Now he placed his arm around both Fay and Charlotte's waist, and looked straight at Francois. "I believe that whilst we have stayed here and worked together, it has not just lead to our successful boat factory, I believe we have all become friends – perhaps, if this new firm is to be successful – we might yet have to become, - er- more intimate friends." There was nothing more to say. Roy left Fay at Fort Pitt and returned to Philadelphia, but not until he had called on Edgar Carroll, to explain what he was trying to do.

Edgar had strongly supported him in his quest. "I shall ensure my son accepts your prolonged absence. Do not worry about the cotton factory, its doing well. If you succeed in this steam power for your boat, I too will be delighted to invest in your company." This pleased Roy, but was intrigued when he continued, "If you should find my daughter, Electra more interesting, - I tell you frankly, I would be glad to welcome you as a member of our family."

Roy very quickly found that John Fitch had patented his plans for steam power in ships. However disillusioned as no one had appeared to want to invest in his scheme. Ironically, having failed to obtain a promise from several men who had shown interest, almost starving John Fitch had committed suicide in Kentucky. With his death the copyright was lost as he had died without a will, and so Roy was able to investigate fully the drawings and scale models John Fitch had made when trying to obtain backers.

However Roy also discovered Robert Fulton who had already built a paddle steamer, which had been used successfully to carry cargo between New York and Albany, on the River Hudson. Roy learned it was easier to use steam power to drive paddle wheels than work a propeller. However as the paddle wheel had to be added to each side of the boat, amidships, in rough weather the entire paddle might be torn away for the boat.

Still Roy felt he could understand enough to feel sure he could replicate these ideas, however he was fortunate to discover Harry Voight's, living in poverty, but as Roy realised, was the man who had developed Fitch's steam engine, Roy knew his importance, knowing even his dividends as a partner in Jensen's firm would be enough, Roy offered to employ him, and sent him to Fort Pitt to await his coming. Now using the metalworkers who had made the steam engines for the cotton looms, he employed them to build two engines, from Voight's drawings and dispatch them, when finished to Fort Pitt. Only then did Roy return and wait for them to arrive.

Meantime Daniel and Michael had returned to the Mansion to await James Downey's arrival, satisfied they had done everything possible to find a solution concerning the transport of the liquor, if Louisa and Anton, considered it suitable. They had not long to wait. Just ten weeks after the board meeting had accepted, in principle, the idea of investing in Bourbon Whiskey, James arrived in a Surrey and they took him to the Albrecht's.

Whilst they waited for Anton to take Louisa and their two children, who were to stay with Claire, James was able to convince Daniel that his investment in horse breeding in Kentucky would be a very profitable one. In fact when James learned of what the consortium would do if Albrecht's confirmed Monica and Antoinette's, good opinion of Dr Crow's distillation, and the possible transportation by steam powered boats, James added an incentive. One problem the five families had encountered was how to extend the market for the sale of their trained horses, beyond the vicinity of Kentucky and possibly a little of Indiana. These boats could also be used to transport horses to the east.

Daniel realised if Roy succeeded in his quest to discover a steam engine and motive power for a boat, it would quickly make Roy a very rich man, as these boats could be used for rapid transport of all goods, to and from the wilderness. There would be an unlimited demand for them.

As soon as Louisa and Anton returned, the next morning they boarded one of their own Surrey's, taking all the necessary clothes for their journey and when they arrived, both Michael and Daniel were there to send them off. According to James it would take them about a week, but everyone would have to learn to sleep rough as they travelled.

Perhaps it was fortunate that Jack Eliot and Manon Lamoignon arrived just as James had come from Kentucky. Not only did they tell Daniel and Michelle the reason for coming to find them, but handed them a letter from Andrew, imploring them to come to Rockville, and to meet the Lady Estelle Carroll, another member of Sir Robert's family, but still living in England. Also to explain to her why Rockville did not belong to her father in England, as Sir Robert's direct descendent.

Just for a moment Daniel had been furious remembering how much he had despised the Hugh Carroll, who had taken possession of Rockville after his uncle had died shortly after his wife, Dina. Remembering the problems Hugh had caused everyone. Then Daniel had smiled to himself. Reading a little of the traumatised happening to Estelle and the death of her mother, he quickly realised what a strong character she must be. He felt she deserved a full explanation, and she would receive one.

With Michelle's agreement they quickly packed their bags and took a Surrey down that Cumberland Road, they had travelled so many times in the past. – Not always a very pleasant journey. It seemed that Jack Eliot and Manon would be staying in Robert's house. The stated reason was so Manon could place on canvas the beautiful vistas awaiting her to paint. However Manon had promised Jack, far more intimate pleasures, than she had allowed him in the past. Perhaps yet he might persuade her to reconsider his offer of marriage. – However she feared this offer was simply the offer she would have been willing to give a suitable boyfriend in France before the revolution.

8

Whilst Roy Marshall was away in the east discovering methods of incorporating steam power into their boats, Charlotte Le Raye had engaged Fay Bradbury in long conversations, which enthralled and amused Fay, as it involved not just Roy but Charlotte's brother, Francois, as well.

It was almost plea of despair from Charlotte. "Fay, though I know you will not like it – I know I've fallen completely in love with Roy. – I'm a Frenchwoman, and I long to yield my body to him. – But since you both came here, I can see just how much Roy still thinks of you." She even sobbed a little with emotion. "I don't think I've a chance of winning him from you. - Even if it were possible, I know he still thinks a lot about Electra Carroll – he's hinted this – for it seems Electra's father thinks highly of him and he knows if he marries her, he will inherit a lot of money. I don't think life's worth living."

Fay could not help smiling. This girl who only a few weeks before had told her she would fight her to the end to win Roy from her, was now confessing she feared she could never achieve this. Strangely her utter despair, seemed to raise some compassion within Fay. She could not help herself. She took Charlotte's sobbing body in hers and pulled her close to her.

Then she said very quietly, "Let me see if I can help. – Firstly, I believe you should know all about Roy and me. How it began. You will be the first we have told and is different from the story we gave when we arrived in America. – You should know when Roy first found me, I was kneeling in the courtyard of Grimshaw's burning cotton mill, in Manchester trying to revive my beloved Trevor Reynolds, my childhood boyfriend who was responsible for my pregnant baby, Terry, but we were not married."

The very slowly she told Charlotte everything that had happened that day, how both of them for different reasons had joined the mob who burnt down the mill, which was causing them to starve. How Roy practically forced her and carried her from the scene, as she would not leave Trevor. Saving her from being captured by the soldiers and probably been transported to Australia.

Then how very kind Roy had been taking her away to Liverpool so as not to be discovered. The amazing way, though, to save expense, they had shared a room at the hotel, but Roy never tried to be intimate with her, though like Charlotte's relationship with her brother, he saw her naked many times. How this continued when they came to America. She admitted she never knew why Roy did not demanded this of her, and at that time it was not what they both desired.

However when at last they settled and shared a house in Philadelphia, herself now very pregnant, they had discussed the situation and decided it was foolish not to enjoy intimacy with each other, which continued until Terry was born, but then afterwards. Her tale finished she concluded, "Charlotte, I still do not know if I love Roy. I know, now, I would agree to marrying me if he asked. – From what I've just told you, you can see just what a wondered man he is. – I know, even if he marries someone else, I know I shall try to somehow continue to have intercourse with him."

Fay now laughed still holding Charlotte to her, though she was no longer sobbing. "Tell me truthfully, if Roy should want to marry you, how would you feel if I seduced him from, time to time to sleep with me." Charlotte tore herself away, then asked, "If so would you want him to give you a baby." Fay just laughed took her hands again and replied, "I don't really know. – That is the trouble – I don't want to lose him but know I should help him to gain another woman, who would make him happy. – I know I owe that to him."

At last Charlotte began to believe that Fay was not her rival. "You are a strange woman to think like that." Fay only smiled and then kissed Charlotte's hands. "Perhaps, but you see I know I still love my dear Trevor. – I cannot accept that I shall never see him again. – it was I who seduced him to make my pregnant. – I knew two years before that, I wanted his baby. It was only because both our families were almost penniless – we were starving – which made me delay – but then the urge became too much. When Trevor discovered my condition, although neither of us had any money, he told me I must marry him. - I agreed – we should have been wed three days after we went to the mill and Trevor was shot dead."

Still holding Charlotte's hands she now gave her a very broad smile, "I still see Trevor – that's why I can't let Roy take his place. – It may be the same with any other man I meet. – I may want intimacy, but not marriage."

At last Charlotte seemed to understand. "Fay, you must have seen how much Francois thinks of you. – I'm sure he is falling in love with you. – I can't understand him. – You know we both had several partners when we lived in France – I lost my virginity when I was fourteen and Francois was the same age. – Yet suddenly, he has become unsure of himself. I would have expected him to sweep you of your feet, soon after you came to stay with us. – Yet he has become so timid. – Tell me, please, what is your opinion of him?"

Now Fay really did roar with laugher. "It has intrigued me the way he seemed to court me, yet when I even encouraged him he seemed to draw back. – Charlotte, I like Francois. – I do not love him – but I'm flattered by his attentions. – Look – Remember what Roy said, when he surprised all of us – including me – when he wanted all of us to be part of his new firm.- his words were 'perhaps we might have to become more intimate friends.' – How would you feel if we both swapped partners in bed, for a time, after Roy returns?" Now Charlotte bent forward and kissed Fay saying, "I'd love that!"

After that Charlotte must have spoken to Francois for he came to Fay when she was alone. "Charlotte has told me what you said to her. Fay, I cannot be sure what my feelings are for you. I know I like you. I am a Frenchman, and have known several girls in the past. – Yet, my feelings for you are different from those I had. – I know I would love to possess you, for you really are a very beautiful and wonderful girl. – I suppose I've thought you were Roy's girl, and he had a priority on you, yet Charlotte tells me that is not true. – Could you consider sleeping intimately with me, without thinking I was abusing you, or believing me vile for wanting to do so."

Fay simply bent and kissed him lightly on the side of his face. "No! Francois, I would not think that of you. In fact Roy and I some weeks ago even suggested we might sleep in different rooms and swap partners. – Then it was just a silly idea for we could both see your and Charlotte's attitude towards us. – Let us wait until Roy returns. Then if he wants this, I will gladly sleep with you. – but I shall be well protected, for I still can't be sure what I really think of you."

When at last Roy did return shortly after Harry Voight had arrived, telling them that Roy had employed him to help him introduce steam power into his boats, as they waited for the delivery of the boilers he had ordered, even as they planned to build that much larger boat, Roy gladly accepted the suggestion made to him and was pleased to welcome a very willing Charlotte into his bed, whilst Fay found the could enjoy sleeping with Francois, as he was a very competent lover, no doubt gained in France. Only time would tell both of them what was their future.

So that last four years had been years of achievements for all the families who had gathered in the United States, including those French Exiles and the four who had come from Liverpool to Philadelphia. Besides the loving partnerships which had developed, particularly those five families, who had married and now settled in Kentucky. The further success of Roy

Marshall, after his earlier achievement in mechanism the cotton mill. Now helping to develop even further the boat building business now established, successfully, near Fort Pitt.

It had been four years in which Daniel Carroll, Michael Casimir, William Holstein, and now Louisa and Anton Albrecht had grown richer from their investments which in turn helped this new country to develop successfully. There were even signs of possible relationships developing between several children from many of these families.

Daniel and Michelle, now satisfied that Louisa and Anton Albrecht were already travelling to Kentucky, to give them advice, and to see if Bourbon Whiskey had a future. As they drove in their Surrey down the Cumberland Road, to Rockville, both were intrigued that they had yet another task to complete. It was not one they really need to have even considered., for in their view, the decision about the future of Rockville they had made seventeen years before, was the only sensible one, as Hugh Carroll had made it a base to be used by the British to help defeat those colonials daring to revolt against their king. His cruelty had ensured his violent end. Neither he nor his family had any rights to Rockville after the United States won the war and became an independent country.

However they both admitted they were amused that this descendent of Hugh had come from England, under unusual circumstances and was now demanding to know why Rockville should not belong to her father in England. The direct descendent of the eldest son of Sir Robert. From what they had been told it seemed that Lady Estelle Carroll, a descendent, had the blood of Amelia, in her, proud of her ancestry. Even now in adversity, surviving what might have sent some women insane, her mother being killed by cannon fire as Estelle held her hand. At least she had shown she was a courageous as Lady Amelia. Daniel felt she deserved a full explanation of his reasons for robbing her father of this inheritance.

Then he smiled to himself. This might even be the greatest achievement of these last few years if he could convince this strong minded woman of the justice of his decision made so long ago. Both Michelle and he were extremely anxious to meet her, if only to meet another in the line of the Carroll's descended from Sir David and Lady Amelia Carroll and even more those of Sir Robert and Lady Dina Carroll, for Michelle had come to love them both, and felt they had helped her to at last realise just how much she loved, her now beloved Daniel

PART 7

CONSUMMATION

CONSUMMATION

"So you are responsible for the theft of this estate of Rockville from my father and his predecessors." Yet as Lady Estelle Carroll made these accusations to both Daniel and Michelle Carroll, she was smiling, as Andrew Carroll introduced them to her. Daniel far from being annoyed, smiled back at her before replying, "My dear Estelle, you should be grateful that this branch of the Carroll family, rebelled against those in England who would have subjugated us. - If not, as your British naval ships failed you, I would not now have the pleasure – and I can assure you it is a pleasure, - of meeting you, - if it had not happened there would not have been any of our Naval ships, to rescue you in the nick of time."

Now he came and offered her his hand, "I should add, that now having had that pleasure, I am delighted that we were able to assist you, only regretting we arrived too late to save your mother. – Dear Lady Estelle Carroll, whatever you think of us, - however you must blame us for the past – whilst you are with us, we hope we can try to bring you some happiness. – I'm certain that both Andrew and Angela, will have promised to help you, but I know that both Michelle and I, would hope we can a least ensure you have a very happy future."

Now he laughed, "Perhaps we may be able to compensate you to some extent, for acting so wickedly in the past. – However, I also believe that such an intelligent woman, as we can see you are, will, in due course, listen to my explanations of the events seventeen years ago. Perhaps then you might even think, we are not the brigands you seem to believe we are."

Now he took her hand and kissed it saying, " I salute a very brave, and if you will forgive me, a very beautiful young woman. How you survived and remained sane after what those French privateers subjected you to, makes me believe, that within you, is the same spirit of Lady Amelia, who herself had to overcome similar terrible adversity. – I know, whatever you may think of me, you will feel as proud as I am of my illustrious grandmother."

Still letting Daniel hold her hand, she also laughed and replied, "I completely agree, and I accept your offer of a truce in our confrontations." Now Andrew led everyone to the large withdrawing room, which was a room filled with the history of the Carroll family, since David Carroll had first arrived to take up possession of this estate, over a hundred years before.

Waiting inside were all Angela and Andrew's seven children. The youngest baby daughter, Olivia, held by a Negress maid, as Angela had only been delivered of her six months before. Daniel, however, was quick to notice the way, their eldest son, Adrian Carroll, immediately came and led Estelle to sit in a chair next to his. He seemed to be particularly interested in her comfort.

Inwardly Daniel smiled, for he knew Adrian was, probably, the same age as Estelle, it might indicate something more than mere politeness. If so he would not blame him for, already, Daniel had seen just how attractive she was. Later he spoke to Michelle about his suspicions. It seemed she had noticed this and even at that early date, he said to Michelle, "You know should this develop. If sometime it became serious and they married. Adrian in due course will inherit the estate of Rockville from his father. If so Estelle might feel it had been restored to her family, as well."

Over pre-dinner drinks, Daniel begged Estelle to tell him about her family in England and little of what had happened since Sir Gerald had died and his second son, Alistair inherited the title. Estelle was pleased to oblige. She showed her anger at her grandfather and his wife, Christine Burke, a daughter of Edmund Burke. She blamed both of them for their flagrant disregard for expenditure.

Looking straight at Daniel she said, "With the lost of the revenue from Rockville, our branch of the Carroll family had little but the returns from Sir Gerald's investment of the large dowry, he received when he married Charlotte Churchill. His son, never seemed to realise the serious change in our finances and both he and my grandmother, spent recklessly, never considering what might happen. So when they died, my father inherited these debts."

She sighed, obviously very sad, "I know neither my father nor my mother are to blame for our present parlous position, and for what eventually forced them to accept James Murray's proposal of marriage. – However much I hated what life with him would have cost me, I still loved both of them, as I do my father now, after dear mother is dead. I do not blame them. – Now I fear for my father's future. It is possible he may land in a debtors prison.-" Suddenly she stopped and clasping her hands to her face bent down sobbing violently.

Again Daniel noticed that Adrian immediately went to her aid and tried to comfort her. Eventually she recovered a little, tried to dry her tears, and managed to continue. "Oh! God! I am a terrible daughter. – I know, however much I hate the idea, I should still continue my journey to the Bahamas and marry James Murray. – I really do feel I must do this. – I cannot sit here enjoying the kindness of both Andrew and Angela, whilst my father, though knowing I am safe and that mother has died, still believes I may save him from prison and still marry, which will remove our debts. – I do believe I must make this sacrifice."

Immediate Andrew and Angela intervened and told her she must not do so. She should not consider this. Angela placed her arm around Estelle, "On no account must you consider doing this. After what you told us of James' intentions after you married, you might not live very long." Then for Daniel and Michelle's benefit she explained that Estelle's future husband had told her to expect virtually annual pregnancies, as he wanted a large family. His first wife having died in childbirth, her third birth in under five years.

Michelle could not help it. Learning for the first time of what Estelle might have been subjected to, she virtually shouted, "Estelle just must not do this. That man is a monster. – Daniel can we help." Now it was Daniel who took up the point. "I entirely agree. We cannot let this happen. However Estelle, apart from this, before I came here, at Andrew's request I asked my son, through his lawyers in Congress to ascertain your lawful position."

Now very seriously he explained, "Since your parents signed the marriage contract and you had to add your name after James Murray's. - We know that is the custom in England. Technically you are already owned by James Murray, or at least his father, the Earl of Dunmore. After we signed Jay's treaty with Britain, it seems that on such a matter as this, the United States would have no option but to return you to the Bahamas for marriage."

Everyone were startled and reacted at what Daniel had said, and poor Estelle, again placed her hands on he face and recommenced sobbing. Then Daniel continued, "There is a possible solution, though dear Estelle, you might feel you could not accept such a compromise. Robert has found that because of the way you were forced to land here in America, the previous reason, for your journey, - is now irrelevant. You could be treated the same as any would be settler coming for salvation to this land and apply for Citizenship of the United States. Robert feels certain it could be granted within four to five weeks – long before any extradition proceedings could be served."

Now Daniel came to Estelle and taking her hands lifted her face so he could look into it. "Estelle, I know just how proud you are of your British descent. – But, so am I. I know I owe so much to my original family at Wookey, just as you do. I am not asking you to recant on your love for

Britain. I swear, if you became a citizen of the United States, I would ensure that you still could believe you were as British as in the past. It would, simply, mean you belonged to both countries."

Now he kissed her hands, "Please Estelle. However much you hate me for what I did in the past. After what we have been told, Michelle will kill me, if I let you go and marry that man. – What I've suggested is the only way we can stop it happening to you – Yes! And if you agree – It, also, means we have an obligation to absolve you from your conscience, of placing your father in jail, by not marrying. – Please tell me how large is your family, besides your father, how many brothers or sisters do you have."

Still not comprehending what Daniel had just offered, she replied, "Only an eighteen year old sister, Julia, for my mother only bore the two of us and nearly died bearing a third child. It seemed that afterwards that mother could not conceive, or at least bear a living child, for she did miscarry further children twice more."

Now Daniel looked at Andrew, "I was going to discuss this matter with you in private but it seems poor Estelle's position, has made it more imminent. Since Estelle feels her families parlous financial condition is due to the fact she believes we robbed her of Rockville. Andrew, you and Rockville are very rich. For once instead of your generous donations to help the people of Maryland, could you not make a donation nearer home. Could you not agree to pay all the debts of Estelle's father and enable her family to have a more secure, even prosperous future. Yes! And perhaps someday come here to America, should Estelle decide to stay here. – Andrew could you agree."

There was no doubt of Andrew not agreeing to this. "Daniel, the only reason Angela and I and my family live in such wealth here was entirely due to your generosity seventeen years ago. Dear Estelle this is the least I can do and might help you to feel we are not such terrible thieves as you at present believe. – I will gladly liquidate your families debts within a month. I shall need your help to enable the transfer of the money to be made."

Now he took hold of Estelle's hands which Daniel had just relinquished, before saying, "If so, as neither Angela nor I could bear the thought of you being forced to live such a terrible life with that man. – and unless you agree, it still might happen. Could you forgive us sufficiently for our past and accept Daniel and Robert's offer and become a citizen of the United States. – Then they could never make you go to the Bahamas and marry. – In fact both Angela and I would hope you would agree to stay and live with us, until you have decided how you would want to spend the rest of your life."

A very relieved Estelle now stood up kissed Andrew on the face then turned to Daniel and replied, "Daniel Carroll, after what Andrew has just offered my family, I can tell you, I will gladly accept your offer and ask to become a citizen of this country. It now seems I may have been wrong in my belief that all of you living in America are not to be trusted."

As she had first done as they had been introduced. Estelle smiled rather disarmingly, "Dear Daniel, really, though I've only met you for the first time, only a short time ago. I think I can now understand why since I came here I seemed to hear so much of this man who it seems helped George Washington to rebel against their king. Daniel, I shall be delighted to hear from you your reasons for robbing my father and yet now, without me making any request, will ensure he, and my remaining family, have a happy future."

2

"I was told you are royalty, and are very rich. You should know I do not approved of Kings and Queens. It was the King of England who cause my parents so much trouble and resulted in the deaths of so many good men in this country." At the first opportunity James Downy acquainted this Austrian couple that he did not hold them in great awe. They had travelled nearly fifty miles that day and now James had made camp and prepared an evening meal for all three of them.

Still virtually challenging them and ensuring that however important they thought they were, he did not hold them in great esteem. "Daniel Carroll told me you have two kids, and beside this land in West Virginia you, also, own a tobacco estate in Florida. – Just why did you come here. Why even come here from Europe if you were so important there. What gives you the right to judge whether the whisky Dr. Crow makes is one we should support. Both Monica Downey, and Antoinette Brady, is a French lady, who learned all about whiskey in France, and confirm our own opinions that it is a very good drink."

James had hardly spoken to them on the journey and both Louisa and Anton were now shocked at his apparent attack on them In fact Louisa could see Anton was very annoyed and feared he would cause an altercation, so she replied for both of them, "I'm sorry that it seems you did not want to come to collect us and take us to Kentucky. I'm sorry that you think that having been born into royalty, it has guaranteed a happy and comfortable life. – I can tell you that you are very wrong."

Before anyone could intervene she continued, "You ask why we came here from Europe. – I will tell you. - If we had not, I should have been sent to live in a convent for the rest of my life, and my first child Antonia, would have been taken from me after she was born and adopted. Anton here would be dead, executed because he had given me that child before we had married. In any case marriage would never have been allowed between our two families, for they disliked each other. - America has given both of us the chance to live and have a family we adore."

It was obvious James knew nothing of this and found it difficult to believe it. "But I was told you were both a prince and princess, surely your position would save you from this?" Now Louisa managed to smile. "It was because we were these things and by my conceiving out of wedlock I created a scandal, which might destroy the name of the Hapsburg, and of all the Austrian line. – No, James we know how much we owe to this country, first Florida, and now even more, to the United States. In fact we hoped by coming with you we might be helping this country we now dearly love."

It was evident that what Louisa had said had shaken James. He did not know how to reply, all his bitterness, what he thought was an imposition in having to leave his estate and come and bring these two, he considered as idlers, now did not make sense. Louisa saw this and tried to offer an olive branch. "Now you know the truth about us - No, we not only so far have done little to repay, but have not attempted to do what you and those other families in Kentucky have already done, we hope now we might help. But please tell us about your self. I understand you met your wife under exceptional circumstances."

James seemed pleased to be given an escape. "Mrs. Albrecht you have just told me you were not married when your first daughter was conceived. Well my dear wife Lilie, has given me two children, though my eldest child, Leila, is a Miami Indian braves child. Yet I believe I am a very fortunate man. Please let me tell you how it happened."

Although both Louis and Anton knew a little of James history from Daniel Carroll, they did not inform him and encouraged him to tell the whole story. When he had finished, they complemented him on risking his life to save Lilie, but added they considered he was fortunate to win a woman who had overcome her terrible treatment. They now told him they looked forward to meeting her and Helga, Paul Eliot's wife who have suffered the same raping and enslavement.

Before they lay on the hard ground to sleep for the first time in the open, all the recent rancour had vanished. It seemed that James now had a totally different opinion of the two he was carrying on his carriage. As the journey progressed James came to increase his opinion of the two of them, when they told him they had never slept rough before. However perhaps the fact that they confessed they loved riding horses and knew a little about horse breeding, from their stable in Austria, perhaps this fact was a deciding factor. They were fortunate with the weather, though they twice were almost drowned by torrential thunder storm rain.

However they arrived safe and sound and received a warm welcome from Lilie Downey, though they were soon introduced to the other four families.

Perhaps because of what James had told them, Louisa enjoyed most having a chance to talk in private with Lilie and Helga, telling them how much she admired them for overcoming their terrible past. In turn when they introduced them Pohanna as Stuart Downey's indian wife they now realised the cost, particularly to women, in extending the boundaries of this new country.

Because of their understanding, but probably even more because they were able to show all of them their ability as horse riders, though Louisa had to explain that having been brought up to ride side-saddle, she still was not quite at home with her legs spread eagled over the saddle, amusing them by telling them in Europe such methods were considered indecent, and even immoral for a woman to ride that way. Laughingly she admitted, it did have an exciting effect on her.

Now it was time for them to introduce both of them to Dr. James Crow and on horseback they took them to Paris. Both Monica and Antoinette had demanded to accompany them, as they felt a little annoyed that these two had been sent for this purpose. In the event, they need not have worried. As soon as Dr. Crow had given them three samples of his distillation, both Louisa and Anton, admitted that this whiskey, though different from the Scottish variety, and certainly missing being heated over peat fires, was quite superior from anything they had drank since they arrived in America.

All four of them favoured one of the three samples Dr. Crow offered them, but still considered there might be a market for the other two. In fact with Dr. Crow's permission and even amusement, they christened the special one they liked 'Old Crow Whiskey'. However both Louisa and Anton told everyone, that when they returned they would recommend investment to enable Crow to build a series of stills to produce all three varieties, but with a greater production of the 'Old Crow' variety.

Now they had to discover a suitable site. As they knew if they gave their approval, the plan was to transport the barrels of whiskey by the Ohio and Monongahela Rivers, this site should be north of Paris. However, though it might be too small for a large boat to sail on it. There was a good tributary of the River Ohio, flowing due north, only a little distance north of Paris.

Since land was being sold and acquired very quickly as settlers poured into Kentucky, feeling sure now that the consortium would approve. Louisa and Anton took the risk and used their own letters of credit they had brought with them to buy a site approved by everyone, most especially by Dr. Crow, who at last believed that his dream of producing his new brand of whiskey in quantity, might soon be achieved.

This settled, and as even if accepted, it would take some time, not only to build on the site but obtain suitable boats to ferry it to market, as the weather was excellent, Louisa and Anton accepted James and Lilie's invitation to stay for a time, even becoming involved in their business of horse breeding.

When out riding on James' estate and Louisa was alone with him he asked, "Am I now forgiven for my rudeness as we began our journey. Really I felt annoyed that I had to leave poor Lilie to run our estate, whilst I came to collect some toffee nosed Austrians, who probably had never done a days work in their lives. – How very wrong I was."

Louisa bent over and took his hand from his reins. "There is nothing to forgive. It was far better you told us what you thought of us. – In the event it pleased me, for not only was I able to tell you of Anton and my escape, it gave me a chance to tell you how wonderful I believed was your wife, for in fact, Daniel had told me how it all happened, before we came with you. – Once again it confirmed my belief that this new country will only survive so long as we have people like you and Lilie, yes and all the others now living here, if we are willing at times, to place our lives at risk."

So after spending a further three weeks enjoying the countryside and the friendly company of everyone, but now, not before Louisa had taken Pohanna aside to tell her how much she admired her and was so happy Stuart had realised what a wonderful women she was, at last they made arrangements to return. This time James insisted that he drove them back as before, promising to come and collect them anytime, if in future they might like to come and spend a holiday with them.

When they arrived they had no difficulty in convincing the consortium to invest heavily in their Whiskey project. However it seemed from what Daniel Carroll had told them the ancillary investment, necessary to build larger boats to transport the whiskey must be further increased, provided Roy Marshall managed to enable the boats to be driven by steam power. This might, itself, be a worthwhile investment for other reasons.

3

With Roy Marshall away in West Virginia both Jansen Carroll and Hugh Foyle were kept busy making their cotton mill prosperous. It was now certain, either they greatly extended the factory or set up a new mill somewhere, they could not satisfy the demands now made for woven cotton cloth. Jansen's wife, Mechia, herself always interested in designing clothes, as a hobby, had seen a further market for women's clothes made from their cotton fabric. She had interested Linda Foyle in this project, herself now bored with little to do.

It had surprised their men folk for what had started, almost as an in house shop, had become so successful, that Jansen had agreed to invest for Mechia, and set up both a small clothes dressmaking suite alongside a large shop to sell their finished dresses. Already it was being well supported by the fashionable women of Philadelphia and the surrounding, growing, cities.

This had not interfered with Mechia's wifely duties to her husband, bearing him another daughter in 1795 and who was now over three months pregnant with their fifth child. This recent event had caused poor Linda Foyle to realise she was nearly twenty three years of age and not yet had the similar joy of conceiving the child she desired. So desperate had she become that as they worked together, Linda had told Mechia, she had thought of asking Hugh to give her a child, as they slept together most nights.

Mechia had smiled at her but took hold of her hands, "Dear Linda, you do not love Hugh, he merely keeps you sane, I believe you need to find a man of your own to father your child. I saw when we were at Berkeley how very much you liked both Torus Scarron and my younger brother Edwin. – I was surprised it did not become more passionate."

Poor Linda shook he head, "The truth is – I did not know how to respond. – in England I never allowed any of my boyfriends to take liberties with me. - - Well my times with Hugh are so different – I still feel wicked doing it, though, you are right, I think I would go mad, if I did not let him take me.

---- But, Mechia, I did not really know how to act when I was left alone with either of them."

Now Mechia gave a kind laugh showing she understood. "I can now see why they both so soon appeared to lose interest in you, for at the beginning, and like when they came here last year, I was sure they liked what they saw of you. – Linda this is America. – You must forget what you were taught in England.- Here both men and girls expect a degree of intimacy in their courtship and quickly lose interest, believing their partner lacks interest in them, if it is lacking. – Linda I slept with Jensen many times and had full intercourse with Jensen, long before we married. I had, also, slept a few times with others."

Still holding her hands Mechia continued, "If you want to win a man here, you have to take a few risks, just like you are doing with Hugh. – You have got to let the man enjoy you, but only if he satisfies your desires as well – at least if the worse happens, here you can easily rectify it with a quick abortion. – Now our dress shop and manufacturing is going well, I will tell Jensen I want to enjoy the company of my family at Berkeley. I will take you with me and you can start again to seduce my brother – and others – I will show you the way."

Linda was delighted, "But will Jensen agree to you going?" Now Mechia really laughed, "Oh! I'm sure he will. He knows, only too well what will happen whenever I go to Berkeley whilst I'm pregnant. – He does not like it – but he dare not try to stop me, or I would stop his similar affairs with others there, as he did when we all went for our holiday there."

Now she astounded Linda, "It always happens when I'm pregnant. I shall go and sleep again for at least a fortnight with Janse Van Braker, as I already know his wife, Eleonara, who was Eleonara Vender before she married him, is already pregnant for the eight time by him, though she is only a year younger than me. You see the Dutch Vender family came to Berkeley with the other Dutch families, as they had lived at Albany, which was soon occupied by the British during the war."

Mechia could see Linda was both amazed but puzzled, "The Vender women evidently love pregnancy, Eleonara's twelve year older sister Annatie, married to Pieter Becker, has had babies at least every two years since they married and though now about forty three, will have endured thirteen or more pregnancies. Well it seemed Eleonara fell for her sister's husband, Pieter, when only fourteen whilst Annatie was recovering from a bad birth, her fourth, in 1780 and Eleonara conceived his child. However she miscarried when only four month pregnant."

Smiling as she watched Linda's face, "Of course Annatie learned of her sister's condition, but Pieter wanted it to continue. She still loved him and so agreed to him sleeping with Eleonara whenever they were both pregnant.. It continues today, sixteen years later. In fact this arrangement, and the demand that it only occurred when Eleonara was pregnant was my own undoing."

"You see at thirteen I had fallen completely in love with Janse Van Braker. I went to live with him for two years. My mother was furious. Well , Janse begged me to give him a baby, but would not marry me until it was born. – I was no fool. I believed his family consider my indian parentage was beneath their own standing and were preventing him doing so. So I refused. Well Eleonara had only recently miscarried and badly wanted a child. She seduced Janse from me, conceived his child and married him when five months pregnant."

Still smiling for she could see Linda was shocked by her tale, "Well I still liked Janse and he liked me. I fell in love with Jensen, but he always knew of my past and that I still cared for Janse. Since I conceived Anne in 1785, whenever I have been pregnant I have always come back to Berkeley and then always sleep with Janse. Eleonara understands, in fact I still feel she loves her brother-in-law, Pieter, more than Janse. She will gladly go to sleep with him probably already pregnant and relieving her sister, also pregnant. – Linda I really love both men – and Jensen, understands and tolerates me, for we do truly love each other."

Linda was still confused and asked, "And would you give Janse a baby?" Mechia shook her head, "I do not think so, though Janse has asked me too, telling me Eleonara would gladly swap with Jansen. However I think that is carrying it too far. No! I shall enjoy a week in Janse's bed, and shall visit Pieter Becker who is also an accomplished lover. Meantime I must first ensure you to have a bed companion whilst I am occupied. In fact I must take you to meet the Becker's. Annatie's eldest son, Petrus, is about your age, and is unmarried, though I know he has had girl friends, including Electra Carroll. I believe you would enjoy a night in bed with him."

Linda could not help herself, she felt her desire for intimacy increasing. It seems that Mechia was far more experienced than she had known before, even being unfaithful to Jensen, although he would know it would happen. Yes, it seems she could teach her a lot more, of how a woman in America should act and expect from a man, even if not married to him. At least her times with Hugh had ensured she would not come to this man as an innocent virgin. She gladly accepted Mechia's invitation to go to Berkeley.

That evening as Linda lay naked in bed with her brother, having enjoyed full intimacy, she told him why she was going with Mechia to Berkeley and what she had been told today. "Hugh – I cannot be sure I would want to do what Mechia suggests – but if I did. – Would you be angry if I slept with a man whilst I was there." She quite expected Hugh to criticise her and was delighted when he once more took her naked body in his arms, though he only gave her a passionate kiss.

Now he smiled kindly at her. "Dearest Linda, of course I would not be angry – Honestly, I would be very pleased. – I know how badly you want babies, just the same as Fay and Mechia. We both agree I should not at present give you one. That is unfair on you. – Linda, if you really could find a man at Berkeley, you could learn to love. – not just one with whom you might enjoy a intimate night in bed. – If you could find a man who you would like to father your child. – Linda – I would be delighted. – You see I want you to be happy. – I know you still care for the man you left behind in Lancashire."

Hugh's words meant a lot to Linda. Both brought up under the strict Methodist regime insisted by their loving parents. Both had been shocked at the sexual freedom seemed to be occurring in America. It had really shocked both of them. However gradually their views had altered. It was this which enabled to do what they would have considered disgusting in England, brother and sister having intercourse with each other. Yet, not having anyone else of the opposite sex, eventually living together in the same house had broken their resistance.

Now they were both delighted it had happened and blessed Mechia who had done everything to encourage them. They now cared very much for each other, far more than just sister and brother. They did love each other, but neither wanted it to be a permanent arrangement. They both craved for a partner, but so far it had not happened.

Now Hugh as he held his sister's naked body to his, felt strangely happy that his sister might soon find that man she could love. He knew he would miss his times in bed with her, but knew he loved her enough to want her to have a full family life. – Perhaps then, he might also discover a woman he could love and who loved him. He was just sorry that so far he had not succeeded, but did believe that Ellia Dumas had shown an interest in him. Perhaps he, too, should go to Berkeley, and see if this might mature.

A week later Mechia went to stay with her father-in-law, though Edgar Carroll had for many years known of the special relationship between his daughter-in-law and Janse Van Braker. He knew it would not be long before she left to live for a time in the Braker household. Both Edgar and Anna knew that Jensen condoned this, and that there was no danger of it causing any chance of a break up of their marriage, for they both loved each other too much for it to happen.

So they accepted this and in turn were pleased to once again entertain Linda Foyle as their guest, knowing from what Mechia had told them, Linda hoped she might meet a man with whom she might grow to love. They would try to help. Meanwhile Linda was wondering if Petrus Becker, or Piety, as he was known, might be someone she might like to enjoy a more intimate life with.

4

Of course after Daniel and Michelle left to go to Rockville, Manon Lamoignon and Jack Eliot stayed on living in Robert's mansion. Now they enjoyed sleeping together with no one else to bother them. Though Jack had once again raised the question of marriage, Manon had just smiled, but would not say yes. In fact Manon had to admit to herself, now twenty four years of age, she did want to conceive a baby. She liked Jack, but neither had much money.

Possibly fearing if they stayed alone too long, she might submit to Jack's pleadings, she suggested they used their time in West Virginia to see the wonderful countryside, giving her the chance to make some pastel etchings as well a paintings which she might sell. Manon, also, knew a number of persons living close by who had close associations with Daniel and others in the last war. She wanted to meet them, if only so that she could include them in the book she was writing.

They knew two such families lived very close to where they were staying. So they first called on Kylie and Adrian Scott. Manon was frank and told them about the book she was attempting to write to cover the entire history of the interesting families and begged them to enlighten them of their past. Both agreed, telling them why they had needed to leave England quickly, their meeting with Neil Reeves and Claire Collins on the boat. Buying two near stretches and settling on this land, their problems with the trees, but the help from Michael Casimir, then how both Claire and Neil left them, so now they owned both lands.

Then explaining that both their two children born in England had now left and had married. How their eldest son was courting and had set up his own business hiring out to felling trees, for the many forest lands around them. How their second son, Clive, had recently left them to attend a finishing school near Annapolis, and hoped to gain entry to University. In doing so explaining about the nearby school run by a high born Austrian lady and her English husband, who was the nephew of the Neil Reeves they had known.

So Kylie had smiled an said, "So we are left with only four remaining children, the last, Elizabeth, if not yet two years old. – Having born Adrian eight children, I doubt if I can give him more." Now Kylie asked if they were married. It was Jack who seemed rather ashamed told them they were not but did live to together. Kylie merely smiled saying, "You need not feel ashamed. Neil and Claire though not married lived together for many years and Claire conceived but lost her child. This happened regularly in these parts."

Adrian now added, "Kylie we must take them to meet the Hobbs and the Reid's. They had an even more extraordinary, though, I should add not unusual, relationship ----" Before he could add more Kylie stopped him, "Adrian say no more. Let us take them there and leave them there. Let them decide how much they tell Manon and Jack ." So after spending a night with them they were taken the next day to the nearby estate to meet these two families.

After Kylie reticence, neither were surprised to find there was only one quite large, almost a logged mansion, on the estate. It seemed the two families lived inside. They were warmly received in what seemed a very large hall-come drawing room by Mary and Brian Hobbs and Erin and Craig Reid, to whom Kylie and Adrian introduced them. Then to all their surprise, both Adrian and Kylie excused themselves, after explaining that their two visitors were compiling a history of the man families who had known each other, during the last war. Saying they must return immediately, but would call on them again very soon.

After they had left they were shown into a large, and obviously communal dinning room for refreshments. It was Brian Hobbs who smilingly asked, "Has Kylie and Adrian told you our own history?" Manon answered, "No! In fact they appeared to be hiding some terrible secret. Before you enlarge on it, let me tell you I am a French woman, brought up in the French court, knowing my father, the Comte, had many mistresses, and I have met several of the illegitimate children born to him. Before I escaped from France, though young, I was no longer a virgin." Now she laughed, "Though I know Jack, here is a little ashamed to admit it, - I now enjoy sleeping intimately with him. – So, nothing you might tell me would shock me, and a truly would liked to know your past, to incorporate it into the book I am writing."

There was no doubt but that Manon's confession had greatly pleased the Hobbs and the Reid's. It was Erin who replied, "In that case perhaps it will not shock you when I tell you, I am very happily married to Craig, as Mary is to Brian. Yet last night I had a delightful night in Brian's bed, whilst Mary enjoyed sleeping with Craig. It happens often once a week, though very occasionally, we sometimes feel the need during the day."

Seeing their surprise she smiled and continued. "I have given Craig six children and Mary has given Brian the same number, our last were born nearly two years ago. All our children are by our husbands but we have always shared a pregnancy together, so we could safely swap partners. All our children knows this happens, and we are not ashamed."

Brian now explained, "Shortly we will inform you of how this happened and why, this building, is really two houses joined together by the hall and dinning room for we often eat together. The Hobbs' residence is on the right of where we sit and the Reid's wing is on the left. This facilitates the way we can change bed companions. In fact both Brian and I love almost equally Erin and Mary, as they both love us. It is true that possibly Mary loves me just a little more than she loves Craig and as Erin prefers Craig. – All this stems for what happened in the past. – Mary perhaps you should tell our visitors the full story."

Manon and Jack sat enchanted as Mary told them of both her and Erin's crime in Ireland and sent to America and bought as an indentured servant to Joseph Quincy. His cruelty, then his murder and then their purchase by both Brian and Craig. Freely admitted they were misused by them, learning to sleep each night with either of them, Their growing love for the two men, each with a slight preference. How Brian and Craig had seemed to not want them as permanent partners, refusing their pleas for babies. How, with Daniel's assisted loan, they had admitted their love and now had enjoyed over seventeen wonderful married years together.

Mary concluded, "Well it seemed that even after our marriage our men folk still wanted intimacy with both of us. So we took pity on them, and it is still continuing. Manon, you confessed your past – yes and your present. – Tell me how do you now judge us?"

Manon did not hesitate. "I think it is a wonderful arrangement. I know, if given the same opportunity, I would have enjoyed a similar relationship." She turned and gently kissed Jack then added, "I really do enjoy living with Jack. If we were rich enough, I would have, already accepted his proposal of marriage. – However, after my upbringing in France, I doubt if I could give me body to only one man. – It is this, more than our lack of wealth, which makes me hesitate, - for before you now, - and I have not said this to Jack before, - I do love Jack Eliot."

Now a delighted but astounded Jack seized Manon in his arms and hugged her body to him. "Now I'm so delighted we came here today. At last she seems to believe what I've been telling her, that I do truly love her. – I can also set her mind at rest, and inform her, should we marry, I would not try to stop her enjoying pleasures, sometime, in another man's bed, though I would hope all her babies would be by me."

An equally delighted Manon poured out her love for Jack and smoothed his face in her kisses. In a few minutes both were overwhelmed by the tight embraces of Mary and Erin. Then the men said, "Come let us sit outside. It seems we four have found two new friends today. Now we all hope you two may find the happiness we have been blessed with, simply because of the understanding and forgiveness of two women we had so misused."

They stayed there that night and were glad to help them supervise their Negro slaves as they gathered a large crop of vegetables and then fill several bags of flour from the granary, telling them they must stay another night, for on the following day they would take all of them to Fort Pitt so they could sell their goods, having a long standing arrangement with several of the stores in the town. There, they would take them to where they knew two other exiles who came with Manon from France had established a very profitable Boat Building Company.

Of course when told their names, both Manon and Jack knew very well Charlotte and Francois Le Raye, and with whom they had shared that perilous journey to Brittany as they had escaped from France. Both Manon and Jack looked forward to once again meeting their friends with whom they had shared fear of discovery and possible death.

5

Of course Francois, Charlotte and, particularly, Fay were delighted when Roy returned from Philadelphia. Charles Voight had already informed them that Roy now had ideas on how, with him, they could introduced steam power successfully into a boat. However when he did arrive they quickly realised that Roy's ideas had developed even further. He told them he was now convinced that their simplest solution was to use paddle wheels attached to the side of the boat, even though propellers might be more efficient. As a speedy solution was essential they must take the easiest route.

However, having explained about Robert Fulton' success, Roy warned them of the possible destruction of the paddle wheels in rough water. They already knew that such conditions often occurred on both the rivers they would have to use. However for a moment they left this question unanswered, as Roy was quickly informed of the decision made by the three people in his absence to, temporary, swap partners for a time, providing Roy wanted intercourse with Charlotte.

A little surprised and wondered if pressure had been exerted on Fay to agree, he first took her aside and made her confirm she was willing to do this. She surprised him, "Dear Roy, I know I want another baby. However, I want to first find a man who I would like to live with for the rest of my life. I cannot be sure that Francois might be the answer, Charlotte tells me he likes me – but he is a Frenchman and has possessed several women when they lived in France. He might see me as merely one more to enjoy."

Roy could see her indecision. "Yet, I feel you would like to try – yes, take the risk. Dear Fay, if this is so, I would approve. – Whatever happens, you know we shall always mean a lot to each other. – After these intimate years together, I would never wish to lose you completely." Fay smiled, pleased at his words, for she still wondered if she could love this man sufficiently to spend her life with him. However she knew an affair with Francois would not destroy this relationship she now treasured.

That night Fay went to sleep in Francois' bed whilst Charlotte was extremely delighted to share Roy's bed. From the start they agreed it would involve complete intimacy but they would try to ensure neither conceived. In fact they found it soon did more to their business relationship. Both knew if Roy should succeed in proving steam propulsion to their boats, then there boat building business would quickly bring them a fortune.

Now Charlotte confirmed Roy's original assessment that she was not only a good engineer but more important, a brilliant designer. She persuaded both Francois and Roy to build one or two model boats of different sizes but to the scale she required. Then for several days she locked herself each day in the drawing office they had built for their earlier designed boats. Although they could see she was working unceasingly on a large drawing board, she refused to tell them what she was doing. Even in bed Roy could not get her to inform him.

Then it seemed she had drawn something they felt correct, but would still not tell them. Now she was obviously doing mathematical calculations, which at times, seem to demand changes in her drawings. Finally after almost a month of continuous work she emerged smiling carrying a large board on which was the design of her creation.

She knew she had their attention and laughed. "I think I have the possible answer to the destruction of those paddle wheels. – We need to give them some support – some protection. We must build boats with two skins. One boat inside the other. Then in between we can rigg our paddle wheels. Not only will it make it very difficult to tear them away, I have calculated, it will actually add to their speed, though they will be much heavier and so not only more expensive to build, but use more coal to power them. – I've checked all the stresses. Honestly, I believe it will work but we shall need to get more investment, for we shall need more machinery."

Both Roy and Francois together gripped Charlotte by the waist and then each smothered her face on one side and the other, with their kisses, telling her what a brilliant woman she was. She undoubtly enjoyed their embrace but then Roy became more practicable, telling them they must first decide how much additional investment they required. Their original investment given to them to set up the boat factory had never been satisfactory established.

Roy told them, whilst in the east he had called on Edgar Carroll, explaining what he had in mind. "It seems Edgar has such confidence in me that he called in his lawyers. Together we established a joint company under the name of 'Carroll, Marshall, Boat Company." Edgar has supplied the capitol to initiate the company, though I have invested half of my quarter-share of Jenson's cotton factory, which I will lose to Edgar if this company fails. – So we already have an existing company to offer to Daniel and others for further investment."

Roy saw the look of disappointment on all their faces and guessed he knew the reason so he went on, "I think I should tell you that the names of the original directors of this company, necessary when establishing a new company. They are Carroll, Marshall, Le Raye and Bradbury. " He was rewarded by a completely changed attitude. It was Francois who stuttered, "But we have no funds of our own to invest."

Now Roy laughed, "Unknown to you, you have already made that investment. The articles state that as directors you agree to use your own expertise entirely for the company without any additional charge. – My friends, today Charlotte has shown that without her drawings and then Francois' ability to turn her plans into fruition, there would be no future for this company. I must ask you to accept the inclusion of Fay Bradbury, for but for her, I doubt if I would have come to America."

That night as Roy lay with Charlotte after she had offered her lovely naked body to him said, "Charlotte you are both an amazing as well as beautiful woman. I cannot thank you enough for solving, - no saving – our company from possible disaster today. Frankly, I believed a woman's desire for a family life and children would prevent her from using her brain from such involved creations."

Now she admonished him, "You obviously have a poor opinion of women. To you it seems you think we are only there to give you men pleasure and conceive and bear your children. My father knew my true value and taught me how I could do many things as well as any man. – Without him doing that I ----"

Roy stopped her in mid sentence. "Charlotte. Though you may be right, today, I considered you not as a woman, but as the brilliant engineer you, undoubtly are. You are far more intelligent than me. I know my limitations. I never had the training you had. – This new company we have established. – Both Edgar Carroll and I knew it would never be successful without your expertise. Of course I know one reason he agreed to invest and help me formulate things, was because he knows his daughter Electra, believes I am the type of man she wants. I think he hopes I might accept her and become part of his family."

Roy felt Charlotte react immediately and had expected it, "Oh! Then you only lie with me because your Electra is not available, as she was when you were at Berkeley. I had thought that Fay was my real rival. – I'm sorry – I hope I did not disappoint you as a substitute." Roy saw tears had appeared and ran slowly down her face. He seized her violently and pulled her naked body hard against him in a passionate embrace. She feared he was about to hurt her, to punish her for what she had just said.

Instead after pressing his lips to hers, so long that he took her breath away, he then released her though still holding her close to him. "No! Charlotte you are very wrong. I did not sleep with Electra and only met her for a minute. – Charlotte - I think I truly love you - I cannot be sure, for I still have deep feelings for Fay. – They will never go. But to me Electra is a very shallow woman. Born into luxury she believes her wealth will ensure she has a rewarding sexual life. – Although I cannot yet be sure of my emotions – You need never fear about Electra. – Dear, Charlotte, please be patient with me. I would like to see if we both could have a future together, for as I said you are a wonderfully brilliant – but also a very beautiful woman. – er – I do suppose, in time, you would want children."

Charlotte could not help herself. Undoubtedly relieved at what he had said, now amused, nay almost offended by his question, replied, "Just because I can plan and calculate things does not mean I'm not a normal woman. – Whatever do you think I was doing whilst you were roguering me earlier. I'm twenty four, of course I want children – many of them, and as soon as possible –either by you or some other man." His answer was to once again embrace and kiss her adding to her delight, "Then I must see about that."

The next day they had a surprise visit from Manon Lamoignon and Jack Eliot brought to them by the Hobbs and Reid families who had made their acquaintance many times before. Charlotte and Francois told Fay and Roy how the four of them had escaped from France when the terror was at its highest, and in great danger. They were also pleased that Manon and Jack had become lovers. They made their visitors very welcome, entertaining them to a new restaurant that had just been established in the town.

Their own house was too small to house them, but the others had expected it and always stayed at the hotel when they came to Fort Pitt. However once the Hobbs and Reid's had sold all their produce they were entertained on the river in one of their own boats, picnicking down stream, and telling them of their plans to enlarge their business and actually start to build much larger boats capable of being driven by steam power. Telling them they must soon go to see Daniel Carroll as his consortium had promised to invest in a factory to make these if they could build one and make it work.

It was when Fay reminded them they should return soon as she had not completed the invoices and financial returns as she had been interrupted the day before. Jack immediately asked if could help. "You see in Ireland, I always acted as my families accountant. I was trained that way, as well as in horse breeding. " Fay was delighted to accept and he did so once they returned.

Then he surprised all of them by being very critical at their own book keeping, telling them, they would have to run these accounts far better if they were to extend their business, and might, already, be being defrauded by companies supplying goods to them. It was Roy who asked if they might agree to stay for a time and help them to put things right, promising to pay him for his trouble. Jack was willing but asked Manon if she was willing to do so.

She had surprised him saying, "I had no idea you had any talents that way. Why if you are good at accountancy, you might yet earn enough money for me to think I might consider your marriage proposal in a different light." Roy and the others had not known of their serious lack of wealth, dependent on Daniel Carroll's generosity since they came from France. Now Manon admitted she did love Jack but refused to marry until they had acquired enough money to establish the family she desired.

Now he surprised both of them ."Providing both of you were willing to stay here and make this your home, I would have a small house built close to ours. I would then employ you, permanently, as the Accountant to our firm. We have needed this for some time. Fay has generously tried to help, for she was far better at this than any of us." - Now looking at Manon he added. "You know what I would be willing to pay him, might this make you believe that he might yet be able to support that large family, it seems you desire."

She did not answer Roy, but pulled Jack to him and kissed him. Then said, "You may not be a French man, but I do believe you would make a good father of my children. – let us see how you progress. Please accept Roy Marshall's offer. I'm certain whilst you work I shall be able to add to our income in painting many views of this magnificent countryside and rivers." It seemed that the population of the river bank around Fort Pitt was going to increase. There was going to be a need for many more persons to help establish this new business.

6

A new century had dawned and New Years Day, 1800, was celebrated in the small and newly constructed log cabins of a settlers in Indiana, Ohio or Kentucky, as in the large mansions in Virginia or Maryland. That year a new capitol had been created for the United States, a purpose build city designed by a French architect, Pierre L'Enfant. Only one possible name could be given to this new city, namely Washington. Though not fully completed it was sufficiently advanced for the centre of government to be transferred from Philadelphia to Washington.

Though a quasi war of a kind at sea existed between the United States and France, President Adams had brilliantly avoided a costly and damaging full conflict. However it now seemed unlikely that he would be elected for a second time in a year's time. What George Washington had feared had happened. The country had divided into two warring parties the Federalist's of which Adams was a member and the Republicans, whose leader was Thomas Jefferson, at present Vice-President to Adams, but fighting him all the way.

Certainly the introducing of centralised taxation, such as the disastrous Whiskey Tax and then in 1798, the Property Tax, leading to two civil rebellions causing numerous deaths. The Fries rebellion against the last tax, and President Adams, sensiblely pardoning of Fries, when sentenced to death, actually destroyed his own party, quarrelling with Alexander Hamilton. Anti-Federalist sentiment was now so strong that it seemed certain Adams would never be given a second term. If so it seemed a certainty that Thomas Jefferson would become the third President of the United States.

However as the century's New Year were celebrated by the five families in Kentucky, as all those English, Polish, Swedish and Austrians living in West Virginia, in fact everyone in Virginia and Maryland, including the recent exiles from France, - what happened next year was far less important than what happened today.

After Louisa and Anton returned and their affirmation concerning

Bourbon Whiskey, the consortium had agreed to invest heavily in its production, recompensing them for what they had spent in buying the land and buildings for its manufacture. Then the consortium were informed that the 'Carroll, Marshall Boat Company', had constructed a river boat powered by steam, and invited them to come to Fort Pitt to test it, telling them if they should want any such boats for the transport of their whiskey, they would have to invest heavily in the company, as it would require specialised machinery to build these in quantity.

Daniel well remembered his words with Roy Marshall, over a year before, and smiled. Roy had warned him then, that if he succeeded it would cost him and the consortium a lot of money. Actually, provided this test boat worked, they had no option. They needed several of these to transport the Whiskey to the east, with the virtual absence of roads suitable for heavy vehicles. Very quickly they all went to Fort Pitt.

They were surprised at the size and shape of the new boat. Roy explained that it contained a double hull and in between, amidships, were built the paddle wheels which when turned by steam power gave it motive power. He told them this was the result of the brilliant design of Charlotte Le Raye, which now prevented the wheels being torn away in rough weather. It seemed they were surprised that a woman could be both a designer and engineer, Roy saw this at once, and interjected. "It seems you men obviously have a very poor opinion of women. I can say to a great extent the future of this company depends on Charlotte Le Raye, who I am pleased agreed to become one of our directors."

In fact the consortium were completely satisfied when the capacity of this new boat was tested, even insisting that that waited until they could prove it still worked satisfactorily when a storm swept down the river. After that, they invested the amount of money Roy Marshall demanded to equip the new factory and then ordered four boats to be built as soon as possible.

It was a very delighted four who congratulated each other after the consortium had left. However it meant that Roy must again travel east to Philadelphia and Baltimore to order the necessary machinery, steam power and the steam boilers for the boats. Their original boat building business was now so efficient that it was possible for Francois, Fay, and now Jack Eliot to run this and control their many employees. In fact even Manon agreed to help. She designed far better forms than the ones they had first introduced.

So to Charlotte's delight Roy asked her to accompany him, warning her if so, she might be asked to help keep him warm in bed each night, a task she admitted she would enjoy. Before he left he spoke to Fay, begging her to continue her sexual liaison with Francois. He knew she was enjoying it, but she still could not be sure of her true feeling for him.

They had now built a small two roomed shack in which Manon and Jack could live, knowing that only one bedroom was necessary. It seemed that it would not be long now, as Jack was receiving a good salary as their Accountant, before Manon relented, and accepted his frequent proposals of marriage. She thought he might now be rich enough to support her – and the many children, she warned him, - she would demand he gave her.

Roy and Charlotte called at Berkeley on their way, so as to inform Edgar Carroll of the success of their joint company. He felt proud as he introduced Charlotte Le Raye, explaining it had been her brilliance which had solved the difficulty of damaged paddle wheels. There was no doubt that Edgar was surprised that it was a woman who had solved the problem. Even more surprised when Edgar called a servant to show them their rooms, Roy had explained that only one was necessary.

However surprised he was he still smiled an said, "It seems that my daughter, Electra is going to be a very disappointed woman. I'm certain that as soon as you arrived she had made plans for some entertaining nights. – She seems she will now have to look elsewhere."

Roy felt he must ask, "Do you mind – I know you considered I might become your son-in-law. Perhaps this was why you gave me your financial support." Edgar quickly put his mind at rest. "No! That is not the case. Long ago when you helped my son, Jenson, to make his cotton mill work, I could see your potential, and particularly after you first went to Fort Pitt to introduce steam power into the boat building. – I admit I'm sorry – but you, and it seems dear Charlotte has helped, to make our investment very profitable."

. Changing the subject, he now told them that Linda Foyle had come with Mechia to stay. "I believe Mechia hopes Linda may find a suitable man, with whom to form a permanent partnership, whilst she stays here. I understand she has, already, enjoyed some intimacies with several of our men friends in the locality."

Roy was very pleased to hear that. He told Charlotte how sorry he had felt for her when they lived close by in Philadelphia. He admitted that he believed she had found some solace in bed with her brother, but she deserved a full sexual life and a family. Then he smiled, "It seems we shall find a very lonely Hugh Foyle, her brother, when we arrive at Philadelphia."

Then Charlotte held him close to her, "Dearest! You made me so happy today, particularly what you said to Edgar. However, you should know, I actually wondered if your strong desire to call on him was so you could renew your time with Electra." He gave her a very hard slap on her bottom but then buried his lips on hers. "Dear, dear, Charlotte, though, even now I cannot promise I would like to spend my life with you. You need never fear that you may have a rival in Electra."

That night in bed Charlotte asked Roy to enlarge on the lives of both Linda and Hugh Foyle. Then as they lay recovering from a very enjoyable hours of intimacy she said to him, "Roy, I want us to act as matchmakers. I must call on Aleia Dumas. She and Jean were very kind to both Francois and me when we stayed with them after escaping from France. Again they took both of us to Fort Pitt where we discovered coal, iron ore and of more important the need for small boats. I know, at one time, her daughter, Ellia had a crush on Hugh Foyle. Let us see if see would like to come with us to Philadelphia, telling her she could stay with us in your house there, and then might meet Hugh again."

It seemed Roy was delighted at her suggestion, so they both went to call on Aleia the next day. By chance they found her daughter Ellia was with her. When they began to tell Aleia at the successful business they had established at Fort Pitt, and Charlotte told her, this would not have happened but for them going with her to meet Tonsac, Ellia asked to be excused. However Charlotte asked her to remain, telling her they wanted to discuss in private, another matter which concerned her.

Surprised but intrigued she stopped and listened to Roy's tale of how they had developed their boat building firm and its now, even greater successful future. Then after refreshments Roy asked if they might speak privately with Ellia and Mechia withdrew.

Charlotte immediately confronted her. "Ellia, I know you were interested in the past, but tell me now, truthfully, what are your opinion of Hugh Foyle. – You once told me you thought he wanted a life with his sister, Linda. – Well Linda is now here in Berkeley. We are going tomorrow to Philadelphia as Roy has some important work to do there. – I wondered if you might like to come with us and stay in Roy's house. It's near Hugh's and you could easily find excuses to meet him. - I believe he may be lonely, with his sister away."

Ellia could not help herself, she burst our laughing. "Are you trying to get me to jump into Hugh's bed?" Charlotte replied quickly. "Yes! For I think you would like it. When I stayed here, I discovered that you enjoyed intimate relations with some men here, so I think a few nights in Hugh's bed, might be a welcome change. But seriously, Roy tells me he knew Hugh found you very interesting each time he met you. – Really, I do hope you will come with us."

Ellia stood up and hugged Charlotte, "O course I'll come. I shall be very pleased. – Yes! I do think a lot about Hugh. In Philadelphia, I will be able to see if I might want a future with him." The three of them left the next day.

7

Of course ever since 1796 America had been hearing of the French victories in Europe. However they very quickly released these were engineered by the General Napoleon Bonaparte, as in Italy, the defeating and forcing the Austrian to make peace, the annexing of Holland and Switzerland, changing their names to Batavian and Helvetic Republics. However when he then invaded and captured Egypt, it seemed he was contemplating driving eastwards, perhaps to India.

The Carroll's were delighted when they learned of Admiral Nelson's fantastic victory over the French Navy at the Battle of the Nile, completely destroying its navy but for four ships which fled. They mistakenly considered Bonaparte was now isolated in Egypt, only to learn he had returned to France and engineered a coup d'etat against the Directory and proclaimed himself as First Consul for ten years. By 1800 he had taken up residence in the Tuileries Palace, then set out to gain a further number of conquests through the Alps into Italy winning the Battle of Marengo forcing the Austrians to again sue for peace.

Re-entering Paris he imposed himself as a dictator , naming himself Consul for life. Then arranged a truce with Great Britain with the Treaty of Amiens in 1802. Everyone knew this was merely a pause, as both sides were tired and needed to recuperate. In fact it barely lasted a year. However this did give the United States a chance to finally stop the quasi war with France in the Atlantic, but it also proved a blessing for those living at Rockville.

After that meeting at Rockville in 1798 arrangements were quickly made to apply for Estelle Carroll to become a citizen of the United States. In fact as President Adams was considering enforcing anyone who applied for citizenship, to wait a number of years, to prove their true allegiance to the country, it took a little longer. Fortunately before it happened before a demand for extradition was received from Lord Dunmore demanding the return to the Bahamas of his contracted daughter-in-law. This did give Daniel Carroll a chance of revenge for an episode with the Lord nearly thirty years before.

Daniel had remembered with anger the reception both he and his friends had received then they had called on Lord Dunmore, then Governor of Virginia, before the last war, attempting to ensure peace in the province. He had insulted them, not even understanding that his own burgesses were against him, swearing he would hang any man who dared rebel against the king in any way.

It was Daniel Carroll who wrote his answer to his demand. "It seems you have not yet accepted your defeat of thirty years ago. You have dared to demand that we send to you the person of Estelle Carroll, a citizen of this land the United States of America, in order to provide your son with the large family he demands. I take this as a personal attack on a citizen of this country, and I shall write to Britain demanding an apology since they appointed you as Governor. – I remain, Daniel Carroll" He showed everything personally to Estelle, who was delighted at his action. After that and after he had written to the Privy Council in Britain, there were no further communications, but unfortunately, no apologises. Estelle now realised how much she owed to Daniel in saving her from the fate she had feared.

Meantime as she lived at Rockville, Andrew Carroll had begun to institute his promise to help her family in England. Like Daniel, Andrew had always been friendly with Robert Eden, a son-in-law of Lord Baltimore of Ireland, living on the Calvert Estate not far from Rockville. Lord Baltimore had been grateful to Daniel for arranging with George Washington that he could still retain his lands, after the war, having as then Governor of Maryland, then been obliged to assist the British. The difficulty was how to initiate correspondence with Estelle's father.

Although she had written to her father explaining that she had no intention of now, travelling to the Bahamas and marrying. Explaining she was applying for United States citizenship, which would prevent her being forced to go to there and marry. Then she told her father of the generosity of the American Carroll's and Andrew, the Master of Rockville, who would use the assets of his estate to relinquish her father's debts. However to do this she needed from him the full details of his debts and to whom, also the name of his bankers, to which this money must be sent.

It was obvious that Sir David Carroll was confused. Not understanding why she had not gone to marry James Murray, then become an American and now wanted to pay off his debts. Knowing Robert Eden was in constant communication with his grandfather, Andrew gave him all the facts of why and how he wanted to help Estelle's father, asking Robert to persuade his grandfather to send a member of his family in Ireland to go to Wookey, and explain matters to Estelle's father. Robert agreed and then Andrew sent Sir David a letter telling him of a Calvert was coming to explain matters to him.

Eventually after the Calvert's visit, at last Sir David understood. In fact it seemed they had acted, only just in time, as proceedings had been served which would have led to him being sent to prison. Soon Andrew learned the size of these debts, which were considerable. However the Rockville estate was very prosperous. Payment would only mean the loss of about three years profit, so eventually financial transactions were made by Andrew's accountants and eventually money was deposited in Sir David's Bank account, enabling him to extinguish his long standing debts.

So, at last, Sir David was beginning to understand everything that had happened since his daughter had, been saved, and landed at Annapolis, but still confused why this Andrew Carroll of Rockville had so generously saved him from jail, and his other daughter, Julia, from destitution. Also why Estelle had become an American citizen, and intended staying in America.

She felt she had to explain to her father the reasons. She told him what James had demanded of her, though it seemed her mother on the ship had told her they both knew of this. "Father, if I had married that man, I doubt if I would have been alive in ten years time. I want children, as much as any woman, but not to conceive and bear one every year. – I hope here in America, I can find a man I like, but who is not so demanding, for it seems here, most husbands let their wives decide when they conceive their children."

Then in a different vein she had continued, "Father I really do believe it will happen – I will not tell you more – but I hope I may have found that man – but, as I say, it may not happen as I would desire. – However I could never had let you go to prison. ----It was when I told both Andrew Carroll, who has given me a home here, - Yes! And Daniel Carroll, who we both have believed for so long was the perpetrator of all our ills, - ---that I must go to James and marry him. Then both told me I need not make this sacrifice and would pay all your debts. – Ironically, it seems that Rockville, which we have for so long felt we should own, has in fact removed your debts and the threat of prison."

Now Sir David, at last understood everything and sent a very apologetic but grateful letter to Andrew, thanking him, for saving him and his family, and especially for giving Estelle a home. Both Andrew and Estelle had begged Sir David and Julia to come to stay for a time with them, offering to pay for their passages. With the war at sea, they both declined. However now, at least for a time there was a measure of peace between Great Britain and France.

So Sir David had written to say he and Julia would like to accept their offer and come on a prolonged visit, as they had no reasons for staying, at present, in England. Sir David, was also wondering who was this man, who it seemed Estelle had found to be one she might accept as a partner. Perhaps he would discover this after he arrived. No doubt, he would be surprised once he knew and the implications it might engender. But all this was still a secret when in 1802 they boarded a ship and came to America.

8

July 1801 was a very sad time for Ruth Tencin had died at the age of eighty three. She died peaceably though she had been weak for sometime. Fortunately her three children by Anton were able to be with her at the time. They were extremely grateful to Jeanne Cristal who had hardly left her bed for the last three months. Of course the Carroll's, Wilson's, Scarron's and Dumas' had known her, when she was Ruth Oldham, and for over fifty years.

Perhaps poor Kate missed her the most. As Kate Tavish, she had sailed to America with Ruth on the 'Colonial Rose' convicted to endure five years as indentured servants. Though they met their future husbands on that ship, they first had to endure four years as virtually the prostitutes, of two men, who, both used them even conceiving but aborting two of their children. Both women had never been able to understand why Anton and Donald had proposed, marriage to them and gave them nearly forty years of happiness.

Ruth had died a very rich woman. Though the majority of her wealth was divided between her three children, she still left a substantial legacy to her protégé, Jeanne Cristal, who had been her constant companion for the last eight years. Jeanne would never have left her whilst she lived but now felt she was a freewoman again.

Though Jeanne had never purposely tried to cultivate any relationship with the many men who called on Ruth, she admitted she was both delighted and intrigued by the constant attention she had received now for almost two years from Henry Wilson. Of course both Kate and Donald had encouraged it, for they felt Jeanne had saved his life after his affair with Fredericka Carroll ended, when she found another man to marry, turning almost suicidally to drink. It seemed Jeanne had made him ashamed and virtually forced him to stop drinking, and report to her each day to prove this.

Gradually a true friendship had developed between them, though for a long time it was platonic. However, pleased that Henry did not try to take her away from Ruth, understanding her reasons, it gradually became more intimate. Jeanne had told him at the beginning she was not a virgin, having as a servant in France to submit to her masters. Yet, in spite of this, their friendship was not completely intimate for over a year and a half. Only then did she invite him to visit and sleep intimately with her.

Jeanne was, also, please at the help he gave her as Ruth became ill, even spending the night sitting next to her by Ruth's bedside. Long before Ruth passed away both knew they had fallen in love with each other, for they were of similar ages. Now with Ruth dead, Henry begged Jeanne to marry him, as she had refused before, but happily lived with him as his wife. As Jeanne was now thirty one, misused so frequently in France, denied then male companionship for some years, Jeanne now wanted children – many of them, so now she gladly agreed providing he promised to give a large family, and quickly.

With her legacy Jeanne Cristal was nearly as rich as her husband. Also, when he found they intended to marry, Ruth's eldest son Francois, married to Louis and Julie's daughter, Anne Scarron, was so pleased as how Jeanne had ensured his mother's final years had been happy ones, built a very large mansion on his land in which Jeanne and Henry could live after they married.

As she lay naked in bed with Henry in this new house, knowing she had got her wish and now carried his child, she marvelled that her, a servant girl, so often misused by the male gentry in France. Escaping, and helping the others to escape, from France, now had found a man of substance who loved her and who she adored, but now was living the life as good as those she had served in France. She knew it was this wonderful new country in which she lived which made it possible.

By now almost every one of those eight Frenchmen and women and the three Irishmen who had shared that nightmare journey as the escaped from France, had settled, found partners and some had married. During their stay with Julie and Louis Scarron once they arrived in America, Jacques Lambelle had quickly come to admire their daughter, Danielle, whilst her younger brother Michael found Louise Lambelle just as interesting.

When they arrived, Michael though only twenty was already relieving his sixty year father, of his responsibilities in his estate. Jacques, himself well trained in France in estate management had readily offered Michael his support. So Jacques and Danielle very quickly became partners, then lovers as did Michael and Louise. Both married in 1797 and now both Danielle and Louise had two children and were hoping they were both pregnant once again. The Scarron estate was extremely prosperous and both Louis and Julie had received much wealth from their families in France before the revolution, so all these families could live together in comfort near Berkeley.

The affair began in 1795 between Jean Condorcet and Kitty Brookes had developed quite quickly. Jean had soon discovered that Kitty, though then only twenty three, was no longer a virgin and had enjoyed intimacy with several boyfriends. The flagrant life of her mother Sophia, after her husband and Kitty's father died, had led to Kitty's early love life, when in her teens as she had lived as a guest in the Casimir household in the Potomac valley.

When only sixteen she had a passionate affair with Karl Wycks but this had ended when her mother brought them all back to live on her, now joint estate, with Colin Chalmers. In fact it was a blessing that Jean Condorcet called on them soon after he arrived in America. Sophia had been very concerned that Kitty, missing her past lover, Karl's, attention, had become involved with a married man, twice her age, who had just lost his wife. But he was a man with few resources, and Sophia felt sure he could not provided for Kitty.

So Sophia had, from the start, encouraged Kitty's relationship with Jean. Fortunately Jean brought up at the French court found nothing strange in the intimate pleasures Kitty bestowed on him. Further more, having heard from Kitty, her mother's previous sexual escapes, found he could admire her. He felt she was fortunate that she had found in Colin Chalmers a man she could love, and replace that terrible longing for her dead husband. Fortunate that Colin found he equally loved Sophia. Very quickly, bored of his new life near Racoonsville, Jean had come to stay for long periods with the Chalmers.

Now Jean offered to help Colin on their large estate, soon taking responsibility for near half, mainly that which had belonged to Sophia before their marriage. At the same time Kitty was now responded to Jean's French seductive manners. Soon they were living on the estate as man and wife. Though careful, in 1799 Kitty conceived Jean's child. Only then did she accept Jean's proposal of marriage, though he had made it several times before. Now settled with their own large house on the estate, and Kitty now the mother of two children, was a very happy and contented woman, much to the relief of her mother, Sophia.

So by the time Sir David Carroll arrived with his daughter Julia, to stay with his daughter, Estelle, at Rockville, all those exiles from both France and Ireland had found permanent partners. Though neither Francois nor Charlotte Le Raye had married they were living intimately with partners they admired, perhaps even loved, and this might develop further. In fact no longer were they French, Irish or English. They were all Americans, and it had been this new country which was responsible and provided a home or all of the to live, marry and raise families. A country spreading westwards to the River Mississippi.

However, suddenly on a single day, April 30th. 1803, the size of this new country doubled. As expected, though after a disputed election, President Adams, the Federalist had failed to be re-elected and Thomas Jefferson, a Republican, had been chosen, with another Republican, Aaron Burr, had been elected Vice President. Jefferson had acted quickly removing many of the tax bills which Alexander Hamilton had introduced., resorting many powers back to the individual states.

France had forced Spain to yield to them the enormous territory of Louisiana in 1800, Napoleon Bonaparte had intended to create a new French Empire there. However the failure of his troops to control Hispaniola after so many died with yellow fever, then the renewal of war in 1803 with Great Britain, he needed the money if he was to control Europe. Jefferson had sent James Munroe and Robert Livingston to Paris to purchase land in the lower Mississippi. To their surprise Bonaparte offered to sell them the whole of territory of Louisiana.

Jefferson, who gave power to the states not liking Federation, now ignored the Constitution and paid fifteen million dollars for this enormous land. At one stroke doubling the size of the United States. Illegal or not, Congress ratified the sale. It was perhaps the best real estate ever acquired for such a little price. It was the decision which was to make the United States a continent in itself.

There were, now, no barriers to westward advance and colonisation, except for the indigenous indians, who most American believed should be annihilated. Now, theoretically there was land for everyone who wished to come and live in America. Adam's bill to make it more difficult to gain Citizenship, requiring settlers to live there for some years before applying, was rescinded. Now this new country wanted and invited the multitudes to come and live there. – It also provided wonderful opportunities for all the families already living and having settled there..

9

The United States had, with some difficulty, tried to number its people and appraise itself of its population. The Census showed it consisted of over Five and a quarter million White population, with White males numbers being greater than females. Also it had a slave population of nearly one million. Of course the greatest density of population was in the Eastern States, though the numbers in the west were increasing rapidly.

However this was not only because of the ever increasing numbers who came from abroad to settle there, but because of the efforts of white females to add to these numbers. Already the five families in Kentucky had each born another child, as Winchester had two very good doctors. But so had all the females who had escaped from France born babies.

Again the long established families had multiplied. Hedwig had presented Robert Carroll with her fourth child and was now pregnant again, whilst Eric and Isabel Casimir now had six children, as had John and Hillary Holstein., as well as Anne and Francois Tencin. But then it seemed most families seemed to increase in size by at least one in every three years. Erin and Craig Reid and Mary and Brian Hobbs, each now had seven children. Claire Wycks, denied for so long of the family she desired, had since her marriage to Philip, she had gladly presented him with five children in fifteen years, and was sorry she could not, now, give him more. All this led to the increasing population.

Now with the territory of the United States doubled, with the Louisiana Purchase, there was room for an invasion of multitudes to colonise and settle there. However this also added to the finances of many of these families. It certainly applied to Francois and Charlotte Le Raye and Fay Bradbury and Roy Marshall with their Boat Building Business near Fort Pitt.

What had begun as one, producing small boats to enable would be settlers to sail to new lands, had now been extended to build steam powered boats, to transport Bourbon Whiskey to the markets in the East. However now the purchase of this new land had ensured a rapidly growing demand for these boats, to carry cargoes and people down the Ohio to the Mississippi. And beyond, even up the River Missouri. It seemed that soon they would start their own Steamship company.

It now guaranteed success for these four people and they, and their investors, would quickly reap large financial benefits. It seemed that in a very few years the four of them might become as rich as those families in the Potomac valley. Fay was now sleeping with Francois every night acting as if she was his wife, just as, in the next room, Charlotte was enjoying a similar life with Roy Marshall. Yet neither of the couples felt they loved each other sufficiently to marry, though Roy had never doubted but that Charlotte would have accepted him, if he had proposed to her.

Both Francois and Charlotte could see that there was still a strong bond between Fay and Roy. Both knew it would continue even if they married others. Perhaps it was after Manon Lamoignon conceived by Jack Eliot, only a month after they married, for Manon had desired this child for so long. In any case both Fay and Charlotte knew their desire for babies were just as acute, particularly Charlotte, now twenty five and still without a child. Together, without their men folk near they had discussed the situation and come to a decision. They would beg their men to make them conceive.

However Fay had been frank with Charlotte. "Whilst I am pregnant with Francois' child, I shall steal into Roy's bed from time to time. You will not stop me. – But, why have you never enjoyed intimacy with your brother, you admit he's seen you naked many times and you slept in his bed. Please, whilst you carry Roy's child try to change this, and see if Francois would be willing to please you, whilst I sleep with Roy."

Charlotte smiled and replied, "I'll see. – Perhaps it is because in France I enjoyed sleeping in the bed of so many men at court, that I grew up never thinking of doing that with Francois. – I must admit after we had settled here in America and was missing my intimate attention, and had not made a male conquest, I did consider asking Francois to help me. – Well I suppose I never had the courage, for we had behaved this way for so long."

Now she knew this. Fay promised that if both men agreed to give them, the children they needed, Fay would quietly suggest to Francois he might ask his sister to help him when Fay returned to Roy for a night. In fact they became conspirators. They would seduce their men, to behave as they would like them to do.

In fact it happened very quickly after Manon and Jack married. Both Francois and Roy admitted they would be very pleased if their women would give them a family, as neither had sired a child until now. As they could not be sure they loved each other enough to marry, they had felt it unfair to ask this of them. However when it was their women who made this proposition, willing to make this sacrifice, they were only to pleased to oblige. Both Fay and Charlotte were pregnant before the Louisiana Purchase occurred.

Soon on Fay's suggestion the two couples would exchange partners for the night. At last Charlotte admitted she enjoyed full intimacy with her brother and wished it to continue. Perhaps it was not necessary, for at present, for either of them, to marry. It was Francois, his arm around Fay's very pregnant waist, as they stood in front of Roy with a similar arm around pregnant Charlotte, summarised the situation. "We have, together, established a very intimate and close business company. Perhaps, since at the moment none of us are interested in anyone other than we four. Perhaps we might establish a Sexual Quartet, just as close as our business, and come to live together as one large family. Perhaps it is not necessary for any of us to commit ourselves to marriage, yet can still continue to enlarge our family." His words were well received by the other three. Both Fay and Charlotte knew they would want more children after they bore their present one.

It seemed that brother and sister, Hugh and Linda Foyle, who had come with Fay and Roy from England, might soon find more permanent partners. Linda was enjoying her long holiday at Berkeley. After staying for a few days at the Carroll household she gladly accepted an invitation to joint Mechia Carroll now staying at the Van Braker household. A very pregnant Eleonara made Linda very welcome. Linda discovered that Eleonara's elder sister, Annatie, now pregnant for the fourteenth time and was forty four years old was coming with her husband, Pieter Becker, the next day. They came with their son, Petrus, who Mechia had specially asked them to bring.

It was quite an experience for Linda, for after a very enjoyable dinner and after a meal and drinks, Janse Van Braker, came and kissed Annatie saying, "Please excuse us leaving Linda with you and Petrus – I shall be glad to fully entertain you tomorrow but I have promised Mechia pleasure tonight." Then he placed his arm around Mechia's waist and led her upstairs as Pieter Becker led his sister-in-law, Eleonara, upstairs. It was obvious the two couple would sleep with each other tonight.

Annatie could see Linda was embarrassed. So she smiled took her hands saying, "When I come with Pieter he always sleeps with my sister, the same happens when Eleonara comes to stay with us. I usually sleep with Janse, but tonight he will enjoy sleeping with his first love, Mechia, Eleonara fully approves of this. – I am grateful that from what Janse just said, it seems he will ask me to sleep with him tomorrow. I always enjoy doing this. – It may seem strange to you but our husbands expect this of us – also the many children we must give them."

Linda was excused further embarrassment as Petrus suggested they went for a walk in the garden. She gladly agreed and they left his mother alone. – Linda could not help but ask if he approved of the way his mother and aunt acted. Petrus just laughed, "They have no choice father and uncle are completely in control of their bodies, who they enjoy at any time." Linda continued, "And when they must conceive?" He laughed, "Oh! Yes! But I doubt if they are ever allowed to wear preventatives."

Now Petrus was very direct, though after what had just happened, Linda was hardly surprised, when he asked, "Linda at your age, have you many boyfriends, and do you enjoy intimacy with them." In fact she felt very annoyed and told him so. "We only met five hours ago for the first time, how dare you ask me such intimate questions?"

Petrus seemed confused then made matters worse, "I'm sorry. You appear to be more my age, - surely you are not still a virgin? - I thought we both might enjoy some pleasure together." Linda was now furious. "Petrus, I am not like either your mother, nor your aunt. No, man would make me conceive and endure so many pregnancies in such a short time. - I'm sorry, I am returning inside, I don't think I want to get to know you. I can hardly believe I could get any intimate pleasures with a man such as you." Turning around she briskly went back into the house and quickly went upstairs to bed.

In fact in spite of what she had said, the next day she could not avoid meeting Petrus. He apologised for last night. "Since you came with Mechia, I assumed, quite wrongly, that you had come for such pleasures as she was enjoying. Eleonara virtually told my mother as much. – Can you forgive me – and let us begin again. Your attitude is a very pleasant one to me, for women here seem to expect me to take them to bed at the first opportunity. – Again, I must make it clear that I completely disapprove of both my mother and aunt's behaviour, though I blame my father and uncle for this. Please let me prove to you that I respect you and your views."

After that Linda felt she could resume pleasantries and what she had hoped might mature from her coming here. Nor was she disappointed. Petrus went out of his way to court her, yet at this time it was only a platonic friendship. However they could talk of their past. She told him why they had to leave England so quickly, leaving the boy friends she loved. In return he admitted the numerous girls he had met and the ones he had enjoyed intimacy. Linda realised he must be a very accomplished lover. So gradually she allowed their meeting to become more intimate, though as yet she had refused his invitation to go to bed with him. Now she knew she liked him.

At the same time, unknown to her, her brother, Hugh, was enjoying a growing relationship with Ellia Dumas, who Charlotte and Roy had brought to Philadelphia. It had, quickly become intimate, for Ellia had wanted this. However, almost to her surprise, she discovered after she had yield her body to him, as she had done to other men she knew, Hugh did not seem to gradually lose interest but, in fact became even more possessive. Ellia could hardly believe her pleasure this gave her, for it did seem that Hugh did care very greatly for her.

She even considered she might yet fall completely in love with Hugh. – But, though she knew, his interest in her might be nothing more than a mere flirtation, she still wondered if he might come to love her. In spite of their nearness and complete intimacy, she did not know. Perhaps it might have amazed her to know, that Hugh, was already wondering if he should propose to her.

It seems it may take a little longer before either Hugh or Linda were certain they had found a partner with whom they would want to start a family, let alone agree to marry. But after so long without it happening, there now was a chance it might occur.

10

Estelle stood up and came and threw her arms around Daniel Carroll. "Dearest Daniel, I think I can now understand why you felt obliged to remove the ownership of Rockville from my great, grandfather's possession. – I never thought I would ever admit this. – Daniel, I've hated you, believing you were the devil incarnate, since I was a very little girl. – You were responsible for my families poverty. My grandfather would never had incurred those terrible debts if we still owned Rockville. – In fact, I was wild with anger when I landed at Annapolis, after the ship was attacked and my mother killed."

She gave a cynical smile, "Wild when those kind men who were trying to help me and others, told me of Andrew's important position in Maryland, and his 'generosity' as Master of Rockville. – Generosity with money which my father desperately needed to pay our debts."

Now she laughed, "Then a few moments later this wonderful man who I had so recently slandered and who I hated, came, took pity on me, and with dearest Angela, gave me a home. – No longer could I hate them, so my real anger was still against you. – Yet when I was rude to you – I wanted to stab you. – You not only showed me how I could avoid this marriage I feared, but asked Andrew to remove my families debts, saving my father from jail. – Now I have both father and sister, Julia, living here with me in this mansion of Rockville. – How could I still feel angry with you."

Now she took Daniel's hands and pressed them to her covered breasts, "Today, - though you had no need to do so, you told me why you felt you must give Rockville to Andrew. – I never knew Hugh Carroll, but can remember his father. –I think I can understand, now, what a wicked man he was. – You were right, Sir Robert would never have wanted Rockville to remain in the possession of a man like Hugh, even more than his father. – Yet, you did not give it to your son, Robert, and today explained why you considered it must belong to Andrew."

Now she bent down and kissed the side of Daniel's face. Still laughing she continued, "Daniel, not only do I forgive you, but I also believe you acted wisely. – In fact it seems that accidentally, by your past actions, you may have provided me with a far better life than if I had stayed and married, anyone, in England. – For it would have been a marriage to improve our position in society."

Estelle now seemed a little in trepidation. "Please tell me Daniel, now you know Adrian has proposed to me, and we are engaged to be married, - You realise this must mean – in a few years, I shall become Mistress of Rockville. – Please tell me – does this annoy you." Daniel's reply surprised her he stood up took her in his arms and kissed her on the lips. "Estelle – That is my answer. – I am delighted it has happened – and more important I believe my grandfather would have fully approved. Rockville is still in all our families' hands. The English and American Carroll's are united again."

In 1803 on the Rockville estate, where so many Carroll's and other Weddings had been held, Lady Estelle Carroll, of the English branch, relinquished her title and married Adrian Carroll of the American branch, and in due course would become Master and Mistress of Rockville. It was an equally happy day for her father and sister, as to all the American families.

Sir David and Julia had come for a prolonged visit. However after Estelle had married, neither wished to return to England. Through the Calvert's, Sir David's possessions in England were sold. He had no son, so when he died the knighthood would revert to the descendent of David's father, Sir Alastaire's, second son. So in fact the titles would remain in England. This was another reason why both Sir David and Julia decided to make their stay permanent. Perhaps the fact that Julia had, like her elder sister, found a partner she hoped to marry, added to those reasons.

It meant a lot to both Daniel and Michelle that things had been resolved to everyone's satisfaction. They remembered deciding, as the lay together in bed, seventeen years before, why they must give Rockville to Andrew. Now it seemed it had proved to be a very wise decision, and they both, now, loved Estelle, as part of their family.

It was the same for those five couples who had come together married and set up their horse breeding establishment in Kentucky , and now this new business producing Bourbon Whiskey. Those three couples acquiring a fortune in building small and large River boats near Fort Pitt. Not to mention those in Berkeley and Philadelphia, now with established and mechanised Cotton Mills, but still providing all with many loving relationships.

But then so had the many other families who had settled here long before it became an independent country, and though had suffered in the war which enabled it to gain this stature. They had done much to enable it to happen and now were still trying to make it a success, whilst it provided for their own comfort.

It seemed that in spite of the terrible global warfare and Britain, often alone attempting to stop Napoleon Bonaparte become the ruler of the civilised world. Genesis had occurred. This land in America, which had only recently achieved independence, had not only survived, but prospered, even if it did not have a ruling king, but elected, every four years one of its people to rule them. It was a New Country but it would grow in stature until it was larger than most countries in the world, with enormous powers.

It provided a home for so many people escaping from the horrors elsewhere, just as it had provided for all those couples who had escaped from France or come from Ireland, now all happily married. Yet it had provided prosperity to people like the Carroll's, Casimir's, Holsteins, Dumas', Scarron's and Tencin's, who had lived here for many years. But it had provided for those two couples who had escaped from a life of hell in Austria. In fact in 1803 Louisa and Anton Albrecht, who still owned their estate in Spanish Florida, were to repeat their pleasurable visit to New Orleans of ten years before.

Now extremely rich and proud American citizens, happy to invest in projects, ensuring the future of this new country, and in return reap its rewards. Now, remembering the present security had depended on the friendships with the members of the American delegation they had formed in those far off days in New Orleans.

Robert Carroll, Eric Casimir, Anton Tencin and several others had invited both Louisa and Anton, to join them and return to New Orleans. Then on November 30th. 1803, in a very special ceremony in that city of New Orleans, the Spanish Authorities, formally, gave possession of the whole of the Louisiana, the area called the Louisiana Purchase, to the new United States of America. A far more important ceremony than the one in December when France, formally handed over possession.

So Louisa and Anton Albrecht, along with the very many friends they had now come to like, even love, in America, now certain that in a few more years that estate of theirs in Florida would, also be part of the United States, and no longer belong to Spain. But now possessing a new holding in a very beautiful part of the new state of Tennessee.

So these friends on that November day, saw this New Country, this newly independent Country of the United States, by a signature, in a single day, became a country twice the size of what it had been before. In spite of what everyone had said, this New Country had not only survived, but exploded in size, with land sufficient to now providing a refuge for any who might want to come and settled here.

Just as it had done so many years ago before in the Seven Years War, when those who came and fought for its independence, and those who so recently, provided a home, loving partners and families for those from France and Austria, but still for those, still needing, to escape from Ireland and England. This first New Country, built on, and ensuring all its decisions would be made by its own people. The true meaning of the word 'Democracy'. It had happened

Long Live the United States of American and all who live in it.

THE END

MAKERE – THE FEMALE PHAROAH – QUEEN OF SHEBA

The passionate love story of Makere Hatshepsut – the only Female Pharaoh of Egypt – with lowly peasant Web-Priest Senmut – and Solomon, King of all Israel

Makere was a very beautiful, intelligent and courageous woman in a man's world. Yet who established herself and was to wear the Double Crown of Egypt for 25 Years, ruling as Sole Pharaoh, The Living God, for the last 10 Years.

Although Fiction, it definitely portrays her true life story 3,000 Years ago.

Made Joint Pharaoh by her beloved father, forced after his death to marry her perverted and evil step-brother, meeting and receiving the love of this Web Priest Senmut who gave her the desire to live. Raising him to positions of supreme important but, though she tried, was never allow to marry him.

After enduring years of hell she eventually becomes Sole Female Pharaoh of Egypt. Then invited by King Solomon, as his 'Queen Shwa – or Sheba', -now because of the proven 500 Years error in the chronology of Egypt – Makere is therefore the legendary 'Queen of Sheba" who travels to Israel.

A story of love and intrigue, though written as fiction, but accurately portrays life and events, in Ancient Egypt over three thousand years ago. Today her two Obelisks stand in the Temple at Karnak, her Magnificent Mortuary Temple now called Deir el Bahri, and is available for all to see and visit on the banks of the Nile near Luxor, as is the engravings on the cliff walls at Syene, placed there by her lover Senmut over three thousand years ago

ROYSTON MOORE
SEE – www.shebamakere.com

284

MARYLAND

This is the story of how the aristocrat David Carroll met and came to love, peasant girl and indentured servant, Amelia Eliot, condemned by an Irish Court to a life of virtually sexual slavery in Maryland, the British colony of Charles Calvert, Lord Baltimore, at the end of the 17th. Century.

It is set in the time when first King James II and then King William III and Queen Mary ruled Britain. It is a Rags to Riches story.

There is no doubt but that Amelia Eliot, was indeed 'Cinderella' and that David Carroll was to become her 'Prince Charming' turning her into his own 'Princess', though it took some time before the fairy tale took shape.

It is the first of five books which form the family sagas of the two Carroll families and their descendents. David Carroll is a young member of the Protestant Carroll family from Somerset going to America for the first time, where the Roman Catholic Carroll family from Yorkshire, have lived for sometime.

Every attempt has been made to ensure the historical accuracy of events at that time introducing into it the lives of several well known historical personages. John Washington was the grandfather of George Washington,. Sir Winston Churchill, was the forerunner of the World War II Prime Minister, and his son, John, was to become the Duke of Marlborough. Charles Calvert was the third Lord Baltimore, and did own not only Maryland but lands in Ireland granted to his predecessor by King Charles I, when he once again became a Roman Catholic and had to retire as a Privy Counsellor.

However enjoy this love story whilst Britain and France continue their wars which have lasted centuries.

ROYSTON MOORE

OHIO

This book is the second book continuing the family sagas of the Roman Catholic and Protestant Carroll's began in book one – 'Maryland'

The story of five couples, five men and women, born in England and France, who find love for each other. Who in spite of the war between their countries, which forces them apart, finding solace with others, go to America, to eventually find each other again. Set in Maryland and Ohio in the 18th. Century at the time of the 'Seven Years War'. Introducing Daniel Carroll, grandson of Sir David and Amelia Carroll, with his boyhood friend George Washington exploring the region of Ohio, where France and Britain go to war to decide who owns it. It may shock you but it is a fact. It accurately describes the true lives of several white woman sentenced for a crime in England, to endure both domestic and sexual slavery, to men without marriage, for several years. Desperately trying to limit the number of children they may bear them. It accurately describes the licentious life at the court of Versailles and the salons where titled ladies bestowed their favours on men for benefit. The love stories of men and women, torn apart, though of different nationalities, virtual enemies, meet, come to know and understand each other, becoming friends. Overcoming their differences helping them to meet again the women they love. Made possible, only, because of this region called 'Ohio'. Though a fiction story, and including many families introduced in the previous book, every event is historically accurate, including the lives of George Washington, as are the many actual governors of the colonies and military persons. Enjoy the love stories and enjoy living in those far off days.

ROYSTON MOORE

LIBERTY

It is the third book written as part of five books, following my books, 'Maryland' and 'Ohio', before Books "Genesis" and "Lebenstraum"

It continues the saga of the Carroll family. Daniel Carroll, the grandson of Sir David and Amelia Carroll, now happily married to his French wife, Michelle. Daniel now helps the friend of his youth, George Washington, married to Martha, living on his estate of Mount Vernon. Daniel having promised to stand 'side by side' with George, when war breaks out, having previously been trying to keep peace in Maryland, Virginia and West Virginia, now with help of his friends, ensures they all support the rebellion.

The main characters are fictitious and includes many families from the previous books. Yet it is' essentially. a love story based on the lives of people living in America, just before and during, the American Revolution However it introduces many new persons fleeing from Europe. Some quite rich like the Casimir's from Poland, and the Holsteins from Sweden, buying estates near the Potomac and land in the Wilderness, but others such as the Scott's, Reeves' and Collins escaping from England, devastated, that the land they were given is covered in Hardwood trees and not suitable for farming, until helped by Michael Casimir for personal reasons, concerning his first love, Carla who committed suicide when Michael was forbidden to marry her, her likeness to Claire Collins.

However there are other couples brought together due to the war, and who discover love. This was not only a war with Britain, but a Civil war, and an Indian war. How France, Spain and people from Europe helped, in achieving, eventual, victory.

It is a romantic story. How the war with Britain brought together many people, who learned to love each other, leading to the creation of land of West Virginia, with exiles coming from England, France and other parts of Europe. How they lost their nationalities, and became Americans, creating the United States of America, when victory was assured in the Treaty of Paris.

ROYSTON MOORE

LEBENSTRAUM
(Living Dreams)

A story of Romantic Love triumphing over all problems, as the new United States continues to expand westward towards the Pacific Ocean. Opening new lands beyond the Mississippi and Missouri Rivers, and into Mexico in Texas and California. Also continuing the Carroll Family Saga as descendents of Margaret Eliot of Ireland, but particularly those of Sir David and Amelia Carroll, who, still, continue to play a vital part in ensuring the rapid development of this expanding country.

Though both Michelle and Daniel Carroll are now deceased, their protégée, Mark and Estelle Carroll of Rockville, and their son Danton, now married to Claudia Albrecht, become part of the Diplomatic Legation in Mexico City. But, also, of the Downey, Eliot, and Reid families who were so greatly helped in the past by Daniel Carroll and Michelle to establish themselves. These were, also, aided by the other branch of the Carroll family, previously Roman Catholics, but who became Protestants when Edgar Carroll married into the rich New York, Dutch families. All fully described in the previous books covering the Carroll Family Saga.

This book "Lebenstraum" is the fifth in the series following the previous books "Maryland", "Ohio", "Liberty" and "Genesis". Though events in those books contributed to everything which happens in this current book, it contains sufficient information, necessary, to explain how important this was in deciding and contributing to their present lives.

Introducing Gordon Taylor from Manchester, Sheila McLean from Northern Ireland, and Rachael Gilbert forced to marry an evil Elder of the Mormon Sect. The escape of Otto Fallon from Austria bringing to this country his knowledge of banking and the investments made by the Ibsen family, coming from Scandinavia, and Otto's growing love for Freda Ibsen. Yet, how, the present long established residents of the United States, was to eventually, after many tribulations, find love and a very happy future.

All historical references are accurately described, when required, in this book. How the expansion west was to add the Mexican lands of Texas and California to the map of the United States, until it became a country stretching from the Atlantic to the Pacific Oceans.

I spite of this, enjoy the many romantic love stories of life in this country from 1828 until after the U.S.A./Mexican War until 1850. Love stories, but which enabled the countries development in river, shipping and the advent of railways, adding to the agricultural wealth, the growing industrial, and economic richness. This, only possible because of the influx of so many new emigrants from Europe. Romance made all their troubles worthwhile, as they established themselves and added greatly to the future prosperity of the United States

ROYSTON MOORE